D0874076

HERMANOS!

STRAYHORN

THE ITINERANT

¡HERMANOS!

A NOVEL BY

William Herrick

SIMON AND SCHUSTER
NEW YORK

PUBLISHED BY SIMON AND SCHUSTER
ROCKEFELLER CENTER, 630 FIFTH AVENUE
NEW YORK, NEW YORK 10020
FIRST U.S. PRINTING
SBN 671-20356-8

LIBRARY OF CONGRESS CATALOG CARD NUMBER: 74-79631
MANUFACTURED IN THE UNITED STATES OF AMERICA
BY AMERICAN BOOK-STRATFORD PRESS, INC.

For
Jonathan
and
Michael
and
Lisa

ABBREVIATIONS USED IN THE BOOK

AIT	Asociación Internacional de Trabajadores
CNT	Confederación Nacional del Trabajo
FAI	Federación Anarquista Ibérica
IR	Izquierda Republicana
POUM	Partido Obrero de Unificación Marxista
PSUC	Partido Socialista Unificat de Cataluña
SIM	Servicio de Investigación Militar
UGT	Unión General de Trabajadores
UHP*	Unión de Hermanos Proletarios (also Unios, Hermanos Proletarios)
USC	Unión Socialista Catalana

* Pronounced "oo! er! pay!" since the *H* in Hermanos is silent.

. . . On the 16th [July 1936] the Army in the Spanish Zone in Morocco rose and occupied Ceuta and Melilla. The [Spanish Republican] Government still had time to act: the Army could have been dissolved and arms distributed to the people. Instead a proclamation was issued to the effect that "nobody, absolutely nobody in Spain had taken part in this absurd plot." That afternoon the officers of the garrisons rose in almost every Spanish city. It was not until midnight on Saturday the 18th that the order for distributing arms to the people was issued. Even then some of the Civil Governors refused to obey it.

. . . The Military Junta and group of Right-wing politicians which rose against the Government in July expected to occupy the whole of Spain, except Barcelona and perhaps Madrid, within a few days. They had at their disposal the greater part of the armed forces of the country—the Civil Guard, the Foreign Legion, a division of Moorish troops from Spanish Morocco, four-fifths of the infantry and artillery officers and a certain number of regiments recruited in the north and therefore reliable. They had also the Carlist levies or *requetés* which had for some time been drilling secretly and the promise of Italian and German tanks and aeroplanes if necessary. Against these the Government had only the Republican Assault Guards and a small and badly armed air force. But the plans of the rebels were defeated by the tremendous courage and enthusiasm with which the people rose to defend themselves and by the loyalty of the naval ratings who at a critical moment deprived them of the command of the sea. Each side being then left in control of one half of Spain, a civil war became inevitable.

From *The Spanish Labyrinth* by Gerald Brenan

. . . and we march up the Barcelona boulevards banners flying red gold purple black red white blue the works a million people on each side of the street and its real quiet as we march and then like the sky opened up and began to let go with a hundred thousand cannon the million people begin to yell and it sounds like the whole world's yelling hermanos hermanos hermanos brothers brothers brothers. . . .

JOE GARMS

Jacob Starr tore about the country with great élan, a swashbuckling revolutionary. A brawny, powerful man of twenty-five, he organized party units among steelworkers in Youngstown, Ohio, black and white sharecroppers in southern Georgia, cocktail guerrilla fighters on Fifth Avenue, New York City. Very successfully. The leaders of the vanguard party of the working class thought he was too damned arrogant but dared say nothing since he was the protégé, if the word may be used in this company, of Carl Vlanoc, Stalin's plenipotentiary to the Western Hemisphere.

In September of the year Spain burst open like an angry boil, torn apart by fascist insurgency and social revolution, Carl Vlanoc ordered Starr to accompany him to Cuba on a mission of secret diplomacy.

At a meeting with the *cubano* party leaders held in a one-room wood shack swirling and stinking with cigar smoke, Jake heard Vlanoc, hero of the Hungarian revolution of '21, one of the organizers of the Chinese Party, old Bolshevik and comrade, order the *cubano* leaders to split their Party in two: one to continue its underground fight in alliance with other parties against Batista, the butcher of the Antilles, and the other to make a *sub rosa* agreement with him. It was the tactic of the unity of opposites. If Batista fell, the Party could claim it had fought him and attract the masses; if Batista held on, as well he might, the Party would have elbowroom in which to operate. All other political parties would in the interim be ground to nothing between them.

As he listened, Starr smiled to himself. An excellent tactic, realistic. Who could oppose it?

Providencio Morales, a scrubby, sullen-faced little bastard with a stubby black mustache, said, "It's immoral, filthy. The comrades fighting underground will be gambling their lives while behind their backs the *partido* will be trading with the butcher."

Jake Starr blushed as he listened. What the comrade said was true.

Vlanoc restated his orders. It was the tactic of the unity of opposites, it was realistic, practical; the butcher had indicated a willingness to make the deal, it would be sheer stupidity to refuse, more, it would be infantile left-wing sectarianism, and, *in último, camarada,* contrary to the decisions taken at the seventh world congress.

Of course, Jake muttered to himself; of course.

"Everything the respected representative of the great Stalin says is true, there can be no denying it," the sullen *cubano* stated quietly. "But it is immoral and that too is a fact."

Two conflicting truths, the young American thought to himself. How would it be resolved?

"We have no morality," Vlanoc stated crisply. "What we do is above morality; therefore, there is no immorality. Only after we have won shall there be morality. To discuss it further is counterrevolutionary."

There was dead quiet in the shack. And Jake Starr thought, Only a man who has made a revolution in his very own soul can possibly find the courage to say that.

But the little *cubano* said, "There can be nothing without morality—no victories, no future, no revolution. *De nada!* Nothing! I am," he said, the words bursting like shot from under the bristly foliage of his mustache, "a moral man first, only after an instrument of the *partido* and of history."

Vlanoc, a short squat man with a shaven head, rose to his feet; the meeting would resume tomorrow.

Before the nagging *cubano* crossed the threshold into the darkness, he turned to Vlanoc and his young aide and said, "A man lives like a beast, he becomes a beast." Wagging his finger, he added, "There are no historical exceptions."

In the late morning of the following day, it was reported to Vlanoc and Starr in their handsome *casa* (who would think to find them in the wealthiest quarter of the city?) behind the black-enameled door that Providencio Morales, the scrubby *cubano,* had been found in a ditch outside Havana with half his head shot away.

Jake Starr had been in the revolutionary movement all his life; he was not naïve. He understood what had happened to Morales and confronted Vlanoc with it. A sad smile on his hard round face, Vlanoc stared directly into the young man's eyes. "Yes, I had him assassinated."

Jake Starr lost his temper, called Vlanoc a murderer, strode shaking with wrath from the handsome *casa,* walked the streets of Havana, ashamed, unable to look a Cuban, any Cuban, in the eye. He walked the city streets for fifteen hours, walked through the slums, the filth, the poverty, walked without eating or drinking. He had known assassinations were to be part of his life but had concealed the knowledge as deep and as far from his consciousness as possible. So he strode through the city of Havana, fighting with himself, with Vlanoc, with the pamphlets and books, hungry, thirsty, tormented with indecision. And wherever he went, there were the stern questioning eyes of his father who had brought him up to believe that a man must live for one purpose—the radical transformation of society—but had died leaving these cunning questions for his son to answer.

Late at night, Jake found himself at the harbor. He could hear the rats amongst the garbage and the whisper of hoarse voices in the dark. Then like an apparition a girl accosted him and clutched his arm; enervated, he permitted her to lead him to a rotting shack in the dark where in some sort of self-hatred he took her skin-and-bones body meanly, a voice screeching in his brain, *Vae victis!*

Woe to the conquered. And the conqueror? What about the conqueror?

Then he smelled the stink about him; his eyes accustomed to the dark saw the rags and sticks of wood which were the girl's home. He saw the girl—eaten and mauled by hunger. Could there be any doubt that hunger was the strongest victor? Justice and morality would have to wait. First there was hunger to resolve.

He dressed and gave the girl all the dollars he had and she tried to kiss his hand. He withdrew it roughly. "Don't kiss the hand that whips you. Shit on it. SHIT ON IT!"

Late that night he returned to the handsome *casa* and Carl Vlanoc. They faced one another under the beautiful Moorish chandelier of curled iron. Jake expected to see hardness in Vlanoc's eyes, but they weren't hard at all. Instead of glittering black marble they were the color of soft soot. Now he's an understanding father. If he were consistent I could hate him more easily. Anger rose to his throat again, but his voice controlled, low, he said, "I apologize, Comrade Vlanoc."

"Get a night's sleep," Carl said without even a nod, "we're leaving tomorrow at noon."

Jake wheeled and ran up the elegantly curved stairway to his room, conscious that Vlanoc's eyes followed him all the way.

The squat, paunchy man turned slowly about. He raised his shoulders, lowered them. Closed his tired eyes. Stood motionless. Began to rub his hands harshly in a quick washing motion.

A few moments passed. He opened his eyes and stared at

his hands which seemed to contain a life of their own. The washing motion became a wringing. Stop it! It was only his hands which Carl Vlanoc couldn't control—and an occasional insight into himself.

Rapidly he walked into the large room, to a cabinet from which he extracted a bottle of whiskey, uncorked it, drank from it until the chill left him.

He made a phone call.

"Yes," was all he said.

"The work is concluded, Camarada Carlos."

"It will operate precisely at noon?"

Sí. We tested it three times, the timing mechanism is in perfect order."

"*Muy bien,* Gonzalez."

Vlanoc called another number.

"Teodoro?"

"*Sí.*"

"You have concluded?"

"*Sí, sí.*"

"Good. Be here tomorrow fifteen minutes before noon. You will come with us to the States. You need a vacation."

"Good."

"Promptly!" Vlanoc said, hanging up.

He took another drink, replaced the bottle in the cabinet. It had been a long day. His work on the island was finished. The deal with the butcher had been sealed with the blood of Morales. A maverick, very erratic—one never knew what they would do next. The second party had been organized; unfortunately several of its leaders had already been betrayed, but defeats must be transformed into victories. Tomorrow the entire city would know of their martyrdom. Betrayed by whom? By Providencio Morales, of course. Vlanoc frowned. These weren't things one enjoyed.

As he passed Jake Starr's room, he paused, shook his head.

Soon it will be just another day's work for the boy. His hands moved toward each other. He restrained them, plunged them into his pockets, and Vlanoc, the old washerwoman as his comrades knew him, proceeded to his own room.

Teodoro, pencil-thin, a yachtsman's cap high on his proletarian head, its peak gleaming new, parked the car at the curb promptly at eleven forty-five. Vlanoc, standing at the window, smiled. Discipline made the difference between *mañana* and today.

As Starr and Vlanoc entered the rear of the car, the older man said, "Through the plaza, Teodoro. Enter it precisely at noon. That gives you exactly eight minutes."

"You want to see the slogan?" Starr asked.

"It's there all right," Teodoro said, and declaimed, "Death to the Butcher! Long Live the *Frente Popular!*" Then he laughed, doubling over the wheel.

"What's so funny?" Starr asked.

"The police are scrubbing away—like devils. What a pleasure to watch them working for a change." Teodoro squealed through his laughter. "They roped it off, but the entire city already knows."

Vlanoc smiled thinly.

One thing about working with Carl, Starr thought, you see results.

Vlanoc glanced at his watch. "Slower. I want to be at the foot of the square at noon exactly."

Starr observed an excitement in Vlanoc, whose hands were moving in that obnoxious motion he so disliked. *What's up now?*

The sun shimmered blindingly off the white and yellow Spanish town houses on the broad tree-lined avenue. Then the car rolled through a narrow street, originally meant only for pedestrians and mule carts. Jake could almost put his hand into the open windows through the black iron grilles. At one sat an Indian girl, her swart head immobile on cupped hands, black eyes wide open, unseeing. The black of her eyes was streaked with white phlegm. Blind from filth, from syphilis, from neglect? No, he thought, a descendant of sun worshippers, she's blind from staring into the sun.

Carl opened his window and peered at the rooftops of the two highest buildings which bounded the north of the plaza, then quickly glanced at his watch. Twelve! Back to the rooftops.

"Ah!" Vlanoc ejaculated. "You see—we make our own confetti parade."

The sky just below the two roofs was suddenly alive with what in the sun's glare appeared to be white-winged butterflies. Jake hunched forward, observed them more carefully. Leaflets. A breeze caught them and soon the air above the public square was aflutter with the white-winged sheets.

"Even the wind joins our cause," Vlanoc laughed.

Noonday pedestrians stopped to gape. The police stopped mopping at the huge red letters of the slogan; leaned on mop handles, heads raised to the sky. Vlanoc laughed uproariously. The car stopped. All traffic stopped. The first leaflets neared the ground. Hundreds of hands reached out to catch them. A slight breeze cut across the square, teasing the leaflets out of reach. As the papers tossed about, laughter spilled from the pedestrians, even the police laughed, and soon thousands of noonday walkers, oblivious of the police, went darting, plunging after the elusive mystery.

There was an abrupt respectful silence as the leaflets were read, folded neatly into pockets. In a few moments the plaza emptied as if sucked clean by a giant vacuum cleaner.

"Get us a few," Vlanoc commanded Teodoro.

As the car accelerated, they read the leaflet. Starr skimmed the words, found quickly what he sought. ". . . Those who represented democracy and peace at the meeting are incarcerated in the Police Barracks of the Northern District. We have no knowledge whether they live or are already dead. They were betrayed by one Providencio Morales, police spy and agent provocateur. The police will find the traitor's body in the ditch outside the city where . . . As in Spain, where our democratic brothers in the *frente popular* are fighting against the would-be fascist dictator, we too shall be victorious. *Pasaremos!*"

Jake Starr kept his features immobile. Executed, then maligned. The dead must be very dead.

Vlanoc studied the strong, rough face of the young man. Big nose, big jaw, big ears, large head, brilliant green eyes. A perfect cross of his father and mother. Intelligent, agile, strong, romantic. For a moment, Vlanoc softened. Why shouldn't he be romantic at his age? An American to boot. But at twenty-five it was time the heart became a mite less lachrymose. It would. Otherwise . . . Carl Vlanoc shrugged.

A few hours later, on the power boat headed for Key West, Vlanoc said to him, "Don't you see, Jake, hunger and justice are opposites. They fornicate and spawn revolutionists. Understand?"

"Of course. It takes a little time, that's all."

"I know."

"Where do we go next?"

Vlanoc smiled. He had been saving it for this very moment. "To Spain."

Jake Starr couldn't restrain the quiver of excitement. "*La lucha por la libertad!*" he exclaimed. They were magic words. For almost, not quite, they erased the etched portrait of Providencio Morales from his brain.

BOOK ONE

I

Professor Rolfe Alan Ruskin was a long, slender man, with a noble head, a grand nose, big, hooked and aristocratic, under which bristled a red-gray mustache. His family crest extended back to and beyond the Magna Carta to the Third Crusades of Richard Coeur de Lion. The centuries had neither thinned his blood nor expended his energies. The Ruskins had never been drawn by their class to the puerile caravan of spas and soirees, but had always preferred the tumult and adventure of intellectual life. It had kept them alive and vigorous, Rolfe no less than his predecessors.

One night in late November, warm in his heavy tweed overcoat from the exertion of his long walk, he steered himself unerringly through a heavy fog along Great Russell Street in London to his Georgian house. He could walk these last hundred meters blindfolded by one of Sarah's knitted woolen scarves. For a quick moment sadness touched his heart. Some day the ancient house would belong to strangers. He and Sarah had no children, try as they had, and when young Rolfe, his son of his first marriage, had left that dismal day a few years before, he had said he wished to be rid of every vestige of the Ruskin institution: name, house, money and heraldic shield. The boy, very handsome, very blond, exceedingly neurotic, had assumed his mother's family name, Keepsake, and associated himself with the fascist Sir Oswald Mosley. A blight. One morning Rolfe had received a card from his son, on it these words and a crude drawing, "This should in all rights be the Ruskin coat of arms," then a bleeding heart encased in a block of ice. A cruel boy. More, embarrassingly mad. At any time of day or night, the telephone would ring. Then young Rolfe's high-pitched nervous voice could be heard, "Have you cried for *me* today, Father? Have you?" Followed by a wild laugh, a slammed receiver. What could a father do?

There was the house now—a light in Sarah's window invited him to hurry. He lengthened his stride. Soon he would be in the room with her, his young Sarah, would relate to her the happenings of his day. There was nothing he enjoyed more, reliving the entire day with her. In that way each day was twice as long. At his age of forty-six, that was very pleasant. To Sarah he would describe the manner in which he had handled the meeting this evening. His speech had been concise, to the point, even when impassioned. Rolfe smiled. Was becoming quite the orator, wasn't he? And he had answered every question without hesitation—a genuine political man, disciplined. It was discipline which was the Party's genius; discipline which made its politics viable. To remold billions of men required discipline and will.

Rolfe opened the front door, entered the vestibule. He placed his overshoes in the closet, one perfectly aligned with the other, hung his coat so it touched no other, set his hat on its customary peg.

When he entered their bedroom, he found her reading, her voluptuous hip outlined by the blanket, her heavy brown hair framing her head on the pillow. She was possessed of a striking beauty, with full lips and a strong, intelligent face. My young, beautiful Sarah. How fortunate I am.

As soon as she heard him, she lowered her book. "Hello, Rolfe." She smiled. "I'm glad you've come before I was asleep.

The Party has assigned me to help with the British volunteers on their way to Spain. I leave for Paris tomorrow morning."

He didn't answer as he approached the bed. First he wanted to kiss her. Gently he raised her head to his and warmly pressed her lips with his. Again she smiled. A fussy man, perhaps too shamelessly taken with his own importance, but he could be gentle and he loved her. And that meant a great deal, for she loved him too.

On a chair near the bed, one bony knee of one long skinny leg crossed over the other, he combed his thin gray hair, which she had mussed as they kissed, into place with his long white fingers. "Yes," he said, "I know you're leaving. I was asked by Comrade Charles—his true name is Carl Vlanoc, a very important comrade—if I thought you could perform the task and leave immediately. I assured him you could."

"Thank you, Rolfe," she said sharply.

Disturbed by her tone, he stared at her a long moment. "You understand, Sarah, these matters must of necessity be impersonal. You know I'd prefer for you to remain at home."

She wanted to say, Then say so before I ask for it, but bit her lip instead, curbed her anger. "Yes, I know, dear."

She observed him as he undressed. A good figure for a man his age, his stomach flat, spring in his long legs. (Rolfe still played tennis three times a week.) When was the last time we did it? She never used to think about it; now she thought about it often. Had it been foolish to marry a man so much older? When one fell in love, who weighed it on what scale? You fell in love, you married. Later you worried about whether it had been foolish. Besides, she hadn't been a very handsome girl; rather plain, she'd say. Then she met Rolfe, a charming man happy to find someone who was pleased to listen, and a very famous scientist. Wife dead, a son turned twenty. Still, she hadn't been a virgin when they were married. Who was a virgin at twenty-one? Even plain girls, with broad hips and large heavy breasts when the fashion of the day called for small breasts like sour white plums. She'd had a messy affair of a month's duration—the boy more frightened than she. He'd run away. Escaped. To study in Rome, he'd said. A year of hope; then the hope gone. And Rolfe Alan Ruskin had swept her off her feet with charm, fame, and a plethora of words. Oh, you love him, she told herself. He's opened up new worlds for you. Rather, has made it possible for you to see the one world. Before there had merely been the cloistered perspective of a well-trimmed lawn hedged in by an old privet. So for a plain girl she had done well. Except now she knew by the stares of men she was no longer plain. What had happened? Men stared at her with desire—and now in her latter twenties the body was more demanding, more often there was the sudden need to feel a man's lips at her breasts, to feel a man's weight on her body. Also there was that most delicious feeling when she noticed a man observing her with desire. Vlanoc had looked at her that way—only for a moment, but it had been there. And though only for a moment, and from a man she couldn't call overly appealing, it had been enough to make a cold day warmer.

Rolfe was now concluding his before-bed ritual: each garment folded neatly, hung away; the shower; the teeth brushed; the hair combed; fresh pajamas; the bathroom light switched off. A shy smile on his face, he approached the bed, his moving shadow huge on the ceiling from the lamp. I love him. He's my husband and I love him. Now his body was stretched alongside hers and she smelled the scent of the soap he used, and she turned to take him in her arms. His hand reached overhead and flicked off the bed lamp.

"This morning, when I arrived at the laboratory . . ." he began, but she stiffened, did not listen.

Without willing it, even against her will, the thought sprung clearly into her head. I'm glad I'm going to Paris. I'll tend those young men going to die for freedom, keep them sober, away from prostitutes and out of the clutches of the French *gendarmerie.* That's what the instructions had said before she burned them. So they can reach Spain to fight and die for freedom. Absurd! But I'll pretend it's not. "Young Hawkins," Rolfe was saying, "thought he'd made a great discovery concerning the missing elements in the theoretic—" but Sarah stopped his mouth with a kiss, her fingers dancing on his stomach. Well, he told himself, moving his hand tenderly to her breast, that's what happens when one marries a young healthy woman. . . .

During the night the telephone rang and Rolfe pretended not to hear it, feigning sleep. To protect her husband, Sarah answered it. It was his son. She spoke quietly to the young man, but all he said was, "Has my father cried for *me?* Has he?" When she attempted to answer, the boy laughed wildly, then slammed the receiver.

In the morning, Rolfe Ruskin went to his laboratory; Sarah to Dover for the Channel boat to Calais.

II

After Havana, New York was cold. It was also a madhouse. It seemed everyone was either going to or coming from a meeting, stopping on one foot to shout either a friendly greeting—"Hey, Jake, how's the proletarian Byron?"—or an epithet—"Look who's in town—that Stalinist bastard!" Everyone also took sides no matter what the issue, proving there weren't just two but a hundred.

No longer Comrade Jacobito, just plain Jake Starr (his party name), he found it difficult to make the transition from protégé of Carl Vlanoc to New York revolutionary. To conceal his anxiety, he remained silent to indicate profundity; firmed his lips and jutted his jaw to indicate determination; adopted a swagger to indicate swashbuckling courage. He was accepted as a peer by his leaders. When he spoke, they listened. While he had been away, he had sent in reports, written articles for numerous party publications. Now he discovered he was *the* Latin American expert. Among those with constipation—he laughed at himself—the man with diarrhea is king. It was this ability to laugh at himself which softened the arrogance.

One thunderous night raining shotguns a few weeks after his return, a group of men raided a German Nazi warship visiting New York harbor and painted hammer and sickles in blood red over the decks and raised the red flag to the top of the radio mast, coincidentally bludgeoning a few sopping supermen. Those in the Party now knew Jake Starr was in town. And when he spoke at a Madison Square Garden meeting soon afterward—"We haven't received our monthly quota of Moscow gold," great booming laughter, "so give, give, give!"—Jake Starr was rewarded with a standing ovation, the spotlights flashing dizzily. He stood there, a figure in bronze, cape and sword, a big grin on his face.

Jake was everywhere. He lectured at the Workers School on the Popular Front, wrote articles on the Spanish Civil War, conducted seminars on Marxism, stayed up nights to read reports, pamphlets, newspapers: from A to Z, Agriculture to Zapata. Was designated Iberian expert—wasn't Latin America related by conquest and tongue to the Iberian peninsula? Read a novel written by an English Comintern agent about the Asturian miners and La Pasionaria and was now prepared to take on all comers. Attended Fifth Avenue cocktail parties to make collection speeches for Spain, street corner meetings for the Scottsboro boys, the Garden for anything. He was a brawny man, very tan, eyes deeply set and speckled green; the girls flocked about him, their mouths open, waiting for the hook. There was always some leggy piece of tail just off the Radcliffe campus itching to scratch her skinny ankles on his big ears. The next day she would be out in front of the Stock Exchange selling the *Daily Worker*. So there was a girl now and then, a quickie. Love on the express train between Grand Central and 14th Street. Exact running time: three and a half minutes.

Spain articulated a million tongues. What came out: anybody's guess. Azaña, Caballero, Durruti, La Pasionaria, General Miaja were exotic names which quickened the blood; Madrid, the International Brigades, *No Pasarán!* engorged the heart. "Fascism will rip itself to shreds on the arid, rocky plateaus of Spain," Jake Starr promised. "*Abajo* Franco! "Long live democracy!" his audiences screamed.

Behind the closed, guarded doors of the party headquarters, a committee of three leaders and Jake Starr interviewed the first volunteers for Spain. Merchant seamen, college grads, union men, unemployed, poets, former hoboes, actors, artists, mostly young men in their twenties, men who had never held a gun, all lying, no one believing, that they had. Among them was Joe Garms who had deserted the United States army to fight in Spain. It had been Joe Garms who on one picket line or another had taught Jake Starr that a tightly rolled *New York Times* could be an educational tool. Smash: the scab had a broken nose. "Saves the knuckles, yuh jerk." Also how to use the stub fur cutter's knife. Slash: the hood couldn't sit for a month. "Always in the ass, Jakey. That way y'ain't in the can wit' a murder rap and we gotta make big demonstrations to spring yuh 'cause y'was framed." Joe Garms, a pug, a wild mop of black hair and exceedingly intelligent blue eyes, had been *champeen* middleweight of the Eighth Army Corps; he had chanced twenty years in the stockade to surreptitiously disperse party leaflets in army barracks and officers' latrines.

Gravel-voiced, "How are yuh, chump?" Joe's famous eye for accurate observation.

"Fine, Punchy."

"A big wheel now, huh?"

"So they tell me on the ninth floor, Joe."

"Where we're goin' bullets don't know the difference." Great laughter, slapping of backs.

The volunteers trained in a famous meeting hall downtown off Third Avenue. Columns left; columns right. Bayonet drill —without bayonets: not even sticks. Joe Garms was the drillmaster, as Jake Starr sat on the dais, observing. Everyone was dead serious.

"Lunge!" Joe commanded.

Splayfooted elephants instructed in the modern dance.

"I'm dancin' wit' tears in me eyes," croaked Joe.

Belly laughs.

One morning instead of reporting to the hall for drill, each squad was sent to a different section of the city to buy American World War I doughboy uniforms in Army & Navy stores: shoes, puttees, breeches, shirts, overseas caps, black ties. *The Yanks are comin', da-da da-da.* The party rep gave each man who didn't have it ten dollars to pay for his passport, and told him what to say on the application. Congress was debating a law to prohibit validating passports for Spain. Starr wrote he was on his way to Poland to visit his mother's parents, using his right name, of course. Garms, on the lam from the army, was to be smuggled on the ship by waterfront comrades; French comrades in Le Havre were to smuggle him off.

Though they made lots of jokes, they were very serious, and very proud of themselves for having volunteered, very proud of their Party and their cause. Now they were going to Spain on the q.t., later the world would hear of their heroism. "Spain," growled Joe Garms, "is the beginning. Then we'll knock off Italy and Germany. After that the world, goddammit, the world!"

And in Cádiz, Nazi military technicians, machine gunners, and expert snipers marching shoulder to shoulder off the gangplank sang, "*Und Morgen die ganze Welt!*"

And the music goes round and round, and it comes out here. Ta ra.

Day after Christmas, 1936, the first contingent, about ninety, embarked *sub silentio* on the *Normandie,* first having been favored with a limp Browderian handshake and wan smile wrapped around a fat capitalistic cigar in the lobby of the Jewish theatre on Second Avenue and 12th Street. Joe

Garms was among them, smuggled on with ease, for the party members among the French crew were both numerous and professional.

"I'll leave a coupla fascists live just for you, Jake."

"Don't be a big hero," Starr smiled. "The best soldier's a live one."

"Yeah, Comrade Starr, I'll dig me a hole in an olive grove an' stay put till the war's over."

"Okay, Joe. But lay off the whores in Le Havre, they're giving short-arm inspection in Perpignan."

"Me? I'm savin' it for when I get hitched." Joe laughed, departed, Jake's eyes following him. Joe Garms passed through life with a laugh, thinking the sound of it would deafen your ears to the screech of fear in his heart. Came from Greenpoint, an Irish slum. At sixteen he'd upended his old man with a one-two combination, hit the road, bummed the world, joined the Party. "Y'gotta be a sucker to always take it wit'out givin' it back." Helped Jake Starr's father fight and beat the gangsters who ruled the fur market and union. Then the Party decided it was time to subvert the American army and sent Joe in. Fast footwork and a murderous right hook earned him an army championship and leisure time to hand out leaflets and read Marx, Engels, and Clausewitz in the officers' library. He was so expert at fighting his fear, courage became second nature. One saw in Joe's face immediately the man he was: a friend to his friends, an enemy to all others. Good guys and shits. His intuition was infallible—or so his friends thought. He followed the party line: it gave him something to hold on to. He would kill a lot of fascists and laugh doing so. And the first commissar who betrayed him. Spain, Jake thought, is going to be very interesting. If any of us live long enough.

"Hey, Joe!" he called. When Garms turned to grin and

wave, he said, "Write me, will you? Your letters remind me I have at least one friend in the world."

"You bet," Joe laughed and ran.

"You're taking the next group over," Jake was told by Bird, the party org-sec in charge, and he nodded assent.

In the group was Gregory Ballard, a fisherman from Cape Cod, where Jake Starr had organized for the Party a few years back. Jake had written Greg, then spoken to him over the phone, convinced him the time for fighting fascism was now. Greg volunteered. He had short legs and a long, muscular body. His hair was bristly and he had a long chin. In between, on a wide plain, were thick lips and a flat nose. When he laughed, his chin became even longer and the point of his nose stuck out like a thumb. His skin was the color of cocoa. The first time Jake Starr had noticed him, he'd thought Ballard was an ugly man. When he really saw him, he realized Greg wasn't ugly at all. The first thing Ballard did when he met you was look into your eyes. If your conscience was clear, you stared back into his and said, "Well?" If your conscience wasn't clear, you turned away, and he sneered. He was laconic, highly individualistic, and tough. When he said *God* you heard it as *guard.* When he said *guard* you heard it as *God.* But you soon had no trouble understanding him.

He met Jake Starr outside the training hall.

"Loney and Ma send their regards." Loney was Greg's sister and it had been through her Jake had met him.

"Thanks. How was the fishing and scalloping this year?"

"Bad. The sword weren't running, the blues disappeared, the bass hid. Besides, who has money to buy fish? And you? Been away a long time." A long speech for Greg Ballard.

"Party work. I missed you and Loney."

"That's your life, I suppose."

"My past, my present, my future. I'm glad you've joined us."

"I'm joining you to fight fascists, but I'm not a party man, you know that. Tell your guys to lay off. I'll join when I'm good and ready."

Jake smiled. Greg hadn't changed a bit. "They won't bother you, I've already told them. Anyway, this is an antifascist organization."

"I hardly believe it, Jake; if you're involved it has to be more'n that. But I'll take your word for it. Also tell them no patronizing—I can take my lumps with the best of 'em."

"We don't patronize."

"Then take that smug smirk off your face." Now Greg laughed and it made Jake nervous, because it was a silly high-pitched laugh, sort of a signal which let Jake know Greg was fighting a battle to keep himself under control. He was familiar with this laugh; still it made him nervous.

"You've just arrived and there you go. Every damn hair on your body's an antenna."

"Yup," Greg snapped, grabbing hold of the laugh and squeezing it into a wry smile, his jaw long. "Each hair smells, hears, sees, feels and even knows, my brain doesn't have to work anymore. That's why I let you talk me into this deal."

"You can still back out if you want."

"If I don't like my pay I will," and he laughed again. Jake squirmed and realized he had better take Ballard inside the hall. As soon as he came to know the men he would feel better, relax into it.

Ballard was assigned to a squad, introduced around, and began immediately to learn the complexities of columns left, columns right, and bayonet drill. He was one of four Negroes training in the hall. It was to be a true American battalion. Later he was given ten dollars for his passport, was bought his olive drabs on Canal Street, was sent for antityphoid shots.

In a few days Jake received a letter from Joe Garms written in his friend's strong hand and unique style.

Big Shot,

In Perpignan now, Jakey, right near them big mountains. What a ball we had. The Frenchie comrades from the crew get me on the boat without no trouble. Half empty. The boat I mean. Not me. I'm loaded with food and champagne. Broads. You don't know nothing. Comrade Phillips our polit-commissar says no drinking no wimmin no talking pretend you don't know me. A pleasure. Bob Gladd the seaman organizer he's with Hammond the military leader. Gladd that big talker he's a stowaway too. Come to the States when he's a kid and he's still a Russki citizen. Anyway he gets himself up to A deck. Next thing y'know he's down in tourist again. Get some a the guys he says. Hurry up I got something goin'. I get Skinny Horton from the Furriers Union, a bindlestiff from way back and a couple other guys. We follow Gladd and Hammond who's a little juiced. Screw Phillips they say. Up we go Gladd leading the way. We end up in a big fancy cabin, the Ritz. And what d'yuh think. Broads from the Folies Bergere on their way home to do a command performance for the Frenchie big shots or somethin'. What a load a beautiful dames. Like in a movies one a them says Ah mon cheree you are goink to fight in Espain. To keel fasceest. Good for you, mon Americain cheree. Come I geev you kees.

They order champagne and we gets down to beezness. Gladd he grabs himself a blond mink and the last I see a them is skipping into the next cabin. Horton's got him a redheaded babe in one fist and a bottle in the other and they vamos. One guy's under the bed with a dame jest heels showing. Hammond's on the bed a bottle in each hand and two dolls on his chest. Me. I get me a big tit blue eyed honey who keeps saying cheree cheree come here and kees me. So I takes a hop skip jump and goddam tuh hell jest as I get close she does a back flip skirts flying. WOW! One a those goddam acrobat dancers. She laughs like a breeze. I say come on baby and make a nice easy grab and shit if she don't do a front flip ending in a split. Hammond and his two dames is heehawing to beat crap. So I dive on this sweet cooze but she's so damn fast I'm on my nose and she's standing laughing like I'm the biggest clown ever lived. I'm getting mad. C'mere you sweet-assed dilly I say real tough. You know me. Up she dances sweet as cherry pie and I put out one a my meat hooks to grab her chin and boom she's standing on her ear and guess what's staring me in the kisser.

Four front flipping back flipping days.

Comrade Phillips comes to look for us. Comrades he says this is shameful. You heard my orders. Hammond's sauced and laughs like hell. Gladd's roaring. C'mon Hammond says to Phillips be human we're soon gonna fight and die. Let's have some fun. No Phillips says this is outrageous. This is not the way for comrades to behave. Shhh Gladd whispers you're supposed to keep your mouth shut we're bizness men going to Europe and the broads begin to laugh. Phillips is standing there with his lips white and tight. So one a the dames comes dancing over takes out her tit and throws it right in his puss.

Y'know what, Jakey, Phillips is human.

O voir, mon cheree.

Joe Garms

III

JAKE STARR's mother still lived in New York, and when he was issued his orders to leave, he dredged up some time to go tell her. She lived in a three-room flat on the second floor of a crummy tenement on First Avenue and 103rd Street, over a candy store. She heard him running up the creaking stairs two at a time just as she began her work. She was a slight woman with strong, tragic eyes the color of green sea glass, and bitter, sardonic lips.

As her son entered, she smiled, not turning away from the dressmaker's dummy on which she had just begun to pin a pattern. He walked quickly to her and bending almost double —he appeared to be twice her height—he kissed her on the lips.

"Are you hungry?" she asked in Yiddish, the only language she ever used when she spoke to him. It was to make him remember despite his Bolshevik disavowals that he was a Jew.

"No," he answered in English, "keep on working. I'll get a glass of milk and a banana."

He sat on the windowsill drinking his milk and munching on the banana, observing her at work. He sat quietly, knowing she loved it when he was in the room while she worked, just they alone and no one else in the world. He wished he could talk to her as he had in the old days, after his father had been killed by gangsters in the fur market and he had promised her some day he would make a million for her and she wouldn't need to sew dresses and alter old overcoats for her neighbors, and she would listen, drinking in his words as if they were the words of her God Himself. How hard she had worked to feed him, to support him while he had gone to college because that had been the greatest ambition in her life, to send him to college. "What you'll be I don't care. How much money you will earn, I don't care. But to be a learned man is the finest gift you can give me. You are a strong, healthy boy, thank God, and you have your grandfather's head, he was a very learned man"—it seemed the grandfathers of all the boys he knew had been very learned men—"and you will be the most intelligent boy in your class."

But his father had been a revolutionary, uncles, cousins, aunts. A distant relative of his mother had been a comrade of Lenin's in exile, had been a brigand for the Bolsheviki, a bank robber for the revolution, was now an official in the Soviet government. So it was in Jake Starr's very genes. Besides, he had known hunger firsthand, shared stale bread with his mother and father, with friends, neighbors. The world was unjust, in disorder, irrationally ruled for the benefit of the rich and the powerful. He rebelled against the old order, would make a new, scientific society, ruled by reason, without privilege for the mighty, classless, where every man and woman would work and eat. And be free. He read the literature of revolution and socialism, was awed by Marx's erudition and logic, his penetrating political insights; was overpowered by Lenin's incisiveness, his adamantine will, his revolutionary genius. So he, Jake Starr, would be. Yet, to please his mother, he worked hard in college to give her the gift for which she had worked a lifetime. That part of his life would belong to her. Not quite the smartest boy in his class, still he had graduated *cum laude,* with a gold medal in European history, and a reputation as a linguist; also as the *éminence grise* of the young Communists in the college alcoves.

He was advised by his dean to seek a doctorate, but he laughed. Yet when they gave him the gold medal at commencement, he heard his mother call out, "That's my son." And he felt badly for her, his mother, who could be so pleased at so little from him, not yet aware he was about to betray her.

Now, as he observed her working so happily in front of him, he bit his lip, for she was showing off her virtuosity with pins and scissors, so oblivious to her son's having been won over by the twin oracles of violence and necessity.

"Ouch!" he heard her cry, having stuck herself with a pin. "You see, I'm a stone; my fingers don't bleed." Then she laughed as she resumed pinning the pattern. He gazed down at her from his perch on the windowsill, hoping he could find the right words to tell her he was leaving again without making her cry. Everytime he had to leave on a party mission she cried. "Get married and settle down. Become a teacher—you'll make a living. Why do you give *them* your entire life? They will hurt you the first time you tell them a truth they don't want to hear."

She was staring at him, so he smiled at her.

"Everytime you have to tell me something unpleasant," she said, "it is hard for you to speak. I cry. Well, tell me, this time I promise not to cry."

Jake laughed and ran to raise her off her feet with a hug.

"And where this time?" she asked after he had set her down.

"Someplace, Ma."

"Someplace, I know. But where?"

"I can't tell you."

"You never can tell me. You're my son, what am I—"

"—a stone?" he concluded for her. "Yes, you're a stone, you don't bleed anymore." But she didn't laugh, and neither did he.

"With Carl Vlanoc?" she asked.

"I don't know."

"Vlanoc," she spat out. "Whatever name he uses becomes a name for filth. I hope he dies like a dog," she said, extracting a pin from her mouth and stabbing it into the dressmaker's dummy's heart.

Her son laughed.

"You laugh?" she asked, looking up at him. "When the gangsters killed your father after he fought them in the union, I didn't even have a dime for the rent and the landlord bothered me for weeks. I cursed him: I hope you die like a dog. The following week he was run over and killed."

"I've told you a hundred times, Ma, that was coincidence."

"Coincidence? Carl, I hope he too dies like a dog. Next week there should be a coincidence."

Jake merely lowered his eyes and shrugged. What was the sense arguing with her? "You'll write to this address," he said, handing her the slip of paper he had prepared. "They'll forward the mail."

She stood her full height, all of five feet. "Starr?" She spat, curling her lips in contempt. "Your own name isn't good enough, I suppose."

"Oh, what makes the difference? Besides, there are political reasons."

"Yes, I know. You think I don't understand, that I'm a fool? I was a revolutionary in Slonim, too. But we used our own names."

He had answered nothing to her last remark, and now she stepped close to him. "Tomorrow?" she asked, and put her fingers to his ear, drew him down to her, stroked his cheek. "You're only twenty-five years old, you don't know everything yet. Not yet. The fact is you are very ignorant, and will die ignorant, as ignorant as everyone else. You want to beat the world—it will beat you, I assure you, will break every bone in your body, and put you in your grave." She said it sadly, and he embraced her, kissed her cheek. She began to cry. And he became infuriated.

"The world will beat me? You beat me with your goddam tears. Stop your crying and leave me alone." In his fury at her he recognized fury at himself and at Providencio Morales for having said to Carl Vlanoc, A man lives like a beast, he becomes a beast.

"All right, I'll stop crying," she sobbed. "I swallowed six pins already. When you are gone I will be able to cry in peace."

They kissed again on the lips, and he left. Then he heard her calling down the stairwell. "Jacob! Come back!" and he restrained his anger.

"Yes, Ma?" he said when he faced her again at the head of the stairs.

"Tell me the truth, please. You are not going to Spain, are you?"

But of course he was a pro now. He had been to Cuba with Carl Vlanoc and had learned to conceal the truth. He laughed gaily. "Don't be foolish, Ma. I'll be back in a couple of months."

And, as always, she believed him.

IV

Jake Starr stood alone on a North River pier, at the gangplank of the *Île de France,* observing his comrades approach singly, look back for a quick moment, then board the vessel. A tall, thick-chested man, with deepset green eyes and a strong mouth, he appeared to be at ease with his strength, a man obviously conscious of every aspect of himself. There could be little doubt as one observed him that he was a man who believed he could mold his very existence, structure it to meet the circumstances of his life and time. Even as he now stood, coat collar turned up against the wind and snow, quietly gazing about the pier, it could be seen that he had already begun to disentangle himself from the complex life of the city he was leaving behind, for his life was here now, on this vessel, which was to carry him and his comrades to another time and place. His strength, he seemed to say, his force of will, would encounter the future *mano a mano,* hand to hand, so to speak, and he would bend it to the requirements of his very own history. He was a professional revolutionary—and time, place, social events were to be utilized for solely one purpose, the lifting of society from one level to another more advanced level of civilization. To fail was to be condemned. And because he believed this with a profound conviction, there was an arrogance, not lacking in charm, about him from this inner dynamism. Yet, since he was an intelligent, sensitive man, he must have been aware of the risks of his commitment, and this accounted for the ambience of sadness about his green eyes and full strong mouth. Strong, yet romantic, for how could he not understand, even against his will, that his victory over the past would at its very moment of attainment become vulnerable to defeat by those like himself who would follow him? And this was discernible in Jacob Starr because as he now strode up the gangplank of the vessel, not once looking back, he himself gave weight to these very thoughts.

Still, if he and the forty young Americans under his command thought of death as the steamer gathered speed for its voyage, it was not of their own. *They* were immortal.

Before they had embarked, Comrade Starr, of whom they were in awe, issued terse instructions. "Obey your political commissars, don't congregate in large groups on board, exercise in your cabins every day, don't discuss politics excepting behind closed doors. And give me a wide berth." He paused. "There are probably Federal agents on the ship." True or not, each man immediately felt more heroic than he had the previous moment. Muscles visibly expanded, so that Starr, whose oratorical timing was phenomenal, said, "You can sleep with all the girls you want, just don't talk in your sleep."

He grinned, and they laughed. All had heard of the first group's encounter with the girls of the Folies-Bergère and had their own hopes. Now Comrade Starr added, throwing it away, "Remember, we're just plain antifascists."

Mack Berg, a lanky, tough-jawed New Yorker with a corrugated face, and the voice and elocution of a radio announcer, called out, "Why? We going to a masquerade?"

"Perhaps—and perhaps not," Starr winked, and everyone smiled knowingly, even Mack whose normal demeanor was sour and harsh. "That's the line, and no infantile sentimentality about it. Besides, there are some who're just that."

"Okay, Comrade," Berg snapped, "if it's the line."

"Forget it, Mack," a couple of men called out, uneasy,

afraid Berg would spoil their comradely esprit de corps, yet secretly agreeing with him. That was Mack Berg's greatest misfortune—people were always agreeing with him and publicly turning him off.

Berg, an obstinate mule of a man who never knew when to stop, said, "Who're we kidding?"

Greg Ballard, suddenly not a disinterested listener, said laconically, "Hope it ain't the Spaniards."

"The fascists are howling 'red' to frighten the timid off from helping the Spanish Loyalist cause. We have no desire to stimulate more howling," Starr said firmly. "Now cut it out. Remember, avoid trouble—enjoy the trip and the girls."

His instructions were assiduously adhered to, though Greg Ballard did slip once. The second morning out he thought he would like to break in his new army shoes. When he hobbled on deck, there were thirty-nine others similarly shod. Forty pairs of gleaming yellow army shoes on parade, and there stood Comrade Starr with his broad back to the railing. Ballard giggled nervously, and for a brief moment Jake Starr looked terribly angry, but he turned to face the sun and the sea, for he also wore new yellow army shoes. The forty men disappeared quickly, and their leader went off to keep a date with a Danish girl whose breasts, though large, never seemed to satisfy his hunger.

In Le Havre, the men were split into small units and dispatched to hotels in the working class quarter for a few days until the French Party sent for them. So many volunteers were surging into Paris now from the countries of Europe that a logistics problem had developed. The Americans encountered each other about the port city, especially in the bordellos, where they were always greeted by someone playing the *Internationale* on the piano.

The same night the forty Americans arrived in Paris they left for the south of France led by an Italian comrade,

Riccardo, an exile whose thinness was quite substantial, a taciturn, graceful man who already had extensive experience leading international volunteers into the Pyrenees. Jake was instructed by Vlanoc to remain in Paris.

They were fed a quick meal in a workers' co-op in St. Denis, then heard a short, snappy speech by Starr. "You're not going to write history, you're going to make it," for to his comrades history was a blood brother—more, they were master, history serf. Greg Ballard shrugged his muscular shoulders, muttered, "Shee-it," for he still hadn't reached any working agreement with history, they were still sizing each other up at arm's length. "The best soldier's a live one," Starr admonished them as previously he had admonished Joe Garms. "Cut out the romantic crap, you're not going to a demonstration on Union Square. Lots of luck. *No pasarán!*"

A bus took them to Gare de Lyon where they boarded a train known throughout Popular Front France as *le chemin de fer des volontaires*. They arrived in Perpignan in the early morning, without sleeping a wink all night. In an old provincial courtyard they were given an orange, a mug of coffee, and a chunk of French bread and butter. Columns right, columns left, bayonet drill; no bayonets, no broomsticks; short-arm inspection. There was one Le Havre whorehouse casualty, upon whom they turned their collective hypocritical backs.

"Can y'imagine, gettin' the clap on the way to Spain?" one pious merchant mariner called out.

"Yeah, the whoremonger," Greg Ballard said drily. No one laughed.

Riccardo led them high into the Pyrenees and in the early dawn, the sun dripping green as it rose out of the Mediterranean, he deposited them in the sure square hands of a Basque, short as Riccardo was long, a rear end as broad as a Percheron's. After Riccardo and the Basque kissed in the

European fashion, and the Italian left, their new guide examined them silently. Then he smiled sadly, said, "*Vámonos,* let's go, the fascists are waiting."

That same day Jake Starr received a letter from Joe Garms, which he saved to read that night when he got into bed:

Dear Jakey,

Here we are. What a goddam country. The people look hungry. They ain't afraid of nothing. When they look at you they're hard as nails but when you look at them their eyes are soft black. Everything's old as hell here, the flat houses—casas they call them—the towns, lots a them with walls around them. It'll be harder'n hell to take a town with a wall around it cause before you get to the wall is open land or mountains. Never seen so goddam many churches in my life. Built like forts, thick walls, with slits for muskets like in the old days. Most a the churches is closed with sandbags in front a them. They was a hell of a lot a killing at the beginning in the towns from both sides. Don't worry our side got their licks in real good.

The sun's hot here, Jakey, but the nights freeze your balls. From Perpignan we come across the mountains in buses. I understand now that's stopped—those sonsabitchin frog bastards going non-intervention and our lousy USA refusin' to give passports even for Spain now or even bullets for democracy, shit! when the fascists are getting ready to take over the world. We're in these buses going over the mts. and when we get to the border the Frenchie guards sure as hell give us the fist salute and boy we yell, and then we're in España and the guards in those berets a theirs and cartridge belts crossed like Mexican bandits with Pancho Villa they give us red front salutes too with their left hands—they're those crazy maniac anarchists—and they're hollerin' long live the revolution viva la revolucion that's what they yell and we yell back long live the popular front cause the polit-commissars told us that's the line. Tell you the truth, Jakey, because you're my friend and a good guy. I like viva la revolucion better, that's for me.

Those fucking democracies ain't going to give us anything anyway so who we kidding? I know the party and the Soviet Union think its better to talk up the popular front now so maybe we can get the bourgeoisie—I can spell that frog word, I ain't read Marx for nothin'—to help beat the fascists but the workers and peasants, obreros and campesinos they say it, like viva la revolucion better. The party says no so okay I go along cause the party's got a line and discipline and cause the party's the party. What else do I got?

Well anyway we come into Figueras and it got a fort with walls twenty foot thick. I read once Napoleon got his ass beat here. Good for him. The town's slanty, starting in the mts. and going downhill. What colors—red gold purple black red white and blue the whole works—every goddam flag you seen in your life. Every initials too—they talk about alphabet soup in the states here they got them all except being catalonia cataluña they got Xs instead of Ss. FEIXSME. CNT UGT FAI POUM (Trotskyite bastards the commissars told us to stay away from them as if we don't know the dumb boy scout bastards) PSUC (our guys but a Spanish kid who talks English told us it's only got middleclass members cause the workers belong to the FAI anarchists and POUM and PS socialists). When you come we'll talk about it. Okay?

The people are happy to see us and give us the food from their own mouths and wine to drink from those leather bags and slapping us on the back and giving us those red front salutes. Its real wild Jakey. Alive. Everything smells twice as good, the broads four times yum! what tits high up on their chest and these skinny little espanolas look so ferocious they can eat you. They'd throw a stick a dynamite as soon as screw.

Jakey, I got into this goddam country I cried. Not in Figueras though. I tell it to you because all the guys saw anyway. I ain't cried in a long time. Since I knocked me old man that drunken sonuvabitch on his ass I ain't never hardly cried. Once when I was on the bum and some bindlestiff pricks beat the livin' crap outa me in a dump outside Detroit cause I wouldn't give them my chunk a bread I couldn't stand for three days and I din't cry.

In Figueras we hopped a train to Barcelona. Christ it went about two miles an hour. The trains full a guys from all over. Italians, Germans, Yugos, Irish lads led by a big bastard from the IRA who fought the black and tans. Dutchmen, Belgians, the whole friggin lot comin' to beat hell out of the fascisti. Jesus how can we lose? We're all jabbering away to each other and understanding believe it or not how I don't know but we understand. Besides there's always some guy who talks the lingo. Y'know we got lots of cubanos and one a them a kid Jaime Ortega says he knows you from when you was in Cuba a couple months ago helps out a lot. We made friends on the train going down France from Paris that night and none of us could sleep we was so excited. On the train to Barcelona españolas give us sausage and bread pan they say and more wine vino rojo they call it from those leather gourds. You raise it up high and squeeze a thin line into your mouth and I almost choked but now I can do it like a pro. Nothing beats me, you know that Jakey don't you.

We got into Barcelona early in the morning. By the way we was wearin' our USA uniforms, Christ we looked like a bunch a boy scouts compared to the others. If you think we're poor in the states you ought a get a load of these Europeans. They're poorer than the okies.

We get off the train in Barcelona and there are these catalans with armbands CNT FAI AIT POUM PSUC UGT USC IR (left republicans what the hell they doin' here) and a million people are out lining the streets to meet us. These guys with the armbands they line us up by country, the Irish, the Germans, the Belgians, us, and we march up the Barcilona boulevards and pass a statue of Columbus banners flying red gold purple black red white blue the works and a million people on each side of the street and its real quiet as we march you can just hear our heavy army shoes pounding the cobblestones quiet like I never heard it in my life a million people crowding the sides of the streets their mouths a little open just looking at us and its so quiet you can hear the guy next to you breathing and your own heart too, Jakey, and the banners are flying red purple gold CNT UGT FAI AIT PSUC USC IR POUM hammers and sickles fists hammers big posters real beautiful too. Dead quiet. A million people and they're looking at us as we march up the boulevards the Irish and the German exiles in their old raggedy clothes and us in our 1917 doughboy uniforms and dead quiet and I don't know what it is. I snuck a look at this redheaded bignosed kid who come to meet us at the station an American who fought already in Madrid wearing dirty coveralls and straw sandals and he all most split a gut laughing at us in our uniforms but who marched with us. I see him sneaking a look at me a strange look on his face as we march under the colored banners and these million people crowding there dead quiet with their mouths a little open. This kid got a strange look on his puss, a tough bastard too, and its quiet all around us and then like the sky opened up and began to let go with a hundred thousand cannon the million people begin to yell and it sounds like the whole world's yellin' hermanos hermanos hermanos brothers brothers brothers Oo! Er! Pay! Unios Hermanos Proletarios and it sweeps over us, takes us in its arms, a million people yelling and this kid who fought in Madrid without any guns he begins to cry and I begin to cry too and other guys too are crying. A million people loving us up and we're loving them up too.

And we all feel like dancing and singing and crying. We're going to make a new world, a great new world, Jakey, where there'll be no poor and no wise bastards who think they own the whole goddam place. We all own it Jakey and we're going to fight for it.

I'm proud I come here to fight and I'm proud of these espanolas, the only ones who said up yours you dirty filthy fascist bastards.

Okay, I cried.

Jake, lying on his bed in the small room of a hotel on rue Lafayette, paused in his reading of Joe's letter. His friend had placed him in Barcelona and now he too saw the multitudes in streets overhung with the black banners of anarchism, the red of the revolution—in streets which the masses had conquered and now possessed. And he envied the seeming uncomplicated emotions of his friend, and for the briefest moment he felt in himself an unease, an unhappiness at the requirements of his discipline, the responsibility of leadership, the proscriptions of his superior, Carl Vlanoc. But as soon as he recognized the symptoms, he forced himself to sit up, to pour himself a glass of wine, to sip it slowly, until the wings stopped beating in his breast. Jake Starr, revolutionary hero. Would he never rid himself of that idiotic syndrome? The need to be where the banners fly, the hunger to eat off the vanity of courage? As far back as he remembered he'd had the need to catch the winning pass, to hit the ninth-inning homer. What was it he was trying to prove? That he wasn't insignificant? That he was greater than all other men? Even as a small child he'd wanted to prove to his father that he was every bit as strong, as heroic. It was an inner need against which he must impose his revolutionary will. The movement was more important than he, the cause infinitely greater. To hell with the hero in history, the man coming out of the mountain who for his very own glory would lead men to their graves. The wine bottle was light in his big hands, the bed creaked under his hard weight. No, he admonished himself, it isn't wise for a dedicated, disciplined comrade to allow himself the freedom of dreams.

He lay back on his bed and resumed reading his friend's letter.

Its tomorrow, Jakey.

Well we marched up the Ramblas between a million screaming people and the other internationals drop off in different places and then its our turn. I don't know how but we get mixed up and a couple of us and Phillips the pol are separated from the rest. We're standing before a big army barracks and on the top a the gateway to the courtyard there's a picture of guess who? You never guess Jakey. Lenin.

Looking down on us with his bald head, a little smile on his lips and those Tartar eyes of his, wise as hell and looking right thru you. Well we march right thru the gates and there's a bunch of hungry skinny milicianos hurraying and hugging us. And guess what again. They're POUMist Trotskyite bastards and Comrade Phillips the polit-commissar he got as white as my ass I'm sure he shit right then. But I got a hand it to him he did okay. He smiled sort of and we went into the messhall and ate beans and chunks of white bread and drank lots a vino rojo. There was a lot a guys wounded there fighting fascist soldiers with pitchforks and clubs and sticks of dynamite. And you know what those guys stand up and sing the Internationale and we stand shoulder to shoulder with those Trotskyites—can you imagine?—singing the international soviets will be the human race. A laugh.

Well anyway we get out a there alive and go meet the rest of the battalion which was in the Karl Marx barracks of the PSUC and they act like we got the syph but screw them and we take a train to Valencia and the Xs become Ss FASCISMO and we ride and we ride till we get to Albacete base of the International Brigades. 400 miles. 24 hours. These trains crawl.

Albacete alongside Valencia is like Sandusky Ohio alongside Frisco. Ugly and hotter'n Wolf's Fang Arizona in an outhouse in August. Lots a wounded International Brigaders. Germans marching like pros, singing We are the peatbog soldiers—Christ it made us feel good.

We take our craps in those stinky Egyptian toilets where you squat on holes plugged with shit, then we get washed and brushed up and we go down and line up for parade again. We march around. Then its quiet. Out comes somebody important wearing clean coveralls and gold braid and the biggest blue beret you ever did see in your life. The more important the bigger the beret I'm told. His gotta be 3 foot across and this guy's fat with a bushy mustache. André Marty. If I didn't know he's a great revolutionary I'd think he was a clown. Marty talks to us in Frenchie English. He tells us we're like the Yanks who came in 1917 to save Europe from the Boche. He must think we're stupid. Lenin called it an imperialist war and he tells us we're like that. We all wanted to puke in his face but Comrade Phillips sings out long live André Marty, long live the hero of the Black Sea mutiny and we chime in.

In Albacete we seen lots a wounded and we begin to realize people are getting killed and lots of the guys is beginning to get the runs. In one of the rooms in the barracks we see a wall full of blood and bullet marks and blood on the floor and I don't say nothing, I know what it is and I don't want to scare the guys. Its good we left right away in trucks before I got the runs too.

Now we're in a midget village in the province of Cuenca, not even a thousand people and they got three real big churches, a monastery and a convent all closed up tight. The Spanish people sure must love their churches.

Anyway guess what, we're barracked in the convent and old Joe Garms, Greenpoint bum, hobo, union strongarm, party pro, champion middleweight of the 8th Army Corps is sleeping in a rickety cot which used to hold a little nun. I kind a hope nobody killed her. You know my mother's sister was a nun and was always good to me just like me mother who died with her tenth kid. Just God wasn't.

We're training very hard with four rotten Canadian rifles, a French Chauchat and a 1914 Maxim m.g. and no bullets. Jesus I know how to shoot but these other guys what happens when they go to the front?

Most of them are good guys, just a couple a shits, and we'll win anyway even if we have to throw rocks and use kitchen forks like that redhead told us the Spanish workers and peasants used to stop the fascists from taking over the country in the first two three weeks of the war. The fascists killed everybody they laid their hands on but they got theirs too. Don't worry. But good.

I'm gonna go to sleep now in my little nun's bed. Dead tired from maneuvers. Wish to hell I had a sweet little ass to keep me company.

I love you like a hermano.

Your compañero (comrade, you chump)
Joe Garms

V

"YOU WILL DIE soon enough—no hurry. Understand!" Vlanoc said when Starr met him in Paris. "Dying is universal," his chief added softly, and Starr looked at him wide-eyed, the softness in Vlanoc's voice a rare surprise. "You will stay here—we need an American who is fluent in the language and someone who can hold the *responsables* in hand. Understand?"

"Yes, I understand." What could he say? I want to die in the open air? Vlanoc would have burst a blood vessel laughing.

"Stepanovich is the boss here, so keep your stupid temper in check. A temper's an instrument of terror. Wasted, it becomes meaningless. Understand!"

"Of course." So are farts an instrument of terror. If all the farts of the international working class were caught up in canvas bags, then unloosed on the world in full volume, the revolution could be won without the shedding of blood. A good subject for an article. A *feuilleton!*

"How is your mother?" Vlanoc asked quietly.

Jake Starr examined Vlanoc a moment. He was hard, squat, paunchy, his round head shaven till it gleamed, his little red-ringed eyes glittering black marble. In the center of the round hardness of his face protruded a nose like an ax blade—thin, sharp, metallic. Jake thought he looked like a squat radiator on which someone had plunked an old-fashioned iron cannonball. Now Jake smiled. "She sent her regards. She's well." Vlanoc knew the kind of regards she would send.

"Thanks. You'll work with Sarah Ruskin, the professor's beautiful young wife. A nice piece. He's important. Be careful. *Salud!*" And Carl marched off to Spain, rubbing his hands.

Jake Starr and Sarah Ruskin slept in adjoining rooms at a party-owned hotel on rue Lafayette near rue Louis Blanc, a working class neighborhood for the leaders of the vanguard. At the office near Place du Combat behind a stone wall guarded by a ladlefaced French workingman, they worked separated by thin lath. On the same floor, in similar offices, bare and stinking of cigarette smoke, worked the other national *responsables.*

They were overwhelmed with work, feeding, housing, entraining the thousands of young men who were filtering into Paris from over the world. Young men with obsessed eyes, nervous, anxious, impatient for the feel of the gun. The Spaniards had drawn the line to the fascist enemy, said no more, *de nada más,* and now the young revolutionaries of the world, the idealistic antifascists, workingmen, students, unemployed, underground fighters from Nazi Germany, the Balkans, Fascist Italy, all headed in one direction, like iron filings to a magnet, the fighting front which shaped like a whiplash led from the Aragon to Madrid to Córdoba to Málaga. There they would meet the enemy head on, fight him, defeat him, change the world, root and all. And though Paris was gray and rainy that winter, these angry and passionate young men warmed it, fired it up so it seemed the sky was eternally red, and there was no night and there was no day, as it must have been when the planet Earth was first born.

The *responsables* were spread thin about the 10th Arrondissement. Only Sarah and Jake lived at the same hotel, and it became custom for them to walk home together after a meeting or after having eaten a late supper together at the workers' co-op nestled among the shoddy little whorehouses on avenue Jean Jaurès.

He told her about himself, boasting a bit about his party exploits, editing out Carl Vlanoc and Providencio Morales. Jake wished he could forget Morales, but he was learning blood is an obstinate substance, sticky, difficult to wash out.

Sarah told him she had been born in Sussex, her father an Anglican bishop and her mother the daughter of shopkeepers. It figures, Jake thought, for he had made a pass the third night home and she said, "No, I'm married." She had married Rolfe Alan Ruskin five years before, and it had been he who'd introduced her to the Party and she'd recently become a member, one of the new sort: for democracy and against fascism. She chose not to tell Jake about Ruskin's prior marriage and his son who was a fascist, but Jake knew since he was privy to the dossiers of all the *responsables*, and had in fact committed them to memory. He even knew about Rolfe Keepsake's periodic calls after midnight to taunt his father about crying for the entire world but not for him.

One gray evening soon thereafter, at the end of a particularly bitter day—the volunteers they had sent off with Riccardo, the Italian mountain guide, had looked extraordinarily young and callow—Sarah invited Jake for the first time into her room for a cup of tea. He sat on her bed and the smell of her scent was on it and he hoped he could sprawl on his back and go to sleep, but he sat upright, stiffly, not wanting her to think he was pushing an advantage. He ate an apple with relish as she puttered about with her small burner, and he couldn't keep his eyes off her. She was a lovely woman, with narrow shoulders and full round hips, the features of her face not small but strong under her heavy brown hair—Spanish almost, except for the eyes which were dark blue and large. The room was little, a twin to his, and her closeness across the room pressed on him so forcefully he almost rose to leave before he made a false move.

She finally handed him his cup of tea, then sat down on the lone chair near the bed. They were silent, and the hot tea eased his tenseness. He couldn't help but think how good it would be if she and he had a sweet run, a respite from the bitterness of the work they did—sending those green kids off to Spain, almost hearing the guns and smelling the gun-powder and seeing the dead in the bombed city streets.

And since it was always on their minds, they began to speak about the war, the atrocities committed by both sides which filled the daily newspapers, and Jake said, "And to think His humble servants bless the enemy guns."

"Not all," Sarah said, "some fight on the side of the Spanish people."

"Very few, and they'll be excommunicated." Then he smiled at her from the vantage point of a revolutionary pro. "It's not necessary always to be so damned honest."

She measured him for a moment. "Why not? Truth can get along fine without the help of lies."

"Because it reminds you that the enemy's human. In war you can't think of the enemy as human—how could you then kill him?"

She said quietly, "Don't you think we must always recognize that the enemy is human? That way we'll remember when we are victorious to remain human ourselves."

They were inches apart, knees not quite touching. "Yes, remain human, treat with him humanly, so that he can re-activate his enmity, his terror, his greed and resume the goddam bloodletting—we're off to the wars, boom boom. In the end that's crueler—but of course sentimentality—"

"It is *not* sentimentality," she said icily.

"—is always crueler. And that idealistic claptrap about truth, virtue, et cetera, has been used to sickening eternity to drain the vitality, blunt the ruthlessness, if you will, of the revolution. Just look about the world. It is the unsentimental, the unjust, the dishonest, the unvirtuous who sit on the thrones of power."

"Thank you for not calling what I've said bourgeois. I appreciate it, Comrade Jacques."

"You're welcome," he smiled.

"But if we refuse to see that the enemy is human," she said, looking at him with her dark blue eyes, "we'll soon forget our own humanity. As my father, the Reverend Dawson, would say, *abeunt studia in mores.*" And it brought him up short. One's habitual pursuits pass over into character. . . . *A man lives like a beast, he becomes a beast.*

But he was an expert in street-corner debates and Union Square tactics and he recovered quickly. He rose to his feet, very careful to avoid touching her, gently placed his cup and saucer on the rickety little table next to the bed. "You're exactly right, Sarah. That's why we have to be even more ruthless than the enemy—so we can win more quickly, before there's time for our cruelty to become a habit." He smiled down at her.

And before she even had time to think what a beastly arrogant male he was, Jake bent down quickly, kissed the tip of her nose, and left for his room next door. Within a few minutes, she could hear his bedsprings twang as he went to sleep.

So they became friends, practically lived together, worked together, were comrades, separated night and day by a mere lath wall.

They became so close so quickly that Jake said one night as they sauntered home, "You know, Sarah, I can hear you undressing every night, can hear you washing, can hear the bedsprings give—even the covers as you draw them underchin. When you turn in your sleep, I turn, too, otherwise we'd be uncomfortable." He waited for her to laugh, but she didn't. Just marched straight ahead up Louis Blanc, never even turning her head. It was dark so he couldn't see her blush. "Sarah, you listening?"

"Yes, I'm listening."

"I even know when you go to the WC on the stair landing and when you return I sort of make room in the bed." Now she giggled and he stopped to face her. "Sarah, we're like an old married couple—married so long we don't do it anymore."

"Good," she laughed, forging past him, "and let's keep it that way."

Another night a few days later, as they climbed the stairs to the balcony off which lay their rooms, just having nodded to Comrade Fishface Marchand who was speaking with the lady concierge who was built like a heavyweight, she remarked that the French comrade seemed to be at the hotel every night.

"Yes. Can you imagine a fish in bed with a weightlifter?"

She laughed.

"Even they do it—but not you and I."

"But we're an old married couple. Remember?"

A middleclass biddy if he ever saw one. But a lovely ass.

Though the days were gray, cold, and icy, Jake Starr began to burn.

Riccardo asked Fishface Marchand, French liaison with the Technical Bureau, for leave to join the Garibaldi battalion. His request denied, Riccardo spoke to Sarah Ruskin about his disappointment. "I escaped from Mussolini's prison camp to fight fascism with a gun, not to be a mountain guide. I want to kill fascists, that's all I think about."

Sarah stared at him, such a gentle, quiet man whose every word to his comrades was a fraternal caress, now quivering with hatred at the enemy. The enemy! Weren't they men too?

Hadn't they feelings of love and tenderness? Difficult to believe when one listed their crimes. "I understand, Riccardo. Why don't you speak to Comrade Jacques?" Comrade Jacques, Jake, an odd man, passionate, cool, sardonic, very efficient, a man who could dissect a political event with fine skill and analyze a battle as though he were Wellington himself—yet a monster, damn him, why couldn't he understand when she said no she meant yes? A simpleton. Where was Rolfe? Why hadn't he come once for a visit? Were they already so long married they didn't have to do it anymore? Be calm, Sarah. At ease. You have work to do.

Riccardo spoke to Comrade Jacques who then phoned Stepanovich on rue de Chabrol. Stepanovich was Stalin's seeing-eye dog in France. But Starr was Vlanoc's man and Vlanoc was no untutored puppy dog, so Starr and Stepanovich spoke almost as equals.

"The Italian wants to fight—don't blame him, so do I. We have the Austrian and can use him."

"The Austrian's worthless," Stepanovich said harshly. "Saw too much blood at Casa de Campo. You're being sentimental."

"Hardly. The Austrian's a good mountain man. It will do him good to get his mind off Madrid. He had a hard time. It's a fair exchange."

"The Italian's a romantic." The greatest sin. "Wishes merely to be a hero."

"They all do. It's our disease."

"Agreed. You too."

"I confess," Starr couldn't help saying.

Silence on the wire as Stepanovich, Jake was certain, wrote a note in a little book in little Cyrillic letters like little romantic bourgeois heroes marching off to die. "All right," Stepanovich finally conceded. "But comrades shouldn't make requests, should wait until they're ordered. Yes?"

"Yes, Comrade Step," as he was frequently called.

Sarah and Jake escorted Riccardo to the train that very night. As the Italian stood gracefully on the iron steps of the train, Jake joked, "Do you need a guide?"

A victorious smile on his lean face, Riccardo called out above the terminal's din, "It'll be a long war—you'll have your chance." The train whistle howled and Riccardo was off to Madrid.

They were quiet on the metro and without thinking held hands, never once letting go until they were in the small foyer of the hotel, where they encountered Marchand saying good-night to the concierge. He stared at them a moment with his bulging eyes, wheeled and departed, a fish trolling. They shrugged, grimaced at his retreating back.

At her door on the balcony, Jake leaned his weight against Sarah, his eyes questioning hers, and she wanted him to lean more heavily, to feel his weight on her, his hardness. He began suddenly to kiss her eyes, but she squirmed from his grasp. "No," she whispered fiercely. "Please. For God's sake, I'm human, leave me alone."

"Then keep your damn eyes off me all day," he said arrogantly, and ran down into the street.

And she didn't sleep all night, because what he had said was true.

For a few days he ignored her, spoke coldly, at times even contemptuously. She was a mid-Victorian, middleclass, petite-bourgeoise chunk of dried-out English mutton who paraded around on a rakish ass with a runted stunted—oh, hell! All his life he had been having his own way. Even his father, who'd loved him with a fierce passion, had said, "Give the boy space. I don't want him to become timid. He has lots of strength, let him dance to his own tune. He'll learn soon enough the world's stronger than he. Perhaps by then he will have changed a little of it." Soon was now. He wasn't accustomed to refusals by ladies. Zip, rip, tear. During college, long after

Annie of the lovely fanny, his first girl, and he had parted, it had become more genteel—to the rhythms of Mozart's *Kleine Nachtmusik* on the parlor sofa while the girl's ma and pa were off to see Charlie Chaplin at the neighborhood movie. When he had become the 1933 revolutionary hero of Union Square, down with the dirty Cossacks, up with the hammer and sickle, it had been in a Village cold-water flat to the staccato beat of the Red Cavalry March, Alexandra Kollontai's *Red Love,* the pillow under the girl's arched back. Love on the run at the New Masses ball, the cock a pole on which to hang a red flag. Come, come, Comrade, move your tail a little faster —faster, I said. Oh, sorry, darling, thought you said you wanted me to suck your O, say can you see the *Bandiera Rossa* on me?

And now where was he? In Paris with a hot nut for Sarah Ruskin and before he went off to the *lucha por la libertad,* finally to meet the enemy head on, gun to gun, he wanted to taste Sarah, he had a very special feeling for her, something exquisite it was, something he'd never felt before. She was no round-heeled college kid lamenting Life and believing she would find it on her back her eyes on the ceiling concentrating on Love and talking the class struggle in the cafeteria on 14th Street. . . . "I'll pay for it, Comrade, my father's a fat bourgeois," said like the boudoir heroine she was, so you finally were forced to say, "If you don't like your old man's money, dear, why don't you give it up?" and she stared open-mouthed at you, betrayed.

Sarah was a mature woman. "The entire world and everyone in it," she said on one of their walks, "seems to have one interest—to corrupt you, to bring you down to its level. I'll be brought down soon enough. Do you mind if I resist just a little?"

He had to respect her. Besides, she didn't construct little snares to trap your foibles so her virtues could by contrast be like shining hunters on horseback. She was, he had to admit, a decent woman, and a lovely one, too. There was a rich opulence about her body which one day he'd seen, barging into her room without knocking as she washed her nakedness from a basin, "Sorry, I wasn't thinking, Sarah"—wasn't thinking?—and found it impossible to forget. Ever. Even when he had an important job to do.

Night work again.

No overtime.

It was ten-0-three.

He sat slumped over the steering wheel of an old black Citroen parked on the narrow shoulder of a narrow road thirty miles outside Paris headed north to Le Havre. The branches of a crabapple tree, nude since it was winter, kept beating the roof of the car to the tune of a gusty wind. No moon, the sky soot-gray. That winter, if it wasn't raining, it looked as if it would.

Across the road, hidden by the trees and their own blackness, were three more cars, each headed south.

Ten-0-four.

Twenty-six minutes more. In eleven he would start his motor. Keep the engine hot and the hand cool.

A lot of trouble for twelve International Brigades volunteers, but twelve men cost a lot of money to bring to Europe. The Austrian, damn him, had led them to Perpignan. Then, to prove Stepanovich a prophet, had got his charges into a brawl with French fascists at a café. The French police had picked them up and then called the American ambassador. But Jake had phoned Pierre Marchand and old Fishface performed a splendid piece of work, dickering with the ambassador. "If you obtain their release, Your Excellency, we will pay for their passage home. You must understand, sir, we wish to avoid any embarrassment." The ambassador had understood —or at least thought he understood. Old Fishface had again bargained—this time with the gendarmerie. The police would escort the twelve men to Le Havre by truck from Paris, an American consular attaché would ride with them and deposit them safely on the *Mauretania* just prior to its sailing for the States. Jake Starr in true American movie style was to hijack them from the gendarmerie and the American consul. He hoped it wouldn't rain, because if it did it would be more dangerous than if it didn't. Simple enough.

Ten-0-six.

He wished it were over. The seat of his pants stuck to his rear, for he was sweating even though the car had no heater and it was cold wet outside. It was dangerous—yet he felt confident his plan would work. Why not? He had planned it himself. The entire business oughtn't take more than two minutes. Zip, rip, tear. Thought of Sarah Ruskin. Stopped laughing. It had become serious—all he thought of lately was how he would like to throw her one. A good hunk if he'd ever seen one. Now, now, Comrade Starr, male chauvinism. A woman's not a piece of ass, she's a comrade-in-arms. Well, that's all I want. Stop the joking.

Looked at his watch.

Ten-ten.

A new element presented itself: rain. Shit!

He kept sweating; his pants, hiking up damp from the sweat, cut into him. He wished he could leave the car a moment and let the rain cool him off, it owed him that much at least.

"No!" he snapped aloud. "The dumb sonuvabitch." The lead car across the road, an idiot, had blinked his headlights. What the hell was he nervous about? He wasn't going to do anything.

It was dead quiet but for the branches scratching the car roof, the wind flirting with the trees, and the rain. Pit pit pit.

No birds, no cicadas, nothing. *Rien. De nada.* Thought of Sarah and nothing became something.

Ten-twelve.

He lit a cigarette. Felt a little tight—loosened his belt a notch, unbuttoned his collar, slacked his shoelaces. Breathed deeply. Better. Small tricks he had picked up from Carl Vlanoc. And what are you doing tonight, Comrade Vlanoc? Had a new name: General Carlos Verdad. How many fascists have you caught so far, Comrade Truth? Leave some for me—I eat 'em like crumpets. Tough guy. Sitting here shitting shit.

The rain stopped. Had been just a patter. He hoped the road would dry in time. A car skittered past. Another. First no cars, now a traffic jam. Raised his wrist to the lit cigarette, puffed up a red light. Ten-fifteen. Started his motor; she hummed; flashed his lights. The three cars across the road responded, then he heard them start their engines with a roar. Good, everything's in order. Another fourteen, fifteen minutes and it would be over. If.

It began to rain again—goddamsonuvabitchbastard. Go away. Wished Joe Garms were here. When Joe was scared he sang songs. Please stop raining. He was sweating and now needed to urinate. Looked hopefully out into the field which bounded the road, didn't dare now. Saw a squirt of yellow light in a farmhouse. Kerosene—no rural electrification in France. The peasantry—de Tocqueville had called them the backbone of the nation—plucked clean as herringbones and the most reactionary class in France.

The rain crashed down in iron sheets—oh! Was startled by a light reflected off his rearview mirror. His stomach muscles tightened—relaxed. Two headlights blinded him. Wrong car.

Ten twenty-five.

Five minutes. The rain stopped. Too late. Every muscle in his body ached from tension. His pants cut into his scrotum and the sweat ran down his brow into his eyes. He wiped his eyes with the sleeve of his jacket.

God, the waiting, the waiting. Any time now. Better concentrate. Women are bad for concentration, very bad for discipline. It was true, she was a splendid woman. Admit it to yourself, you like her a lot. You more than like her. True. I respect her. Respect is another name for it. All right, I love her.

He kept his eyes on the rearview mirror, stepped on the clutch, guided the gear stick into first—blinked his headlights again, received an answer. When I get back to the hotel, I'll break the bloody door down and put it right to her. He realized he had an erection, scared or not, and then his eyes caught the flash of light turning the bend about a mile behind him. He wet his lips—one light! He heard the rumble of the onrushing tires on the bumpy narrow road and he slowed down his breathing. Let out the clutch, began to roll till he was a car length beyond the last of the three cars across the way. The speeding truck approached—almost upon him. He swerved right into its path, gassing his car quickly, feeling the rubber under him slip on the wet asphalt, but the car jumped ahead, the gear in second. He heard the truck slam on its brakes, rubber slapping and squealing, slipping with a terrifying whoosh, right on his tail—catch hold, catch hold, catch hold. Horns screamed. Jake braked fast, the old Citroen slid, stopped, and he was out the door as the truck, tires shrieking, caught hold, smacked into his rear bumper, stopped.

He was shouting filthy French at the gendarme behind the truck's steering wheel, the American consular aide at his side paralyzed white in the darkness. There was yelling, cursing in American, hurried footsteps, laughing, a mellifluous flute of a voice singing, "Goodbye Chicago, hello Madrid," someone calling, "Hey, Archie, c'mon!" Doors thumped—three cars tore back towards Paris and sundry points south.

Jake Starr still stood at the cab of the truck shouting French obscenities, cut it short as the gendarme winked, ran to his car, and all he thought of now was how he wanted to pee.

Not Sarah. She sat in her room, waiting for Jake to return. They had walked together from the office that late afternoon and had stopped on Faubourg St. Martin where she'd bought bread, cheese, *pâté,* apples, and a bottle of red Bordeaux. "I'm not hungry, Sarah, my stomach becomes upset when I'm scared. Oh, for God's sake, don't look so concerned. I've been trained for these things, it's part of my life."

In her room they ate quickly, without speaking much. Then as she rose to put the table things aside, she heard him rise from his chair, then total quiet, then his hands were on her shoulders and his lips burrowing beneath the collar of her blouse, his lips hot, and then he patted her behind and was gone. Without once turning she finished cleaning her room, his footsteps across the balcony and down the stairs having long since disappeared. Then she undressed, washed with the ice-cold water from the porcelain pitcher, and then, her woolen robe about her, she sat on the chair, his chair, a book open on her lap, one of Rolfe's beautifully written essays on nuclear structure, and didn't read a line, because she kept parading images about the sundrenched courtyard of her brain. There was the brawny hulk of Jake Starr, and the distinguished handsomeness of her husband.

Rolfe's urgent need for tidiness and order had led him in his youth to the submicroscopic world of nuclear physics. A pioneer is a lonely man and a lonely man is a man freezing for want of warmth, so in the early days of his youth he left the laboratory just enough to find a wife. She bore him a son, and there were a few warming years. But the laboratory was his life. The same year he was awarded the Nobel Prize for the discovery of one of the *fundamental particles* of nature, his wife died of too much whiskey. After she was buried, he realized he had given her very little else. An honest man, it was he who told Sarah of his neglect of his wife and his son.

The son became a man as the father became an institution, honor upon honor as brick upon brick. Then the son revolted against his father, the family line, even the family wealth, and became a Socialist, but of the Nationalist breed. As his son found fascism, Rolfe found the Party.

Still a vigorous man, with tremendous energy, he met her, Sarah Dawson, a girl of twenty-one. Rolfe could, when he wished, be a charming man, and of course to an intelligent girl from a parson's parish house in Sussex, a Nobel laureate, and a Ruskin, could be a sun as blinding as any. Their marriage, never a passionate one, had its disappointments, but they learned not to maul one another, and that, she had already learned, meant it was better than most. More happy than less, they lived a busy contented life.

As a young man Rolfe had been a creative researcher, and the thrust of his compulsion to order the world neatly and precisely had pushed his imagination to great heights with the obsessiveness of a mountain climber. He stormed unconquered mountain passes, gained a foothold, pushed on, conquered a few hitherto insurmountable peaks. Yet, always elusive, there stood still another, higher peak. In middle age his imagination failed him: a mountain climber crippled by sclerosis. The genius of his imagination waned but his obsession for tidiness persisted. He turned to philosophy, to the unifying theory of the universe: there must be a solution, a giant eraser which would wipe away all filth, a machine which would penetrate the mystery of all untidy packages with loose strings.

He returned to the plains. Pondered. Time ran swiftly. He must hurry. The younger scientists politely granted him his moment of awe and respect, then pushed on themselves. They would storm higher peaks, through passes first opened to man by Rolfe Ruskin. His obsession generated a great reserve of energy, made him restless, but his restlessness alone could not reactivate his imagination. Cornered by the relentlessness of the one and the immoveability of the other, he became bitterly frustrated.

One day he read the *Manifesto,* skipped immediately to Lenin. It was as if he had peered into the microscope to examine a nuclear emulsion and exclaimed: My God! a perfect theory for the creation of matter! There before his startled eyes in neat phalanx marched the unifying theory of man's history. And that history led ineluctably in one direction: to a neat and tidy world—from each according to his ability, to each according to his needs. Just like that—with a loud snap of the fingers.

Rolfe Ruskin and Jake Starr, thought Sarah, what an odd comradeship.

The center, a giant nebula, enveloped Rolfe, and he soon believed himself an integral element of its swarming growth, its movement. Movement is action: action replaced the need for imagination, provided an outlet for his restless energy. His frustration concealed itself; having confronted an imponderable massif, he had conquered it.

He became enamored of the poor.

They, alas, already overburdened with poverty, must now bear the impossible weight of sainthood.

Rolfe was a man, a mere man, composed of the same chemical elements as that arrogant, intelligent hogshead of pulverizing brawn who slept every night separated from her by six inches of wall. She could feel his hot breath—no, it was Rolfe she was thinking about. Rolfe was a gentle man, and in his neat and precise manner loved her, needed her. And she loved him, too; of that she was certain.

And Jake, this flaming sword of a man, this—she smiled wearily, the images in the bright courtyard of her mind marched gallantly to the fanfare of trumpets, and she had to laugh at herself. An odd young man who took himself so utterly seriously, yet knew how to laugh. Once he had likened her to the eighteenth century. He spoke as if he were the proprietor of history, as an antique dealer is a proprietor of period furniture. *This chair's Empire, my dear. You're eighteenth century, honey. Reason and morality. . . .* She wondered how he looked asleep. We are all like little children when we are asleep, she thought, innocent in the face of night. She heard a stair creak and for a moment she stopped breathing, it was he—no, nothing, but it was as if the thought of him were the same as touching him and desire caught at her, and she moved her hand to her breast. No, she cried out to herself, the echoes caroming off the walls of the courtyard of her wide-awake imagination, desire is a cheap fire easily burnt out. Oh, it was Rolfe's fault; he himself had given approval of her assignment in Paris, sent her long letters detailing every minute of his day, fifteen-, twenty-page letters, always remembering at their very end to ask, "And how are you, my dear?" My dear. Honey. Darling. No, it was not Rolfe's fault; it was no one's fault. It was desire.

And what is desire? she asked herself, holding her breast. A flicker, a tease. You took a cold bath and it disappeared. The following morning, there it was—a jolt. Dazed, you sat quietly, closed your eyes, rested. Ah, gone. To return in a few moments with the door's slam. "Meeting at four, Comrade Honey. Leave your brains and bring your ear muffs, Fishface's going to talk." Another slammed door.

Desire. It is the insufferable wish to be nailed to a bed by the brawny weight of love. It is the incessantly insistent image of him on her, entwined, curved, molded—it is a need, a terrible terrifying need to have hunger assuaged. It is a moment of vanity: to know a man, not any man, but that grinning bull of a man, who wanted, cajoled, cunningly planned, laid traps to ensnare your female nakedness, and you gave your hair a few extra whips of the brush and took a second's extra care with your lipstick.

Desire is wanting and not having.

Sarah did not know how long it was she sat in the dark, completely and starkly awake waiting to hear Jake's steps—when with an abruptness which made her gasp there he was, running up the stairs, those powerful thighs, tiptoeing across the balcony to her door, then silence. Total silence, her heart a hammer. She willed her eyes to see through the darkness, to cut through the door. *Open the door, my love, it is unlatched. Open it! Open it, please.* Then she heard him sigh, a very long sigh, and then *his* door squeaked. And she hated him and herself, especially herself for being a coward, for putting the entire burden on him when she desired as much as he.

She heard him quietly undressing in his room, the quiet considerate splash of water, the quiet yielding of his bed to his weight and she wished she were his bed, his pillow, and she told herself to stretch out on her bed so she could be near him, to rap on the wall, to call to him, to go to him—*go to him, you coward.*

No. It would be a lie. Just a little lie—but a lie nonetheless. *Little or great, I will not lie.*

It was then her door opened and shut, and he stood before her, a tender smile on his face, looking down at her.

She slept, he couldn't. They were still in a deep embrace. He felt an excitement such as he had never before in his remembered life known. A strange, exotic excitement, and he couldn't quite understand it. It was an excitement derived from the peace of having at last encountered an emotion which he had never believed could be his. This is love, I suppose, he thought. This is what it's all about. There wasn't at this moment a tense nerve in his body. Complete and total peace and satisfaction from the tender and gentle love Sarah had given him. The passion had been intense and wild, breathless, but the emotion had been one of absolute yielding of each to the other. Each kiss, every caress of hers had said, Love, I love you, though the words had not been uttered. And the kisses and caresses he had given her had also cried out with love. I give you all my love, all my tenderness, all my gentleness. There had been no hurt, no violence, nothing but love. They had given it to each other as if they had loved one another all their lives and had been awaiting a proper moment in their combined history to yield up this love to each other. They had embraced each other without hesitation, as if with a lifetime's familiarity. It seemed incredible to him now as he lay entwined in her sleeping arms and thighs. Her body under him was soft and had a sweetness which went beyond all time, and even asleep she held him firmly to her as if to say, You are mine, never leave me, and he was utterly content with the thought, No, I will never leave you. Never, my love, my Sarah.

Still, his bravado, his swagger, the revolutionary hero he pretended to be in one tiny cell of his brain sneered at his discovery of love. Cut it out, Jake thought, you're being romantic, gushy, she's only a sweet-assed woman you admire.

No, no, he answered himself, sex is something you have in your balls, this is something delicately held in the very marrow of your existence.

In her sleep, almost as if she had heard him, she embraced him more tightly, kissed him, moved her thighs under him in a manner to draw him deeper into her, and he yielded to her, kissed her throat softly so as not to waken her. And he suddenly remembered what this reciprocal feeling of love reminded him of, the love that his father and mother had given one another. His father had been a violent man and his mother a woman of quiet, yet determined stubbornness so that their personal quarrels could arouse strong antagonistic emotions in one another. His father would pound the table, his mother would reply with sharp irony and the very air about them would tremble with anger. Then his mother or father, one or the other, would suddenly reach out a hand to the other and smile, and abruptly they were in a tender embrace, laughing or kissing, unashamed before him, as though unconsciously they thought, he is our child and he must learn that those who love may quarrel but that love is greater than all quarrels. Hunger, the bitterness of their social or economic existence made life an endless struggle, but their love had been so profound and so satisfying, had yielded up such peace to each other that their marriage had always given him, their child, a feeling that he had been born out of and was part of a life of great beauty. And this is what he now felt with this woman whom he knew for so short a time but whom he felt he had known forever. This is what my mother and father had, and this is what I can have. He could barely believe it. Perhaps he didn't want to believe it. Again he remembered—he had thought at times, observing their love, that he would never be capable of finding anything to match it. His father had been a man of powerful personality, and how could he ever match him, and where would he ever find a woman to equal his mother's ability to love, to overcome the tumult of life which his father created by his mere presence.

Sarah, in her sleep, must have felt his presence wandering, that he was thinking of others, not her, and in the complete selfishness which intense but satisfying loving brings in its aftermath, she wanted his total presence for herself. It could have been, of course, that as his mind wandered to his parents he had relaxed his embrace. Whatever it was, she awoke.

"You're not sleeping?" she whispered.

"No," he answered. "I can't. I'm astonished at our familiarity, as if we belong to one another—as if truly we're married."

"Yes," she whispered. "I don't understand it myself."

They were quiet for a few moments, he at peace, she abruptly aware of reality. She was being unfaithful to her husband. My God, what am I doing? Yet she could feel no shame. What would her parents say? They had reared her strictly, one must be true, loyal—one must be honest with one's spouse. (They hadn't been as much as they'd pretended.) Vows are made to be kept. A woman must not give herself cheaply. Well, she hadn't. Though she had not kept her marriage vow, for some uncomprehended reason she felt deeply in herself that she had not been unfaithful to herself. Desire had been strong, perhaps her feeling for Jake was only an infatuation, but somehow she knew profoundly in her very depths that she had done, was doing, something which was not against herself, so it could not have been done cheaply. This man who lay with her, despite his apparent arrogance, his almost theatrical stance of the professional revolutionary, had made love to her, had responded to her own giving of love, with an almost innocent tenderness and gentleness. It was that man who now embraced her, not the impersonal revolutionary who spoke so often of his total commitment to the cause. Still, Rolfe was her husband, and she loved him, had never doubted for a moment that she did and she owed him complete fidelity. She had committed, was committing, an act of dishonesty. But not to myself, not to myself. Rolfe would be terribly hurt if he discovered her infidelity and she had never wished to inflict pain upon him. To inflict pain was evil, and it saddened her. What have I done? How will it end?

She felt Jake's arms tighten about her, his entire body press upon her, and the pleasure she derived sharpened the knife of guilt, made more acute the chagrin. "I'm sorry," she now said, "but suddenly I feel sad. Our presence here has become real." And she began to cry. Under him he could feel her thighs become tense, rejecting.

He tried to soothe her with soft words, to calm her, but she said, "Please," and he stopped. "I've never done this before. The thought of sleeping with a man other than my husband repelled me, it almost made me ill. I like the attentions of other men, what woman doesn't, and why shouldn't I? But I've always believed myself to be incapable of being with a man who is not my husband. Maybe it is old-fashioned but I have never been attracted to the idea of having an affair. And now I've given myself to you. I have wanted to for days, for weeks. I feel guilty, but I am not ashamed and I would be terribly unhappy if you left me now, Jake."

He embraced her strongly, kissed her shoulder, the softness of her breast. "Let's not think about it now," he said.

"Yes, let's not," she whispered. She felt his weight on her, his strength, and the intensity of her emotions, her desire, overwhelmed her, so that her guilt hid. "Will you kiss my breast," she whispered.

He caressed her breasts, kissed them gently, lovingly, and she ran her fingers through his hair. Under him her thighs again relaxed, opened to him, as if asking for his love. And she, as he before her, was incredulous at the intensity of her feeling for him and yet at the exquisite pleasure derived from the tranquility which pervaded her entire being, a feeling which she, too, never before in her life had known. And for a moment, but only for a moment because she could not accept yet her infidelity to Rolfe, she wondered: Is this the love one always reaches for, is this it at last?

And then all thought was lost as his lips became unruly, kissing her breasts, her throat, her lips, eyes, her body, where he willed, and her hands urged him to come to her, her thighs beseeched him, please hurry, come to me, come to me, and then her hands clasped at his hair to draw him up to her, to force him to give her his weight.

And when they both fell asleep, there still rang in their ears her sublime cry, "Please, hurry, burden me with the weight of love."

VI

"Y'GOTTA DO IT, it's politics. We gotta prepare to take this cruddy country over once the fascists are beat," Joe Garms muttered, then turned toward his cot on the other side of the barracks room, Skinny Horton and Bob Gladd following him without a word.

Greg Ballard had just finished telling them and Mack Berg, tall, lean, and mean-mouthed, a Harvard College grad, about what he had seen that morning during maneuvers. As Ballard crept into his cot in the dark, he heard Berg laugh harshly to himself.

"What's so damn funny?" Greg whispered sharply.

"I keep learning every day—expanding my knowledge of man and his culture, just as my professors at Harvard said I should. Dollars to donuts the same trick works among the Ubangi. When I first enrolled my gaunt scarred head in the vanguard of the revolution, I believed I was joining forces with the lowly amateurs of the world. If we're amateurs, what are the professionals like?"

"I'm beginning to wonder," Ballard whispered.

Greg Ballard lay sleepless on the straw mattress of his cot which once had bedded a nun. She must have been a slight bundle of bones because the mat had no curve in its center as had many of the others. There were nineteen other cots, ten to a row, in the large room on the second floor of a two-story stone structure. On one side of him slept Mack, and on the other Bentley "Peanuts" Murchison, Texan, Freudian, vegetarian, revolutionary, and peanut eater.

Ballard tried to sleep; he tossed, turned, squirmed, couldn't. The events of the past few days had erupted like a rash of infected pimples, to which he, Ballard, was often prone. He wanted to squeeze them out, expunge them, but was unable to. Like he was unable always to ignore another man's hurting. Unable anymore. He didn't need anyone to tell him that what he was he'd be forever. He had wounds which were unhealable. He was able to be a man among these men but he could never join them as absolutely as they seemed to require. With them it seemed always to be all or nothing. It would mean giving up the inner privacy necessary to his existence. That's why he loved fishing. You wake early before the sun's out, you go to the dock which stinks of fish (and you love it), turn the motor over, let her run, adjust the oil mix, smell the weather, read the forecasts, happy the fog is up so you can cast the lines off the capstans—they were called niggerheads, he didn't mind anymore, that was the least of it—and head her out to sea. He loved the sea most when it mulled, was heavy gray, rough heavy surf, not choppy, the sun barely showing through dark gray clouds, a crisp breeze, and he had to wear his old red mackinaw, worn and patched by his mom. All alone on the sea. Complete in himself and his boat, feeling the sea through his boat, its power, its mystery, its life source. Feeding him too, and mom and Loney and aunts and uncles and cousins. His boat was deep-prowed and deep-stemmed, of ancient oak, nondescript, a boat which he'd reclaimed half-sunken at the wharf, reclaimed with his own hands, vouchsafing percentages of future fish catches for lumber, for motor parts to Machine & Marine. All alone on his boat he could pick his nose, he could fart, he could sing, he could dance, he could daydream freely, wildly, sullenly. No one there to laugh or say. He could sleep on a calm day, the wheel tied down, let the currents and tides take him where they would. Or feeling the wind on his back or on his face or through the triangular little red canvas sail when the wind was on his back to help the old diesel in its work. He loved the wind running behind him. Watching the gulls, the greedy clumsy birds fighting each other for every clam or mussel—just like men. Stealing a sandwich out of his hands. No matter. The real joy of being alone. Talking to himself, singing some blues song, figuring the sea, figuring his life. On the sea no one could hurt him. No one but the sea itself. The sea could destroy him, beat him, kill him. But no man anymore could break him. Never. A man could kill him, but no man could break him. He had found that out himself. Found it for himself. They could call him every name—and they had—and they could turn their backs on him, boys he'd played with, gone to school with—and they had—and the pain had embittered him, but he had learned no man could break him, only he himself. Oh, yes, he'd built his defenses, he was a cautious man, he smelled out a man like he smelled out the wind or the sea, his body a litmus paper; if a man had that hatred in him, his, Ballard's, body turned purple inside where it couldn't be seen. Like it had been whipped. It had made him careful, had taught him to move more slowly. *Don't show too much to a man before you know him,* he always said to himself. If he loved being alone so much, loved the sea, why was he here? Since the first day he had read of Hitler, his, Ballard's, body had become purple inside. He ached and he pained and he writhed so his mom had said once, What's ailin' yuh? Y'look like Jesus on the cross, but I weren't no Virgin and you're a heathen. What's ailin' yuh? And it was an ailing after reading the news stories and seeing the newsreels. There was so much hatred in Hitler and his kind that the entire world ought to feel purple inside. He went on the sea to be alone, to be where no man could laugh or curse at him or do him harm, but a man can't live on the sea. He has to live on land because that's where men make their lives and a man can't separate his life from other men. Even from those who laugh and curse, belittle him, humiliate him. That hatred has always to be fought, and that's the way he, Ballard, had learned no man could break him, only kill him.

Someone down the line of beds talked gibberish in his sleep, Peanuts snorted, another coughed, still another sighed sadly. At the opposite end, where Skinny Horton slept, a straw mat creaked faster and faster, and Ballard smiled wryly to himself. Life's little pleasures.

Otherwise it was quiet, and he fell asleep.

For more than a month they had been training in Villanueva, an ancient peasant village curled angularly like a scrawny dun-colored cat in the softly rolled hills of the province of Cuenca—mud huts, three churches, one a gigantic fortress, two monasteries, two convents, two Moorish manors magnificently wrought, all guarded by tall graceful poplars.

They still trained, as Joe Garms had written Jake Starr, with several old Canadian rifles, no bullets and no bayonets, and one 1914 vintage machine gun.

For the past week they had reached their full complement of men—five hundred. No columns right, no columns left, but much crawling. Amidst great rejoicing, each man was given two bullets to shoot at a target of sandbags set up in the convent chapel so they could accustom themselves to the noise of exploding gunfire close to their ears.

In the weeks they were in Villanueva no passes were issued for leave to Albacete, the International Brigades' base and the closest big city to Villanueva. Many asked; none were received.

"But we gotta get laid sometime," complained Joe Garms.

"Hear, hear," echoed the battalion.

It became a problem. Had to have a meeting.

They held theirs in the convent chapel, altar dismantled, plaster saints carefully wrapped in burlap and stowed in the stone cellar. Comrade Charlie Flagg, a handsome fullback, clefted chin, strong short nose, charming smile, cynical blue eyes, a riot of wavy blond hair, just a born leader, chaired the meeting. He had become battalion commissar after Comrade Phillips was forced to return to the States because of illness. The men weren't sure yet whether they liked Comrade Flagg because he always seemed to have his hammer jaw raised above his broad shoulders ready to smash a poor rank and filer's head. Now he stood easily on the dais as the men sat quietly in the pews before him. He made a short speech punctuated by exclamation marks enumerating the reasons why they could not go to Albacete to get laid, concluding with the golden words, "It's against the party line in Spain to encourage prostitution. Bathe in cold water from the barrel!"

"Yeah," shouted Joe Garms, the gravel of his voice almost shattering the stained-glass windows, "we'll pickle it."

Even the commissars laughed. Very unusual.

Comrade Flagg introduced the sandy-haired doctor who had just arrived. An academic smile on his face, he gave a highly technical discourse on the degenerative effects of spirochete and gonococci on the human corpus.

They listened politely.

Then, in all seriousness, he concluded, "Comrades, I realize the psychic disturbances resulting from sexual abstinence are debilitating. But you need not abstain." Everyone moved to the edge of his seat, slyly eyed his bunk buddy, tongues salivating. "You can masturbate."

They cheered, applauded, stamped their feet, gave him a standing ovation.

He became known as Doc Jerk-off, and thereafter was consulted only if a man thought he was dying.

The anarchists of Spain, true revolutionists, went the Party one up. They plastered Free Spain with exquisite posters which proclaimed: No Prostitution and No Masturbation!

Thus they vied for the minds of men.

So they crawled *mucho,* stripped and reassembled their old rifles and lone machine gun, laughed *mucho,* complained, had many meetings. And despised the commissars. *Mucho.*

The military commander of the International Brigades base at Albacete, Comrade Vidal, Spanish name but French crony of André Marty, visited briefly. On a yellowing knoll outside the village, in the shadow of a kingly poplar, he brought the volunteers greetings from their leaders in Albacete, from their International comrades at the fronts, spoke a few minutes about the progress of the war. Excellent. Then he admonished them to maintain an iron discipline, to obey their political and military leaders without question. With a thin smile, authoritatively, he concluded, "You will receive new rifles, bayonets, good machine guns, ample ammunition before you leave for the front." They cheered. "And when you take your positions in the trenches, Comrades, you will discover that the fascist soldiers do not have their hearts in this war, are cowardly most of them, and in the face of your guns and bayonets will flee in wild disorder." A rousing ovation from the green recruits. "*Salud!*"

"*Salud!*" they echoed.

So thrilled by this comradely wisdom was one of the American commissars, a former leader of antimilitarist demonstrations at Columbia, that he was impelled immediately to pen his wife a letter, closing, "And, my darling, when we arrive at the front—God! I hope it is soon—all I will have to do is pull out my gleaming Colt .44"—*sic!*— "and the yellow fascist dogs will turn tail and run. Jesus, how I love my gun!"

Another day, another meeting.

"Tomorrow," said Comrade Flagg, "a group of thirty Irish volunteers are joining our battalion. The British had no room for them. I must remind you that these comrades are not long since from Ireland. Some might be those very Irish who marched with our first contingent in Barcelona. However, they're probably Catholics and will be easily offended by the careless anti-Catholic remarks that comrades make. So watch your tongues. You are also not to use the prayerbooks as your source for toilet paper. The Irish might not like that."

There was scattered laughter. A few days after the Americans' arrival at the convent, a secret cupboard had been found containing hundreds of prayerbooks. Their soft, tissuelike pages, it was immediately discerned, were more suitable for the above purpose than the old much-read copies of the *Daily Worker* and, when those weren't at hand, the leaves of trees and bushes.

Flagg, only slightly disconcerted by the laughter, continued. "This is no joking matter. They will probably find it offensive, and we're not anti-Catholic at this time."

Hunt Carrington, a tall Chicago Negro with red-brown skin—his mother was a Cheyenne—sang out, "They'll find the *D.W.* and the leaves even more offensive, that is, if they end up being sensitive at all."

The meeting ended in boisterous laughter.

The Irish were a ragged, impoverished-looking crew. Most were from Dublin, and many had fought with the Irish Republican Army against British rule. Some had served with the British colonial army in Asia and Africa. Those loved to regale the Americans with tales of adventure and danger among the Sikhs and Gurkhas. They were expert gunsmiths and boasted knowledge of any gun made. All wore holy medals under their shirts and made the sign of the cross before embarking on maneuvers—all but Sean O'Hara Levy, who spoke Yiddish with a brogue, having been born and bred in Dublin.

They had been training with the English but one day a new Irish war for independence broke out. The English comrades had treated them like colonials, they said, and it became too much to take. One morning the English awoke to find their barracks completely surrounded by Irish volunteers for liberty, armed with guns, knives, and cobblestones. A hasty truce was reached before André Marty shot them all, and agreement made that they be transferred to the Americans. Here they were.

The Americans did not know whether to believe this story, but it was so often repeated, with such generous interspersals of "bloody limeys" and "bloody bastids," that it did not seem hospitable and comradely to express any doubt.

Three days following their arrival, the prayerbooks reappeared, found by one of the Irish, who gleefully declaimed his great discovery to the world. Without hesitation, he was congratulated by all but the sour-faced pols. After sufficient time had elapsed to permit intimate questions, he announced, "A mon carries his faith in his heart, not on printed bits of tissue paper. Besides, me arse is raw."

Villanueva was a village of several hundred people, most of whom worked the vast fields which previously had been part of the ancestral estate of a *marqués* and his family. The fields were tilled by hand and burro. The earth was arid and hilly, and the acreage yield very low.

Before the February election of 1936, the Villanueva peasants had worked for the *marqués* under the supervision of the field bosses, *caciques.* The villagers had voted overwhelmingly for the *frente popular,* which listed among its campaign promises land to the landless.

Victory in the election brought no discernible change in the six months prior to the fascist revolt. The fascist rebellion had been challenged by stark paralysis on the part of the People's Front government, but the workers and peasants of Catalonia and the remainder of Spain had risen in vigorous, almost gleeful, anger and defeated the fascists in every major city but five. This had so frightened the *marqués* and his *caciques* that they fled, followed by the priests, monks, and nuns. Villanueva was notable for the fact that no atrocities had been perpetrated by either side.

The land was then equally divided among the peasants by village meeting and tilled cooperatively. The storekeepers and the blacksmith continued, as before, to ply their respective trades. The churches remained as they had been left, untouched and unused. The schoolteacher, self-named Espartaco, leader of the few Communists in the village, moved his family into the massive fortress-church which dominated the town. By a sort of psychological transference, he dominated the village; also, as Mack Berg said, "Because he is literate, energetic and ruthless."

The battalion saw little of the peasants, thin, hard-working, fragmented angular faces, their reserve a wall. Their women the volunteers saw even less. Their daughters not at all. Though at times a young merry eye was caught sneaking a look through a shuttered window.

And there was Daniel Nuñez:

A young man in his late twenties, short, thin, a gentle mouth and burning eyes, a consumptive peasant who had lived his entire life in Villanueva; a hard-working peasant who had since the age of eighteen been the villagers' spokesman in dealings with the *marqués,* a tough, unrelenting spokesman who never knelt to the man whose land he tilled; he had a wife, two children, a burro, was self-educated. He had once been a Party man, had quit in 1935 when the line changed from revolution to *frente popular*. He no longer was spokesman for the village, had become leader of a very small minority.

One day the village council decided to have a town meeting and invited the Americans to witness their ability to handle a democratic tool. It was Lincoln's birthday.

About seventy-five Americans, including numerous Cubans, attended and took the rear benches in their very own convent chapel. The front rows soon filled with villagers. Only men. Politics in Villanueva were not for women, not yet. Each peasant as he entered removed his cap and unwound the shawl which covered half his face and all his chest against the sharp cold nights of Cuenca province. Excepting one, who kept his shawl tightly wound and his cap on his head.

The meeting was chaired by a village elder, small, thin-shouldered, wiry with age and six decades in the fields, a mighty *hidalgo* nose darkening his already swarthy face in shadow under the sickly yellowish bulbs.

"Friends," he said, "before we go ahead with our meeting I would like to say a few words to our American brothers. Before you arrived in our village, I must admit we were concerned with how your alien presence would affect our lives, our village, our customs. You are young, you are vigorous, you are all brave to have come to help us in our fight against tyranny, but we are a small village, unsophisticated, and you are foreigners. We were frightened. I must tell you that your behavior, your courtesy, your considerateness, your respect for our customs and ways have made us ashamed that we should even for a moment have been frightened of your alien presence. We are very proud that our village was chosen to be your training camp. And as a token of our respect for you, tomorrow our daughters will give a dance in your honor. The entire battalion, of course, is invited to attend. There will be cakes and wine—and—" with a shy smile— "our daughters to dance with."

As he concluded, all the Spaniards present rose, turned to the Americans, and applauded. The volunteers, because they deserved the praise they had just been given, were doubly pleased. But, before they could become smug, the meeting began.

It opened with a discussion of cooperative business, so many acres plowed and prepared for seed, so many acres fallow, in a few days the olive harvest would begin, and so on. Questions were asked, were answered, all in a spirit of freedom and comradeship.

Then Comrade Espartaco reported on the fighting fronts: Madrid is still holding, Toledo will be ours, Málaga wavers, the Basques are firm, and in the Aragon, with a sneer, "*fútbol* is played in no-man's land." A thin arm, belonging to the villager who hadn't removed his cap and shawl, was raised in the front row. Espartaco waved it aside and continued. "The Popular Front government is now forging an army which will destroy the enemy, and though the democratic world does not sell us arms, from its factories and fields have come the brave young men of the International Brigades, true antifascists all, many of whom have already shed their blood defending heroic Madrid." Enthusiastic applause from both Spaniard and American. "But there is one country which doesn't permit us to perish without aid, the great socialist land which stands with Free Spain as a bulwark of democracy against the fascist horde and infidel Moorish blacks who murder our Spanish people."

Again the thin arm punctured the air above its head, an exclamation point asking a question. Espartaco continued, impassioned.

"There are those who raise the slogan of all power to the revolution. It is a slogan of betrayal because it is a slogan which would further divide our already sharply divided country. It is common sense to know that only together, bourgeois and workingman, landowner and peasant, Communist, Socialist, Republican, Basque, and Catalan separationist, that only together shall we find the strength to defeat the fascists of Spain and Italy and Germany. I know you will reject these false revolutionists, these false messiahs, as you reject the fascists, for they would lead you to the gallows. Have faith in the *frente popular,* have faith in its leaders, have faith in your ability to work and fight together, and the war will be won. The Republic will be ours.

"Abajo Franco! Arriba España!

"No pasarán!"

The mixed audience applauded with great vehemence, joined by Espartaco himself in emulation of Stalin.

Now the exclamation point, Daniel Nuñez, was permitted his question—more accurately, a series of questions, which it soon became apparent was a Socratic oration.

He rose and turned to his audience. Slowly he unwound his shawl from his face, tucked it in at his chest. He was a frail man, with sunken cheeks, whose pallor heightened the blackness of his bright passionate eyes.

First pulling at the bill of his cap, he began to speak in a clear pure voice. "Why is the front of the Aragon quiet, Comrades? Could it be that the troops defending the soil of Aragon have somewhere misplaced the courage with which they stormed huge walls of stone to wrest Barcelona from fully armed soldiers just last July?" A short staccato spurt of a cough so raspy its grate made everyone in the chapel wince stopped him; then, wiping his lips with a large red kerchief, pulling again on his cap, he continued. "Or is it perhaps because they have no bullets and guns? But it is known to all that since November our great ally, the Soviet Union, sends us arms from her factories, transported perhaps by cart and burro, for it has taken six months to arrive."

A murmur mulled across the room, and Mack Berg felt Joe

Garms seated next to him stiffen as Jaime Ortega's voice rumbled in Joe's ear. Espartaco jumped to his feet and was hurriedly talking and gesticulating. It was impossible for most of the Americans to understand.

"He's calling him a dirty renegade Trotskyite fascist dog," Jaime Ortega whispered loud enough for those around him to hear.

One of the boys muttered, "Then let's hang the bastard." Some of the Americans tittered. Among the Spaniards there was loud shouting.

Nuñez stood calmly, a smile about his mouth. The village elder who chaired the meeting pounded the table with his bony fists, and order was restored.

"Everyone must be permitted to speak freely," the old man stated. "All here are friends. There are no fascists. This is democratic Spain."

Most of the Spaniards applauded, though some among them did not; the Americans shrugged and wriggled on their uneasy butts, not knowing what else to do. Ballard felt embarrassed, a guest at a family spat, and thought of leaving. Mack Berg sat motionless, his face stony; Joe Garms seemed to be dancing on his buttocks. Ortega, called the lone *vaquero* because of his silent, lean leathery look, seemed to be enjoying his role as interpreter.

The heretic continued, his voice fresh and clear. "Perhaps the democratic government of Russia does not trust the false revolutionaries who beat the reactionary dogs while the *frente popular* government sat panic-stricken upon its hands, as cringing and as timid as the rabbits of Estremadura? Perhaps it desires that they die, so there would be none to say no as its agents devour the parties of the *frente popular* one by one?"

Dead quiet.

"Now the great anarchist leader Durruti is dead and the

leaders of my party are being slandered and maligned by those Hungarian assassins, Vlanoc and Roegen. *Verdad* and *Ernesto.* They laugh at us with their names. And to replace those who have died and who are hunted, Compañero Es-par-ta-co," he laughed, "welcomes Stalin's most courageous and loyal corps of ambassadors: the agents of the OGPU."

Espartaco leaped to his feet, livid, pounded the table with his fists, and spoke so rapidly and loudly—POUM POUM, mimicking the acronym of Nuñez's party—that his words bounced off the *azulejo*-tiled walls, then rolled along the floors like bowling balls, almost upsetting a pedestal on which a plaster Virgin and Child had once stood serenely. Shouts of anger rose from among the villagers planted among the audience, and though not understanding the words, Joe Garms seemed to understand the pattern, for Ballard saw him smile knowingly, then heard him whisper, "A setup." Mack Berg muttered under his breath, "Pros even in this hick town."

The old peasant was on his feet. Slowly his eyes moved from one shouter to the other. Without a word, without a sound, his eyes raging, he stared the shouters down. Now Espartaco was the target of his eyes. That boiling kettle—POUM POUM, it *was* a funny name, yet oddly no one laughed—subsided. Daniel Nuñez stood coolly, his arms akimbo, his own impassioned eyes staring into space, disturbed only by his own consumptive cough.

Again the village elder spoke, each word spoken distinctly so even the Americans to whom the tongue was strange could understand. "Compañero Daniel will be permitted to speak until he has concluded. I am truly unhappy that our friends from democratic America should be witness to this spectacle on Lincoln's birthday. The democratic town meeting is a gift they have bestowed upon the world.

"Proceed, Daniel."

Mack Berg, who labored hard to keep his corrugated facial

muscles immobile and his small brown eyes indifferent, saw Tom Demo, a one-man battalion OGPU, a bull of a man with the face of a Fra Lippi angel, sitting coldly on the far side of the chapel. Demo, for democracy, worked his jaws, teeth gritting teeth, his jaw muscles balled like steel agates trying to break through the skin.

Nuñez resumed. "I apologize for having spoken carelessly. I did not mean to imply that those of the International Brigades who have come to fight against injustice and for liberty are agents of the OGPU. I admire you as I admire all men who risk their lives for justice and freedom. I merely ask you to keep an open mind and a clear eye and to listen to what I have to say. It is rumored in Albacete that even your comrades have already received cruel notice of the arrival of that quiet band of diplomats, those gentle lovers of humanity, the OGPU. Ask your international comrades, perhaps they will speak."

Tom Demo, the one-man OGPU, stood up like a shot, sat down with a bang. The Americans dared not turn their heads; they sat and stared into nothing. Greg Ballard remembered the rumors Joe had picked up from an American kid who had gone AWOL in Albacete to join a Spanish battalion. "André Marty is nuts, the Gaypayoo is all around, and you guys will have to asslick commissars to keep them off your back."

Nuñez was again speaking. "The Aragon front is quiet because the revolutionary militia of the FAI and the POUM, Workers Party of Marxist Unification—yes, a very humorous name, ha-ha—are without weapons. Only those who kneel to His Holiness, leader of all the Russias, receive arms. My comrades will not kneel, for they are revolutionists and Spaniards.

"First the war and then the revolution is a slogan of absurdity: without the revolution of July there now would be no war. The fascist hangmen would this very moment be erecting their gallows for the lot of us.

"The shops of Madrid, Valencia, Murcia are fully stocked, yet our troops at the fronts are hungry and sleep thinly clothed in ice-cold trenches. A revolutionary government would put an end to such cruel stupidity.

"The exploited, colonized Moors—infidel blacks, what an ugly term for a revolutionist to use"—Nuñez turned his head to stare contemptuously at Espartaco—"stream daily into Cádiz from across the sea. Why does not our so-called democratic government grant Morocco freedom and so dam the stream? A revolutionary government would not hesitate to institute a policy of self-determination, this time in fact and not in fancy, self-determination with freedom and justice.

"In Villanueva we have taken the land and we till it together as brothers. This is possible for we are a small village and are forgotten. From Valencia I have heard that the government refuses to permit such economic justice, and the peasants must return the land to the landowners, even to some of those who have fled. If they refuse, the Communist Lister sends his troops to force them to uncollectivize. And as Minister of Agriculture in our democratic government we have the great Bolshevik Vicente Uribe. Bah! He will believe in collectivization only when it is imposed by the state—*his* state, backed by the guns of the secret police: *his* secret police. Well, we shit on his secret police: we shit on his state.

"I must remind you that only during the days of the revolution in July and August were there victories, and only since the revolution has been thwarted have there been defeats and no victories.

"I say to you only a government which is moral in all its acts, only a government which is just, only a government which never bows to blackmail, which itself has clean hands, can recapture the minds and hearts of its people and go on to victory. I say that to you—and my comrades join me. And no matter what our enemies say, whether they be wearers of the black of the *marqués* or the red of Espartaco, we will continue to shed our blood in the struggle against injustice and slavery."

Nuñez paused as he reached inside his jacket with a trembling hand. The chapel was deathly still, tense. He drew out a rumpled sheet of notepaper, stretched it taut before his eyes, and resumed. "Two months before Durruti died, he was interviewd by a Dutch journalist, who said to him: 'You will be sitting on top of a pile of ruins if you are victorious.' Durruti answered: 'We have always lived in slums and holes in the wall. We will know how to accommodate ourselves for a time. For, you must not forget, we can also build. It is we who built these palaces and cities, here in Spain and in America and everywhere. We, the workers, we can build others to take their place. And better ones. We are not the least afraid of ruins. We are going to inherit the earth. There is not the slightest doubt about that. The bourgeoisie might blast and ruin its own world before it leaves the stage of history. We carry a new world, here, in our hearts. That world is growing this minute.' "

Daniel Nuñez paused for a moment, looked proudly about the chapel, broke into one of his hacking coughs, the kerchief catching the bloody sputum. It was painful even for his enemies to observe. The cough subsiding, Nuñez looked about the room, his eyes in pain. "Durruti was an anarchist who was beginning to learn of the necessity for cooperation with other political parties, to learn that freedom without law to discipline one's actions also led to unfreedom. He was killed some say by one of his own comrades who feared he was compromising his anarchist principles, others say by a Stalinist who feared his leadership among the working class and peasantry. I do not know so I cannot say. He was not, of course, a member of my party. But I, and my comrades, have learned from the tragic experience of other comrades in other lands that no party, no man, has a monopoly on the correctness of any one course in human behavior or in politics. A simple thought which seems to so many to be impenetrable." Nuñez smiled. "Because the party of which I am a member has made it an integral principle of its program, it has earned the hatred of Stalin and the sharp criticism of Trotsky. We search for a path which will lead Spain to a democratic, just, socialist society. We will listen to anyone who will illuminate that path.

"*Muchas gracias, compañeros,* for hearing me out.

"*Abajo Franco! Arriba la revolución!*"

Nuñez sat down, his head drawn into his shoulders to ward off the blows which must surely follow. A goodly number of the villagers applauded with passion; Espartaco's men sat thin-lipped. None of the Americans applauded, many of them not having understood a word. Espartaco, rising, his jaw sharp as a Thracian axe, nodded to Charlie Flagg, the battalion commissar, who in turn signaled the Americans to leave. The peasants wouldn't do what had to be done with strangers present.

Quietly the volunteers retired from the chapel; those who had understood were angry, but some, like Mack Berg, showed no emotion, wore a blank stare. Greg Ballard did, too, to mask the excitement the speaker, via Jaime Ortega's interpretation, had aroused in him. Nuñez's was the first revolutionary speech he had ever heard anyone but a Communist make, and he hadn't heard one from a Communist, not even Jake Starr, to equal it. So this was a Trotskyite—no, the man had indicated he wasn't. Still, it was one thing to be warned of the devil, another to be confronted by him.

As they stood along the latrine trench behind the chapel, watering the stones, they could hear Espartaco chopping out short staccato sentences. "He has humiliated us in front of these fine American boys. He has embarrassed us. He has insulted us. His beautiful phrases mask his growing sympathy for the *fascist Falange*. He must be expelled from the village." "*Sí, sí,*" from his claque planted about the room. "POUM POUM" pounded like a battle-ax. "*Expulsión, expulsión*" exploded through the convent roof. "*Sí, sí*" echoed in geometric pattern off the tiled walls.

Down at the end of the latrine, Tom Demo squatted, a beautiful angelic smile softening his gorgeous lips.

The following day passed quietly, maneuvers, crawling, and an afternoon tea dance with the village maidens, each protected by one heavy dress, sixteen petticoats, and a score of mothers, grandmothers, great aunts, and baby sisters and brothers. Fathers were off working in the fields, big brothers fighting at Madrid, Córdoba, Toledo. There was great politeness, a multitude of smiles, and a genteel pushing-shoving about the dance floor to music supplied by two ancient guitarists who had never heard that Spaniards are supposed to excel with the instrument. It was pleasant, and the girls remained untouched. Except one, it was said. There's always one who breaks loose.

On the morning which followed, while defending Villanueva against an imaginary attack, Ballard peered through the sights of his ancient machine gun, Joe Garms at one side, Jaime Ortega at the other, when a very real enemy entered his target area, coming from—not into—the village. It was an enemy whose determined jaw petrified his fingers on the trigger of his bulletless gun and struck like an iron shaft into his gut.

It was the consumptive Daniel Nuñez. On foot he led a burro and cart laden with household goods and bedding. On top of this ragged lot sat a woman cradling an infant with one arm, the other encircling a staring white-faced child. Ballard followed them as in slow motion they trundled down the road between two beautifully symmetric rows of poplar trees, which stood a majestic guard of honor on either side of the road.

For a full thirty minutes Ballard lay behind his gun, his eyes following the length of the narrow road beneath the trees. Joe Garms alongside him was quiet for once, Jaime his usual silent self. On occasion Nuñez would stop, the cart and burro not waiting, to cough his hacking cough, his back humped like a penitent's at a station of the cross. Inside Ballard felt purple, as if he had been whipped, and no longer able to bear the sight lowered his head to the cold harshness of the gun until he heard Ortega whisper, "They are gone."

When Ballard raised his head, he and Joe Garms avoided one another's eyes.

That night after Ballard related what he had seen to Mack and the others, Joe Garms growled, "Y'gotta do it, it's politics."

The following morning, the volunteers of liberty asleep in the convent were awakened by the tin-eared bugler's reveille, and someone yelling, "Rise and shine! Pack your gear, the trucks are here. Tomorrow we start killin' fascists!"

VII

"THESE KIDS are on their way to fight and kill fascists," Jake Starr said snappishly that same morning at a meeting of *responsables*. "And I won't lie to them. To the whole damn world, but not to them. I'll steal, I'll forge passports, I'll even—I'll do anything for the Party, but I won't lie to or steal from my comrades going to Spain."

Fishface Marchand had just submitted a request from the Tech-Bureau. Comrade Jacques was to collect the passports from all arriving American volunteers to Spain. He was to inform them they would be held in safekeeping by the bureau until their return to France after the Civil War's end.

An obvious steal.

"No," Starr said quietly. "I won't do it."

"Don't be naïve," Marchand said coldly.

"But all Americans are naïve," muttered Heinz Brucker, the Hamburg dockwalloper pre-Hitler, a party pro. They called him the Liverwurst, a solidly packed man. He had worked in the German underground for two years, and the Paris assignment was a vacation before he went on to Spain. "They think revolutions are made by honest-to-goodness truth."

"Sssh," hushed Peter the Czech; Peter Rabbit, long pointy ears, timid brown eyes, frozen rabbit face.

The others in the room snickered, save for the English lady, who bit her bruised lips.

Comrade Starr merely snapped, "Shut up!" and the snickering froze.

Marchand stood, a parabola, reached for his coat, opened the door. Giving Jake one last chance, he said, "Is that your answer to the bureau?"

"I told you once, I'll tell you again: I'll ask them for their passports, but I'll explain that they are to be used by our agents, and to get them back, if they come out of Spain alive, they'll have to go to the American consul and either inform on themselves or perjure themselves. Then if they give up their passports, they'll be doing it voluntarily. That's as far as I'll go—no further."

"And you worked with Carl Vlanoc?"

"Yes, I did. And that is none of your business."

"Then you're not only arrogant, you're a fool."

Starr rose, banged on the table with his fist, and red in the face shouted, "You stinking fishfaced bureaucrat, I'll hang you by your heels!"

Marchand stumbled through the doorway out of Starr's reach, and the latter stood, feeling the idiot. It had been childish and he knew it. Wished he could retrieve it and do it another way. Too late. Lost his temper—what was eating him?

The others in the room said nothing, though Heinz found it difficult to repress a sneer.

Starr grabbed his coat and left. He had better hurry or he would end with his head in a noose coiled by Comrade Step's agile strong fingers.

As he passed through the gate of the courtyard to the street, he felt a hand on his arm. It was Sarah. He stared at her coldly.

"You were right," she said.

"We'll soon see," he bit out. A fine thing, receiving affirmation from the most bourgeois of them all. It was an apparatus matter and had nothing to do with her. He lengthened his stride, wanting to lose her.

She ignored his rudeness, kept pace with him. "Do you think it will rest there?"

"No, Sarah. Now please go away."

He was overwrought, this wasn't like him, so she walked with him toward the metro on Place du Combat. Since her hand had touched his sleeve she had not withdrawn it. Now it nested, a warm bird, in the crook of his arm. It felt good and he was glad she had ignored his bad temper, but he had work to do, and quickly, there was no time for this love bit. He had twenty kids holed up in Le Havre, another thirty were on the Atlantic headed for France, and if their passports were expropriated—it was nothing else but—they would never see them again. These damn bureaucrats, couldn't they wait until the dead were buried?

At the metro he excused himself, tried an apologetic smile, but it went awry and his face looked like a chipped gargoyle. "I'm sorry, Sarah, I have work to do."

She withdrew her hand from his arm. He was caught up short by the void it left. Quickly, he took her hand and kissed the open palm, then left her standing in the middle of the Place du Combat near a kiosk plastered with posters reading in large black letters on a red background: SOLIDARITY. In six languages.

As he entered the metro he looked back and saw her still standing there, lost, a bird in the wrong nest. He wanted to run to her, to take her in his arms; she looked forlorn, unhappy, lost, truly lost. What the hell did she get herself involved with him for? He wanted to comfort her, to crush her warm soft body in his arms, *Don't worry, my love*—not now he couldn't, had work to do and he had to do it fast, because he was in trouble and *he* could be crushed, his warm body, and he knew it, because of this stupid, bureaucratic venality. The revolution wasn't supposed to be like this, it was supposed to be barricades and flowing crimson pennants and a million people yelling *hermanos hermanos hermanos* as you marched down the Ramblas in Barcelona. In a couple of days there would probably be lots of dead Americans outside of Madrid—they would have plenty of passports without stealing and lying.

He located a telegraph office on rue Saint Honoré. "French dealers demand letters credit for consignment Stop Have refused Stop Await instructions today Stop Immediately Exclamation point Starr"

In Paris it was noon; in New York it was still early morning. He would have to wait a few hours. Found a café nearby, nibbled on some cheese and bread, drank Pernod till he was half-tight. He was in trouble—so what? What could they do to him? Demote him and send him back to the rank and file? Perhaps that would suit him best. They would send him to Spain. Vlanoc would have a fit. Well, up his with a hammer and sickle. Greg, Joe, the battalion were probably in Albacete by now, being outfitted with guns, bullets, bayonets, helmets, even gas masks—he would meet them at the front. He didn't need any training. And Sarah? Now, why did she have to intrude? All woman and no feminine blackmail. After his rudeness she probably thought he had been lying that morning. No, she wouldn't. She wasn't simple-minded.

As he had sat on the bed, putting on his shoes, he had said, "You're not just a woman to sleep with. I've been running around with an empty space inside me, and you've filled it. Amply," and he smiled. She was lying there, soft-bosomed and round-bottomed, her hair spread wildly over the pillow. "My love for you has filled me all up."

"It's too soon to talk of love, Jake."

"I suppose," he said, feeling suddenly flat.

She touched his hand, and he looked at her. She was staring

at him intently. "Now I know what my body was made for," she said. "To carry your weight. That seems to be its sole purpose in life."

It sounded good, her saying that. He stood at the side of the bed, half dressed, and she laughed. "Look, there he is, a jumping jack." Without bothering to undress again, he gave her all his weight.

"I love you, Sarah. I've known you for about six weeks now, that's a long time."

"I'm sorry," she said wrinkling her brow, "but right now I feel terribly guilty and disloyal," and she moved from under him.

She would feel guilty, of course. "I understand," he avowed, rising to his feet. He finished dressing quickly and left.

Now he ate more cheese and bread, drank from his Pernod. Gently but obstinately she had filled the vacuum in his life. How was he going to dislodge her? . . . Ah, *merde.* It was good he would be leaving soon. He remembered Carl and Eva and the sadness and crying. Eva was his mother's sister; Vlanoc had been her husband. It was late at night and they'd thought he was asleep. He was only a kid. Eva hadn't seen Carl for four years; he had come home from China via Moscow and would be leaving again after a few days.

"I can't wait any longer," he heard Eva say to Carl. "I want to begin living and it's impossible without my husband." *Mein Mann.*

How sad it had sounded when Carl said, "Revolution can't wait for us to love—for us to live."

Carl must have begun to wring his hands—that was the first time, the first visit, they had noticed that ugly little motion of his—for Eva said, "You cannot love, you cannot live," crying out, "because your hands are filthy with blood. It is not the revolution, it is the blood!" She began to scream and wail, became so hysterical Carl had to slap her hard.

Then he heard his father holding his mother down in the next room. "Stay here! She has to settle it herself. It's their life, and it's not ours to interfere with."

Oh! what was the use thinking about it now? He had Sarah to think about. He hoped she wouldn't cry. Ah, women cry, so what! He was glad he had been honest with her, too. During the night he had told her the Party came first with him. First, last and—she couldn't say he hadn't been as honest as she, could she? Perhaps he shouldn't be so vain, she would be as glad as he that he was going soon. Glad. So glad. Maybe he would die. His stomach quivered involuntarily, curled. No, not me. I haven't lived yet.

Ordered another Pernod. I'm drinking too much. Good for the soul. In trouble with the bureau, to wit, Comrade Step, ergo Joseph Stalin; and Carl Vlanoc, General Carlos Verdad, was in Murcia busy chasing down fascists and Trotskyites and with no time or inclination to bail out his boy. *I am not only drunk, I am scared.*

When Jake entered the metro, once looking back, Sarah felt her heart tremble. She stood for a moment gazing after him, her hand in midair, and she realized how truly frightened she was for him, for herself. Desire—pure desire. Is that all it was? Her knees were quivering, and she could feel the beating of her heart in the clamor of the midday traffic. A bicyclist stopped alongside, smiled gallantly, "Are you lost, M'mselle?" "*Non, M'sieur, merci.*" Not lost, merely mislaid.

She entered the station—where in the world was she going? —shook her head, stepped back into the street, struck her way north to Louis Blanc through the midday bustle. It's not fair, Rolfe, you've never come to visit. I'm a woman and I desire a man. A man? *Any* man? A weight? No. One man—a big, burly young man who is being torn apart by the unity of opposites. Thinks the quickest way to heaven is via hell. "You're not just a woman to sleep with," he had said. As if she didn't understand. Oh, he always stripped her naked with his words or his eyes—she could swear when he looked at her she had gone completely mad and forgotten to wear her clothes. But a woman needs that reminder that she's a woman with a naked body. And she also was torn by the unity of opposites. Was marriage, and peace, and love so cheap? What more did she require in order to live? Aside from her life with Rolfe, the work she did had an intrinsic value. And she was part of it. Not merely ingesting it through books and music and paintings, but doing. There was lots wrong with their politics, yet it gave one something greater than its parts: a chance to act, to do. And to do was Comrade Jake Starr.

She was at the *pont* over the muddy St. Martín canal, and she stopped to stare into its blank waters, its current as imperceptible as the flow of time and she knew exactly who and what it was she wanted—and recognized she had lived every single day and night of the past several weeks knowing it would become reality.

She tore herself away from the blank waters of the canal and began quickly to retrace her steps to Place du Combat. She would wait for him in the office and let him know immediately upon his return that it was not merely an infatuation, it was not merely satisfying desire, it was satisfying the flawless weight of love.

Happy because she had at last arrived at a decision, she typed reports in her office as she waited for Jake. But the happiness became impatience as the hours of the day reeled past to the clicking of the keys and Jake did not appear. Impatience displaced by fear, an uncomprehending fear (for she still had not acquired a profound knowledge of the inner workings of the revolutionary Party to which she gave adherence) as Comrade Step—himself—phoned.

Coldly, "Comrade Jacques? No? When he arrives, have him wait."

Once, twice, three times—and no Jake. The silver of afternoon was grayed by the black of evening. Still no Jake.

Again the phone rang. Fearfully, she raised the receiver. "Jacques! No? The fool! When he comes—immediately! Yes?"

"Yes, Comrade Stepanovich." She was terrified. Where in heaven's name was Jake?

Rolfe Alan Ruskin that afternoon had crossed the Channel. The weather had been nasty; the Channel mean. The steamer arrived late. Now he rode in a taxi to the Tech-Bureau and was restless and frustrated with himself as if he were at fault for not having been able to control the fog, the sea itself. It was childish, he realized, and the realization further increased the frustration with himself. It seemed to feed on itself. There was this untidy business with Sarah. The British general secretary had told him. It had been very embarrassing to him at first, and at the end he had spoken as if that too were Rolfe's fault. And Rolfe had wanted to apologize.

What nonsense! The organization brooked no frivolity. Rolfe had given his approval of Sarah's assignment—more, had recruited her into the Party. Here he was thinking only of the Party, himself forgotten. There were violent revolutionary changes taking place within himself. He was expunging the individual ego, overthrowing its dominance, its monopoly control over his actions, and in so doing destroying centuries of tradition, the tradition of personal freedom which had helped form him as a man, and doing so for the universal good. To change the world totally was to change man totally

—western man at any rate. Would he, Rolfe Alan Ruskin, be destroyed as well? The thought sickened him—or was it the nausea of the rough Channel crossing? In a laboratory one is isolated from the world, intent only on the search for a specific truth. He was changing all that, was entering into the world, deep into its roots, in order to change it root and all for the general truth of man's social existence. Before revolution could build it must destroy. Not only the old order, but the self. Still, when he had been informed that Sarah had a lover he had wanted to die. His lovely young Sarah, who never in the years he had known her had even gazed on another man coquettishly. She had been a good wife and a fine comrade—it was confusing, devastatingly confusing. First his son betrayed him, now his young wife. Yet the firmness with which the general secretary had spoken after the initial embarrassment had starched his spine. There could be no doubt: discipline had a salutary effect. What would Sarah say? He was certain she would be truthful . . . that it was only a nasty rumor.

For a moment he bathed in the relaxing warm tub that it was only a rumor. No, they didn't deal in rumors, facts were their tools. Of course, rumors were at times spread for good reason, and he couldn't repress the cunning smile which insinuated itself between the frustration and fear, honesty cringing in some dark corner. He must accept the fact. Sarah had a lover. A young man.

Rolfe began to freeze. That mean wind on the Channel had frozen his bones. Yes, a young man, an American comrade with powerful friends in the International—too powerful to reach. Now what was he thinking? *To reach?* A corrupt bourgeois practice. The American, he had been told, would cause no trouble, he was a disciplined professional—having his fling with his, Rolfe's, young wife, just another party woman to him, a camp follower.

Rolfe felt a sharp pain in his chest, had a panicky yet hopeful thought he was going to have a heart attack. Sarah would nurse him. Nonsense. He would not have a heart attack, the Ruskin men always had strong hearts. He was proud of his heritage.

He had been frustrated, frightened. Now he became angry. Whether or not it was true she had a lover, they would command her to stop. The Party would tell her they had great plans in mind for Professor Ruskin and his wife. Together they were a charming, personable couple. Teas would have to be given, cozy dinners, grand dinners. Not at once of course. Sarah would have to continue with her assignment in Paris, as he would have to continue with his in the academic life of England. But at the proper moment, at the proper historic moment, he smiled slyly, the plan would unfold. Professor Rolfe Alan Ruskin, Nobel laureate, staunch antifascist, would be put up by a committee of the arts and sciences for a seat in Parliament. As an independent, naturally.

He beamed. Sarah, his lovely wife and ardent comrade, would stand with him on the dais as he spoke. That's what the general secretary had said. They would make a splendid couple, and there must be no breath of scandal. *They* would put a halt to this idiocy. Besides, the general secretary had also said, if she balked, Starr would not. Starr was a selfless, dedicated comrade. If Starr would not—and the British leader had smiled cunningly and not concluded the sentence, merely smiled, and he had returned the smile in kind. My God, they were ruthless. It chilled his spine—and thrilled him. In this day and age one *must* be ruthless. He too could be ruthless.

But it would not be necessary with Starr. He thought of Comrade Starr as one of those legendary revolutionary heroes he had encountered occasionally at the King Street offices of the Party: silent men, powerful men, iron-disciplined men who knew no fear, who performed their work in the dark, alone, fearlessly. Rolfe envied Starr and hoped he also one day would become a legend in the movement. Was he not descended from crusading knights, from men who had fought in England's great battles, had helped to mold its destiny as a world power? Now he would add to their valorous history—and at a higher level of history.

He was shaken from his reverie by the cab's lurching stop. These damn French drivers, discourteous, slovenly. A national characteristic. No order.

The cab paid and sent off, Rolfe entered the austere Romanesque structure of the Technical Bureau on rue de Chabrol for his engagement with Comrade Stepanovich.

As day became night an hour later, he closed the door of the building behind him, his shoulders squared, his grand aristocratic head held high, a swashbuckling swing to his stride. He descended the stairs; a broadshouldered, burly young man ascended. They passed with a comradely nod, since each was aware that only comrades crossed this door's threshold, each unknown to the other.

As Rolfe sat in the cab he had hailed he kept marveling at the honor which had just been bestowed on him. He, too, was going to be a hero. How quickly they worked, how efficiently. That man Stepanovich was a dynamo, the new socialist man. It would take a few days, and then, and then—his head whirled. As the cab turned into Place du Combat, reality abruptly asserted itself. In a few minutes he would be standing before Sarah. He came to quick decision. He would speak quietly with her, maintain his composure. There would be no dreadful scene. It was not becoming to a man of his position. In any event, he despised scenes, they were untidy. Words were spoken which flew off into space aimlessly. They were modern, rational people. Jealousy bespoke a possessiveness of another's body as though it were private property, a relic of a society rooted in the holiness of Adam Smith.

As he climbed the rickety stairs to Sarah's office, his heart began to beat furiously. Hat in hand, he ran his fingers through his thin gray hair, made a courageous effort to control his excited breathing; soon he would see his lovely Sarah, hold her in his arms. Oh, my God, he loved her, she was his very life.

He entered the office, saw her. "Sarah!" he cried hoarsely, his eyes momentarily blinded by tears.

As they embraced, husband and wife, to his exquisite pleasure, she wept.

At the cable office earlier that afternoon, Jake Starr, fully and completely drunk, received a reply from New York. "Your refusal approved Stop—" he heaved a deep wet sigh—"Inform French dealers letters credit being cashed in Base." Albacete. Why the dirty bastards. Stealing—comrades—on their way to front—to die. Damn them—who the hell comrades going to die. Romantics, just stupid romantics. Bastards. Must go to Stepanovich. Must show him cable. Drunk, drunk. Catch hold. Think. Stepanovich holds noose. Tighten noose. Dead Jake Starr—dead revolutionary hero. Best kind, dead heroes. Ha-ha. Everybody screwed. Screwed tightly dead. Catch hold of yourself. Must save neck for revolution. Hell with scum. Went and lost cherry at the altar of Stepanovich's noose. Ta ra. Catch hold. Bolshevik will. Stop playing fool. Will. WILL!

With the preciseness of a guilty drunk he stalked through a heavy drizzle to the metro. In the subway he concentrated totally on becoming sober. And as he stood at the bottom of the flagstone steps to the gaunt structure which housed the Tech-Bureau, he *was* sober. He instructed himself before he mounted the stairs to be courteous and obedient to his superior. No more trouble, he merely wanted to get to Spain. The cable would soften Stepanovich's anger. How much, he didn't know. Still, he was one of Vlanoc's men, and that counted for a lot, unless of course they were out to give a little squeeze to Vlanoc too. One never knew. He would apologize if necessary, beat his breast, utter words of self-criticism, he knew the party catechism by heart. As he climbed the stone steps, he spied the tall lean figure of Ruskin immaculate in tweed topcoat and shining Scotch grain brogans leaving the building. We even have the rich on our side, Jake thought as he passed the man. All kinds.

When he stood before Stepanovich, he was relaxed, even a bit obsequious.

Marchand was also present, but he sat, as did the boss. Stepanovich had a lean cold face under heavy curly black hair. When he smiled, which was rarely, he showed a mouthful of rotten teeth like chipped chiclets; when he was silent, also rarely, he had a habit of biting on his thumb.

So Jake stood; they sat.

Step had his little black book open before him on the highly glossed Empire desk, but he wasn't reading it, he had it all in his mind. Memorized cold. He began simply enough, speaking in his coldly quiet voice, listing the numerous infractions of discipline Starr had committed, from the petty to the most heinous, which of course had been his calling Vlanoc a murderer in Havana. (Though Carl had understood and expected the novice's reaction, he of course had found it necessary to include the incident in his report. Carl Vlanoc took his job seriously.) As Comrade Step enunciated each breach of discipline, he concluded in his customary manner. "Yes?"

"Yes, Comrade Step."

". . . Threatened to hang Comrade Pierre on a wall hook. Yes?"

"Yes, Comrade Step."

Now Stepanovich had concluded but for the latest. He snorted, Jake catching a glimpse of a couple of chipped chiclets, gray at the edges. "When I give an order," he began, and it was then Starr handed him the cablegram.

Step read it quickly, tossed it aside. "That doesn't settle it, does it? Yes?"

"It doesn't, no; yes, Comrade Step." Just play it straight, Starr, you'll soon be out of here. Sarah's at the hotel by now, probably waiting, wondering.

Stepanovich studied Jake Starr, his thumb being ground down by rotten teeth. He read Starr's face easily. Arrogant Jew, the independent kind. Meanwhile, Marchand stared into space. Now Stepanovich curled his lips contemptuously. "The American Party—chicken heads! Never in the entire history of the revolution has there been a more stupid, mendicant, inane, sentimental, venal leadership." Yes, Comrade Step. "I GIVE THE ORDERS! Yes?"

"Yes, Comrade Step."

"You've been a good comrade, Vlanoc thinks highly of you, it seems you think so yourself." Then like a power saw, "But no one is that good. No one. Not even Vlanoc." And he laughed, the chipped chiclets rattling in that red box of a mouth.

Jake stood rigidly, staring at the picture of Stalin on the wall behind Comrade Step. *They don't like Carl either, it seems. I'll have to let him know.*

Stepanovich observed him coldly, decided to use a little terror. He pounded his desk, machine-gunned words, for a moment Jake thought—hoped—a chiclet would yank itself loose and stick in the man's throat. The terror exhibited, stowed in the cooler, Step stopped playacting, and got down to business. "Have you ever heard of Comrade Rolfe Alan Ruskin, my dear Comrade Fool?"

Jake twitched. What was this?

"Have you, Comrade Starr?"

"Yes, of course."

"And you have read the reports?"

"Yes. Comrade Stalin said he is one of the new men, that he is worth an army to the Party."

"And you have dared twiddle his piece of baggage between her legs?"

Jake's mouth went dry as every muscle in his body tensed. Catch hold. Scum. He groped in a grab bag. "She held me off. I did try."

"You more than tried, Starr."

Comrade Concierge told Comrade Fishface told Comrade Step. Vlanoc, the old wise man, had said to be careful. Comrade Fool is right. "She loves her husband, is loyal to him. There will be no trouble. She believes marriage vows are made to be honored, not broken."

Step's mouth dropped, the chiclets rattling, and a laugh beginning at his feet and roaring its way upward like flame through a flue convulsed him. "Vows are made–" Choking, he jumped from his chair and had to lean against the wall behind him, all the while stamping his feet, making such a racket that two guards ran into the room, for it sounded as if he were being strangled. Marchand had risen and was pouring him a glass of water, as Jake stood at attention before the desk hoping the man would die.

The convulsions over, the guards dismissed, Marchand reseated, Stepanovich stood behind his desk, a sly smile on his still trembling lips, tears running from his eyes, seeing Jake Starr in decadent bourgeois cubist fragments. "We don't want a scandal, Starr. Her husband's being appointed scientific consultant to the Spanish Republic. It's a great coup for us, since they don't know he is one of ours. It's good we were watching you and her. Another week and she probably would have been demanding a divorce which of course the control commission would never have granted. We want a good, solid bourgeois couple in a high position. Understand?"

"I understand." Jake felt the tension go.

Stepanovich smiled. "Relax, Starr. No harm's been done. Tell me," he grinned, "is she a good lay?"

His guard down, caught unawares, Jake quickly leaned across the desk—the revolution attracted all sorts of trash—and raised his huge fist, impatient to knock a couple of chipped chiclets loose into that flapping red box. Comrade Step, a brave man, merely jutted his jaw and stared coldly into Jake's angry green eyes. And Jake remembered the revolution was the altar of his life. What the hell was he so indignant about? He straightened, lowered his fist. "I'll report this little conversation to the Central Committee of the Comintern, Comrade Step. There's a point at which even a leading comrade must stop."

Stepanovich imperceptibly shrugged. Worked with Vlanoc a year and still a naïve fool. Quietly he said, "You'll leave tonight for Spain. Report to the office in Figueras. At the fort. Don't speak to her again. Pick up your papers in the front office."

Jake Starr nodded, and left.

Behind him Stepanovich sucked his thumb; his brain whirled and whizzed, clanged and tolled. The total on the white tape revealed itself clear and precise.

These Jews, no matter how harsh the discipline, underneath they wear their independence like their very own skin. The best way to temper steel is with fire. Vlanoc was too close to the snot—besides, Vlanoc, the old washerwoman, could himself use a little spurring. Aaa, these Jewish comrades (Vlanoc, like Jake Starr, had stopped thinking of himself as a Jew at the age of eighteen, he was a Bolshevik) reminded one of the boastful fly in the Russian fable. Having sat on the ear of an ox which had pulled a plow through frozen soil, the fly could boast it too had plowed. Comrade Step smiled sadly at the image of the Russian people who like oxen broke the soil for the eventual harvest of a new world. He sucked his thumb, bit his nail, jarred a loose tooth, the pain a screech! Well, he was one of those who held the reins—at least today, he thought, removing his thumb from between his lips, for tomorrow who knows, the revolution's so erratic. He caught himself, glared quickly over his right shoulder at the image of The Brightest Sun behind him on the wall—glimpsed again the clear precise total on the white tape. The young snot would never learn their discipline.

Aloud he muttered one word. "Roegen."

And from the corner of one cold yet satisfied eye he noticed Marchand flip a fin, then lower his protuberant eyes. To himself Step smiled. Roegen. Would make Vlanoc jump too, like an old stud its tender belly raked by a sharp Cossack spur. Stepanovich smiled, the edges of his teeth where the enamel had eroded showing a softish gray. Roegen, the Hungarian assassin. Also, the shiteater.

The young fool would learn or die.

Sarah Ruskin, haggard, her hair a ruin, frantically searched for a taxi in the rainswept Place du Combat. The square was deserted, all the store shutters down. She must inform Comrade Step that it was all—what? It was not a lie and it was not the truth. They had slept together one night—it was after all their own affair. They had been thrown together so constantly it had been a marriage of sorts, without the biology—what was she saying? There had been great desire and they had succumbed. That did not mean she was going to leave her husband and it did not mean Jake Starr had asked her to. They both had understood it was a passing fancy. An infatuation, she herself had called it. Rolfe was mad—literally mad.

Jake had told her the Party came first, last, and always. He was married to the Party. And Rolfe was insane. What would they do to Jake?

"I know about Starr, Sarah, and I find—find it difficult knowing you do not love me," were the first words Rolfe spoke after she had stopped weeping and they stared into one another's eyes.

"But I do love you, Rolfe, and there was, there has been—" She was a bad liar.

"Please, Sarah, you were observed."

She should be angry, but he looked all at once so frail, so utterly destroyed. In his way he loved her deeply. But she must tell him the truth. "Not love, Rolfe. We—yes, we did. One night. It was nothing, Rolfe, an infatuation." Oddly, she felt like a liar. She raised her eyes to Rolfe, recognized the pain, his face was a startling white, his hands trembled, his lips. She swept him into her arms, embraced him violently, attempting to warm him with her love, her body. For a few minutes his trembling became worse, but slowly it eased off, and she could feel strength returning to his body. She kissed him and he responded.

They gazed at each other. He had control of himself now, and he stared deeply into her. "Sarah," he said quietly, "you treat me like a child. You are not telling me the complete truth."

The complete truth. Could it be told so easily? "The truth is that I desired him, we lived very closely for some five weeks, we became infatuated, and last night we—well, we slept together. There's no more to it. Nothing more to tell."

Now that she had told him what it had seemed he wanted to hear, he began to tremble violently again. First pain, then anger distorted his face. "I'm a power in the Party," he drilled harshly, and it sounded so completely unreal and alien to him she had to keep reminding herself it was Rolfe, her husband, whom she had hurt terribly, "and he will be made to suffer!"

It hurt to hear him speak this way. "For what, Rolfe? You asked for the complete truth. He has done nothing—nothing that any young man wouldn't do. We have done nothing which should alter our relationship. What do you mean he will be made to suffer? You have never in your life consciously hurt anyone. That is not like you." She could see he really wasn't listening.

"You've never known my anger, Sarah."

"True. Come with me to Stepanovich so I can tell him there was nothing. Jake is a decent, considerate young man—completely devoted to his cause—it was I who wished to smash—Rolfe, for heaven's sake, I am utterly confused, I don't know what I'm saying anymore. I love you. You are my husband."

"You love him, I can see it in your eyes. He will regret it."

"Even if I did—" she almost wished to acknowledge it—"would you have him punished? We are civilized human beings, or at least up till now I've thought so—perhaps Step is a barbarian, but we're not."

"Comrade Stepanovich is a most enlightened man. He was very understanding. He is a true son of the revolution, a rational man who does not permit sentimental drool to come between himself and his duty to the Party. Starr is an anarchist—perhaps even a Trotskyite."

"Have you lost your senses? Become untidy?" She knew what hurt him most.

He blanched, the white prow slashing through an unruly sea. "He'll be disciplined for this, I will see to that."

"Are you permitting your injured vanity to corrupt you? I always believed you to be a man of integrity."

"*You* speak of integrity? And it is not my vanity. I view these sexual matters as a scientist. It is the decision of the

Party. He is not to see you or speak to you and you are not to see him or speak to him again." Did she really love this man?

"Enough, Rolfe. I am going to Stepanovich this moment."

He followed her quickly and interposed himself between the door and her. There were red spots like rust marks on his white nose. "Don't make a fool of me, Sarah."

"You are making a fool of yourself. I'll merely tell Stepanovich the truth. Jake and I were merely—"

"Were merely!" Speaking slowly, emphasizing each word, her husband said, "He will certainly regret his little love affair, my dear." The door behind him opened and a young woman, a secretary from down the hall, entered, only to stand suddenly paralyzed from embarrassment at the sight of these two angry people. Rolfe in slow motion patted his tie, pulled down his jacket, observed with satisfaction the high polish of his shoes, and, flipping the brim of his hat—for the fresh young pretty face stared—jauntily made his exit, nonchalantly saying over his shoulder, "I will wait for you at your hotel, Sarah. We must return to London; we leave for Spain in a fortnight." Very proudly he added as he turned to face his wife and the young girl, "I have been appointed scientific adviser to the Spanish Republic."

Sarah barely heard a word he spoke. She was obsessed with a desire that he leave, that he disappear, vanish from the face of the earth. *Jake! What would they do to him?*

After enough time had elapsed for Rolfe to have left the building and courtyard, she herself descended into the rain-swept streets. In the square she finally found a taxi which drove her to rue de Chabrol.

Ushered, half soaked, into Stepanovich's office, she saw that he paced behind his desk with a controlled tension which was frightening. He was a quivering steel splinter of a man. Hurriedly she searched with her eyes about the room for Jake Starr, but he was not present; gone, she wondered, where?

"Yes?" Stepanovich asked curtly, continuing unabated his tense pacing.

"I've come to explain—"

"No explanations, Comrade Sarah," he said calmly enough. "Biology's biology. The matter is out of our hands now." In the hands of God, she thought. "Return to your hotel, your husband's waiting." He saw she still wished to speak. "Please, go," he said, impatience thinning his lips.

Sarah held her ground. "I'll go when I have concluded. Comrade Starr was no more culpable than I. It was merely, well, a passing fancy." She no longer believed it herself. "He himself told me there could be nothing more. He is totally committed to the Party."

Stepanovich halted his pacing to stare at her. How absurd that a revolutionist had to waste his time on the flirtations of middle-class women. "It is expected of him. Of you, too. And hereafter no passing fancies, please. The Party will in the future let you know for whom to spread your legs. Good-night."

Sarah stood petrified with shock and disgust. She had humiliated herself, but that had not been enough. She felt immersed in filth.

Stepanovich smiled his eroded smile, wondering how she would look spread out beneath a man. A guard entered to his ring and he nodded at him to lead Sarah from the room.

From the Tech-Bureau, Jake Starr went directly to the hotel. Rolfe Ruskin, waiting for Sarah's return, hearing his footsteps on the stairs, opened the door, thinking it was she. Jake saw him, recognized who it must be—as did Rolfe. They nodded to each other, and Rolfe closed the door and Jake went into his room. Obviously Sarah was not present, and Jake wondered where she was.

He washed, changed clothes. Perhaps he should go to the

man, say something to him, apologize for having hurt him. But what could he possibly say? *Sorry, Comrade Ruskin, for having slept with your wife?* No, it was best left alone. Though if Ruskin wished him harm he could hardly blame him.

The humiliation he had suffered at Step's hands bit at him. It had been unnecessary. Stupid. Inhuman. He hoped Sarah would be spared—she wasn't built for this kind of discipline. Dammit, where was she? What was keeping her? It was perfectly all right that the Party should make these petty decisions, but that did not mean humiliations were painless or palatable. When he had made his decision to become a professional activist, he had understood these personal affronts would be part of the game. In the past he had learned to accept them, and would again. To be an activist one has to live in the world, not outside it, enveloped completely in oneself. He had accepted the gamble. For the chance to be part of a movement dedicated to uprooting the old social order with its chaos and injustice, he had to accept the risk of losing his personal liberty, even his life. Those in this world who wanted to move, to change, to discover, always had to take chances. Everything he had done since having made his decision had been in preparation for Spain. His personal feelings mattered little—or Sarah's, for that matter. Or Ruskin's. . . . For the briefest moment it occurred to him that he had no right to risk anyone else's life but his own, but he hurriedly turned the thought aside. Tomorrow he would be in Spain. He began to pack his bag, gather his papers. What would Roegen do to him? Not kill him. Not for this idiocy. They did not kill aimlessly. Vlanoc had repeated this a hundred times, his metallic nose sharper each time he mentioned it. "Nothing without purpose. Words, deeds, everything must be done with one thought in mind: advancing the time for seizing power." The worst Roegen could do was exactly what he, Jake, wanted: send him to the front. It seemed he had waited for this opportunity a lifetime. So to hell with his own feelings. He loved Sarah. It was no infatuation. He knew himself too well. When he committed himself, he went all the way. No half measures. He loved Sarah fully, deeply—he had known it quickly and found it impossible to forget her for a moment. She filled his inner life.

He was dressed, his bag was packed, he was wasting time. Where in the world could she be? Stepanovich had ordered him not to speak to her. Pure rhetoric. Step was playing out the game. If Ruskin loved his wife so much, why hadn't he once come to visit her? Sarah wasn't made of ice—he remembered what she had said that very morning: Now I know what my body was made for!

No use waiting around. The ticket they had given him was for a first-class sleeper—only the best for a man ordered to report to Roegen. He smiled. Steak and potatoes for the condemned's last meal. Roegen the assassin, he was called. Also the shiteater. "Why do you call him that?" he had asked Vlanoc. Laughter. "None of your business. Learn not to ask questions like that."

He picked up his bag, put out the light, his body refusing to hurry. Would go to the station, get a bite to eat, board the train, go to sleep. In the morning, there would be the Pyrenees. His heart leaped. Where was she? In the next room he could hear Rolfe pacing back and forth. Was he wondering too?

Valise in hand, he left his room, strode across the balcony feeling Ruskin's eyes on him, slowly descended the stairs, said goodbye to Comrade Concierge, her weightlifter's shoulders hunched noncommittally. Marchand's apparatus.

It had stopped raining, was dark and quiet. He stopped at the corner, put his bag down, debated whether to take a cab or use the metro. Looked at his watch. Eight-thirty. Had lots of time to kill. Oh, stop fooling yourself. You're waiting for her. Accept it. You want to say goodbye.

He stepped into a doorway, lit a cigarette, and decided to wait, feeling simultaneously defeated and elated.

Sarah, numbed and confused, walked slowly from Chabrol towards the hotel. A long walk but time was meaningless. Rolfe waited; she did not care. Let him wait. They had said Jake was leaving that very night and she wondered if he had.

Her shoulders as she walked trembled. She had come face to face with a reality she had not known existed. The Party will let me know for whom I am to spread my legs.

She hastened her step. Her husband waited. In her room. Maybe that night he would want to sleep with her. She could still smell his clean male scent. His? Jake's. After he had left that morning unaccountably she had turned and kissed the pillow on which he had couched his head. A romantic schoolgirl. She did not give herself to a man lightly. Never had. Said from the vastness of her experience. She smiled. Becoming a real woman of the world. They would tell her whose pillow to kiss, whose scent to smell. She wished she could make the whole affair smaller than it was. She loved Rolfe. She loved Jake Starr. She hated herself. She held back the tears. As she passed the dimly lit doorway where Jake Starr stood waiting, he gripped her shoulders firmly, whirled her about, and she was in his arms, her back against the wall. "Sarah, Sarah," he whispered between kisses. And she bit at his lips, her heart pounding mercilessly, her head dizzy. "Sarah," he whispered, "my love." It echoed in her skull like a cry for succor. She became faint, heavy in his arms.

He blew cool breath on her temple. "We can't do it against the wall," he laughed. "It's against the law."

She laughed now, too. "I would do it anywhere with you," she said softly.

He held her at arm's length, breathing heavily. "Even against the wall?" he asked, his hand falling against her breast, gently caressing her.

Then she remembered, stiffened. And he remembered, too. Let her go.

"Your husband's up there," he said, nodding in the direction of the hotel.

"I know."

"Tell me where you've been?"

She told him down to the very last humiliation.

"He's a barbaric sonuvabitch, Sarah. Forgive him. Forgive us. Sometimes the bureaucrats get carried away. Forget it."

"You forget it," she said coldly. "I shan't." He stood speechless before her in the little vestibule. They were close. He wanted to take her in his arms again. Then with impossible imperturbability, impassivity even, she said, "You will be careful, won't you?"

"Sure, I'll be careful." Right then he wanted to die.

"The best soldier is a live soldier is what you always tell them." She smiled wryly.

"Yes."

"We will be in Valencia, or do you know?"

"I know."

"Will you write?" she suddenly asked softly.

"No. Neither will you," he said forcefully. Didn't she understand?

She wanted to be angry, tried to be angry. "Are we permitted to *think* about each other?" Words which should have been said with bitterness, sarcasm heavy, they sounded vacuous, blank. He only shrugged—she could feel he was slipping away, would soon no longer be present. In truth, so was she.

"No," he said humorlessly.

"So be it."

His bag in one hand, her elbow in the other, he led her out to the street. They were strangers now.

"It's time to go," he said quietly. "Goodbye, Sarah."

"Goodbye, Jake."

He started to move towards her, stopped. They touched fingers, their last embrace.

He headed towards the metro, and she to the hotel. Before he turned the corner, he waved, but it was too late. She had already entered the hotel.

VIII

"OLD ARON is dead! Oh Jesus, Aron is dead!"

Mack Berg stood tall and sour-faced at the ridge of the shallow trench with the others and forced himself to look at the dead man. Old Aron's skull had been cracked open during the night's artillery bombardment by a shell fragment—there it lay by a clump of dry earth, unobtrusive sheared piece of iron junk. How strange—the oldest man in the battalion had been the first to be killed. Natural justice, Berg thought. There's a God.

Aron was—had been a man in his late forties, skinny and wrinkled from a lifetime of work in the old country, Turkish-slaughtered Armenia, and then in the textile machinery factories of Worcester, Mass. "Goddam sonuvabitch open shop town. Blackball all my life for trying to organize worker. They kick me from shop to shop. Best tool'n diemaker in New England." Larry Hillman, a thin bespectacled kid from the same city, told them Aron's wife had died this past year and that Aron also had wanted to die. They left no children. The fascists with willing kindness had granted his wish. Dead. No one had ever spoken ill of the man, except perhaps his bosses. "All he ever wanted was fair pay for fair work," Hillman said. Who could have been so mean as not to recognize his virtue? Aron was dead.

The urge to turn away from the corpse was violent, yet Mack refused to budge. He was a stubborn mean-mouthed man from Saratoga Avenue, Brooklyn. Hot and cold, very, very bold. Every day for him was a new war and had always been—with his sisters, his brothers, his mother, father, Hebrew teacher, schoolteacher, kids on the block. He wanted what he thought everybody else had. Since it was impossible, life became one long lost battle. He hated himself for it, and thus became his own enemy: wily, mean, unjust, unsentimental, sardonic. He became an atheist and radical the day, at age fourteen, when he walked in on his old man eating bread and butter in the toilet on Yom Kippur. The sanctimonious mean old hypocrite who daily drove around with a horse and wagon buying and selling iron junk, waiting for a war so he could become a millionaire like Carnegie and Frick.

Aron's was the first corpse Mack had ever seen close up and he wanted to vomit, even to cry. Instead he said loudly, "Looks like a rag doll with its head chopped off. Why don't they bury the old bastard?"

Nobody listened. And it infuriated him.

Greg Ballard had seen other corpses before. One he remembered with special terror: a drowned man on the beach at Menauhant, washed up from the sea, his bloated scrotum being eaten by two long gray rats. He had vomited and run. Ten he'd been. There had also been another corpse before. His father's. Eight years old he'd been then. His father had come home to die. He'd been home before, Greg supposed. To lay with his, Greg's, mother—could hear the goddamned springs twang, the bodies whacking across the dark room. Then the man would be gone—a month, a year, who counted, who cared? Returned again. Twang, whack. Gone and not returned even when Loney was born. Loney because momma was alone again and alone remained until Ballard came home to die. T.B. They uncovered the pine casket before it was lowered into the sandy earth and his mother had screamed and fought for one last embrace of the man she'd known only in embrace. "He made mah body wawm," she cried. He had wanted to spit—he was eight, old enough to know everything there is to know—because they'd been alone and alone again would be. But they sealed the casket and lowered it into the carved-open ground, and he had become terrified with the thought he would be next. Into the ground it went, the adults weeping, his mother shrieking, wailing, the fool, the little white-haired aunt rocking her round buttery-sweet brown body to some sad soft rhythm as he pressed between her thighs. It had remained with him for years, a terror to hide from in the dark. Until he grew up and learned there are people who yearn for that terror, run to meet it head on because they find the terror of living even greater. And soon, now, he and his comrades would be killed and killing. It was something one had to get used to.

So he was insistent that his eyes unflaggingly focus on the broken skull. The stone features of the familiar wrinkled face now seemed less wrinkled. Death. Look at it. It can't hurt you.

Greg Ballard stared until his stomach relented, until he was able to see the dead Aron in his peace. By then volunteers had gathered to act as a burial squad.

"The right guys," Joe Garms laughed, to interrupt his high beelike humming of Life's just a bowl of cherries. "When it comes to buryin', the Irish is always front'n cenner. There'll be extra vino rations."

Old Aron was buried in an olive grove on the other side of the road.

Joe Garms lay on his stomach in his trench on a hill east of the Chinchón-Madrid road. With a little stub pencil he was writing a letter to Jake Starr who he imagined was still in Paris, though the address he sent Starr's mail to was in Figueras. Joe enjoyed writing letters, he felt freer than when speaking to a person directly. He could say what he wanted to say without fear of interruption, and besides the person didn't hear his lisp. Joe spoke with a slurping lisp, each word drowned in spit. Because he was a man of great personality, his listeners usually forgot the lisp, but he himself could never forget it. It was his blight, his shame. As a kid, he had punched senseless any boy who'd teased him about it. He wrote, intoning each word to himself . . .

Jakey,

What a fuck-up. Can't they do nothing right?

Five days since we left the convent. We left it nice and clean, real ship shape. The bung holes full a lime. Somebody told us Dutch socialists was going to make it into a hospital. That's the diff between socialists and us. They make hospitals, we make soldiers. Good ones too. This is going to be one goddam good battalion. If not for the fucking commissars. Mack Berg calls them comic stars. All a bunch of prickfaces. Nagging bunch a fucking women. Don't realize you got a give men a little elbow grease to have some fun. Can you imagine I ain't got a chance to get laid yet? Nobody. Not even the fucking commissars. Must be a bunch of fags. Everybody beating meat. Balls.

All right, Jakey, I feel real mean. I'm laying in my trench sunning me feet and crotch. I'm growing a beard, the sun's slitting me eyes, I'm getting ready to kill fascists. I get a hardon everytime I think of it. Ha ha ha. Peanuts Murchison tells me it's normal, it ain't because I'm a killer. Thank you, Professor Murchison. Up his.

Anyway we line up outside the convent ready to hop on the camions, we have a meeting. Can you imagine that? We leaving for the front, we gotta have a meeting. Charlie Flagg introduces this guy who showed up a couple nights ago Schlepp from Philly as the new battalion comic star. Then Charlie ups and joins an infantry squad and that's it. Nobody tells us nothing. Charlie's got a stone look on his face staring straight ahead. Ain't said a word to anybody except maybe Mack Berg in five days. Mack says he don't say nothing much but we all know he's boiling mad about something. So we got us a new polit-commissar, a fat round little bastard just as we leave for the front. Anyway we hop on the tailgates and a bunch of villagers come to see us off. Men, women, girls, children. They bring us flowers. The women are crying, the kids are screaming me cago en Franco I shit on Franco and the men are giving us fist salutes yelling Abajo Franco and Comrade Espartaco our leading comrade in Villanueva gets ready to make a speech but just then my truck backfires, a real bellyfart, and takes off so I don't know a thing he said and I don't give a shit. He stinks. Thinks he's big. All these fucking bastards get a little power think they're bigger'n everybody else. I know the party's full of them. Not you, Jakey. You're one a the few who keeps his prospective. Well, I'm a party man, I tell you, nobody else. Some day you become too big for your britches you'll blow the whistle on me maybe even shoot me and I'll fuck you. Right now I see things in the party make me puke. But I button me lip, keep my cock hard, me ass tight—nobody's fucking me in the ass. Not yet.

We go to Albacete. A big city after Villanueva. We see girls, International Brigades girls, nurses, comrades, wiggling their asses, bouncing their tits, wiggle wiggle bouncey bouncey Christ we want a jump off the trucks and go screwing right in the streets. Five nofucking weeks and we're going to the front. But we got discipline. We get off in the bull ring and whaddyknow André Marty's there to hand each of us a brand new Russian carbine taken out of the crates right in front of our eyes. Beautiful Communist guns still all greased up. Then Russian bayonets beautiful beautiful sharp things, helmets, webbed belts, bandoliers, gas masks fucking gas masks! and guess what? bullets. We start screaming, howling, dancing around the bull ring like a bunch a wild Indians laughing and yelling big grins on our puss and that clown the chief comic star André Marty leader of the I.B. hero of the Black Sea mutiny member of the exec committee of the Third International he raises his fat arms above his head jumping up and down like a fucking witch doctor. We're really ripping it up.

They blow the whistle and we calm down. Line up.

Marty speaks to us thru his droopy mustache real sweet like old foxy granpa "We weel your passports hold in see-cur-i-ty" and the guys line up to hand theirs over to a guy sitting at a little table right where the last bull shit. Not me. I ain't got one, remember? And if I did I tell you only for your fucking ears I wouldn't give it in. I'm no easy mark. A few other guys didn't give theirs and who they are is none of your biz.

Jakey, you can see I'm in a real fucking mood today waiting for the Capronis to come drop their bombs on little unprotected us.

We get a hot lunch a rice and some kind a fish. Greg says it's codfish. Tastes like fried wood. I like the black son of a bitch. Quiet moody baaaastid. Everything he does he does like a pro. Studies the m.g. night and day, sleeps with it, strips it, assembles it with his eyes shut. Watches everything with his little black eyes, sopping it up. He'll never be one of ours, I'm tellin' you. He don't like power like I do. Party power. Stalin power. I love it. Not the shitass power of these punk commissars who are more interested in what we're saying about them or the commanders than anythin' else. They got their ears all over. Schlepp. Shit. I say that once to Mack and he laughs. Schlepp shit. Carry shit, Mack says. Ha ha ha. Our battalion comic star.

The trucks leave Albacete, stop go stop go stop go the whole goddam day and night. We was freezing but we get close in the trucks, everybody touching everybody else, buddying up, we're all scared, we're cold, we warm each other, we got a feeling of comradeship. Hermanos hermanos hermanos. We're going to the front. All the guys are worrying whose gonna get killed first. We sleep off and on. Whisper to each other. Sleep. Stop go stop go. Brrr it's fucking cold. Sleep. Leaning against each other. A whistle blows. The sun's coming into the truck. The truck's stopped. "Everybody out. Line up for rollcall."

We jump out. I'm creaking like an old man. The sun blinds us. We look around. We're on a narrow macadam road running through rocky hills. In the distance is a valley—

somebody says Tajuña valley. Hill and dale, a long flat plain, thousands of olive trees, a couple a cypress tall and very dark green. Jesus it's beautiful. It's early and we can see peasants already and their burros. Nothing else is moving. The air is thin and you can spot a man miles away. I'm already looking sharp. I'm alert, Jakey. Like you said, the best soldier's a live one.

We line up. Have rollcall. Shit. A truck's missing with about thirty guys. We was quiet. What the hell? Guys begin to whisper. The truck took the wrong fork in the night and went toward the fascist lines or the truck was driven by fascist Trotskyite spies and slipped away in the dark to the fascists.

Captain Hammond the batt-commander calls us to attention. He talks quiet, no bull shit like the pols. He tells us it's no use wondering what happened to the truck and our missing comrades now. The chances is they went up ahead and we'll find them later in the day. We hope. Well Jakey it's four days later and those guys ain't showed yet and nobody knows where they are. It's my bet they got lost and ended up behind the fascist lines. If they did those guys are dead men, killed, murdered. They don't keep no I.B. prisoners over there. Well I ain't gonna keep none a them either.

Then the captain says this is the Chinchón-Madrid road, part of the Valencia transport link from Madrid, and he smiles shy like, you know the kind a guy Hammond is, no crap, and he says we're about forty kilometers southeast a Madrid. It's our mission to protect this road. The fascists have been attacking for days to cut off Madrid and this is the last highway open and our troops have counterattacked. The dirty fascist bastards took the road at one point but our guys chased them back. Then we get hot coffee and a big chunk a bread. Then each company goes off by itself. Right then and there after five shitting weeks of training, the day we come to the front lines we organize our companies all over again. Everybody got somebody different in his fucking squad. Real good for morale I call it. New comic star, new everything just like we never trained. You ever see a fuck-up like that in your life? The captain of the m.g. company Cord, a real pro, can hardly look us in the eye he's so mad. Horton his runner, you know the kid from the Fur Union, told me Cord's been taking nips at the bottle because things are fouled up and he thinks we're a bunch a fucking amachures going to the slaughter. Horton says not to say nothing about it. I don't except to you a leader of the vanguard. We look around and all the other companies are doing the same like us, choosing up sides for the war. They make me a section commander with three squads so maybe they know what they're doing. Greg is one a my gunners, probably the best man in the battalion next to me. I got Karonian, company pol, which is my luck because he ain't no comic star. We understand each other. He's not the guy to give a political lecture in the middle a battle. Keeps his mouth shut.

The order's given everybody's to shoot five bullets at the rocks in prone position. I shoot my five and then have to go around showing guys how to load their carbine, how to aim, how to shoot, don't jerk you dope squeeze. About ten of us know what we're doing with a gun. We hit what we aim at. The rest a them Jesus have mercy they couldn't hit Fatso Goering at ten feet. Then I remember where the hell is our machine guns we're a machine gun company. Captain Cord makes a face and he leads us to a truck where there is nine world war I Maxim m.g.s. The gunners stripped them down and reassembled them. They look in working order but we don't shoot them. Cord says make sure your gunners hold on to their carbines and I know what he means.

We get back in the trucks. They move like a snake through this little narrow road to a town called Morata de Tajuña, slow through trucks, ambulances, tanks, men. We wait. Then somebody yells hey bombers! Heinkels. We head for the ditches like we was told. Everybody's okay. Shit I almost loaded me drawers. It happens real fast we hardly have time to get scared. But we're all a little paler than we was before. Real quiet we starts marching singlefile thru the hills and the guys are pulling those mgs on wheels behind them. They're those heavy buggers. I'm a son of a bitch if Greg don't take his apart and put the heavy chassis on his back with the rest a the junk giving the barrel to another guy and off he goes.

He's alright that black bastard. Studies everything, watches everybody, keeps everything in. Moves real quiet. Makes sure he knows where he's going. He don't like to get hurt so he sort a sends patrols out with his brain to get info for him. I can tell he don't like to give up anything of himself to anybody unless he's sure he can trust him. He trusts Mack and me but just so far. He's tough and strong and independent. Jesus he's independent. I wouldn't like to take him on in a fight, I'd have to get real dirty to beat him but I got an idea he can be dirty if he has to too. He got a tight ass too. But one day he's gonna let go. Then watch out, the shit will fly. The blood too. He learned himself how to read and write. I never had the ass for it. He told me I have a high I.Q. and if I tried I could stand up with any guy who went to college. Me. Son of a bitch. Like Mack Berg—he could talk the balls off a burro. Real hifalutin. Worked for the New Masses, went to Harvard college. But he's a good guy. He's in the trench next to me sunnin' his nuts. Greg's on the other side of him. We're all snoozing in the sun. Hot as hell. Some dumb bastards got so hot walking thru the hills, beginning to hear machine gun fire, the BAROOOOM of cannon they dropped their sheepskins and three hours later was crying they were so fucking cold. Now I'm writing this little note to you it's hotter'n hell and I'm airing me feet in the sun. Soon the fat Capronis will come and drop their bombs. Every day about this time—yup, Jakey boy, you'll be reading this I might be dead cause here come our daily visitors the big black Capronis. They're gonna drop their bombs, big fucking Italian shitass eggs on us. Hey, Jakey, they're coming closer, closer, got the whole sky to themselves and we're all naked underneath sunning ourselves in our open trenches. . . .

Joe was forced to stop his writing. The silver bombs, glinting in the sun, fell away from the bomb bays. Cromwell Webster, Negro leader from Gary, Indiana, and Chicago, Illinois, just arrived the night before and already on the m.g. company commander's staff, called out in his shrill choirboy's voice, "Leaflets, as I live'n breathe." Cord, the company commander, had to yell, "Shut up, you damn fool, they're bombs. Everybody down!"

Joe Garms turned on his back so he could observe the bombers in their tight drone overhead. His stomach knotted, and he kept moving his hands first to cover his head, then his groin, he didn't know which he wanted most to protect. Goddam them, goddam them, there they come, silver eggs littered the sky, whining, whining, whining. And he observed them, the bombs falling so limpidly almost, slowly, shining silver bombs, whining down at him alone, and deep inside him he had a vague wish that they would obliterate him, send him to his peace, and yet the fear belied the wish for obliteration, and he forced himself to focus his eyes on them as they approached the earth which not quite sheltered him, and he began to sing Life is just a bowl of cherries, don't take it serious, don't get delirious and there they were upon him and quickly he turned to bury his head into the ground, the whining ripping his eardrums, arching his back, and then they exploded shaking the earth, pebbles falling about his head and his naked feet, then another explosion, and another, until he was almost lifeless with fear, numb, and he was embracing the earth and himself. And he was alive. Life is just a bowl of cherries, don't take it serious, don't get delirious, ta da ta da ta da rara. RAAAAAAAA.

Yeah, it was real romanticlike.

Jakey, this is the next day.

They was closer than ever yesterday. Three days running and nobody hurt yet. Crazy thing. The more they bomb the madder we get. Just like Spaniards. You get so mad you say you dirty scum we'll never give up. NEVER! Go ahead and bomb. NEVER! Well, anyway, I'm sunning me balls today. Oh, yeah, where was I? After we marched across the mountains singlefile the first day we come out on the road again. We been hearing bullets zinging, guns ratatating louder'n louder. We come out on the road it's sundown.

The road's constipated like most a us ain't with trucks, ambulances, a couple a tanks, Russkis. Jesus Christ the ambulances are loaded with wounded, blood all over the place. Guys moaning, crying, screaming. Nobody pays no attention to us. We sit on the side of the road and watch the ambulances stacking up the wounded. A lot of the guys can't stand it and turn around not to look. Me and Greg we're sitting there watching everything. We wanna know.

A wounded guy comes down off the hill shaped like a dried-out titty leaning on another guy who's okay. English. They say they come up to the lines a week ago with a full battalion 500 men and got 125 left. Holy Jesus, Son of God. Our bellies flop. The captain asks if he can help and they laugh crazy like and keep going. As we follow them with our scrunched up eyes we see a white stone house and on the side it says Madrid—32 kms. We scrabble up that dried-out titty of a hill. It's getting dark fast. Take positions. Begin to dig trenches with shovels, helmets, bayonets, sticks, everybody working fast, scared, way up ahead they keep shooting like a battle's going on. We dig fast. Horton's lucky. When he's scared he just lays down and falls asleep. Not me. Scared, real scared. I hear shots from one of my gun positions. What the fuck? I hear a guy yelling his stupid head off in Spanish. I run over there. A couple a Spanish soldiers are pointing guns at some a my men who are pointing theirs. "What's cooking?" I ask. Kovacs, my number 3 gun, he says, "Shit. These guys approached and I asked them to halt. We haven't got a password. They kept coming. I shot my rifle over their heads. They stopped. They're Spaniards." "Yeah, I can see," I tell him. Rodriguez one a the Cubans come over and speaks to them in Spanish. He says they say we're just as fucked up as everybody else in this goddam war. They spit and slump down the hill to the road, sorta skipping hippity hop over the rails of the narrow gauge railroad running around our hill from the lime quarry up a ways.

I tell Kovacs he's trigger happy, we're in the third lines and these milicianos just walking straight up. Kovacs says, "What kind of army are we? We should have passwords." "You're right," I says. "I'll find out."

I go down to battalion h.q. and nobody can give me an answer, the commissars and the commanders is too busy chewing the rag, having an argument. Ah, shit, Jakey, wish you was here. I go back to dig with Mack and Greg. We dig till we're dead on our feet and fall asleep.

Every day we dig deeper, eat rice and bread and lousy café con leche. Way up ahead we hear shootin'. Down on the road we see trucks coming and going, ambulances filling up, the two Russki tanks clanking into the lines in the morning and coming back up the road at night. In the afternoon we sun ourselves in the trenches, the black shitass Capronis drop bombs on us and never hit a fucking thing.

We eat rice and bread and café con leche for supper. Tuck in my little fuckers, return to my trench alongside Mack and Greg and after it gets dark the artillery comes after us. They're after the road. Searching fire. One long one short. Jakey, artillery is the worst. Goddam it you're just sitting there and they keep sending shells out searching us out. Closer, closer, and you begin to feel like you're in a vise. Killed old Aron from Worcester a couple nights ago. Just chopped off a chunk a his head. Clean. Not the first guy killed. Before him one of the observers got killed showing a guy how to observe. And before that there was those guys in that lost truck.

Oh Jakey last night and this morning was a time to remember. After the sun took a dive, cold as hell, the battalion was ordered out a the trenches to a flat plain on the front side of the hill. As we sit there wondering what's up, Captain Hammond, Captain Richard Jordan Prettyman who come to us direct from the Lenin Institute in Moscow and company commanders Cord, Raleigh and Avila are talking all the time. Hammond and Prettyman are arguin' it seems to us. Good for the troops. No orders come back to us so we just sit and talk. A half hour goes by and still no orders. The enemy must of got wise or heard our talking or what not and started giving us m.g. fire. We stopped talking fast. Ten minutes later they stop shooting.

Finally an order comes to follow the commanders in double file. My section for no reason is at the head of the column. We're marching thru the fucking mts. again. Hills. Ahead of us I can see Hammond, Prettyman and Cord gabbing away. They're arguing. I can't hear what the shit they're saying but holy mother of god they're throwing their hands around wild. Cord turns and with his hand orders me to come to him. I run over. The other two commanders are up ahead. The moon and stars light the whole damn sky. Everytime we march over a little hill I'm sure the whole world and the enemy too can see us clear. Cord just told me keep close behind me for orders and then he ran up to join the other two guys. Every few minutes he turns and tells me to order the battalion down. I had to shout my orders to the battalion and I'm sure they can hear me in Berlin.

We march for hours I don't know I lose track a time, over hills thru barrancas olive trees and scrub oak and pine. Once we went thru a grape orchard, they're like scrub oak, and some of the guys grab a hold a grapes. Green. The noise we make sounds like a giant army being moved. Must of scared the enemy so much they ran because we stopped getting any fire at all in our direction. Nobody seemed to know where the holy shit we was. All of a sudden we're back on our dried out titty but I don't know till Captain Cord tells me to get the men to sleep and set the guard. I'm so dead I just lay down and die. Everybody the same.

I feel I gotta take a leak and wake up. Early dawn. The Tajuña valley looks beautiful with the groves and the cypress trees and the quiet. Jesus you never think there's a war goin' on. I go down the hill to the latrine trench. Pass the batt. h.q. and see the commanders and comic stars still arguing. Blah blah all fucking night. After coffee section and company commanders meet at h.q. Schlepp tells us Hammond had a nervous breakdown and was sent to the hospital. Richard Jordan Prettyman was our new batt. commander. Prettyman smiled with his big teeth like graveyard stones. Bob Gladd the big talker from the merchant marine tells us we shouldn't buy that crap. Hammond told him Copic the brigade commander didn't know his ass from a hole and Hammond argued we shouldn't be used for daytime battle until we got some experience at night attack which is better for raw troops. Copic accused him of being a yellow bastard and Prettyman licked Copic's ass the Spanish runs and all, cause they both was on the staff of the Lenin Institute experts in diabolical metabolism and Hammond was just only a lousy U.S. Marine officer and instructor in the Chinese Red Army and what the crap do they know, but Hammond ain't got no pull in Moscow and Prettyman and Copic got no experience but lots a pull. Hammond kept sayin' he ain't gonna lead us in no daytime attack and Copic called him a lunatic. That's that Jakey. Come quick before we're all dead.

Last night while they was arguing and we was waiting a couple a guys got wounded. This a.m. two guys shot their toes off accident like. The yellow pricks. If they didn't want to come to Spain they didn't have to or ought to of come. None of us could look at them when they took them away. There's a big battle every day in the first lines way up in the Tajuña valley off the San Martin road which comes off our road at the foot of the dried out titty near the white stone casa with the sign Madrid 32 kms. The ambulance duty does plenty overtime. We're getting meaner and meaner. Fights keep breaking out. I even had a fight with Raleigh one of the infantry commanders. He says I'm a bad example for the troops cause I don't crawl around. Jesus Christ, Son of God we're in the third lines. But he's right I'm acting like an amachure. Greg says I'm being a brave fucking hero and oughtta cut it out. Hey, we just got our orders to pack gear, we're moving up. It can't be no more fucked up than where we are.

Hurry up before we kill all the fascists.

Hasta la muerte, compañero
José Garms

IX

Jake Starr lay on a straw pallet in a stone cavelike cell, windowless, almost airless, in the fort at Figueras to which he had reported pursuant to Comrade Step's command. He had arrived in the mountain town the morning of the day the American volunteers first saw the rolling Arcadian beauty of the Tajuña valley. He had alighted from the train, been overwhelmed by the freshness of the mountain air, the flowing colorful banners, and the montage of heroic posters, and then ascended on foot the long hill to the fort which dominated the city. Ancient gray stone, musket slits, Napoleonic cannon showing their black mouths, a red flag with the hammer and sickle. He had presented his pass to the International Brigades guard, asked for General Ernesto, *nombre de la revolución* of Roegen, Hungarian underground party leader, a man who had spent half his life in airless cells, tortured, beaten. Called the shiteater by a few, assassin by many, to his comrades he was known as a man who carried his threshold of pain to such heights that his torturers had never been able to break him.

The I.B. guard took Comrade Starr's message to Roegen, returned shortly, led him through serpentine underground passages damp with the centuries into a stone cell. Said, "Wait, Comrade," closed the heavy oaken door behind him. Standing under the single light bulb at the end of a gnarled electric cord, Jake examined the blank stone walls, the low domed ceiling, the straw pallet on the cobbled floor, the iron grate on the floor which was to be his urinal and pot, a pitcher of dirty water on a wooden chair. Starr shrugged, smiled ruefully. He understood; he would have to wait for his interview with Roegen a day, two, three, who knew? Unless Vlanoc were already in disgrace or dead, and perhaps he was, they would not touch him. Roegen was close to Stalin, Vlanoc closer. In the hierarchical chart of the apparatus, Vlanoc stood a few brackets higher than the shiteater, even higher than Comrade Step. He, Jake Starr, was Vlanoc's man. If they touched him, they touched Vlanoc. Would they dare? Jake was frightened but already knew how to prepare his body and mind for the onslaught of fear. "Keep your bladder and intestines empty, that's the first rule," Vlanoc had instructed him against the day the *enemy* took him. "Loosen your belt, your shoelaces, your collar. Free yourself to breathe slowly, tensionless, find a good andante beat, count off the time. Lie down. Keep your mind loose and free. Clear. Do a problem in mathematics, recite some verse to yourself, a passage from Marx. If they beat you, fight against tensing your body. Sway with the whip, don't wait for it, accept it fully. Make it part of your body, your blood flow, your heartbeat. Enjoy it. Yes, enjoy it. Then they can never defeat you—only kill you. Understand?" "Yes, Carl, I understand."

So now with trembling hand he unbuckled his belt, opened his trousers, removed his tie, unbuttoned his collar, loosened his laces, urinated and voided his bowels over the grate, relaxed on the straw pallet, and, concentrating to the utmost, cleared his mind of fear by an *andante* intoning of whole passages from *The Eighteenth Brumaire of Louis Bonaparte*, the work of Karl Marx he most honored: *Hegel remarks somewhere that all great, world-historical facts and personages occur, as it were, twice. He has forgotten to add: the first time as tragedy, the second as farce. Caussidière for Danton,*

Louis Blanc for Robespierre, the Mountain of 1848 to 1851 for the Mountain of 1793 to 1795, the Nephew for the Uncle. . . . Starr for Vlanoc. Jake laughed. He was calmer already. He resumed, like a monk, his prayers. *Men make their own history, but they do not make it just as they please; they do not make it under circumstances chosen by themselves, but under circumstances directly found, given and transmitted from the past.* On he intoned, losing himself in the rhythm, not even thinking of the words, thinking of another time, when he was a young boy and had suffered a mild case of claustrophobia. He used to sleep in a very narrow room, barely wide enough to contain his bed. He began to wake nights, frightened, the walls of the room closing in on him, and he would cry out for his mother, run from his bed to her and his father, and they would soothe him until he fell asleep. But one morning he awoke—he was about twelve—and called out for his mother. No one responded. Scared, his heart beating violently, he felt the walls coming closer, closer, the very room shrinking about him. Filled with a terrifying panic, he ran to the door and grabbed at the knob. It wouldn't give. Now completely embraced by terror, he flung himself at the door, trying to break it down with his shoulders. The panic and terror shut him in so viciously he could barely breathe and though he began to shout the sounds were merely gasps which scraped harshly at his throat. Even then, at that age, something inside kept at him to control himself, kept after him to throw off the panic, to be sensible, and, to be sure, in a few moments he stopped his senseless pounding on the door. He forced himself to stand perfectly still, to breathe slowly, to see the room as it really was. Holding on tightly to himself he willed himself to relax, to sit quietly on the bed. He stared at the door and was suddenly certain it wasn't locked. How could it be—he hadn't locked it. All you have to do is walk slowly to the door, turn the knob easily, and the door will open. That is what he did, and of course the door was not locked, and he walked victoriously from his room. Thereafter he never suffered from claustrophobia again. That had taken courage and will. Now, strangely, it had reversed itself. He *loved* the closeness and narrowness of the Party, and precisely because it contained him, held his fears in check, kept tight rein on his strength. He was afraid of his strength, its violence when let loose. And he remembered another time, when he was about fifteen or sixteen, with a strength beyond his years, inherited from his father. One day, after a stickball game in the city street, he had started home exuberant at his having hit a couple of long ones, when he bumped into a man working with another on one of those street excavations which go on interminably in the city. The man he bumped into cursed him harshly. "Dirty Jew kid." He stopped to look at the man, who returned his stare. "Beat it, Hebe." He could feel the hatred for the man surging through himself, he could kill the bastard. Suddenly he swooped down and picked up a short crowbar lying at the man's feet, and with one movement on his way up smashed it into the man's face. He could feel the man's jaw crunch—and for a moment, a very short moment, he enjoyed a stab of satisfaction and relief deep in himself, a pleasure almost. Then he became frightened and ran. He'd always had that love of violence in him, and knew he had to control it, subjugate it to his will. Make it work for him for good purpose. Disciplined, controlled.

So now, too, by force of will his body and mind were free of panic and fear. He smiled victoriously, turned about, and fell asleep. Later, when he was brought his food on a tray—good food, he was still a leader, bean soup, pork, bread, hot coffee—he awoke, dispatched it hungrily, placed the tray at the foot of the oaken door. Settled again on the straw pallet. When the events of the past few days began to edge themselves into his consciousness, he rejected them. A lightheaded weightlessness pervaded him and he was proud of his ability to conquer his fear and his environment. He was prepared for Roegen the assassin and whatever Roegen's decision would be.

Yet, when he slept again, he dreamt of Sarah Ruskin, of her voluptuousness, of her full lips, a large blue eye into which he walked openhanded, and then the eye began to whirl, faster, faster, and all meaning was lost but love's.

X

South of Madrid, in the equilateral triangle formed by Arganda, Chinchón, and San Martín de la Vega, in an area approximating forty square miles, there was little thought of love as fifty thousand men found themselves engaged in a strange combat. In the battle which had already coursed for several weeks, tens of thousands had lost their lives, been buried in mass graves among the graceful rolling hills and valleys carpeted with gorse, marjoram, olive, and grape, an occasional aspiring green cypress, pine, and silver oak, under a miraculous blue sky through which sailed a white-yellow sun to the nagging shrill song of magpies. No perfume bottle ever secreted a more exquisite scent than the soles of a man's shoes from the pressed gorse, sage, and marjoram. The day's slaughter enveloped by night, a man could fling his aching nerve-quivering body to the earth, place his shoes near his weary battered head, sniff, and smile sweetly, war almost, but not, forgotten. Nature's very own justice.

The enemy—Spanish and Moorish infantry, German machine gunners and snipers, Italian Capronis, Savoias, German Heinkel 111's, Junkers, competent generals, and line officers, not a polit-commissar in the lot—was professional. Sometimes, it is true, the line officers bullwhipped their men when a trench was not deeply dug, a reactionary method for saving men's lives, but efficacious. The Loyal Spanish and Interbrigade troops were not as well trained, were amateurs in fact (save for the German exiles), whose trenches were not as neatly or as deeply dug, whose lives did not seem to matter as much. After all, they had right on their side.

It was the enemy's mission to cut the roads leading from eastern Spain to Madrid before the rains inundated the valleys of Tajuña and Jarama in March. The enemy fought with competence, heavily armed, their fire power on the ground, in the air, three, four, five to one over that of the resisting Loyal forces. The enemy would attack, break through; the Loyal troops would counterattack, repulse the enemy, but rarely if ever regain the ground the enemy had won. The graves were bottomless.

The troops of the Republic had poor commanders, worse line officers, bad communications, amateur troops who were led to fight the type of war the enemy wanted them to fight. Army to army; front to front. Though caring little for life, still they had will, and they had decided almost intuitively, collectively, not to yield The Road. The mass graves grew larger. The Road remained open, cluttered day and night with caravans of trucks, ambulances, staff cars, and a few Russian tanks used for mobile machine gun and light cannon fire. Overhead a sparse flight of Russian Moscas—flies—harried the enemy.

The fascist fire grew more ferocious, insistent; the Loyal and Interbrigade troops became more obsessively willful, stubborn. No! they cried. Despite our officers and our political leaders, no! Fascism took Italy without a fight; Germany was handed to you on bended knee. Only here have men fought and here we'll all die.

By the uncounted thousands they died. No one kept an accurate score.

As José Garms wrote his friend, Jake Starr, it was truly badly fucked up.

First they fought with will. And now that February approached an end, they fought with hope. It had already rained a few times, but in March there would be a deluge. Friend and enemy would sleep in their trenches, cooling their fevers with rain, healing their wounds with mud.

The hill on the Chinchón-Madrid road behind them, the American volunteers were camped in a gully shielded by its own high banks and an olive grove. To their left the narrow San Martín road, once macadam, now macadam and dirt, wound like a fish line strung out to dry through the hills and spacious flats of the Tajuña valley. To the troops in the sector, both enemy and friend, this was The Road.

To the peasants it was just another. Fearless, industrious, motivated by poverty and hunger, they could be seen daily with their burros and carts almost into the battlefield itself harvesting their olives. They too raced the deluge.

In the barranca shielded by an olive grove, Greg Ballard, his head resting on his gear, spoke quietly to Jaime Ortega, the lone *vaquero,* as Mack Berg slept and Joe Garms played crap with the others for the condoms they had never got to use. Ballard was becoming a soldier. He had not come to Spain to die a romantic hero's death, but to fight fascism. In the few short days they had spent on the hill, his trench had become a fort and a home: deep, spacious, neat with shelves and pegs for all his soldierly possessions. Shipshape. "Any man working a fishing boat who isn't well organized is taking his life into his hands. A fishing boat's little, the ocean's big." You asked, he answered. Then he became embarrassed because you gave him all this attention and he giggled his high-pitched way until you squirmed. After a time you became accustomed to it, as you did to his long-jawed head on no neck on broad shoulders on long body on short legs, and the smashed nose, the thick lips, and the big white teeth. Slowly over the weeks he had quietly and studiously explored his new comrades. Learned that if they had prejudices they concealed them securely behind their politics. If they suffered from a fault in their relations with him it was the one of patronage, they were just a mite too good, except for Joe Garms, Ortega, and, after he'd been set straight, Mack Berg. Mack was a little too prone to include him in his, Mack's, Jewish troubles. As Greg learned he could trust these men, he became less laconic, giggled less, began to assert himself. He was a man among men.

It was with Jaime Ortega he was most at ease and he admitted to himself it was because the Cuban boy was even more bashful, more afraid of people than he. When Jaime spoke it was as if he were walking a tightrope, and one became afraid at every word he was going to topple over and break his neck.

"Soon, *amigo,*" he said to Jaime, "we'll be doing what we've come to do. The other side of the gully's the enemy. Four hundred meters, Cord said."

"*Sí.* Gregory . . . the . . . enemy. Are . . . you . . . a . . . fraid?"

"Yup."

"We . . . are . . . as . . . one. I have pissed enough to have flooded the valley."

Greg smiled. The lone *vaquero* grunted.

They hadn't heard much rifle fire since settling in the barranca. Now a bullet snapped in the distance. They ducked. Every time they heard a snap they ducked. Captain Cord informed them they would soon learn to gauge the distance of every sound.

Greg and Jaime looked back toward the hill and the road beneath it. It was becoming dark now and they could barely see. What they could see was enough. The ever-present trucks, ambulances stacking their wounded, two tanks like armored beasts clanking away toward their night's lair, the day's hunt in the field done.

"I'm gonna take a nap, Jimmy. We probably move up tonight."

"You . . . sleep. I'll . . . try."

"Yeah. Either there's never enough or there's too much."

They napped.

Greg was wakened by a soft touch on his shoulder. It was Joe Garms. The sun was completely gone; it was freezing. As Ballard wrapped himself in his sheepskin, Joe Garms spoke. "Special duty squad. Wake Mack and Ortega. Get your gear. Meet yuh down below, the edge a the gully. Don't ferget your machine gun." He smiled.

"Okay, Joe."

When Ballard, Ortega, and Berg arrived, Garms, unusually silent, was there with Horowitz, Carrington, Dempsey, Leonidis, Bederson, and Parker. Skinny Horton had an m.g. squad there, too. Captain Cord was conferring with an English officer whom they had seen around, stiffbacked and *muy correcto*. When Cord saw they were ready, he motioned them to follow.

They marched singlefile for thirty minutes, always in the shelter of one hill or another. No one spoke. They made very little noise. It was very cold but everyone perspired. Everytime they stopped, someone had to take a leak. Captain Cord tried a joke. "Don't take it, leave it." It helped.

Night had fully arrived; the sky was a blank slate, the quarter moon like the unerased curved half of a question mark.

Garms's squad waited, leaning on one another for warmth and comfort, as the captain and the Englishman led Horton's squad up the side of a hill. Fifteen minutes later Cord and the English officer returned and the singlefile march resumed. They were now in a scrub pine wood, sparse and dry, the crackle of broken twigs a monstrous din echoing off the massive blackboard of night. Without anyone saying, Joe Garms's squad knew they were at the very edge.

First Joe and the English officer intermittently crawled and ran until they reached some stone breastworks. Ballard, the heavy carriage of his Maxim on his back, his rifle slung beside it, Jaime Ortega, cradling the machine gun itself in his arms, and Captain Cord followed. Mack sent the others in pairs and finally himself.

Captain Cord—a lean, handsome Tennesseean—the English officer, and Garms spoke with a tall slender comrade who talked with a Dutch accent, commander of a company of the famed Franco-Belges battalion. He was all business, curt and quick.

Under his orders, the Americans were positioned, the machine gun emplaced, Ballard going methodically to work. Cord smiled warmly and with the English Comrade wished them luck—"*Suerte, mucho suerte*"—and departed.

If the squad had been asked life or death to spit, everyone would have died.

Greg Ballard, with Ortega and Berg at his side, worked as quietly as possible emplacing the ancient gun firmly and solidly between some large stones. As they worked they heard Joe whisper, "Lookit those bastids smokin'." Sure enough, to their left, they saw the gleam of cigarettes. Must be nuts, with the enemy up ahead. Garms found the Dutch commander, queried him about it. The man smiled through his heavy beard, color unknown in the darkness.

"It is very well iff your camarades are smoking. We are goodt coffered by stone breastworks. So long as your men stay down der will be no trouble."

Joe thanked him, returned to his squad. Mimicking the commander, he told them they could smoke as long as they stayed down. Mack Berg began to laugh, soundlessly at first, but it got away from him and soon he and the rest of the squad were burying their mouths in the earth to muffle the guffaws.

Garms set up guard duty for the night, starting off with Ballard and Ortega, then ordered everyone to sleep. "Tomorrow when yuh wake up, right in front of them stones, up that shitass hill, is the enemy. He got guns and he shoots bullets. You been listenin' to the bull shit of the commissars that they're yellah, that they'll run as soon as you aim your guns at 'em. Y've seen those ambulances, y've seen the blood and the wounded, so you gotta understand y've been told a load a shit. They got the guts you and me got and they got more fire power. There's one difference. We're one hundred percent sure we're right, they ain't so sure. Goodnight, Comrades. Jest remember, little old Joe'll be here to help yuh." He laughed, the gravel running, they grinned, and then all turned in.

As Ballard sat near his gun he smoked a cigarette. Ortega asked for a light. "I . . . can . . not . . . sleep . . . even . . . if . . . I . . . try," Jaime said. "I keep thinking of Havana, schools, my mother and father." Greg looked at him sharply. Jaime never spoke about himself, about his family. He was one of those shy boys who couldn't believe anyone might be interested. Greg merely grunted. Hesitatingly, teetering ever on the tightrope of embarrassment, Greg remaining absolutely quiet so as not to throw him, Jaime continued. "I keep thinking about death. Last year I engaged with other students in a revolutionary action against Batista. We made some bombs and threw them into the police chief's home. I wasn't afraid that time. I didn't even think of death. But now I keep seeing the faces of comrades who died that night. I suppose I am very much afraid."

"We all are."

"I come from a wealthy family. Most of the students in the Cuban revolutionary movement do. It is strange: the richer the family, the more revolutionary their children. Very un-Marxian." He laughed.

Ballard smiled. He remembered once putting the question to Jake Starr about some of the sons of the rich joining the Party in Boston, but Jake had shrugged, passed it by. Jake Starr didn't like doubts, and questions which didn't fit flush with his economic determinism created doubts and he passed them by.

But Jaime Ortega was speaking, less rapidly now, and Greg stopped thinking of Jake Starr to listen.

"We have a beautiful old hacienda outside Havana. There I lived with my parents, three sisters and two brothers. I am the baby," he said shyly. "My father was proud of my revolutionary activity but couldn't understand my interest in the international movement. He lives only for a free and democratic Cuba. After that affair with the police chief I had to leave for the States. Before I left for Spain I wrote my father to explain my views . . . we left before I received an answer." He was abruptly quiet, then the words tumbled out. "If I am killed, will you write them?"

Greg was stunned by the request. Why ask him? No, he didn't like putting his nose in other people's business.

Jaime urged, "Will you, please? I want you to do it because I have great respect for you—you will write a letter, not a pamphlet."

"Thanks," Greg murmured.

"I will give you their address . . . just tell them I died bravely."

Greg's hands began to shake, he grabbed hold of himself, he didn't know what to say. "You haven't died yet. Oh, of course, I'll write them." Suddenly it occurred to him he could die too. "You'll do the same for me. I'll give you my sister's address . . . she'll break it easy to my mother."

"*Muchas gracias,*" Jaime whispered, biting his lips.

Each retired into himself.

Then Jaime said, "If you speak about death and make the practical arrangements, it becomes easier to face." He spoke as though he were certain he was going to die.

Greg stared at the lean leathery face. Jaime was nineteen years old and already making the practical arrangements. "Yeah. When I bought my ma a plot and a funeral she was happy for days."

"I feel better now," Jaime said.

"Good." A moment later, "If I die let Jake Starr know. He must still be in Paris. I'll give you his address."

"*Sí*. I saw him in Paris, too," Jaime said, as both became busy with their stub pencils. "But I met him once before in Havana, at a meeting at someone's house. He told us it was time we stopped behaving like wild anarchists, it was necessary sometimes to crawl as in war. He spoke Spanish very well and we were impressed. We did not listen, however, we made that attack on the police chief like wild Indians. It was foolish."

As they exchanged the slips of paper, Greg said, "He's a good man. He learns fast."

"How did you meet him?"

"He came up to the Cape for the Party. Met my sister Loney at a meeting and they became friends. She belongs, I don't. He told me he was colorblind. I told him, too bad you are, I got a real beautiful color. He became mad and I told him to stop patronizing me, it was jimcrow upsidedown. Out he slammed from the house. A big fish. I waited for a day when small craft warnings were up and took him out on my boat. The wind came up, twenty, thirty, the sea became rough just as I figured it would and he got so sick he thought he was going to die. I laughed like hell. When he was a real Kelly green I turned her about and brought her in. He stumbled off, fell on the ground and just lay there heaving. Finally he sat up pale as boiled sole. You're white as a sheet, I said. He gave me a sickly grin. And you're black as coal, he said. You caught on, I said. Yup, he said. We shook hands. Now he's not color-blind, though Loney thinks he still is. But he saw *me,* that's all I want. You understand?"

Jaime grinned. "Yup."

They smoked in silence. The night was totally quiet. Very dark. Some of the Franco-Belges were sitting guard, also smoking. The air seemed very light, dry.

Jaime said, "Something very dirty happened when Starr was in Havana. I don't think he was responsible. There was another man with him, an older man, from the Comintern. I think it was this man."

Ballard looked at Ortega hard. A man starts, he ought to finish. "What was it?"

"Better . . . not. I . . . shouldn't . . . have . . . spoken."

"Yes." A man oughtn't do that, start and not finish. But Greg was curious. "The same as happened to Nuñez in Villanueva?"

"Worse. We were all very unhappy, but we did nothing, said nothing."

"That made you an accomplice," Greg said sharply.

"Then you and I are accomplices about Nuñez too."

Ballard bit a thick lip. "You bet."

"Our dreams are so bright, Gregory."

"Is that good enough excuse?"

"I don't know . . . the enemy's so cruel."

"Agreed."

"So we become."

"And the enemy wins after all."

"I hope not."

"Me too, Jaime."

They'd made themselves unhappy, and had no more to say. First carefully extinguishing their butts, they then wrapped themselves tightly in their sheepskins and stared over the stone breastworks to where the enemy slept.

A half hour later they woke Dempsey, a merchant seaman from Mobile, Alabama, and Horowitz, a pants presser from the Bronx, to do guard duty. Then Ortega and Ballard spread a common poncho on the ground, lay down back to back, and fell asleep.

Dawn, orange gray streaked with alarming blue, woke Joe Garms's squad. Now they could see where they were. The stone breastworks were at the foot of a long easysloping hill covered with gorse, sweet marjoram bushes, some stray grape trees. At their rear, an open plain; to the left and slightly behind them, the scraggly pine wood through which they had come the night before. To their right, parallel to the wood, another hill which Joe Garms figured was the one being defended by Skinny Horton's squad.

In the line with them were sturdy blond- and red-bearded soldiers, a ragged, filthy lot. Indifferently they nodded to the newcomers in the line. They spoke little among themselves. From their lips drooped crooked Canary Islands stogies, removed only for food or drink. Plenty of drink—red wine. They had been in the lines incessantly for three weeks. Before that they had fought at University City.

Their commander seen in daylight was imposing: a tall man, freckled and tanned, a mane of flaming red hair, beard no less flaming and covering his entire chest like a burning bush. The hill up ahead, he informed Garms, was held by Moorish infantry and German machine gunners and snipers. "Very goodt fighters. Excellent!" The enemy had been attacking every day for weeks, been repelled each time with heavy losses. At night the dead were buried. "No shooting unlest I give der order. *Me entiende usted?*"

Joe said, "Yeah, *entiendo.*"

The commander smiled. "Position your men. Be always ready." Joe was dismissed.

As he strode back to his squad, he heard the commander call out, "Soon the coffee will be coming."

Garms ordered Ballard and Ortega to remain with their machine gun and to sight it at the top of the hill in front of them. Greg sprawled on his stomach behind his gun, sighted it at four hundred meters, as Jaime lay down beside him to feed the belt. Garms had the remaining seven men sit in a semicircle with him in the center. They looked nervous, dirty, white-lipped. Piss-ass scared. He was too. Never been so fuckin' piss-ass scared in his life. Worse than before goin' into the ring for a fight. So scared his scrotum hurt. Like blue balls. "You guys—which ones besides Parker and Dempsey know how to shoot?"

Horowitz, a big black-bearded kid, raised his hand. Garms laughed.

"Yuh fuckin' liar. A pants presser from the Bronx?"

Horowitz smiled darkly. "I was captain of the rifle team at Morris High."

Garms grinned. "Sonuvabitch. Take the position at the right flank at the end a the stones." Horowitz obtained his gear and rifle and loped over to the furthermost point behind the stone wall. "No shootin' unlest I give der order. *Entiende?*" Horowitz nodded. "Dempsey, take yer gear and set yore li'l southern ass near that meanlookin' Dutchman on the left." Dempsey, a bulletheaded blond man, rose gracefully to his one short and one long leg—he wore a shoe with a built-up sole and heel—and moved lithely to his position. Joe sent Mack Berg next to Dempsey, and Leonidis, the Greek furrier who was great with a fur-cutter's knife, a cold potato, next to Horowitz. "He'll learn yuh fast, Skippy." Then he positioned Parker, a blond hard-nosed ugly man all of eighteen years old, a squirrel hunter from way back when he was three, next to

Mack Berg who was looking meaner by the day. He placed Bederson, a twenty-year-old baldheaded boy with steely blue eyes behind steel-rimmed glasses, a City College grad, next to Parker. Hunt Carrington, the big brown fullback from Morgan U. and Party organizer from Chicago, he placed near the machine gun.

All in position, he called out, "Remember, squeeze the trigger, don't jerk it. Save that for your rolled beef."

Mack Berg, already the dirtiest soldier in Spain, said drily out of the side of his thin-lipped mouth, "Topkick Garms thinks he's Victor McLaglen in *What Price Glory*."

Everybody laughed and Garms became red in the face. "Screw off, yuh mean-mouthed bastid."

"Up yours with a meathook," Mack retorted.

Joe balled his fists, and Dempsey drawled, "Ten-shun!"

Garms plopped to his seat and started counting, "One, two, t'ree," up to ten, and he and Mack were friends again.

The blue widened, the orange reddened, the gray disappeared, dawn became day. The Franco-Belges spoke among themselves, smoking their stogies; the Americans fidgeted, staring through slits in the breastworks out into no-man's land at the invisible enemy. Not a shot had been fired.

From the scrub-pine wood two men and then two more brought hot coffee and bread. Devoured with relish, smacking of lips.

Chatter, waiting, snoozing, waiting. Noon: sweating. Two men broke from the pine wood, flopped, crawled, ran, crawled. Crossed half the one hundred fifty yards, flopped on a slight rise. Snap! snap! Right in front of their eyes one man lay dead and the other twisted and turned, screaming. A medic detached himself from the wood, running and flopping. Joe Garms, fists clenched, ready to go, was pinned down by the commander's order. "Don't move. No shooting. I have neider men nor bullets to spare." Garms and his men watched dry-mouthed as the medic reached the wounded man, gave him a shot of morphine, then started back with the man on his back. Snap! snap! The medic and his wounded man lay still.

"Fools!" the commander snapped out.

"Breathe slow," Joe Garms said. "Jest breathe slow. It helps. And lookit those guys."

The Franco-Belges calmly reclined behind the stone breastworks, smoking their stogies, drinking *vino*.

The Americans chatted desultorily, sweated profusely. Waited. Hunt Carrington said in his mellow bass voice, "We've been in the lines a week, been hit with artillery fire, aerial bombs, been shot at, seen lots of dead and wounded, and we ain't shot a gun in anger yet. I feel myself getting real mean. I would just love to kill somebody."

Silence.

Ballard said, "A week." He giggled nervously. "It's Washington's birthday. The twenty-second. Hey, let's have a parade."

Silence.

They waited. The afternoon passed.

Nothing from the enemy. Just silence. Not even a wind through the gorse. The sun began to set, and it began to get cold as it does when the furnace goes dead in midwinter.

"I'm hungry," Mack Berg said, scratching dirt out of the corrugations in his face.

"You always say the right thing," Leonidis glared.

Ortega passed Berg a square of hardtack through four pairs of hands. As Mack ate it sounded like the cracking of wood under a heavy strain.

If these guys is scared as me, Joe thought, they're gonna run. He was prone five paces behind his men, dead center. And his scrotum still hurt. Somethin's gotta happen. It jest gotta. Too fuckin' quiet.

Singing! Shrill, skincrawling, weird, like a geyser of wailing oboes. Joe turned his head towards the Dutch commander who also lay prone behind his men. The man nodded affirmatively. Called out, "No shooting till I give der order." Joe signaled assent.

"The Moors," he called to his men. "Take a piss, y'll feel better."

The line from Horowitz at the extreme right to the last Franco-Belge at the left arched like a cat's back ready to spring. Smoke rings spiraled above the heads of the veterans like smoke from a hardclimbing locomotive.

The Moors seem to be screeching and Joe can feel his skin become taut. Jesus Christ, me balls hurt.

Waiting.

Joe is breathing heavily, sweating—now it's cool and I'm sweatin'. He can see his men fidgeting with their rifles, can hear them cursing under their breath. The veterans are alert, puffing away on their stogies. Leonidis calls out, "Let 'em come! Let the fuckers come!"

Parker screams, "What the shit they waiting for?"

Joe Garms holds on tightly to his voice, still it's like gravel spilling down a chute, "You will not fire until I give the order."

At the machine gun, Ballard giggles. "Did you hear Joe? His enunciation was perfect. The bastard's scared as we are."

"Stop . . . giggling."

"Yup."

Still the Moors sing. All else is quiet, except Joe Garms's heart which beats a helluva tattoo.

The shrill singing stops.

Total silence.

Dempsey begins to scream. "Mama, mama, let 'em come. Mama, mama, let 'em come. Mama, ma——"

"Shudt opp!"

Dempsey clamped his mouth shut.

Suddenly bullets were around their ears and everyone dug his nose into the ground. Even the veterans. Then they heard the ratatat ratatat of machine guns. A deadly racket. Shattering. Bits of dirt and stone began to trickle down around the stones, tufts of earth and gorse danced a drunken jig about them.

The Dutch commander signaled Garms into the line with his men. "Soon," he called. "Soon."

"THERE THEY ARE!"

A horde of shrieking Moors loped gracefully down the hill, bayonet-fixed guns held easily, helmets strangely high on their heads.

"Helmets, for chrissakes," Joe yelled. He grabbed for his, plopped it on his head. "Put your helmets on!"

"I hate it," he heard Mack Berg mutter.

"Put it on!"

Mack conceded.

The Dutch commander stood behind them in the open, bullets skipping all about him, standing easily, his hands folded underneath his red beard, a pensive, sad smile on his face so it looked as if he were eating his way through his beard. The Moors looked like giants, unreal giants, not men. They loped gracefully, their black capes flying behind them, their bayonets ribbling white in the rays of the sun, blinding the eyes of the defenders of the line.

Horowitz way over to the side screams, "I can't wait, I'm gonna shoot."

"NO!" Joe shouts. Scared, so fuckin' scared. Oh, Christ, my balls hurt. There's a constriction around his heart, and now his rectum hurts too. Too tight.

Half-blinded by the sun, looking up at the loping, flying Moors coming down at him, they look like giants. Some of them are wearing white turbans like towels wrapped about aching heads on which they have placed their helmets. It ain't real, Joe says. He wonders why the enemy machine gunners aren't shooting high to keep them down and then of a sudden he realizes the noise is fantastic, frightening, and he knows the enemy is shooting except his fear has made him deaf. Soon they gotta stop shootin', he says to himself, for the Moors strung out in an uneven line are fast approaching. The singing has stopped. The enemy machine guns have stopped shooting. It is quiet in the valley.

Ballard's mouth is dry, his tongue sticks to his palate. Through his sights he discerns the features of a Moor. Very real eyes. Shining black skin. Black beard. A very deadly bayonet pointed straight at him.

"FIRE!"

Greg closes his eyes, hunches his huge shoulders, presses his thumbs on the machine gun trigger.

Nothing. Not even a click.

The Moor's bayonet is at him but Joe Garms shoots the Moor dead.

The battle has begun.

The veterans of Madrid and The Road, the Franco-Belges raise tin cans with black fuses to their smoking stogies and heave them with great accuracy. Joe Garms climbs to the top of the stone breastworks and is pumping lead, his carbine already hot in his hands. Ballard follows him. Mack Berg is already there. The entire squad is perched on the stone wall. They are moaning, Parker is crying, but they are shooting. Moors are falling. The Franco-Belges are flinging dynamite. Moors are exploding. Dempsey screams. He is hit, stands straight up, falls on Mack Berg. Dempsey's face is a bloody pulp. Mack vomits. Ortega pulls Dempsey off Mack and gently lays him aside. He gives Mack a large kerchief; resumes firing. The tin cans and dynamite are being thrown swiftly, with great accuracy. The Moors turn tail, and as they do a machine gun on the hill behind the Americans shoots a burst of three, sputters. Dies. Nothing. Horton's machine gun. But his squad takes up the slack, sends fusillade after fusillade at the retreating Moors, black capes flowing behind them.

Greg Ballard is shooting madly, wildly, numbly, holds a running Moor in his sights, is ready to squeeze the trigger. Suddenly the Moor stops, leans over, raises a fallen comrade to his shoulders and returns to his flight, now a semistumble like a gull with a broken wing. Ballard swings his rifle, finds another target, fires. But out of one eye he follows the stumbling enemy. Of those making it back to their trenches, the Moor with his burden is last. Ortega aims his rifle, his shoulders stiffen, his finger squeezes, the enemy and his comrade sprawl to the sage.

Ortega sees Ballard staring at him, coldly returns the stare.

The battle is over. It has taken ten minutes.

They are all laughing hysterically. They didn't run. Dempsey is dead. Several of the Franco-Belges are dead. Joe's singing,

> *I went down to the St. James Infirmary*
> *To see my sweetheart there.*
> *She was stretched out on a long white table*
> *So white, so cold, so bare. . . .*

Some of the veterans of the Franco-Belges battalion straggle over to shake hands. One, a blond-bearded, redheaded behemoth named Struik, dirty and grinning, waggles a stubby finger like a pendulum run wild under Joe Garms's nose. "*Mucho loco, americanos; mucho loco.*" They laugh. Very proud. Horowitz has had the tip of his nose shot away—he could afford it. It has stopped bleeding. "A cheap nose-bob, a cheap nose-bob," he roars. The commander is sprawled on his back staring into the twilight sky, bold orange streaked with black.

Bederson's beaming, his glasses fogged, yelling, "I'm alive. Holy Moses, I'm still alive."

Parker is sobbing. "I didn't run. Y'get what I mean? I didn't run."

They are all alive, excepting Dempsey, of course, whom Mack Berg has covered with his poncho.

Joe realizes he is freezing, his hands quivering like a spastic's. He notices the others are beginning to tremble as well. He orders them to sit down against the stone wall. They do, swaggeringly fling their helmets aside, light cigarettes. Their voices are shrill, high-pitched.

It is not yet night and it is icy cold. Hot steaming coffee is brought in urns from the pine grove. They crowd around, use their helmets for cups, as Jaime Ortega, a self-appointed mother hen, ladles out his share to each man. Bullets are zwinging overhead, but who cares, the coffee's great. They're alive.

An explosive bullet smashes into Jaime Ortega's head and his brains splash into the coffee urn.

Mack Berg whispers to himself, though they all hear him, "Shit! There goes the coffee."

For two hours as the sun disappeared, the night lit by a squiggle of a moon, they sat against the stone wall waiting for the commander to tell them when they could bury their dead. For two hours Mack Berg wept, inconsolable, intermittently cursing himself. "No fucking good, have never been any fucking good."

Garms kept everyone away from him. "Leave him cry it out, it's good for 'im. He oney said what we all thought."

At Jaime's death, Greg Ballard had run to the pine wood—to cry, it was assumed.

When night had come to stay and the commander told them they could bury their dead, Garms sent Parker to find Ballard. They waited and in fifteen minutes Parker returned with him. Greg immediately went to Mack and said, "Come on, Berg, help me carry him."

They took Jaime Ortega, and Joe and Horowitz took Dempsey, the rest of the squad following. At the foot of Horton's hill two graves were dug and they buried Ortega and Dempsey.

Later, as they sat with their backs to the stone wall, they heard the muffled cries of the earth as it was pitted with shovels. The Moors too were burying their dead.

Before they turned in, a battalion runner appeared who spoke to the commander, who came to the Americans himself, commended them, and advised them to return to their battalion, which on the following day was to go into its first battle.

On the afternoon of 23 February, their battalion commander Captain Richard Jordan Prettyman sat in the gully surrounded by his staff and the battalion. They were waiting for zero hour. They were going over the top.

Captain Cord, just juiced enough so that his intelligent gray eyes showed their contempt for the commander, advised Captain Prettyman that eight of the company's nine machine guns were defective. Horton, a slender curlyheaded kid with a long nose and a dour disposition, was given the one good gun and sent with a few men to a flanking position close to the San Martín road. Captain Cord withdrew his remaining machine gun squads from the line. They sat away from the battalion near the end of the gully chatting idly, not unhappy.

In no-man's land, on the overside of the gully, hidden from view, the enemy kept up an incessant machine gun fire. The two infantry companies, under the command of Raleigh and

Avila, a Cuban, sprawled in a conglomerate group, their packs on their backs, helmets on their heads, bayonets fixed to rifles clutched in white bony fists, their eyes intent on Prettyman and his small staff.

They were scared, nervous, white-lipped, and impatient. Were waiting to do what they had come to do: to kill fascists, to save Madrid, to become heroes, to die. Not a few wondered out loud what in the hell they were doing there.

Two Russian tanks crawled to opposing flanks and began immediately to shell the enemy lines. They, with Horton's machine gun, were to give covering fire for the over-the-top bayonet charge.

Twenty-five minutes after Skinny Horton was sent to take his position, Karonian, the machine gun company polit-commissar and Horton's gunner, returned to the battalion, which still awaited its orders, and advised Captain Cord that Horton had been killed and that his gun too was defective. "Before he died," Karonian said, "Comrade Horton called out, Long Live the Communist International!"

Poor Horton. Joe Garms cursed, Ballard screwed up his black face so it was all chin, and Captain Cord went to stand by himself for a minute. Horton had been his runner all through training at Villanueva. Bob Gladd, the battalion's linguist and loudest laugher, a man whose every boast proved true, cried. Horton had been a member of their gang.

At three o'clock Captain Richard Jordan Prettyman signaled to Raleigh and Avila. They ordered their companies into battle formation. A great sigh, a quiver shook the infantrymen. Silently—only the clanking of rifles could be heard—they lay themselves on the bank of the gully.

The sun shone. The two Russian tanks kept their small cannon pounding. Va-room! Va-room! The enemy machine guns never for a moment halted their wicked fire.

At three-0-five Prettyman stood, raised his right hand high

over his head. Again a great sigh, a giant quiver shook the riflemen. Prettyman brought his hand forward and down.

The American infantry, led by Raleigh and Avila, clambered up the gully bank and went over the top.

No cameras clicked. No movies were made.

The enemy, perhaps astonished, held their fire for thirty seconds as some three hundred fifty Americans advanced on the run, flopped, ran thirty yards. Larry Hillman, straight out of Clark U., old Aron's comrade, forgot to flop and running like a gazelle reached the enemy trenches. And was killed. A few others, envious, made a similar attempt. With a similar result. One was a company commissar, a gleaming Colt .45 clutched lovingly in his fist.

It was a lovely afternoon. Spanish to the core—olive and grape trees, an occasional slender cypress, gorse, and marjoram. The air was light, dry, the sun a rolling ball of fire. Visibility was perfect. Americans never fought or died on a more beautiful battlefield.

The enemy raised their rifles, sighted their machine guns, their mortars, and killed these immortal Americans by the score.

An Irish boy, a laggard, stood in the gully screaming and with maniacal strength ripped his skin from forehead to jaw. For a moment he stood like a torch of blood. Ran berserk. An Irish comrade killed him with one shot.

Three Americans and one Cuban, standing on the summit of the gully and seeing the slaughter, wisely turned tail and fled.

The machine gun company, at rest, counted its blessings and shrank into its collective self.

Captain Cord advised Richard Jordan Prettyman to order the battalion back. "You can't send green infantry into that kind of fire without cover."

Captain Prettyman stared at Cord with his blue steel eyes

and said, "The Spanish and the Bulgarians have gone over too. We can't let them down."

First Captain Cord spat. Then he said, "If you look to your right and left you will see that they haven't. You've sent green troops on a bayonet charge all alone."

Prettyman turned away, deep in thought.

On the other side of the gully the blood ran. The screaming was like that of a hundred head of cattle with their throats slit. Wet and gurgly.

Richard Jordan Prettyman faced about, his decision made. "Send runners to Raleigh and Avila," he ordered Cord, "to beat an orderly retreat."

The runners, one an Austrian boy who had fought brownshirts in the streets of Vienna, closed their eyes and plunged over the gully wall.

In twenty minutes, by some miracle, the Viennese boy traversed the thirty yards out and the thirty yards back. His lips thin, his hands trembling, his voice harsh, he reported that Raleigh was badly wounded and Morrison, his second in command, as well. But they had sent word to their men to beat a retreat. Help would be required to bring in Morrison. Raleigh himself refused to move without his men. Then the boy added, "It might best be if they wait until it iss very dark. They can't move forwards and can't move backwards. They are pinned by a terrible fire. And when a man is on top of the gully it iss like on a stage being with all the spotlights on."

Prettyman looked at Cord as if to say, "You see!" Then he clamped his big white teeth in a grimace, thought a moment. After all, it was rumored he had studied in the Frunze Military Academy in Moscow under Tukhachevsky and Gamarnik. "Raleigh and Avila will have to decide on the battlefield. I have given them orders that they may turn back."

The Viennese boy slumped away, Captain Cord stamped

about, and Richard Jordan Prettyman stood thinking, his large tomb-white teeth gleaming.

Joe Garms, who had come up and listened to the conversation, ran up the gully bank and dove over headfirst. He lay slumped on the earth, screwin' the ground, lovin' it up, smellin' it, till I fergot the bullets, the screams, learnin' the ground, hearin' it, becomin' a part of it, vomitin' too, givin' it back what it gave me. Then I opened me eyes, scrunched me head around and saw what there was tuh see. Holy Mother of God, they was busted open, each man hit by three different guns. Closed my eyes again. Says to meself, jest ferget it and move. I become a part of all the screamin', the bullets, the mortar shells, the dyin', and the wounded, and I went tuh work. . . .

Inch by inch.

By the time he brought Morrison in with the aid of a medic it was dark and he had vomited every last particle of both undigested and digested food. And blood too. Then he went back in the dark—the enemy fire had if anything intensified in a sweeping fire, low, cutting the grass—and again inch by inch Joe Garms hauled Raleigh in. Two men helping him were killed. By this time those who could move were moving themselves, like a horde of wounded turtles, their shells cracked open, trailing insides. Still the enemy kept cutting the grass, scorching it, burning it. A third time Joe Garms threw himself out of the gully, crawled out there, this time brought Gonzalez in, a bullet through his jaw. Sprawled under an olive tree, protected by a shallow trench, muttering curses on friend and enemy alike, Joe heard that Raleigh had died, and Morrison, too, though no one knew for certain. "It's harder savin' guys than killin' 'em," he said, shrugging.

About ten-thirty that night, the enemy closed up shop and the machine gun company labored with the medics to bring in the dead and the wounded. Some eighty men.

The corpses were buried in mass graves.

As the remaining men of the American battalion set up their guard, prepared to catch some sleep, in the midst of their greatest despair, they heard a rumor of a man, a voice, who had saved the day, prevented the Chinchón road from being cut by the enemy in the north, near the Jarama River bridge. A real hero.

"Bull! shit!" Joe Garms growled before he keeled over and fell dead asleep.

And Mack Berg said, "We don't need any other heroes, we have our own. If ever a day belonged to a man, this day belongs forever to Joe Garms."

XI

THE SUN HIDDEN: blackness. White days: black nights.

Darkness arrived, the grave battalions crawled from the battlefield with their burdens. Digging vast pits, soldiers on guard could hear the shovels breaking earth, the long sigh of dirt as it whooshed from shovel through air, they dumped the hundreds of dead into the sour coldness, emptied bags of lime, and then again those on guard could hear the shovels and the sighs. It was work which took the night's hours.

During the last few days of February the Loyal Spanish troops and their Interbrigade allies did the attacking, the Nationalist enemy the counterattacking. It was the mission of the attackers to stall the enemy for a week, then, March in attendance, the rains would be a flood. The Road saved, Madrid, the symbol now of Free Spain, would survive for at least another month. And then? Then.

There were many heroes. But one man became a legend.

On the evening of 23 February, in the twilight, just as the German Interbrigade forces began to give ground and it seemed the Jarama River bridge and the Chinchón road would be lost, rumor had it that a huge Hispano-Suiza limousine, a polished black palace of a car, rattled over the narrow steel-girdered Jarama bridge, came to a halt, its rear door was flung open, and a man thrown out on his face. The limousine made a quick U-turn, almost hitting some wounded on the side of the road called Death Valley, and disappeared with the running sun. The man picked himself off the ground, found himself a rifle, and barreled into the lines.

He made his presence known first with his voice: a raging, ringing, clear voice, strong, commanding.

He spoke in German. "*Halten die Schweine!* Stop shooting wildly. STOP THE PIGS! HOLD THEM!" It was an amazing voice, ringing high above the battle clamor. It bellowed forth from a gray figure, a helmet plunked on his head, a broad mass of back, his rifle carried like a toy. To those who heard the voice, it seemed unconquerable, unbowed. No one knew whose voice it was; after the battle they would find out. They relaxed their stomachs, forgot their fatigue, controlled their fire, became the pros they were. They held the pigs.

Night dropped quickly, the sun had absconded, the enemy retired to his trenches defeated another day. A day closer to the flood.

The voice disappeared. It seemed a ghost's voice, but of course it was a man's, what sort of nonsense is that?

The second day of battle, farther south, after having attacked and been repulsed, the enemy counterattacking, the Spanish and Hungarian Interbrigade troops, their backs against the last hill before their sector of The Road, were on the verge of disaster. Again the voice commanded—this time in Spanish. "*Por la lucha por la libertad! Por el honor de la vida!* For yourselves, your manhood. HOLD THE DOGS!" It was a powerful voice. And its rage could be heard above the crackling bedlam.

The Spanish and Hungarian battalions held; the voice had revived their will.

Again he disappeared. No god—a man in a gray poncho, his helmet down over his ears. No god—what kind of bull! shit! was that?

So another day passed, The Road remained open, one could

almost smell the rain. It would come, a deluge, even if the voice had to wring it out of the heavens himself.

25 and 26 February were quiet days: attacks, counter-attacks, nothing of great moment. Men were wounded, men died. The grave details worked only half the night. The pits were smaller, fewer lime bags were used. The French, the Slavs, the Yugos heard the voice for a moment, then it was gone.

From Chinchón to Madrid itself, the bedraggled amateur soldiery of Free Spain regaled themselves with this romantic tale. Who was it? Someone would say perhaps it was a famous German comrade who'd disappeared a few months before in Madrid for having broken discipline—what, no one knew—and he'd been thrown into the line to die. Men smiled. The rantings of battle-fatigued soldiers. Shellshock. It was their courage and their will!

Two days closer to the flood. It rained a bit, stopped. Soon, however, soon. The Road would live! Madrid, Free Spain, the soldiers in the line would hoot at the fascist.

27 February. Not even a spit of cloud. "Aaa," Joe Garms sneered, "the goddam rain can't read the calendar."

"Of course not," Mack Berg snapped. "This is Spain, illiteracy rampant."

Again it was the American's turn. Some four hundred fifty men, seventy-three replacements, arrived the night before as green as newborn grass; men who had never held a gun, let alone shot one, they waited for Prettyman's command. The machine gun company was now infantry. Their mission was to take a ledge of rock a mere, a trifling, three hundred meters away. Their cover would again be the two Russian tanks and an invisible air force. They had heard of the voice, snickered at it, now they prayed for it. They didn't care if it were the voice of ghost, god, or man. Beggars aren't choosers. And if not the voice, perhaps the rains would flood. How the hell did it know it was 27 February and not 1 March?

"The sky's as clean of clouds as a baby's ass of hair," Mack Berg muttered.

They were now positioned on the left of the road, flanked by British, Slavs, Spaniards. A battery of 75's began slapping shells into the enemy line before the Spanish battalion. Ah, cover. Where's the aviation? Where are the tanks? The Americans were led by Prettyman, Cord, Avila, Cromwell Webster. Schlepp had spoken to them once. "This is war, Comrades. We must learn to take the bad with the good."

"What good?" Mack Berg called out. Everyone laughed. A black mark was put down against Berg's name. Schlepp disappeared, as did Barrel. Comrade Patrick still survived, as did OGPU Demo.

Prettyman called Brigade. "Where is our aviation cover, Comrade?"

"Have you placed your aviation directional arrow? No? Well, place it now. Don't worry, the aviation will arrive. Follow your orders."

Two men are sent to lay out the arrow for the *avión*. They are killed, murdered, assassinated, cut to ribbons.

Prettyman called Brigade. "Where is our aviation cover, Comrade?"

"Just do as you were ordered. This is not maneuvers, this is war."

"*Salud,* Comrade Commander."

"*Salud!*"

The sun shining, the sky azure, the enemy waiting, drinking tea perhaps, led by Prettyman himself the Americans hurled, wrenched, dragged, stumbled into no-man's land. Alone. In the entire sector. The enemy had a ball.

The American boys lay there for hours, the sun burning their tails, the enemy professionals putting them into a deep cold sleep. It was just as senseless to turn back as it was to go forward. They screwed the earth, smelled it, vomited on it, but it did not help. Time was an endless road, the screaming of the dying and the wounded red mileposts marking off the mileage to nowhere.

Mack Berg felt dead, though he knew he was alive because he could hear himself breathing like a rattle. The explosions were like spikes being hammered into concrete at the rims of his ears, yet after a couple of hours he could hear a pin drop.

It was late afternoon. He was still alive—waiting to die. Only make it clean, he prayed. I don't care if I die, so long as it's fast and clean. The difference between life and death's only a philosophical abstraction. Yes, *Herr Doktor.*

Suddenly there was a lull. He raised his head from the earth, spied a clump of olive trees twenty feet away, decided he wanted to live, lowered his head, shouted "Follow me" to some men nearby, forced himself up and ran crouched towards the trees, threw himself behind them. The enemy fire resumed and it was like sheet metal beaten by an avalanche of rocks. Grateful to the olive trees and their jumble of uncovered roots, he screwed his head about and counted five men. Wondered where Joe and Greg were. Not for long. He began shooting his rifle, and the kick of the gun, the heat of the barrel, the work of reloading made him momentarily forget his fear. The five men near him were now shooting too. He hoped they were all shooting in the right direction. The enemy gunners meanwhile were taking their time, sawing the olive trees down one by one. The enemy's a pro, we're just amateurs, five, six days, still amateurs.

They were making a mistake and didn't know what it was and no one told them. Each group was an island by itself, a little bunched island, all contact lost, every man his own commander.

Others had now crawled and run up to the olive tree and they were fifteen men. No longer trees, stumps. Each stump was no thicker than an old woman's arm, but it was cover of a sorts and besides it was becoming darker by the minute. If we can hold out, we'll live. Mission not accomplished, but another day will be gone, and we will be that much closer to the rain. Mack didn't really believe the rain would intervene in this daily horror they were being put through, but it helped to believe it would. They were beginning to breathe easier at the clump of sawed-down olive trees, ignoring the screams, talking to one another.

About thirty meters to their left one of the Russian tanks blasted fifties into the enemy line. Now the sun was gone and in Mack's mind's eye he could see the vast ruin, the monuments like black gnarled bodies, then the darkness, then safety.

Suddenly with a rush like kerosene thrown on a bonfire the tank was in flames. A torchlight. The enemy must have laughed. In silhouette the Americans were better targets than before the sun had begun its descent.

It lit up their sector, revealing islands of *bunched* comrades in an area of a couple hundred meters.

Within the tank there were shattering explosions. Three men were in that burning steel can. Mack drilled the earth, his cheek pressed against a ripped tree root, numb to the sharp edges tearing his skin, his eyes hypnotized by the turret of the tank. It flung open and a head emerged, hair like burning snakes. Mack thought he could smell the man burning, his face seemed to be melting like tallow and he was screaming. Oddly, though Mack couldn't hear the firing, he could hear the man's screaming. The man's head hesitated, then his shoulders emerged, his uniform smoking, his hair on fire. Suddenly he was heaved out by the man below. An enemy rifleman put an end to his screams before he hit the ground. The technical invincibility of the modern superman. Mack spat and the wind made by the burning tank splashed it back against his face. Then there was the second head, burning like the wick of a candle, and he melted in front of Mack's eyes. The third man was never seen.

And still no command.

The tank continued to burn, lighting the sector, the enemy fire cool and accurate. There were only eight men left alive near the stumps—now like pencil stubs ground down to their erasers.

Only one thing to do—tear yourself the hell out of here. Can't, just can't move.

He drilled himself into the earth, waiting to die, hoping it would come quickly when it came. It was then from the sky itself he heard a voice—a roar it was, a haunted unrecognized yet familiar voice. "DON'T BUNCH UP! SPREAD OUT! RUN! SPREAD AND RUN YOU'LL MAKE IT!"

It was a commanding voice and none could say it nay.

So Mack ran, crawled, now alone, driven by the howling, carried on the wings of that commanding voice which still roared "SPREAD OUT AND RUN YOU'LL MAKE IT!" shooting incoherently at the unseen terror, the howling, the nogood fascist scum, over the top, go get 'em, PASAREMOS! the fight against fascism is the fight for freedom, for equal rights, Madrid the tomb of fascism and of heroes, better to die on your feet than live on your knees, dying on their bellies, running, crawling, driven by the screams MAMA MAMA OH MAMA MAMA I'M DYING IT HURTS OH GOD IT HURTS MAMA PLEASE I'M DYING, running with wings and then there was the ridge of solid rock, Joe Garms hugging him, "Dig, *puta*, dig!" Mack dug behind the rock with his bayonet and helmet, shovel forgotten. Captain Richard Jordan Prettyman—the dirty incompetent bastard couldn't even remember to order them to take trench shovels. About seventy men were digging with their bayonets and helmets. But a huge wraith, gray, separated himself from others down the line, "I'll get the shovels, keep digging." The voice in a lower octave, familiar yet strange, and he was gone, and Mack resumed digging, listening to the howling, and then next to him he heard a man gasping, holding himself from crying, and Mack became enraged and couldn't prevent himself from grabbing at the man, punching him, beating him, screaming at him, "Cry, you sonuvabitch. Cry! You have a right to cry. Cry if you want to cry. Go ahead you stupid sonuvabitch. CRY!" Joe Garms had to lock him in his arms, to hold him tightly so he couldn't breathe, and Mack caught hold of himself. It was Archie Cohen who'd come up just that day twenty minutes before they went over the top and who had never held a gun in his life and who hadn't shot one bullet out there. He cried now, sobbing deeply, and he dug with his bayonet, and Mack hugged him and begged his forgiveness. Then Mack began to cry, a man who hadn't cried in years. And Archie Cohen cried more and said it was all right, it felt good crying, and his voice was a flute. He and Mack became friends *hasta la muerte* and resumed digging, Archie singing, Goodbye Chicago, hello Madrid. Then the gray ghost was back with a fistful of shovels and Mack turned to him, but he was gone, a gray wraith, a god, a ghost, a man. The enemy found their range only forty, fifty meters away now, and the ridge of rock sounded like a chute of coal emptying into big tin cans. So they resumed digging—faster, no one wasting time on words.

Abruptly the enemy stopped his heavy fire; the silence was ragged with a spotty pattern of rifle and machine gun chatter. It sounded like the ticking of a looney clock. Crack. Crackasnap. Crack. Crack crack crack. Crackasnap. ZWINNGGG! And the terrified crying of the wounded and dying sounded like rasps filing on the edge of glass.

The man, the wraith, did not return. Mack and the rest—Greg Ballard had a strange look on his smashed black face—wondered who the man was, where he was, kept expecting him to materialize like a ghost.

Hours passed, more shovels were brought, more men showed up, some with coffee and bread. And they wondered to themselves, afraid to ask, how many lay out there. They dug. They were still alive and had learned what mistake it was they had been making. They had bunched and the voice had seen immediately. They had won a victory. The ridge of rock was theirs. They were a day closer to the rain. Each man counted those near to him, wondered where familiar faces had got.

An hour after coffee and bread were brought, a brigade runner appeared out of the dark. "Return to previous positions."

"WHAT?"

He repeated the order. None of the other battalions had gone over and the Americans had fought themselves into an exposed position.

Joe Garms grabbed at the runner's throat and now it was Greg Ballard's turn to haul him off. "Save it, Joe. Save it for the commander."

The runner, an English boy with a face like that of a sleepy owl, stated, "He's been wounded, Cord is dead." They moaned. "Avila is dead, someone brought him in, a very big man, but he died. In fact, as far as Brigade can determine, most of your officers are gone. We're searching for Webster. If he's alive, he is next in command."

"Leaflets Webster," someone said.

"Deaf'n dumb," Garms said. "The guy never talks."

"He can't be worse than the last one," Mack shrugged.

"Hardly," Ballard muttered.

Archie Cohen piped, "What about the man with the voice?"

"Yeah," Joe smiled. "A live ghost. An American too." But the Germans had said he was German, the Spaniards Spanish.

The runner smiled patronizingly. A wraith. These poor shellshocked troops. But they knew he wasn't a ghost, they had seen him.

Silently, haggard and weary, not a few weeping, they shambled back across the corpse-strewn field, picking up the wounded, burying a few of the dead in shallow graves. They searched for the man in the gray poncho, but could not find him. He must have gone to Brigade. Must be a leader.

In their trenches they made another count. Concluded, couldn't believe it, made another count. It was true. They had one hundred twenty-three men left. They had lost about three hundred thirty that day. Counting the men lost in the truck outside Chinchón, the eighty on the 23rd, in ten days they had suffered a loss of close to four hundred fifty men. Now some cried out in anger, some merely wept, all were scared—no, this was not the way it was supposed to be.

They chose Joe Garms to command them. He set up a guard for the night and told them, "Tuhmorra we haul ass up to Brigade and talk to ole Carryshit. We needa reorganize."

Mack Berg, depleted of strength, even of anger, found his slit of trench, kicked soft flesh, heard a shuddering sigh. Must be a hurt comrade.

The man huddled against the side of the trench, his head buried in his arms. Mack's hands soothed his back. "Are you hurt badly, Comrade?"

A shuddering sigh for answer.

Mack turned the man about, peered into his face. It was Cromwell Webster. The man wasn't hurt, just frightened. His handsome face was a shudder, his eyes frozen with fear. "You didn't go over?" Mack asked quietly, his hands continuing to rub the man's shoulders and neck to ease the tenseness.

"I jus' couldn't, Mack. I tried, honest to God, I tried, Mack but I jus' couldn't."

Abruptly Mack took his hands off the man. A vicious rage invaded him. He wanted to hit the man, to kill him. Before he knew it he found himself thinking, dirty fucking black yellow nigger. Stop it! he yelled at himself. The man huddled in on himself, shook violently, his eyes never leaving Mack's. And Mack fought with himself. Courage isn't everything, you barely have enough for yourself. No! He's a dirty yellow nigger hiding while we all went into that hell. Decimated. Massacred. Coward! he wanted to scream at Webster. The man was panting hard, staring up at him with his frightened eyes. Shame and guilt overtook Mack, so his rage intensified, and he was overcome with hatred for this man, hatred for himself, for every man dead and alive in the sector, and suddenly he raised his rifle by its barrel to use like a club.

"NO!" Webster screamed and brought his hands up to cover his head.

Mack began to bring the rifle forward, hesitated, flung the gun to the side, and threw himself into the trench, beating the earth with his hands, expending his rage wildly.

Under control at last, he sat up and turned to Webster who still watched him with his scared eyes. "Look—we're all scared. Even Joe Garms is scared. There'll be days when you'll be less scared and will help us because it's our bad day. Someone said you're to be our new battalion commander."

Webster huddled deeper into himself. "I told them I didn't want to be an officer, but they wouldn't listen. They want a colored commander." He lowered his head in his hands.

Yes, of course. Instruments of history. Willing victims of history. "Let's hit the sack. When you wake up go to Brigade and tell them you don't want to be commander. Insist on it, they can't make you. Don't be afraid to tell them you're scared, they are, too, the dirty cocksucking bastards. Then come into the line with us. We'll cover for you. We're comrades."

Webster was silent, thinking. Said, "I'll go, Mack." He began to breathe normally, his handsome face whole again.

"Great," Mack said tiredly. "Very good." St. Mack.

They stretched out in the trench, head to head, gazing up at the moon shining like a tin pie plate.

"Go to sleep, Webster," Mack whispered.

"Ace—my name's Ace."

"Okay, Ace."

The surf off Dogfish Bar roared, and Greg Ballard's long brown head—he was catnapping after the net had been hauled in that early morning—kept pounding into his arms. Goddam, must be a squall coming up.

He awoke. It wasn't his head pounding, but bullets into sandbags. Christ! not again! Damn. If they come over now we're gonners. He sat up, his thick-chested body creaking like a rusty winch. He stretched his short muscular arms. Flexed them. Strength gone. Never in his entire life had he felt so tired. Empty. Not even when Ursuline Washington had run off to New York to wiggle her small hard ass and little girl tits in the Cotton Club for customers looking for a change of luck. Empty. So was the trench all around him. All those dead and wounded. Can't go on without replacements. Impossible.

Ten meters away Joe's helmetless head was glued to a gun slit.

"Put your helmet on!"

"I hate the friggin' thing," Garms spat without turning. With his crop of jumbled curled brown hair and two-week beard he looked like an ashcan on which someone had plopped a discarded dirty mop.

"Remember Jimmy?"

"Yeah; a hunnerd years ago. Between him and now over four hunnerd men."

Bullets kept slamming into sandbags. Must be some trigger-happy fascist killing time. Greg looked into the sky. A gray haze. Dawn hadn't quite arrived and night hadn't quite gone, just its tail showing. Ah. Is that a cumulus cloud—that one over there like a stuffed haddock? Would it really come down or wouldn't it? The heavy rains lasted a month they had been told by the Spaniards. Was it another fish story? A month! To give themselves a chance to build a new battalion, to really learn something. He felt like praying for it to rain. Mom, pray for me today, will you? For an easy never-stopping rain and good fishing. You hear me, Mom? You're a heathen, she smiled brightly, a tolerant woman. Did the whitingest waaash on the Cape. Jest a little black heathen. Yup.

"What do you see?" he asked Joe, coming up to him, Joe's head still glued to the slit, that fascist still killing time.

"A hand."

"A what?"

"A hand," Joe murmured, not turning.

Greg pulled him away, looked for himself.

Gray streaked early dawn like an oyster shell still dripping with sea—a good sign, maybe it'll rain—and forty, fifty meters away above the moist gray yellow sage: a hand. A thick wrist, five fingers stretched to the sky. It was a human hand severed at the elbow, stuck upright into the earth, just the wrist and five agonized fingers showing.

And an enemy rifleman was taking target practice. The visibility was too gray for his distance, for he kept missing the hand, overshooting, his bullets pounding into the sandbags.

The dew-wet yellow sage and still moist dark gray dawn combined with the pale bloodless hand to give off a shimmering aureole of citron gold about the petrified fingers. Like the old print of a painting of Lazarus' hand emerging from the earth which hung in Mom's church.

He shook the image away, laughed harshly at himself. A man had been killed, rigor mortis followed, his body had rolled stiffly into a gully, and the last agony of his hand showed, that's all.

Still the hand held his attention.

He heard startled mutterings along the trench. Others were now eye to slit. They had seen the hand. A dead hand.

The rifleman two hundred meters away paused. Perhaps he was giving up the game. Poww! No, just reloading; no hurry, the hand was dead.

Ballard wanted to turn away from it, but his head refused to budge. He felt an ache in his heart for the hand, an awesome mystical feeling filled his body, something which whispered in eery ghostly echo, It's alive.

"No, dammit," he muttered aloud, tearing himself loose, leaning with the back of his head to the slit.

The enemy's rifle still rattled away, crackasnap, the bullets pounding into the tightly packed bags. He's shooting too high, or maybe the hand's unnerved him, just as it has me.

Joe Garms, a few meters away, stayed glued to another slit, a mop with ears. Dirty.

"Come on, Joe," Ballard called impatiently, "let's see about coffee. We gotta have a meeting, remember?"

Garms didn't answer, continued to peer into the ghostly gray field.

Ballard raised his heavy shoulders to his ears, lowered them slowly; he closed his eyes, screwed up his face so that the point of his nose protruded like a thick thumb. He'd had enough of this nonsense, similar visions had appeared to him at sea during great fatigue; he started up the trench, stopped abruptly, dammit, drawn again back to the hand.

"It *moved!*" Garms shouted hoarsely, "it *mov*-ed," his voice cracking.

Greg trembled as he stared through the slit, found the hand. Frozen stiff. His voice shaking, he yelled, "You're loco —plain loco."

"It moved, it moved," he heard voices call.

Mass hypnosis. War crazy.

Then he saw the hand waver, hold still. Frozen. A gust of wind must have caught it or it's a mirage from the dew and moisture crystals of the early dawn.

"IT MOVED!" crescendoed up and down the line.

Damn if it hadn't. No doubt about it. It had moved.

The hypnotic spell shattered, Joe Garms pulled away, called to Ballard to keep watching. "If that sonuvabitch's alive we gotta haul him in—in daylight too goddammittohell."

Again Greg saw the hand move. Yeah, got to haul him in. In daylight—an oyster gray early dawn, but daylight. Under that fascist rifleman's eyes. Then he realized the shooting had stopped. Had the rifleman seen the hand move and himself been moved by it?

No, too far in this light. He remembered the enemy had binoculars, telescopic sights. Perhaps the man has a heart—maybe. Or a trick up his sleeve. The English had told them that one early morning a company of Moors had approached, hands high, surrendering. They had been permitted to come forward. For their generosity the English had received a fistful of grenades in their faces.

Garms gathered the remainder of the machine gun company, about thirty men, to discuss the man with the hand. Mack Berg was present, looking thoughtful, wondering if Webster, who had not been in the trench when he awoke, had gone to Brigade.

"We can't bullshit, it's gettin' light," Garms said. "Ballard and me'll go. I want anudder man."

Silence.

"Even wit' three it'll be rough," Garms said, "but we can't spare no more."

Silence.

Garms looked at Berg. "Not me," Mack snapped. "I don't want to be a dead hero. I've had enough."

Karonian, a bullface with two knobs high on his forehead where the horns once must have grown, said in his quiet voice, "It looks like heavy rain. It will be safer then."

"It might and it mightn't. We gotta get this guy."

Fidgeting silence. It was just too fucking much. Mack Berg thinned his lips, jutted his jaw, stared into the distance.

Archie Cohen, the new kid, his sandy hair wet, his face pale green, his knees water, said in a barely audible whisper, "I'll go."

"Oh, no, for God's sake," Mack Berg bit out.

For a moment the boy's face lit up hopefully, perhaps he wouldn't have to go. No, it was too late to back out. "I'll go," he said quietly. Then blushing under the stares of his comrades, he said, "That's the guy with the voice and the shovels."

Ballard observed him sharply: Was the kid unhinged?

"How do you know?" he asked.

"I don't know how I know—I just know."

Ballard didn't know why, but somehow he knew that Archie knew. He believed him.

The others were nodding their heads, dirty, rancid with stale sweat, stunned with fatigue and hopelessness. They also believed that he knew. Everyone's stark raving mad this morning. Ghosts, wraiths, voices, hands, they knew. War crazy.

The dawn shone gray, moist, no fog, visibility deceptive. The entire sector was as silent as the winking of an eye. How to get the wounded man and then return, that was the question.

And there was one enemy rifleman who knew what he knew.

"We gotta take a chance," Garms reckoned. "We'll do it wit'out coverin' fire. Wake up that stinkin' enemy line an' we're dead men. Jest tell the rest a the guys to keep their eyes open an' their peckers stiff."

"I think you should take a litter," Karonian said. "I'll go get one."

"Nah," Garms argued. "We ain't got the time. That stupid sun'll break through an' wake everybody up over there. We'll turn the trick, don't worry. Jest get some medics an' Doc Jerk-off to be ready." Turning to Ballard, he laughed. "You go first, you're the hardest tuh see in this dark gray stuff."

Greg slipped over, Archie, then Joe, who remembered at the last moment the first-aid kit, which he jammed into his jacket pocket. They heard someone in the trench behind them say, "They'll reach the guy, he'll be dead." Then they heard a hard slap and Mack Berg's harsh whisper, "Shut up!"

Mack Berg always at war with his guilt, Greg thought as he began crawling, the others behind him.

Dead quiet. Yes, maybe the fascist rifleman had a heart. Or an ace up his sleeve.

They crawled ten meters, a quarter of the way, stopped behind the corpse of Rodriguez, one of the Cuban officers.

They were breathing hard, sweating. Archie's face was puce.

"You're a good kid, Archie," Joe whispered. "More guts than all a us."

"Let's go," Ballard urged, "before I lose my nerve."

Again they crawled, using corpses for cover. The silence was massive, oppressive. Shattered by a magpie's shriek and flutter of wings among the smashed olive branches. It made them deaf. Archie vomited, choking to restrain the rasp which followed the gush. Niagara Falls followed by a foghorn.

Ballard and Garms waited until he recovered. Now he would feel better. He didn't, but urged, "Okay, let's move." His face was the color of dried putty.

The sage was heavier now, better cover. They crawled more rapidly; stopped at Levy's body, the Dublin Jew.

Ten meters to go.

Ballard was stopped five meters away by another corpse, that of Leonidis the Greek. He had been with them the day Jaime was killed. Greg remembered the letter in his knapsack to Ortega's father, he had never got to mail it. War the breaker of promises. I'll do it today, he thought. If—

Garms and Cohen were waiting. Ballard bypassed Leonidis, went ahead.

The silence as they approached the hollow in which lay their wounded—not dead, they hoped—comrade had the immeasurable weight of all the dead the world over:

A shot stung out.

They flattened, not breathing.

Far in the distance; their sector remained quiet.

Ballard began to laugh his high-pitched nervous laugh, it squeaked and whined. Garms crawled to him and clouted him hard on his long jaw. Dazed, Ballard shook his head, sighed deeply, whispered, "Thanks."

They resumed crawling and soon were at the bank of the hollow.

And in.

He was a heavy man, about six feet, longer perhaps, lying there on his face, his hand still grotesquely upright, a hole the size of a soup plate under his right shoulder blade. Hit by an explosive bullet, the flesh and bone had jellied with the congealed blood. A gray poncho, a broad sweeping back, helmet to his ears. "I told you," Archie whispered. "The voice."

Garms, followed by Ballard and Cohen, slithered round,

stared at the man's face, swallowed hard. Archie kneaded his lips with his teeth; Greg gasped. They merely stared, unable to speak. The man's eyes were open and from between his teeth, in flagrant heroic movie style, protruded a flattened slug of lead on which he had been biting to keep from screaming. Joe Garms was breathing heavily; suddenly unable to restrain his emotion he cried out, "Goddam sonuvabitch Jake Starr! I love you like a brother." Gently he lowered Jake's upright hand; then no longer able to control himself he took Jake's head in his arms and kissed him.

Greg, on his stomach alongside them, had to close his eyes a moment, force himself to breathe slowly. Barely able to speak, he whispered, "C'mon, Joe, give him a shot and let's get him out of here. Jake looks like he's lost lots of blood."

"Yeah. Okay." Slowly, Joe Garms lowered his friend's head, then administered a shot of morphine neatly, quickly. Archie just sprawled there, incredulity marring his boyish blond face. He remembered that a month before he had been making speeches for the unemployed in Bughouse Square in Chicago, that a week ago this man Jake Starr had helped hijack him and some other comrades on the road to Le Havre, he remembered the voice, the hand, and now he, Archie Cohen, was also a hero. Life was strange, wasn't it?

Drugged, asleep, Jake's jaws slackened and the lead slug fell to the ground. Archie reached for it and without examining it placed it in his pocket. Ballard smiled. And the sentimental shall inherit the earth.

Joe cleaned the wound. "They'll be pickin' bone outa him the resta his life," he whispered.

"If he lives," said Archie, who had taken Jake's thick wrist in his hand, feeling the pulse. "Slow and just alive."

He saw Ballard and Garms staring at him. "I was a boy scout—an eagle."

"He'll live," Ballard muttered. "If we get back. Let's go before the cave-in."

Archie and Joe, flat on the ground, raised Starr and as gently as they could placed him on Greg's broad back, then each slid under one of his legs. They tried crawling that way, but got nowhere fast.

"Goddam jerk I am," Joe muttered, "shoulda taken a litter."

They were compelled to stop.

"If that *puta* out there was gonna shoot," Joe said, "he'd a done it already. Nobody could be that much a killer, to wait and do it now. I'm as much a killer as any man, so I know. Let's pick Jake up and run. It's oney a hunnerd twenty-five feet."

Greg and Archie agreed. Besides, it seemed there was one fascist with a heart.

They heaved the two hundred pounds of dead weight off the ground, began a slow dogtrot. Passed Leonidis—thirty-five meters to go. Made another ten: Sean Levy. Stopped for a little kosher meat.

They were breathless, speechless, unbelieving. Fantastic luck! Could the entire enemy sector be asleep? The one enemy rifleman a Christian? If one fascist rifleman was a Christian then it could be said that even in defeat the war would not be wholly lost.

Jake's moaning was a file on the bone of Greg's ear. Greg stared at their trench twenty-five meters away. It bristled with guns. Now he knew what it meant. Looks formidable, Greg thought. Now I know how an approaching enemy sees it. Must be as scared every time as we are. The thought gave him strength.

Garms signaled to Ballard and Cohen.

They made it to Rodriguez.

Ten meters to go.

Greg could see impatient hands waiting at the sandbag

parapet—Mack Berg's mean, stony face, Karonian's hornless bullhead. Put your helmet on, you dumb Armenian bastard.

He started to say, "Heave," when they heard a crackling at their ears—sharp and snapping. Crackasnap. They remained perfectly immobile. There it was again. Crackasnap. Sharp and nasty.

"Lookit!" Greg heard Joe say, "to your left."

A black crow perched on the back of a corpse. It was eating off the dead man. Sharp and snapping. It was Murchison, who never ate meat, just peanuts. Murchison's knapsack had opened, and the crow was eating peanuts. Crackasnap.

They began to laugh hysterically.

Archie recalled them to their senses. "This guy's pulse is just about zero."

"Heave," Joe ordered.

They were running quickly now. They were at the sandbags. Hands, eager, friendly hands stretched out to them—lifting Jake Starr, moaning a gibberish song in his morphine dream, off Ballard's aching bones.

Greg dove over, followed by Archie and Joe Garms.

They heard the yap of the machine gun a split second after Joe was hit, a clean bullet hole bored through each cheek of his ass.

Like a signal, it rained.

XII

THE AMBULANCE was driven by an old Córdoban. Alongside him sat an English poet with a face like a beaten prize-fighter's, wrinkled and old before his time. In his jacket pocket the poet carried a letter given to him to mail by the Negro who had helped load the wounded American.

Dear Señor Ortega (the letter read):

Jaime and I were friends. We respected each other. Before he went into battle to fight for the things he lived for, we exchanged family addresses. Now I must write you.

Your nineteen-year-old son was a man. He died fighting for justice and liberty. It happened some thirty kilometers south of Madrid, on the San Martín de la Vega road, at sundown on February 22, 1937.

We buried him and marked his grave with our tears.

Respectfully,
Gregory Ballard

Jake Starr was wakened in the ambulance by the taste of a heavy sweet liquid on his lips and tongue. It dripped from the stretcher above him. It was blood. The man above him moaned pitifully, *mamita mía, mamita mía.* There was the heavy smell of urine and warm feces in the ambulance and it made him retch. The pain in his shoulder, now that the morphine was wearing off, entered more deeply, as if a hot coal were being driven into his flesh. The ambulance bumped along slowly, and every bump quickened the dripping of blood from above him onto his face and lips. He ordered himself to move his head away and drowsily wondered why he had taken so long to do this simple thing.

He heard the rain outside slashing into the sides of the ambulance and somehow it helped to cool him and he suddenly remembered he was at the front, south of Madrid. The driving rain would be welcomed, wounds would be cleansed, the dead buried, the blood washed away. The hot coal was being nailed into his shoulder more roughly and it burned and hurt terribly. The man above him was crying and Jake wondered if it helped if one cried. By God, his shoulder hurt and he wanted to cry. Abruptly he did. *Mama, mama.* He tried to stop himself from crying and realized he had to urinate and he didn't care if he didn't restrain it. He permitted the hot urine to flow and somehow it helped, warming his groin and his thighs. The pain was now unbearable and the blood dripping from the man above seemed to flow faster, splattering on his face, and the stink in the ambulance was so sticky and thick that Jake felt it encrust on the inner walls of his nostrils. And he realized he was screaming. MAMA MAMA, it hurts, it hurts. And the man above him was weeping, *mamita mía,* and the ambulance bumped into every pothole in Spain. Now the man above began to call *Dios, Dios,* then was suddenly quiet, only his blood dripping, and Jake became certain the man had died. He began to strike the side of the ambulance with the back of his hand, hitting it harder and harder, trying to hurt it so much he wouldn't feel that hot coal being driven deeper and deeper into his back. Then he lost consciousness.

An hour later the ambulance pulled into the front-line hospital southeast of Chinchón. It was more like a slaughterhouse, choked with still warm flesh, running with blood. In the back there were galvanized tin cans into which were dumped the amputated arms, legs, hands; the cans were taken every morning to be buried in a mass grave with the bodies.

When Jake came to, a plump little Spanish nurse stood over him, smiling patronizingly and wagging a dirty fat finger in front of his nose. "No, no," she was saying, and he didn't know why.

"*Qué pasa, bonita?*" he muttered, and she pointed to his chest. He sighted his eyes along his nose to his chest and saw his hands clasped as in prayer. He returned his questioning eyes to her.

"No, no, *compañero,*" she said, "there is no God."

And he said, "*Sí, bonita,* there is no God," unclasping his hands. Suddenly she screamed, for he had gone chalk white and fainted dead away.

BOOK TWO

XIII

LA VOZ Y LA MANO MUERTO read the headlines of every newspaper in Loyal Spain. The man whose heroism and inspired leadership had helped save Madrid from falling to the cruel armies of international fascism had died. Madrid lived. Jacobito Estrella had not fought and died in vain. From city to city, village to village, man to man the tale of his exploits on the battlefields of Jarama and Tajuña was related with pride and with sadness. To live in freedom men must die. And they would all die if necessary, as had the voice and the hand, so that Spain would live in freedom. Even in defeat, they would live in freedom because of men like Jacob Starr. Each newspaper story surpassed the other in its recitation of the details of his heroism and his inspiration to the Spanish and Interbrigade troops on The Road. His voice had been a godlike roar, his rifle aim unerring, his leadership on the field dazzling. Bone weary, shaken by defeat and the slaughter, yet no man had been able to resist his command and his unyielding will as he led them gun in hand, bayonet flowing with blood. The Road remained open, Madrid stood proudly free, Spain fought on.

The voice and the hand was dead.

In Valencia, Sarah Ruskin, newspapers in a heap about her, lay on her bed dressed only in a robe, her hair in two braids down to below her shoulders, reading glasses on nose, a hand clutched at her breast. It was morning, Rolfe had already gone to his laboratory a few hours earlier. She stared into space, a constriction about her eyes and temples because somehow Jake's death could evoke no tears. Loyal Spain had little else, so it created legends, myths, fictions. Symbols. *La Voz y La Mano.* How can one cry for a symbol? Jake Starr had died from loss of blood at a frontline hospital, and had been buried in a mass grave.

Sarah wrapped the robe tightly about herself. Removed her glasses, folded them away in their case. She closed her eyes. She wished to cry to ease her suffering. A sharp, clear black-lined image, tall, brawny, tense, with a serious full-lipped mouth, large strong nose, deeply set green eyes, intelligent, smiling, angry, a large face on a large head, with brown curly hair. Sarah, he had said, all of a sudden I feel whole, complete.

She bit her lip, wanted to mourn him. To weep. To tear her hair—and yet she didn't, here she lay on this elegant bed, in this elegant *casa* in Valencia, a marvel of tower and turret and space, her husband off, at his laboratory, at a meeting with Vlanoc or Roegen or La Pasionaria, 90 percent myth, 10 percent rhetoric, and Jake Starr lay in a mass grave. And it all seemed unreal. Her feeling for him had been real enough, profound, but she had never believed his feeling for her to have been more than transitory, and this had helped to lessen her own emotion about him, created a self-protective shield. Even in Paris when they had walked home together completely at ease and he had spoken so openly it almost hurt to hear him. "Sometimes, Sarah, I begin to think I haven't even begun to live, when do I start? When did you start? You seem so at ease with yourself." Yes, at ease.

If I cry, she thought now, it will be better. Tears to cool the brow. If she mourned him it would be mourning the death of her one short fling at great passion. She had learned quickly with him that she possessed a passion beyond all reason. Just like him, violent and raging. Her inner life had been quiet, rational, and then she had met him and she had found her rational self to be but a matron's gown. Stripped off by Jake Starr, she stood revealed naked. And alive in a way she had never been. No, it hadn't been he. It was merely that she had finally emerged from the shell constructed by her mother and father and Rolfe, that genteel generation. Once emerged, she saw herself no longer as a rational being with a vestige of the animal, but animal with a gloss of tradition, civilization, so-called human. And Jake—he too had thought of himself as a rational being. Scientific.

He had been driven by his own inner force and needs. Foolish man, he had thought it was the logic of his ideological beliefs. But in truth he and Rolfe were similar, and must she love men of this nature?—they were directed by a striving to live in an orderly world, who could not abide disorder.

They had tasted each other as if both had known it would be the first and last time. And she hadn't even known his real name. Who had mothered and fathered him? How had he come to run the race he had? Whose bullet had killed him, bled him dry? This vital young man who had cried I want to live, goddammit, biting her shoulder, impregnating her with the weight of his love. It was astounding how the weight of a man's love could lighten a woman's heart.

If she could only cry, uncask the sorrow, the sadness of his short life, of hers. They had owned a miserly moment, that was all. Now Rolfe and Step could no longer stand in their way. No one could object to her love of him dead.

Sarah lay silently on the bed, allowing herself to submerge into her mourning of Jake, to sink into her grief for him, for herself, for her husband. She wanted her mourning to be mythic, heroic, to equal his death. And she couldn't make herself weep. Because she knew it was for herself she most wanted to cry. Not for the dead. They were dead. It is for oneself one cries. She had known him so little and there wasn't enough of him in her for which to cry, unless she invested it with more—the entire world, it seemed. False woe, she said to herself. False heroics. False myth. False Sarah.

For a long time she lay on the bed, turning, moaning, tearless. Then suddenly he was there in the room with her, she could see him above her, tall, passionate, his strong hands reaching out to her from his grave. Sarah. Sarah! My God, how I love you. I didn't want to die, Sarah. I wanted to live. And she became mad with grief, crying, Oh, my life, my shortlived life. How I want you. Her moaning became a violent sobbing, wrenched from her heart, as if all life were being torn from her, leaving her empty, and she began to cry loudly, lost, letting herself go completely, wailing. Oh, my love, you are gone. She could see the grave and cold lifeless corpse. And her breathing became difficult, her sobs like a pulsating surf smashing through the stone levees of her life until she was inundated with a grief so profound she drowned into unconsciousness.

As she slept, Rolfe entered the room quietly and saw her lying there, the newspapers heaped about her. LA VOZ Y LA MANO MUERTO.

He stood before her gazing with his own sadness down at her. He loved her and these past weeks he had lived only on the exuberance of his new work, the meetings at which he counted for someone, the flying banners, the *camiones* with their singing *milicianos* waving their raised fists as they left for the front, the unease at the chicanery all about him, the civil war within a civil war which raged in and about the government as each party vied for naked power or subtle power, all had buried the hurt of his love for her at her absence. Her absence. That was it—she had been absent. Her heart had been off with her onetime lover, a young man, heroic it seemed. At odd moments the past few hours how much he had envied the man's heroic death, wished it were he instead. And when he had read the headlines and the stories how his heart had leaped with joy—yes, joy. She would in time forget Starr and again love him.

Her face in sleep was cast in deep mourning. Her fists were clenched at her breasts. She sighed deeply. Wake her and tell her of your love. Wake her and tell her the truth. Don't permit her to carry this sorrow. Be an honest man again. You were born an honest man, have been reared gently, must live gently. She is more than your wife—she is a woman whom you love. But he remembered the pleasure at learning of Starr's death and wished to savor it a moment longer. Still, mourning him, she would love him more. Wake her and tell her, she will sweep into your arms.

Gently he shook her. "Sarah."

She awoke with a start, a cry of fright. Better the sleep of peace than the awakening to reality. She took both Rolfe's hands in hers, held onto them with a grasping selfish need, brought them to her breast.

"Hold me tight, Rolfe, I'm scared," she whispered. And her grief shook him. He couldn't endure her grief. It was greater than his at having lost her.

He drew her hands to his lips. "Sarah," he said at last, "these papers are misinformed. Starr lives. Norman Bethune's blood bank saved him. He is in Murcia."

Now she wept, fully, with deep, and to Rolfe's ears, harsh sobs.

XIV

WHEN Capitán Jacobito Estrella was finally escorted by two *pistoleros* to Comrade Roegen in the fortress of Figueras, he found himself confronted by a tiny man with a long narrow head, with cheeks so flat and smooth he resembled a horse, huge yellow teeth kept bared in a picador smile. He also was proud possessor of a wild mane of black hair. Before the Moscow Master had chosen him to grace his stable, Roegen had been a poet. A true leader of the proletariat, he had been born into the upper middle classes. His father, a Budapest banker, was a great huntsman, and the only callus he ever developed was on his trigger finger. Like father, like son. In Spain Roegen was known as General Ernesto, a rear-echelon commander who deployed his disciplined troops with professional efficiency and deadly stealth.

Upon reading Stepanovich's instructions concerning Jake Starr, Roegen laughed triumphantly. Not that he cared one bread crumb either way for Starr, but Starr was Vlanoc's man, and Vlanoc was leading Roegen—and Comrade Step—in Stakhanovite competition: more bones. Now he would have an opportunity to catch up.

He examined Jake Starr with interest, was a little surprised to see the boy's composed features, his relaxed stance, a smile in his eyes, the old washerwoman hadn't done a bad job. "You're going to the front," he said, and, as Starr grinned, Roegen smiled slyly. "*Salud!*"

So the rumor heard at the San Martín road was fact, except of course it was not the German comrade who had disappeared from Madrid—and never been heard of again—it was Jake Starr. When Roegen's *pistoleros* threw Jake out of the Hispano-Suiza, they did not bid him *adiós,* which was then taboo in Loyal Spain, but did manage, "Go fight, Comrade Hero." And they departed, four of the great antifascist fighters of Spain. Since Jake Starr had the hero syndrome, it was assumed he would manage to die; and everyone knew, it's a natural historical law, the best hero is a dead one.

Thus the legend of *La Voz y La Mano* was, despite him, a Roegen creation.

He was supposed to die; he should have died; he almost died for lack of blood one frantic night. Blood ran in that charnel house by the barrel, over its tiled floors, out into the mesa of Castile and, diluted by the rain, was sucked into the insatiably thirsty earth of Spain. Jake Starr would have died but for a Canadian doctor, Norman Bethune, headquartered near The Road, who had just recently discovered the secret of banking blood. And a blood transfusion was given to Jake Starr and he lived that night.

And such was the exact science of Roegen's theory-practice.

And the very inexact science of Dr. Norman Bethune.

More dead than alive, Starr was placed on a pallet, the pain monstrous, the doses of morphine heavy, and shipped by hospital train to Murcia where the wildly bending Segura River flowed doltishly under the furnace sun, garbage and human offal like a fleet of old barges lolling in its torpid currents, bringing cholera, typhoid, and dysentery to the wounded who filled its hospitals.

A poor town, a rich town, of seventy thousand, Murcia was the marketplace for the lush green *huerta.* The Sangonera and Segura rivers conjoined in the valley to give it water for irrigation. It was a city of narrow streets, dirty yellow and white stucco *casas, mudéjar* manors, baroque and Moorish palaces, the ubiquitous sandbagged empty churches, also a cathedral, its spire the sole challenger to Monteagudo, a soaring purple-black basalt peak in the smoldering sky. Bazaar was raucous neighbor to marketplace.

Murcianos of city and province were a sullen, swart people, as proud of their *pistoleros* as of their dates and figs, mulberries, *pimiento rojo,* maize, barley, wheat, and great sweet onions. No gang of hoods in Spain could expect to exist without a Murcian *pistolero.* And it was Murcianos, driven earlier by drought to Barcelona and Valencia, who with dynamite sticks hidden under *camisas,* under belts, in pockets, strolled calmly to fortress walls, set match to fuse and exploded dynamite, walls, soldiers, and selves. *Por la libertad. Por la revolución.* Oo! Er! Pay! Oo! Er! Pay!

Unios, hermanos proletarios!

And the sun, from the moment it rose insolently over the Espuña range until it sunk beyond man's sight to bake the mangy mesquite-ridden *mancha* of Albacete and Castile into solid rock, was neither orange nor yellow, but white flame. Murcianos, having lived with it since birth, gave it no mind. The wounded of the International Brigades—the sole reminder in Murcia that there was a war in progress (though the poverty and the profiteers should not be forgotten)—cursed it, berated it, and loved it. Because its heat healed those who would be healed more quickly, it seemed, than elsewhere. For those who died it did not matter. For those who had lost a hand, a foot, an eye, and there were many, its savagery was a topic to discuss on waking and on going to sleep. For those without a face, plaster of paris their mask, there was hope its heat would burn them to ash.

To Jake Starr, the sun was an added burden; he sprawled on his stomach in a semicoma, unable to move, the hot coal being twisted into his flesh; the sweat from the sun burned his sores and wet his bed.

He was barely alive.

He would wake on occasion from the seemingly endless pain, the nightmare of steel instruments probing his wound for bone chips, and he would stare dazedly about. There was a constant uproar in the hospital, from the dead celebrating their return to life with *vino rojo* and from the market huzzahs in the square. He would stare with wonderment at his comrades who hobbled through the corridor on crutch and cane, or dragged their smashed limbs encased in plaster of paris, and sometimes they would stop to return his stare, the voice of The Road. Once a blind soldier was led to him to touch his hand, hoping perhaps for a miracle. And there was Joe Garms, his friend, gabbing, singing, laughing, complaining, a man who held on to life with two horny fists. It was on Joe's great audibility that Jake Starr depended for the direction signal which would lead him back to the living.

Joe Garms, his ass in a sling, and Skinny Horton, stiff-necked with a bullet in his spine, a man who had also returned from the dead, stood in the corridor ward of La Pasionaria hospital in Murcia staring sad-eyed at Jake Starr, wan, immobile, eyes slitted against the hot Murcian sun, an African white.

"Cunyo," Garms growled, "yuh been dead t'ree times. Every crappin' paper in the world wrote you was dead. Now you're alive stay alive. C'mon now, you big sonuvabitch. I tole everybody they was nuts, nothin' can kill Jake Starr, he loves cunya too much. Lots of stuff around, Jakey. Get better an' me an' Skinny'll show yuh. He beat the devil too an' to show his t'anks he's been screwin' night 'n day. Fact, Jakey, this town's the biggest whorehouse in the world right now."

Jake issued a weak smile. Wished Joe would shut up. Still,

he wanted him to go on talking, too. Anything but the terrible pain in his back. "Tell 'em I wanna shot, Joe. Please. Hurts."

"No more shots, y'had too much already," snapped Dr. Garms. "Pain's good for what ails yuh, lets y'know you're alive."

True.

A thin, weary nurse rushed up to them. "Enough," she said in Spanish. "Let him sleep. The entire hospital stops to bother him."

"Gi' me shot, please," Jake begged.

"I am very sad," she said, "but I cannot. You will have to bear the pain. Go to sleep."

"What a noisy place," Jake muttered thickly. "Sounds like Times Square on New Year's Eve." Again he fell asleep, but for the first time in weeks he could enjoy the sun warming his face, investing him with life. The pain, though, holy hell, the pain.

Horton, with a bullet in his cervical spine, sauntered long-nosed and stiff-necked out into the city. Garms lay in his cot on his belly and began to write a letter to his friends at Tajuña. He was lonesome for the front, for his buddies, and besides had gossip to tell. . . .

Dear Cunyos,

Me an' Skinny Horton's havin' a ball. This town's the nuts. The sun's hot, the food stinks of olive oil, the dames of cologne—and do they screw. No rush rush with them. Slow as crap climbin' up a hill in Mobile, Alabama. Horton's out to see if he can do it to all a them. So far 32. Me I gotta muchacha. I can't sit or lay on my back. I used to have one hole but now I got one in each cheek a me ass plus the old one so that makes three in case you can't count. Three holes where before there was one. Freak a nature. They're healing pretty good so soon's I'm all better I'll be back to take care a you.

I call on my muchacha early in the morning before business starts and crawl into the sack with her. I can't sit or lay on my back but I can screw standing up or on my belly. Varoom! Me I'm monogamous Skinny says when he says. He's like old Jaime Ortega, the quiet kind. He gotta bullet in his neck and walks around with a stiff neck and a stiff cock. He says when you been dead and come alive again you want to live and to me screwing is living. We kind a hope Jake comes out of it soon and starts living too. The whores come from Malaga, refugees. Some a the boyscouts say you shun't make whores out a them but if we don't pay them they'll starve to death so what should we do let them starve? This place is all screwed up. The rich campesinos getting richer, the poor poorer. And the I.B. runs the town. What a laugh.

Every day the peasants come in with their pushcarts in the big square near La Pasionaria hospital and the big hotel Reina Victoria and sell figs and dates and vegetables from the huerta. That you big bunch a dopes means garden. What a big racket they make selling and buying.

Me and Horton's in the same ward with Jake Starr. The doc says he's a big healthy sonuvabitch strong as a burro and will live. We hope. Guess who's in the next ward? Prettyman and Hoopes. They got their arms in big plaster casts like wings. We hope they fly away. Me I don't talk to Prettyman but I call him Murderman and Horton spits everytime he passes our cots in the morning to go out and eat in a good restaurant in the Reina Victoria with the rest a the rich.

There is four I.B. hospitals in this town all loaded to the roof with the wounded from The Road and from the Cordoba front and from the early days in Madrid. We keep finding guys we thought was dead alive like Horton and Jake. But we keep hearing of guys we thought was alive dead. So it evens out.

Every big wheel in Spain who comes to Murcia comes to look at Jake when he's in a coma. I love the bastard but he ain't the only guy who was brave on The Road. We all had to go over the top like a bunch a greenhorns led by the likes of Murderman and Schleppshit. But they sure make a lot of Jakey. One day a whole camp of them come into the ward,

General Verdad and André Marty the prick and Prettyman and Professor Ruskin and his wife—what a broad, Jesus I'd love to put it to her—and they look at Jake and she starts to cry and has to go away. Skinny finds out there's a rumor she was in charge a the English in Paris when Jake was there and they was lovers or something causing a great big scandal. Leave it to Jake Starr to get himself the classiest head around. He was always like that in the States.

Horton's gonna get a operation on his neck to get the bullet out. His hands is getting paralyzed again and he's so skinny I can see thru him. We eat lousy fried fish every day. Prettyman and Hoopes they took officer's pay. Me and Horton said no, give us what you give the rank and file. Seven pesetas a day. We never even thought a pay but they give it to us so we take it. Can you imagine in a proletarian army getting more pay than your comrades? What would Lenin say? Shit! That stuff's for Prettyman and Hoopes wearing stripes. Hoopes said me and Horton's infantile leftists. I told him go blow it outa your ass. An army needs leaders, needs good discipline but we ain't come here to get more money than the rank and file.

You think the front's bad, me cago you oughta see it in the rear. The asslicking just like that American redheaded kid told us in Albacete when we first come to Spain, the back knifing the crazy politics where the guys who call for revolution and socialism are called fascists and the guys who call for bourgeois democracy are Communists and good guys like us. Everybody screwing everybody else a man can't make head or tails of it. I'm coming back to the front soon's I can to fight fascists so a man knows what he's doing then. If Jake was all right I would talk to him about it cause he's a square guy, no chickenshit like Prettyman.

Guess what? Horton and me run into Bob Gladd that big-talk who's with the Russian tank corps in Archena on account he capish Russki. Horton likes him even though he's a loudmouth. Says he never caught him in a lie yet. But he sure knows everybody there is to know. He told us how you guys mutinied against Schleppshit at the meeting after I got hit and demanded to be withdrawn from the line for training and new officers and how he and Mulveen and Aaronson went to brigade to present your demands. He says they bribed Mulveen with the job of battalion commander, made Aaronson adjutant commander of the m.g. company and promoted him Gladd to the Russians cause he speaks real good Russki. End of mutiny. An old trick in the party. The leaders always win. Gladd says he lives like a millionaire with the Russkis, eats pork chops and bread and butter, can you imagine, and drinks real scotch and soda and vodka. Lucky bastard. Got himself a beautiful tweed suit just like the Russki officers, and wears a Russian Nagar pistol on his hip and sometimes comes to Murcia in a limousine with a chauffeur and got lots a pesetas in his wallet. When anybody asks him what his nationality is he says he's Serbian just like the other Russians, then laughs. Horton ran into him in a whorehouse where Horton spends most of his time.

Hey what do you think a those Garibaldis? They took the fascists real good in Guadalajara. If they had enough materiel they'd a gone all the way to Portugal. Shows what you can do with good officers and well-trained men. We oughta give the fascists Prettyman to even things out. Ha ha ha.

The nurse just dressed me ass with alcohol and clean gauze. She's real gentle but ugly as hell. Next to me's this kid from Segovia who had his cock grazed by a bullet. Lucky he's still got it. 15 yrs. old. Everytime the nurse comes to dress it he takes it outa his fly and pulls the skin back and holds it up for her to clean it with medicine and he got a big grin on his little puss. This morning we told him me and Horton'll take him to a place this afternoon where he can dip it into the best medicine in the world and he laughs like hell. Then he gets all red. Says he's a virgin. Well he's waiting for us now all dressed up in his new uniform, his straw sandals all shined up, his black hair plastered down and his black eyes shooting fire. We're gonna get him fucked with one a Horton's hottest broads, an Andaluz with those high hard ones could cream a guy. Wow! When his peter's all better he's going back to the front to kill more fascists. He told us the fascists in his town killed his father and mother and brother and two uncles and three cousins but he and some other guys killed fifty a them all in one afternoon. He said he didn't kill the town's priest cause he was with them all the way not all the priests was bad just most a them. He said they'll never believe the church again as long as they live cause the church showed whose side they was on. I asked him if he belonged to the party and he laughs. No, he says, he's for the workers and peasants and he's a leftwing socialist and Caballero's his leader. I say shit, those yellow socialist bastards like Norman Thomas and he says shit on the milk a your grandmother I don't know Tomás but I know Caballero's for the workers and you shitting Communists are for the bourgeoisie. So we get in a yelling fight the whole hospital's in an uproar. I always said this country's all screwed up. Everybody's in the wrong corner.

But it's funny as hell him and me blabbing. He don't talk inglés and I talk broken Spanish—I'm studying real hard and I talk with my whore muchacha all the time. This guy Horton don't talk at all. He's got a bird brain he says himself. But he's learning German talking to the Thaelmann guys. Well, anyway me and this kid Santiago—Shanti—we seem to understand each other perfect even when I don't understand all his words and I use American and Spanish and my hands. I'm laying on my belly with my ass bare and he on his back his cock bare for the nurse. Now we're gonna take him to get laid for the first time. Me and Skinny bought a gallon of Bonjour cologne for our whores and we sprinkle this kid's cock with some and it burns like hell but he's laughing to beat crap.

I understand from Bob Gladd you guys are doing nothing at the front but fighting with Mulveen the battalion commander all the time and that his adjutant commander Cromwell Webster never says a word and never shows his face. He said on the 14th of March when Mulveen was in Albacete getting his handmade boots fitted and the enemy made an attack on your trenches Webster never showed and Gladd and Mack Berg and Greg and Hunt Carrington took charge and then Greg and Hunt after the slaughter carried a picket sign Equal Rights for Whites. Jesus, what the hell's going on with you guys? Well, soon I'll be with you. I decided I'm gonna be a rank and filer, nothing else. Our leaders all stink.

What happened to Carryshit? Is he still around?

Me cago on all the big brass but Jake Starr and I miss all you guys.

Salud,
José Garms, Hero

P.S. Listen, cunyos, on the 27th when we got murdered, killed, hell beat out a us, we think we're the only ones. But on the other side of the road, just to the right a us, around where we was on the 23rd, the 17th Spanish battalion lost 500 men in one day. Jesus, we always forget the Spanish is fightin' too, all we think of is the great, famous good guys from the movies the International Brigades. Well everytime we lose one man they lose ten. The goddam Spanish is fightin' this war, we're just here helping out. But one thing is for sure, the enemy's the same—fascists. And our commanders is the same—in com pe tento.

JOSÉ JOSÉ, UN HOMBRE HEROICO

XV

One morning, the white hot sun sliced through the long iron-grilled window opposite Jake Starr's bed to bathe him with its healing power, and he fully awoke, his eyes wide open, and he knew he was alive. He saw Joe Garms and Horton, dour, intense, thin, slightly mad, gazing sympathetically down at him. Joe smiled. Horton grimaced. Jake grinned. He was alive. He closed his eyes and slept peacefully. To hell with the pain.

The following morning the sun again woke him. There was an organized bedlam about him. Nurse, orderlies, wounded came and went. Life continued.

Next to his cot Shanti sat up, holding his penis in his hand, the foreskin pulled back, a smug grin on his little face as the nurse swabbed with alcohol.

Two beds up a Pole sang a love song in soft consonants as he stared from sightless sockets.

At the corridor's end, a radio blasted a Mahler *Lied* and two German Interbrigaders swathed in bandages from waist to shoulder danced a grotesque *pas de deux*.

PASAREMOS! in six languages sparkled in red block letters through a splintered black twisted cross on the white wall behind them.

Biting his lips, Jake sat up. The pain was good. Everyone stared at him. Why don't they go away? Someone called out in German, "Look, he's sitting up." The refrain swept over the entire hospital, "Jacobito's sitting up." He retreated, returned to the peace of sleep.

Next day, there was Joe Garms again, Horton out adding to his score.

"Your friggin' fault, Jakey. Me wit' bullet holes in me ass like I was runnin' from fascists. How'll I ever explain it to anybody?"

"Just show them the clippings, Joe. Bet you're a big hero."

"Jest as big as you, you bastid—hoggin' all the glory."

"That's because I'm a leader, Joe. Everyone knows leaders get all the attention."

They laughed.

"What goes?"

Joe told him about the town, what Americans there were, the continuous and endless feuds between the French doctors and the German, who everyone was sleeping with, what he had heard from the American battalion at the front. "Did y'get my letters?"

"Yes. I enjoyed them very much. You write the best letters I ever read. One of these days you will be shot for writing them and I for reading them."

"Screw them. Did yuh—? What's the matter?"

Jake had winced. "Bitch of a pain."

"Bullet gets so hot, the first thing it hits, it spreads—boom," Joe said dryly. "Rotten wounds, a long time tuh heal." Joe had become an expert on wounds, the belly wounds, the intestinal hemorrhages which blew a man up, left him in a semicomatose state, death slow; the shoulder wounds, the head, the ass. He gave everyone advice, including the doctors. His curiosity about wounds was never satisfied.

"Why, Joe?"

"Because I wanna know which ones to avoid, yuh jerk."

Jake was suddenly tired. "Go out and see the world," he told Joe. "I want to sleep."

He slept. Joe went to see his *muchacha.*

"Good bone, healthy animal," Dr. Poissin, head doctor of La Pasionaria, told him. "Your shoulder will sag when you stand, bone chips will work themselves to the surface for which we shall have to probe every week or so, your fingers will become less numb and your arm regain its strength. You'll live." And passed on to Shanti, the Segovian boy.

Jake Starr grunted, retreated to sleep. Sleep was for him surcease, escape from thought, an emptiness, there was a gaping hole where his heart had been. She had it; held it in her strong slender hand. Sarah? Oh, yes, where was she? Her lips had been like honey. Joe had told him of her visit during the days when they thought he was dying and how she had wept and left. And where the hell was Carl Vlanoc? Somewhere in all this bedlam he'd heard Carl speak—or had it been a dream? And Stepanovich and Roegen?

Go fight, Comrade Hero. Yes, he remembered.

But he was young, and how long could he withstand the obvious adulation of the wounded, the hospital staff, the important visitors from Valencia? Young enough still to believe his not having died was due to his immortality. How could *he* die? Be dead? Without him there would be no world. As a secondary proof, he could rely on the legend which he had become in Free Spain and half the world as the savior of Madrid. For as he began to mend he began to read the newspapers and the internal party reports, which were still his due and were forwarded to him from Vlanoc's office in Murcia, and from these he learned further about his immortality. Madrid owed him its freedom. And though at first he said to himself it's just a load of crap, still he smiled secretly and acknowledged to himself that he loved the adulation, as he had always loved it at home. He had always dreamed of being a hero, had always known he would be a hero, and now he was a hero. Yeah, *go fight, Comrade Hero*. The scum.

He thought of Sarah often, and when he did it was each time with a feeling of grief—what might have been if not—and then he would induce himself to think of other matters such as the Party, or the purges in Russia (were the old Bolsheviki really fascist traitors?) or progress of the war in Spain (poorly since the victory at Brihuega in mid-March), and he would ask for party bulletins and reports to functionaries so he could keep abreast with party activities throughout the world. And then again think of Sarah.

He was in love.

She was a gentle, indomitable woman, he saw her clearly, and immediately knew life still flowed strongly within himself. Then he thought of her and him sitting at the edge of the bed, laughing, having made love. That night—how marvelous it had been, the long, deep kisses, the insatiable curiosity to touch, caress, delve, the holding off, the flying.

He loved her.

She was in Valencia with Rolfe Ruskin. Would she come again to Murcia? Many women of the International Brigades came there to nurse the wounded. Why not Sarah? If she wanted to come, she could find a way. She must have read about him and he was secretly proud until he realized he was being self-indulgent with all this wishing and in the end he suffered greater pain than that which lacerated his back. Pain. Grief. They were the same. There were more important things to think about, such as the sharp steel speeches of Comrade Stalin—fascism is a symptom of the weakness of the working classes and of their betrayal by the—Everybody betrayed everybody.

No one but he, Comrade Jacobito, and the apparatus knew how he had come to The Road; the reports had been written, filed, and, hopefully, forgotten, for André Marty had sent a courier to Murcia with a note for *La Voz y La Mano*, "You are one of mine," which Jake Starr received one morning as he squatted on a bedpan. History, the grand jester.

As he read and reread the note, he realized he was now a printed page of history, his immortality assured. His chest expanded, a Samsonlike strength pervaded his entire body, he even forgot he sat on the pot. The Party has made a place for me, he said to himself. There's no place else for me to go. The chicaneries, the venalities, the murderous bloodletting are only interludes in the grand design. Stop kidding yourself. Acclaim is cheap in history. Vanity is surplus profit. The honest fact is you've cut all ties with the past. If you're one of André Marty's, you're one of Stalin's. Have been since Havana where you did your bit to help cement the unity of opposites. A great euphemism for the doublecross. Accept it now. The destination's worth it.

Beside him on the bed was a huge picture of *La Voz* staring up at him from the front page of *Mundo Obrero*. The glory, the acclaim, the speed of the express train of history were too much for him. Yes, he was now a printed page of history, immortal.

His labors concluded, he wiped his behind with André Marty's note—toilet paper was the scarcest luxury in Spain—and imperiously called for the nurse.

So Jacob Starr, also known as Jake, alias Jacobito Estrella, *La Voz y La Mano*, recently returned from the dead, curled in his cot like a babe, slept, thought on occasion of Sarah Ruskin, ate his bread and dried fish without complaint, used the bedpan, and suffered the pain in his back as penance for having momentarily failed in his loyalty to the vanguard Party. He became obsessed with one aim, one goal, one dream, and resolved to do better in the future, to become one with the Party, the monolith, the catapult of history. Underneath it all he understood—against his will—that it was not because his ideological concepts led him inexorably to that end, but because his vanity and his inner being (that part of him which all his life had responded to, perhaps even exulted in, action and violence) found union with the powerful hypnotic idea of becoming one with history, in the world, a god on earth, immortal. It might be madness, but he excluded it as an important factor because he had once come upon the idea (and half humorously, half seriously accepted it) that all human life on earth was absurdly irrational.

Resolution brought peace and strength, and, in the words of the French Communist philosopher Garaudy, he lived in the world. Yes, man makes his own history. But of course the Party is the midwife of history, so Comrade Starr wrote a letter of self-criticism to Stepanovich in Paris, who acknowledged it only by the addition of a few more straight-backed Cyrillic soldiers in his little black book: Starr will be useful for a time.

Jake slept well, the placidity of his dreams disturbed only by the occasional sweet-sad intrusion of Sarah Ruskin's splendid presence.

Only Joe Garms, professional proletarian and hard guy, had the interest to see. "What's up, Jakey, what's eatin' yuh?"

Jake would gaze up at Garms from his pillow, stare into the pug's face, ears protruding like the handles on an ashcan, smile gently, "Joe, you're the only friend I've had time for all these years." Jake had reached the age of twenty-six in early March. "If I had anything eating me, I'd tell you. I'm tired, this is the best rest I've had in ten years, leave me alone."

"You say so, okay, *puta.*" Whore. Joe's observations were always accurate. "I gotta date wit' my broad. *Hasta la muerte.*" Out he stomped, walking like a man with bad piles.

In April, when Jake was at last able to leave his bed, get into a new brown corduroy uniform, ski pants and jacket, Joe took him out to see the sights, got him to buy *alpargatas* so much more comfortable in the heat than the heavy army shoes. Took him to the brothel where his girl worked. As Jake waited among the ladies chatting to them in pure Castilian, learning their provincial dialects, Joe would take care of his needs.

"She's real good," Joe growled respectfully.

Out again they would stroll along the crowded bazaar streets with their wounded on cane and crutch, the young Spaniards from the tank school in Archena come in for the day, the cadets from the aviation school out in the *huerta,* the peasants in their black round trousers and the old women in their black guimpes and shawls in the heat, and the girls in all the live colors of the sun, cerulean, flamingo, cypress green, chestnut, and all smelling to high heaven from cheap Eau de Cologne. The languages made bedlam, yet everyone seemed to understand each other: besides the tongues of Europe, those of Spain: gallego, valenciano, castellano, andaluz, navarro, vascuence, catalan, and a half dozen others. Yiddish, too, the Esperanto of the International Brigades. And they talked, Joe Garms among them—but not Jake Starr, he was mute. There was nothing he could speak to them about. With a startling abruptness he realized one day that he and they were as separated as the upper classes from the lower in any stratified society. He was one of André Marty's, or Roegen's, or Vlanoc's. Oh, he bartered words for smiles. He spoke to the girls in the whorehouses he visited with Joe, and on occasion Horton. He spoke to Joe about the fronts, the battles, about Prettyman who had already left, arm in winglike cast, to train a battalion of Canadians and Americans outside Albacete. "Poor bastids," Joe said when he heard. Comrade Jacobito spoke to the doctor, to the nurse who tended him, a long skinny *madrileña* with a gentle tawny face—Joe was wrong, she was not ugly, her gentleness made her lovely—and whose hands, poor girl, were like steel wool. He spoke a few words to the wounded Americans, most of whom he knew, since he had sent them through Paris and had managed to speak a few words to each. Now when he encountered them, he said, "Hello, good to see you're alive." "Yes, Comrade Starr, the best soldier's a live one." He would laugh, from the gullet, never from the chest. "Yeah. Have some fun. *Salud.*"

Joe Garms kept trying to loosen his friend up.

One day Jake remained in the hospital; it was the day of the week they tweezed bits of bone out of his wound. Joe went out by himself, returned in an hour.

"Pregnant," he said.

"Who's pregnant?" Jake asked from his cot.

"My whore."

"Oh, I thought it was you."

Joe laughed.

"Now stop pretending you're unable to speak English. Tell it to me in a sentence."

"When I met her she was pregnant. A little round belly. I like it."

"In sex everyone has his own tastes, Joe. You have yours, so what?"

Not listening, impatient, Joe said, "If you'd get yourself laid, gotta little *muchacha,* you'd come out a—out of the funk you are in."

"I'm not in any funk, Joe, you're just looking for something that isn't there." That's right. His heart. Sarah had it.

"Well, if you don't like girls, maybe you can get yourself a little Spanish boy. Not too hard to get around here."

"Oh, shut up, will you?"

"For chrissakes you're the oney one in Murcia ain't got laid yet, includin' the ten-year-olds. They pulled the no prostitution posters off the walls long ago."

Jake sighed. "You're making it worse, Joe, not better."

"I know, Jakey. What I'm gettin' at is yuh ain't—you are

not yourself. In New York before you went off to Latin America for the Party you was—were alive, y'could drink and screw wit' the best of us. Now you're dead. Yuh might as well of—have died. You're beginnin' to look like a fuckin' pol."

Jake sat up fast, ignoring the pain. This conversation was getting out of hand. "I am a pol. And don't you forget it!" Joe's fists balled, came up to his chest, and his eyes slitted. Jake said slowly and quietly, "Remember, Joe, and remember it well. In the Party friendships are secondary. So you had better watch what you say and to whom you say it." Joe's face was mean and nasty, murder in his eyes. Jake smiled. "If you're not careful, you dumb bastard, André Marty will get you and cut you into little pieces and feed you to his harem in that grand *palacio* he lives in."

Joe stared hard at his friend for a moment—what he says is the trut', the livin' trut'—then laughed halfheartedly, defeated. He felt sorry for his friend who was a good guy—he would bet his last peseta Jake Starr was a good guy.

As those in the ward were having their orange, *café con leche,* and bread one morning, General Carlos Verdad appeared, gun on hip, braid on cap, the same old paunch, the same sharp metallic nose and tired, red-ringed black marble eyes; strung out behind him an entourage of doctors, nurses, two *pistoleros.*

The same harshness. "Feeling better, Comrade Starr?"

"*Sí,* Comrade General." The *general* following the *comrade* sounded like an obscenity in Jake's ears.

"Fingers numb, I understand?"

"A little."

"Too bad." Now he smiled, the nose like a paring knife, for the entourage, the entire ward observed them. "I recommend work therapy. You will come to my office."

"*Muchas gracias,* Comrade General."

"*De nada. Salud!*"

"*Salud!*" Yeah, health.

The following day, Jake moved—the clothes he wore, his toothbrush, toothpaste, a cake of soap, his comb and brush—to a dingy office with a cot, desk, and chair adjoining Vlanoc's on Calle de Trapería, over a café from which wafted through the floorboards the stink of frying olive oil. He was issued a pistol, holster, and cartridge belt, all of which he hung on a wall hook.

Vlanoc sat at his desk examining Jake Starr, his eyes lit by some sardonic glint. "You were a fool in Paris," Vlanoc said with contempt.

"I admit it. Wrote Step a letter of self-criticism." *Mea culpa.* He felt like pounding his chest with his fist.

"I know." Vlanoc studied his aide's face, read the man's eyes, was positive he read correctly. There's a new cynicism in his eyes and mouth. Perhaps Step had been right—he had needed a hot flame. Now he's a hard egg. Vlanoc smiled to himself. He had known it to happen that way before. Year of resistance to the discipline, to the immorality, then a crisis, and there it was—a hard egg. He also knew there would be self-flagellation, but it would soon dispel itself in action—physical action. The mind would learn to detour those nagging questions—we'll settle them when there's more time, not now. Suddenly Vlanoc shouted angrily, "You endangered *my* position, you understand."

Starr sighed contritely. "So I guessed. In Figueras, when I was finally escorted to Roegen, I could see he was lapping it up like a happy dog. Let's get it over with. I made a mistake. Won't again."

"Not the same one anyway," and Carl laughed. "Coming out alive, it's good you're a hero. Lead flattened between teeth, the voice, the hand—a hero! What dreck. For the suckers—not for professional revolutionists. All right. Now I can rehabilitate you."

And yourself. "Before you do, I would like you to answer one question for me—if I may?"

Vlanoc knew what it would be. "Yes," he said.

"Havana, that meeting and Morales—does one ever forget it?"

Vlanoc closed his eyes for the merest second. "You won't. I won't. Roegen would. Step, too." He pointed with his thumb towards the *pistolero* outside the door, a Franco-Belge who'd fought alongside the Americans in their first battle with the Moors at Tajuña, "Red Struik would forget it; Heinz, the German, wouldn't. It doesn't matter."

"That's what I thought," Jake said quietly, revealing no emotion.

Vlanoc again read and was pleased. "You will work here," he said. "Do as I instruct. We have enemies in the Party—and that's as it should be. The hardest, the strongest lead. That's the meaning of the liquidations, you understand that. The soft, the romantic fall. Make a mistake—HORSE MEAT!" He shouted so loud his face became swollen and his little marble eyes were swallowed by their sockets, his sharp metallic nose gleaming in the white sun. Jake merely stood, waiting for him to come out of it. Something new. Carl Vlanoc began to rub his hands, faster, caught himself, stopped, began to bite his lips, stopped. Said softly, "You understand, don't you?"

"Yes, Carl, I understand." And he did understand. The closer the bullet gets to him, the louder he's going to shout, the harder he's going to rub his hands. Poor bastard, time is pressing down on him. And me?

Now Carl spoke with concern. "Have you written your mother?"

"Not since Paris."

"Write her a note, she must be worried—picture in the papers, dead, alive, name on everyone's lips."

"I'll write today, Carl." And why haven't I without being told? Am I becoming worse than he that he has to remind me?

Harshly again, "You'll work in the office, learn our routine, read our reports. The Spaniards already hate us, especially in the government, but we have them"—rubbing his fat little hands like a butcher who's just got away with a heavy thumb on the scale—"you know where. Caridad Mercater is a scourge. Dolores, La Pasionaria—ha ha—is as tough as the lot of us. You want matériel, she says, pointing to the Russian freighters in the harbor, give us more commissars in the army. No? she says; the freighters will wait out at sea. And they wait. When the government concedes, the freighters move in." This time he clapped his hands and laughed.

"I guessed," Jake said with a little smile.

"Roegen and I are preparing a little surprise for the POUM and anarchists in Barcelona, we've had enough of them. In May. We're going to take the city away from them. You won't be too deeply involved, and then only in an emergency. We will use Spaniards. Interbrigaders will be in trucks outside the city to be brought in only if needed. Meanwhile you will work here. Later you will be given real work."

Jake Starr was excused.

As he opened the door, Vlanoc called out laughingly, "Get yourself a *muchacha,*" just as Joe Garms had said it. "Have some fun."

Yeah, have some fun. Rub it against a wall. He would live without it, to hell with the lot of them.

Jake went into another office and began his work therapy, good for the fingers.

Learned to roll a sealed envelope between index finger and thumb, rolled until the point of the flap loosened, pulled gently, rolled again, pulled gently, rolled again, pulled until the flap came free. It was easier and quicker than steaming them open. He withdrew the letter and read it quickly. He was reading the mail of a number of I.B. men who were under suspicion of being Trotskyites. He found nothing. His job bored him and he did it poorly. "There's nothing," he told Vlanoc. "Everyone knows his mail's being read. They're cagey. Nobody likes the line. Neither you nor I. They follow it. We follow it." Vlanoc laughed. True.

When Jake became fatigued, he read reports, bureau decisions, what Stalin said on this or that—the man covered everything from peanut growing to cosmic research. He was a genius.

Before leaving the hospital, he told Garms where to find him and Joe came every day, waited in the tiny antechamber until Capitán Jacobito emerged neatly dressed in his corduroy ski pants, clean khaki shirt opened at the throat, *alpargatas.* He was tall, lean, tanned, laughed less and less. He found pleasure in the pain in his back.

To the doctors and nurses, to the Interbrigaders who worked for Vlanoc, to the Murcian police who came to visit, the old police, they worked for whomever paid, he was *el capitán.* To Joe he remained Jake. And to Joe Garms Jake was like a drunk pretending he wasn't. He spoke slowly, enunciating each word carefully. He walked a straight line—just as slowly, as carefully. Jake didn't betray himself even to himself. But Joe Garms knew different. Pug, hobo, bum off the streets, scat singer—Minnie had a heart as big as a whale, skiddlee-at—Joe spoke to Jake with affection and his friend returned it somewhere deep inside. Joe knew. He knew what Carl Vlanoc did not know, what Jake Starr himself did not know or if he knew didn't show.

Jake Starr was a Molotov cocktail. Some day somebody was gonna t'row a lit match. The blood would splatter.

Whose?

That was a question Joe Garms could not answer.

A few days before the first of May, Vlanoc left for Barcelona and Jake Starr for Sitges, south of the Catalonia capital. Starr spent about a week with a battalion of picked Interbrigaders, living out of trucks as they awaited the call which never came. In Barcelona, Ernö Gerö known as Pedro, Vlanoc, and Roegen, with the help of the Spanish police and militia, backed by the Party and the rightwing elements in the government, made their surprise move against the anarchists and POUMists who since defeating the fascist rebellion there controlled the city. For a few days it seemed civil war had taken over the streets of Barcelona. But Pedro, Ernesto, and Verdad won. As a consequence it became apparent the Caballero government would soon fall and the Party would move into the army with greater strength than ever before.

As Vlanoc later told Jake Starr in Murcia, "We provoked them, and they began to beat the living hell out of us. But they were hampered by moral questions. Should they or should they not recall their troops from the fronts. They decided not to do so. We of course weren't hampered by moral questions. While we coined the slogan all firearms to the front, we held on to our firearms in the rear. No one else did, of course. They wished to turn the war into a socialist revolution, make Spain into a socialist state, a position detrimental to the foreign policy of the Soviet Union, so we had to destroy them. The POUM—POUM POUM, funny name—has been driven underground, their leaders have been dispersed, some have been jailed, a few shot. The anarchists have more or less conceded—for the time being. Anarchism seems to be indigenous to this *arschloch* of a country. Even Díaz and Hernández, the two top leaders of the Spanish Party, are angry with us. But the Italian Togliatti is running the show for them, and the great La Pasionaria's doing his bidding. Better to die on your feet than to live on your knees, she said. So she squirms on her belly every time Togliatti wrinkles his nose. A heroic lady. A great orator. We are the only ones who can supply organization and arms, so we have blackmailed the government's leaders into looking the wrong way. Now, after the fact, they are sorry, a little weepy. Caballero will fall. We will find someone legitimate, but more amenable. We control the foreign ministry, the war commissariat, the police, propaganda, every day gaining greater control of the army. Out of modesty I do not mention the secret police." Vlanoc smiled dryly. "Now we can fight this war our way. Understand?"

"Yes, Comrade Vlanoc." And he smiled as cynically as his superior.

"Any questions?"

"None, Comrade Vlanoc."

Vlanoc nodded modestly, dismissed him. "*Salud!*"

"*Salud!*"

A few days later, without a goodbye, Joe Garms left to rejoin the American battalion at Tajuña. Just a note for Jake. "Gone to the front. Back to one hole where before there was three. Keep your pecker up and your powder dry. José." Jake sent him a captured German Luger and holster as a gift.

Jake now had withdrawn completely from his Interbrigade comrades. He rolled envelopes, read other people's mail, that of Spaniards as well as that of the International Brigades, found not one tittle of fascist propaganda or one Trotskyite or even anarchist, usually the most candid. If the men and women of the I.B. had any political doubts, they concealed them. How long does it take to learn that the security police are about you, in your hospital wards, in your cafés, in your streets? He did, however, have to ask Vlanoc to intervene for two American comrades who had gone to André Marty's Albacete office to request a poncho for a comrade who suffered from a head wound and was not properly garbed. Marty called them fascists accustomed to luxury and wealth and threw them into prison. He himself lived in a manor house outside Albacete surrounded by a stone wall, guarded by French *pistoleros,* made love to by voluptuous ladies. Vlanoc said Marty was insane. But he and Roegen were rational, coldly efficient, and their men well trained and as ubiquitous as the Murciano sun, present even in the black of night—the baked mud huts, adobe, cobbles ovening its heat. They were recognized by the guns on their hips and cynical arrogant faces.

Soon Vlanoc prescribed a more vigorous work therapy for *el capitán:* to hunt, trap, and execute fifth columnists in the provinces of Murcia and Alicante.

Jake Starr proved to be exceedingly adept, for he had a keen nose and a great intuitive sense. Pure bloodhound. Thoroughbred.

The first man Jake personally executed—an elegant fascist he and his *pistoleros* had rooted out of an Almería potato cellar choking with stolen weapons—stared up at him in inelegant grotesque death from the bullet *el capitán* had deposited in his brain and he vomited all over himself, some of the previous day's codfish splashing on the dead fascist's face.

No man, he learned, was an executioner by birth. It is an evolutionary process. Red Struik, a redheaded elephant of a man, covered with freckles from head to toe, a perpetual nervous grin on his face, laughed at Jake through his grin. "You won't vomit the next time, Comrade Jacobito. They're only fascists." Struik, a Belgian miner and amateur puppeteer, had already traveled the evolutionary road at the end of which an executed man was merely a sack of salt.

Struik spoke the truth.

The next time it was a pitiful ragpicker of a fascist, a limp bony hairy little thug with hateful red-shot eyes, a bit of scum, a human rat, an indiscriminate murderer of any loyal Spaniard, man, woman, child, who went out of his way to offer him a piece of bread. Jake Starr and Red Struik hunted and found him in the mountains of the Espuña range which ringed the *huerta* outside the city of Murcia. Jake didn't vomit after he shot him, he merely stared long at the thin bony corpse and suddenly saw the man and felt a desire to cry. My God, how absurdly frail.

"You suffer melancholia, *Capitán?*" Struik asked pitilessly. Grinned. "This man's a fascist, a murderer of comrades, a dog. Only his mother will cry for him, and even that will be a waste. *Aie,* Jacobito, the next time you won't cry."

Struik proved a prophet.

He did not cry, but he couldn't help thinking that when human life is purchased cheaply, the purchaser begins to find his own life cheap, and with a lowering of value comes a brutalization and tawdriness of feeling. There must be a point where terror must stop, or else one ends wringing one's hands. Like Vlanoc. In uncontrolled pity for oneself—not for the victim.

Soon the horror of it became less horrifying, became even tedious; it was such a simple operation: the captive was asked to turn, to walk toward the door, *el capitán* raised his gun, pressed the trigger, an ounce of lead smashed into the captive's brain, he stiffened, sighed, fell, a twitch, perhaps another, was dead, a nothing.

At midnight the nothing was flung into the square for the populace to see upon rising the following morning, a headline, a warning that the Party was ubiquitous and inexorable.

Comrade Starr discovered no joy in work. It was a dull job. After he had worked his way up the ladder, a Horatio Alger among revolutionists, to the top occupied by such as Carl Vlanoc, others would perform this menial task. It would take some time before class lines were obliterated.

For a short time he developed an eczema, Marat's disease, and scratched till he bled. The doctors could discern no organic malady. *De nada, Capitán.* Still he scratched, bled, scabbed up. By the assertion of great will, Bolshevik will, on which he prided himself, he learned to restrain his fingernails, the itch stopped, the eczema vanished.

His jaw became a jut, his eyes learned to conceal all inner feeling. The revolution at the present stage of development required coldblooded action; emotion, abstract thought, morality would have to abide their time. He would do the job required of him. He was a hard.

His shoulder sagged, bone chips were probed for weekly, yet the wound healed. And he never for one moment could forget Sarah. She had invaded him, it seemed, an antibody to the disease, the unease, which nagged at him behind his cold, cynical eyes. In the dark of night he would awake in his furnace of a room, and see Sarah complete and total, her splendid self, that miraculous curve of hip, her eyes soft with longing, her full passionate lips, the fine dignity and strength. He could hear her voice and smell her perfume, and he would mutter curses at himself because here his will deserted him.

So he had an affair with a Brazilian nurse who worked at the just completed Socorro Rojo hospital. She was a warm round soft beauty who gazed up at him with awe, then flew at him with clawing fingers, her passion a clutch for survival in the midst of the ugly wounds and dying. She gave him ease for a time, a sexy piece with ball bearings for vertebral discs. One, two, three, boom. He treated her shabbily, with a degrading violence to which she seemed to respond with a violence of her own.

In the morning he would send her from his room. "Please, Comrade, go away, I'm busy."

Herself depleted, a little nauseous from a too-violent, too-quickly-spent passion, she would slink away, and he could hear her sandals clapclapping down the broken wood stairs.

He gave her up, she was too demanding.

An American nurse became infatuated with him, a tall, dark beauty with piano legs. Every morning, still sleepy from night duty, she would slip into his room and fling herself on his bed as he worked at his desk, writing or reading a report or studying a map. A modern young woman, she would sprawl on his cot in a position calculated to reveal the nakedness under her white uniform. A bore, she had one redeeming feature, a cast in one blue eye which somehow promised more than could possibly be there. One morning he tried her, only to find she was a clumsy girl who simulated passion no more sincerely than a whore. He abruptly realized Vlanoc had sent her to serve him, to take care of his boy, and, upon questioning her, learned she was in love with an American who drove a supply truck from the *Intendencia* in Almería. He told her not to return and she ran, poor girl, blushing more from anger than shame. Now he met her on a crowded *paseo* during siesta, she lowered her eyes and bit her lips as he nodded and passed her by. He didn't want a party pussy to satisfy a vagrant itch or biological urge to spit.

He wanted Sarah Ruskin.

In the night he would awake, think of her, and his body would begin to tremble. He wanted her love, her warmth, her gay humorous smile which wrinkled her not-small nose and highlighted the dark blue of her eyes, the peacefulness he felt at her side, or that passionate turmoil he used to have when they would go to sleep at night separated by a wall.

Sarah. When they had made love she'd kissed his eyes, his fingertips, had placed her gentle fingers on the back of his neck and drawn him to her breasts. He'd wrapped her in his arms and held her so tightly she had cried out and then bit his lip. That damn first time when she had revealed herself under the night light and he had sung, "I'm flying, Sarah, flying," and she had held on until they flew together. Flying.

Romantic love. Kid stuff.

Was he to live a lifetime without it? He was getting older. Was already twenty-six.

Go to sleep, take a pill to kill the pain.

Comrade Estrella and his *pistoleros* became occupied with a search for a new enemy of the people, one Daniel Nuñez, the peasant heretic from Cuenca province whose rhetoric and flight from Villanueva had so moved Greg Ballard.

When Daniel Nuñez was expelled from the cooperative of Villanueva for heresy against the *frente popular* and for allegedly insulting the American volunteers, he, his wife and children, the cart and burro trundled their way—it took the goodly part of a month—to Alicante where Nuñez had cousins who a generation before had exchanged the earth for the sea. There Nuñez left his wife and children, retaining for himself only the cart and burro. He disappeared.

Vlanoc's men kept the Alicante house under constant surveillance. If the Cuenca heretic ever visited his family Vlanoc's men never saw him. Nuñez had in fact gone to Barcelona where he worked for his political party writing leaflets and tracts on peasant collectives. But of course that was not enough. One day he joined a group of *milicianos* on their way to the front of Aragon, near Huesca, where he shared his comrades' lack of food and clothing, settled disputes as to which militiaman would receive the spare bullet—"We'll cut it in two, comrades"—and daily coughed up more blood. The fighting in Aragon was sporadic, as it was now at The Road, for the fascists were busy mopping up the Basques, securing their northern flank before their onslaught on eastern Spain. Nuñez' presence was not required and his comrades finally petitioned that he return to Barcelona. "Comrade Nuñez, we don't need you here. And if we are to die from lack of food, the cold nights and an occasional fascist bullet, are we also to die of consumption?"

He left and returned to Barcelona, where in early May he fought in the streets against Roegen-Vlanoc and the government's Assault Guards. He was among those who voted in his party's councils against recalling the troops from the front to help protect their party's headquarters and the Lenin Barracks in which Joe Garms and a few other Americans had once eaten lunch. Nuñez was taken prisoner, escaped, disappeared.

Reappeared in the province of Murcia, where he organized a small band whose mission it was to disseminate the words written by their leader: in red paint across the cobbles of one public square or another, or on paper under a doorstep, a poster stuck on a wall. "Only truth can convince us."

He was a rebel, a noble spirit, a *castizo*, as the Spanish say it. Not once did he retreat from his position of antifascism, not once did he call for treason against the Loyal government, not once did he even suggest a laying down of arms against the Franco nationalists. Yet these were precisely what he was accused of by Roegen-Vlanoc; in addition, that he had made an alliance with Franco. All he said—all he ever said—was that victory against the enemy must be won not only with arms but with morality. His leaflets were found everywhere and, as Vlanoc's men led by Jake Starr closed the iron ring tighter about him, the gentle consumptive alternated his demand for truth with a wry contempt for the general and his *capitán*.

The populace read what Nuñez wrote and began to respond. In the shops, in the bawling *paseos* and *calles*, murcianos no longer greeted those of the International Brigades with clenched fist salutes and friendly greetings. It was true, as Nuñez wrote, that these men had left their families, their native lands to come to fight against the enemy, but they were led by the manipulators of the pincers, Roegen to the north and Vlanoc to the south; Franco possessed arms and planes and tanks and even troops sent by Mussolini and Hitler—for the ancient glory of Spain—and carte blanche, it was bitter to admit, from der Fuehrer and Il Duce to do with these arms and men as he thought best for his dismal cause. But Free Spain's ally sent a pair of pincers and the tactic of the unity of opposites—befriend, the easier to destroy. And pincers of course are made to pinch, and they pinched in a very delicate area of the human anatomy. The gland pierced, Free Spain howled in anger. So the laden black freighters from the ports of the Crimea idled at their moorings outside the harbors of Barcelona, Valencia, Cartagena, and Alicante in easy view. But if Free Spain received no matériel, it would die. So its leaders gagged the anger. Roegen and Vlanoc smiled, La Pasionaria made a speech, the pincers relented, and the black freighters lifted anchor, steamed into the harbors and unloaded their cargoes. Prepaid with the blood of the revolution.

"Why exchange black fascism for red?" Nuñez asked. "To the devil with them, we'll fight a guerrilla war and draw our strength from the soil and factories of our people. Army to army, we cannot win. They are a trained army, led by experienced frontline officers. We are a rabble led by ill-trained, incompetent frontline officers, many of whom have lost their senses in the indecent lust for more and more gold braid on their caps. Then there will never be arms enough to match the enemy on the open field." As an aside, wryly, he asked,

"And where, *compañeros,* are the lands of the Magna Carta, the Bill of Rights, and the Rights of Man?" And all Spain, both sides, answered with him, "Shitting!"

He continued, "We are hunted, my comrades and I, because we believe in a revolution which has as its core human freedom—human decency. Words to be ridiculed, I know. I also have studied the dialectic, have believed in its alleged science, and, since habit is strong, its words still flex in my throat to motivate my tongue. I am no different from any man in that I find it as difficult to unlearn as to learn—perhaps more difficult. Yet a part of me which has all these years remained untouched snaps a warning finger. Man's learning, his art and his science, even man's love for his brothers are like grit to be washed from the greens grown in the Murcian *huerta* if they by one word alone intrude upon a man's right to justice. Learning is but an arid earth, art and science stones, overweening love a burned seedling when they are put to the service of degrading man, already degraded enough by the bitterness of his mere existence. Man is neither angel nor brute, and his misery is that he who would act the angel ofttimes acts the brute. Man is no simple matter to be casked like wine, ground like wheat, molded like iron by the inevitable dynamo of history. Man remains a mystery to science, to the dialectic. His spirit can be crushed one moment—give him one free breath and his spirit is revived and not even death can stamp it from our earth. It lives, this mystery, as all mysteries, untouched, untasted, unmolded—its strength revived from man himself.

"General Untruth is also a mystery and, alas, he leaves me but little time in which to learn what makes him what he is—assassin of the innocent; and what makes me what I am—rebel against both the bullet and the lie. Comrade Untruth says I have become a romantic and that romanticism has turned me sour like curds in the Spanish sun. So it has always been: a man cries out for truth, and the cynics laugh, 'A romantic.' Well, I am not romantic enough, Señor Untruth, to forgive you and your comrades for your daily slaughter of Free Spain. I know you do not ask for forgiveness; whether you do or not, I do not forgive. Jesus, Who believed he could intervene for man, perhaps saw no difference between the murderer and the murdered, and could forgive. But no man or God can intervene for man. Each must intervene for himself—so that he can resume his search for justice which is man's greatest virtue."

So wrote Daniel Nuñez, *castizo,* and of course was adjudged an enemy of the people. Many in Free Spain objected, including not a few in the government. Vlanoc and Roegen smiled sadly, spoke quietly: He who is an enemy of the Party is an enemy of Free Spain; and he who is an enemy of Free Spain must die a traitor's death.

With revolutionary arrogance, Jake Starr added, "Even if he's telling the truth, he's lying, because he doesn't understand the concrete truth of the Party. He's an objective fascist and must be silenced."

It was not that he had forgotten the words of Providencio Morales—*A man lives like a beast, he becomes a beast*—but that he had merely relegated them to the ash heap of history (his terminology), where could still be seen half buried the rotted bones of those romantic, not quite forgotten creatures of another age, the just and the virtuous.

XVI

ONE MORNING early in June, *el capitán* returned to Murcia angry and not a little frustrated. He had decided to use Spaniards to find Spaniards—young Spanish peasants from the *huerta* who, sick to death of the spirit of *mañana,* had been attracted to the Party by its harsh discipline and its spirit of doing yesterday what could easily be done tomorrow. He sent them into their villages. "It'll take a month, two, but they'll find Nuñez," he told Vlanoc. "He's not in the cities, he's too smart. He knows city people talk too much—only peasants know how to keep their mouths shut." A few days before he had received word that Nuñez was holed up in a farm near Yecla, and he had chased after him there, but in vain.

Now he washed from the basin in his room on Calle de Trapería, literally Street of Ragshops. Red Struik entered asking, "Any luck?"

"Not yet."

"Come, he's played a joke on us."

"Good. I like jokes." Jake dressed hurriedly and followed the Belgian *pistolero* out.

They walked quickly through the streets mobbed with the ambulatory wounded and marketing women. Soon they entered into the market square with its bawling burros and hawkers' cries. There *el capitán* read the huge letters printed in dripping crimson: "LONG LIVE TRUTH! DEATH TO THE LIE!" under which was drawn crudely a life-sized dog with a man's face, labeled *el capitán.*

There was a hush in the market and Starr knew the peasants and marketers were observing him, so he laughed aloud. Now they grinned, shrugged, went about their business, selling and buying figs, oranges, and sweet onions.

"Crude, but a good likeness," he said to Struik. "Well, let Nuñez have his fun. One of these days we'll find him and you can go to work on him." Struik, a magician, smiled coldly through his grin, and Jake began to scratch his chest—noticed it, forced himself to stop. "Get Tomás with his paints and brushes, I want him to change Jacobito to Franco. Return with him, and bring a few others. While he's working, laugh —loud, all of you."

"In front of them?" Struik asked icily.

"Why not? Treat it like a joke and they will too. They know how to laugh," he said dryly. "In fact, they're people, try to remember. *Salud.*"

Struik departed, heavy muscles sweating, brain thinking, What's he so patronizing about, his bullets kill, too. *El capitán,* his fresh khaki shirt already purple with sweat, strolled to the corner of La Pasionaria to lean against the old stones and smoke a *papaross.* As he stared into the riot of carts and burros and peasants crowding and clamoring in the square, at one point a gap opened and he could see the off-duty doctors and nurses drinking coffee or *naranjada* in the Reina Victoria's sidewalk café under the torn blue canopy. Recognized the undulating figure of the Brazilian nurse at one of the tables. One, two, three, boom. Hey! A very talented tail. The gap closed, and he noticed a young Interbrigader he had never seen before skipping by on two crutches, his plaster-encased legs swinging jauntily between them. The boy sweetly sang,

Here on his back doth lie Sir Andrew Keeling
And at his feet his doleful lady kneeling;
But when alive he had his feeling,
She was on her back and he was kneeling. . . .

then stopped when he recognized *el capitán* whose picture he had often seen in the frontline edition of *Mundo Obrero,* the party newspaper. "*Salud, la Voz.* The comrades at Tajuña send their best."

"Thanks. I miss them."

"Not me. Here there are women."

"How do you manage with those legs?"

"Easy. Here on his back," he sang, "doth lie Sir Andrew Keeling and at his feet his doleful lady—"

Jake laughed, and waved him on.

"Cheers, *compañero,*" the Englishman said, and swung cavalierly away on his crutches.

Starr finished his cigarette, tossed the butt aside, looked again into the bedlam. Saw Hunt Carrington who'd come from the Tajuña valley to repair his piles which had been rendered asunder by terrible food, the Spanish gallops, and trench warfare. He had been operated on, recovered, been appointed American pol for the wounded, a decent pol, too, human, treated his comrades with respect and was thus in return admired and respected. Carrington was with Skinny Horton and two Interbrigade nurses, a Lithuanian and Hungarian, all on their way to the Alhambra-like casino on Tra-pería. They disappeared into the crowd, and Jake again saw the Brazilian nurse. She was soft and warm and wild. A burro brayed in his face. He was lonesome and tired. Ought to run up to San Juan for a few days to swim in the Mediterranean. Well, he'd meander over—perhaps she would forgive him his boorish behavior the last time he had spoken to her. He eased his way through the crowded market, emerged into the clear, and saw she had gone. A mirage.

All these comrades, yet he had been alone for weeks, and now he was seeing things. If there were but one person he could speak to, a human being he could feel at ease with, someone warm and fresh and alive. Joe—why the hell didn't he write? Or Sarah. She was in Valencia, keeping house for her husband and giving dinner parties to which were invited the notables of international journalism and belles-lettres, entertaining sincere, brave, intelligent leaders of the vanguard of the working class like Verdad and Ernesto and Gallo and Gomez and Pedro, and not a Spaniard in the lot. Why didn't she come to Murcia? There was a need for nurses, especially since the increase in typhoid and cholera cases. And there she was living and entertaining like a *marquesa* in a fancy *palacio moro* in Valencia on the sea. Suppose she's forgotten me completely. What the hell, one screw. Middle-class, that's all she was.

He sat down at a café table and ordered American coffee and toast and guava jelly. Nodded to Horton who had returned with his Hungarian nurse, a beautiful Magyar girl whose husband was a frontline commissar. Comic star—a new coin minted by Mack Berg. Mack Berg was earning himself the hatred of the entire leadership of his brigade—the voice of the rank and file. They were permitting him to get away with it because he had become the smokestack through which the men spouted their pent-up steam. Berg seemed to understand and took advantage of it. One of these days if he wasn't careful some pol would bomb that smokestack out of existence. Horton had enough sense to keep quiet, except to his nurse, Boeshka Haas, who though having an affair with him had informed Vlanoc the kid was sympathetic to the POUM. Horton had huge purplish-red scars on his neck since his operation which had been unsuccessful—the bullet still lodged in his spine. He would have to be called up one of these days and given hell, which would shut him up completely.

Jake heard laughter in the square and looked up from the point on the blue tin table at which he had been staring. Tomás was changing Jacobito to Franco, and Struik and the boys were laughing hysterically—joined by the peasants who had gathered about to observe the painter at work. The market seemed to empty as they all swarmed around Tomás, craning their swart scrawny necks to see, and the painter, warming to his job, began to improvise, floppy ears here, longer tails there, the *pinga del perro* lengthened so it reached into its own mouth. Spanish comics.

Jake looked away, frowning. He could enjoy nothing. There was something nagging at him, something he could not understand. He realized he had lost the habit of thinking about himself—and that was exactly what he wanted. Being taken with himself was after all an adolescent gambit he could do without. A man could begin to think about himself so completely he forgot the world he lived in. He smiled to himself. He didn't want to forget the world, that's all he wanted to think about. And wasn't that a device, too, fabricated to conceal himself? The easiest place to get lost is in a crowd. He gazed about the square, the marketplace, saw the lean, tawny faces, the wares they sold and bought. With a start his attention was suddenly held by a woman standing at a peasant's cart heaped with large sweet onions and strings of garlic. Even lost, he thought, a man required a warm hand to hold, a soft breast to kiss, the sweet moist secret of a loved woman's body. His heart beat quickly. For the woman was the most beautiful he had ever seen, with the most shapely legs, the most splendid breasts, the brownest plaited hair, and she was staring at him with astonished dark blue eyes. His heart spun and his head fell into vertigo. He felt himself rising to his feet and beginning to walk towards her. She merely stood staring at him, her eyes opened wide, biting her lower lip. Finally he was as close to her as he could get without touching, and all he saw was her eyes—the pupils, he could see, were like murciano suns in a vivid burning blue sky. He heard himself from a great distance whisper harshly in

Spanish, "*Vámonos,*" and he turned towards the Paseo del Malecón. Without words, without touching, she followed slowly behind him the length of the stone promenade to the outskirts of the city, between fig and orange trees, then over a metal stairs and into a *casa moro* which this morning shone extraordinarily white. An old woman, a Goya caprice worn gray with time, closed the door behind them on the persistent white glare and heat.

He led her immediately to a large room on the second floor, still not speaking, not daring to speak, not touching. He turned from her to close the long floor-to-ceiling shutters. When he faced her again, she was sitting upright on the bed, her eyes lit by a soft warm glow, and he could hear his own heart pumping wildly and he was filled with a joy such as he had never before known.

There was an agony to the joy, and he somehow wished to hold on to this agonized joy for an eternity, but he also wanted to touch her. Slowly he moved towards her and dropped to his knees before her, and placed his head on her lap, and then he felt her fingers on his neck.

"I almost died when I read you had died," she said.

"You kept me alive," he said simply.

They were silent again, and there was nothing in the world but them.

When at last he began gently to undress her, she threw her arms wildly about his neck and began to kiss him and to laugh, and soon he joined her.

They made love laughing and crying at one and the very same time.

XVII

When Sarah had been asked by the celebrated Dolores Ibarruri, La Pasionaria, who came often with her lover, Antón, the commander of Madrid, to the Ruskin house in Valencia if she would go to Murcia, they were badly in need of nurses, she knew it would mean seeing Jake Starr again and couldn't wait to leave. Yes, she had answered, and Dolores smiled her famous white smile. Sarah would have gone to Patagonia to be near Jake Starr. What surprised her—perhaps shocked was more accurate, she had to admit to herself—was Rolfe's attitude about her leaving him and Valencia to go to a city where it was known Jake Starr worked with General Verdad. Now neither Rolfe nor Roegen seemed to care. Roegen especially appeared to wish to be rid of her.

Rolfe had become insufferable—no longer spoke as a man speaks, but as a megaphone in a trick moving picture from which words are shouted at the audience yet no human form is discernible. Her husband had convinced himself that he was a great revolutionist—and Roegen never permitted him to think otherwise. In front of her, laughing at her from the corner of his large equine eyes in that horse's head on the body of a sallow dwarf, Roegen constantly flattered Rolfe's already overindulged ego. For a short time Rolfe resumed his old ways with her, was gentle, was repelled by the naked power moves of the party leaders in Valencia, the capital of Free Spain, was satisfied to work in his laboratory and to advise the government on scientific matters. Of course, in the laboratory, Rolfe Ruskin was a great man: motivated only by truth, there no one and nothing in the entire world could sway him but truth. But outside the laboratory, in this world which to him was really an alien world, he began again to permit himself to be puffed up like a falseface balloon fabricated, perhaps, in one of Roegen's dungeons at the headquarters of the Servicio de Investigación Militar, the dread SIM. Murcia for her would be a happy change; she would nurse the wounded of the International Brigades, and Jake and she would be lovers. She had decided that very coldly and deliberately, after which, again an admission, she smiled wryly to herself. Perhaps the Party was succeeding in making her one of its own.

Now it was so; she and Jake became lovers. Every day that Jake was in Murcia, they met at the Reina Victoria under the torn blue canopy at the edge of the sea of the square pelted with white sun, and then strolled arm-in-arm, casually, openly, to the white Moorish *casa* cooled by delphinium blue *azulejo* tiles, shuttered windows, high ceilings, and the pure white stucco of the outer walls which repelled the sun. Jake told her that before the war it had been the home of a rich Murcian grain merchant whose belly had been sliced open before he had been dumped into the Segura at the outbreak of the fascist rebellion, but not before he himself had pumped six bullets into the heart of a socialist leader. The *casa* was now owned by the people, that is, General Verdad, an exceedingly nervous tribune since the Tukhachevsky purge in Moscow in mid-June. Already the Russian commander of the tank base at Archena had been recalled by his Maker in Moscow, and several Russian *consejeros,* advisers, as well.

Vlanoc gave Jake use of the house. Jake bought a phonograph, collected records, and every afternoon for three hours he and Sarah wove a wondrous cocoon for themselves. Then put it to flame and by some miracle came out alive.

Jake needed her to comfort him in his terrifying loneliness; she needed him to satisfy her femaleness. It was, of course, her obsession for him which blinded her to what he had become; just as it was his obsession for the Party which blinded him to what the Party had become and what the future most certainly would bring. So for three hours of every afternoon of every day Jake was in Murcia—the days he was not out searching for Daniel Nuñez, another obsession—they gave one another a breathless joy and a wild peace; yet each soon became aware that they were living with an unspoken sense of unhappiness, a sort of ferocious, passionate despair.

"I love you totally, without the slightest reservation," he told her one afternoon as they lay in bed in their shuttered room.

She kissed his ear, then said softly, "I love you, too."

"Do you love me more than you have ever loved anyone before?" he asked her, looking directly into her eyes, and he saw her flinch, and he knew he shouldn't have asked this question. But he continued to look into her eyes, which seemed to want to find a place to hide. He knew he shouldn't press her, but he couldn't stop himself. "Do you?" And it sounded like a demand.

She avoided his eyes, stared at the huge iron candelabra in the far corner of the room. She knew she must answer, and she didn't want to be unfair to Rolfe, he was still a very intimate part of her life, but Jake had demanded and she realized he now had a right to demand. "Yes," she said looking at him sadly, "I love you more than I have ever loved anyone else."

He smiled, and he couldn't help but know it was a vain smile, one of victory, but still that was the way he felt. She read his smile for what it was, and immediately was even more guilty about Rolfe than before, but she did not blame Jake for it, that was love, one element of it, the feeding of one's vanity. Now he said, "I have never in my life loved anyone or wanted anyone as much as you." And now it was her turn to smile victoriously, and she did. "I missed you so much, I felt lifeless without you. I tried with others, but it was no damn good."

For a quick moment jealousy made her ill, but it left as abruptly as it had arrived.

"You have no cause to be jealous," he said, having recognized the discomfort in her eyes. "Do you ever think of that first time?" And he placed his weight on her side, their legs intertwined.

She gazed up at him, a small smile playing about her lips. "Do you think I can ever forget it?" She took his head in her hands and kissed him, then bit his lip and wouldn't let go.

Later in his room on Trapería, outside of her presence, he added to himself that he loved her enough to know she would be hurt by their love and it would be best if she left both Murcia and Spain and returned to England to make a new life for herself.

It was a thought which made him unhappy and he began to read the reports on his desk, to try to lose himself in work.

That night he could not sleep. It was hot. The smell of fried olive oil was especially noxious. First his ankle itched, then his back. His wound hurt. The bed became wet from his perspiration. The guards at the bottom of the stairs spoke too loudly and he yelled at them to shut up. He drank wine from his gourd, and it was tepid and too sour. Took a couple of aspirins. No sleep. That damn nag in his belly. No, it wasn't Sarah. What was it?

He slipped from his bed, doused himself with water from the basin. Tried to regulate his breathing. Emptied his head. Returned to bed. His stomach quivered. Began to quote a passage from Marx as he had that time in the Figueras fortress; however this time it didn't work. It wasn't fear he was trying to conquer.

What was it?

If a man can't identify what is obvious, he thought, it's because he has been staring at it too long. He jumped from the bed and stood in the dark, his head in a whirl. What the hell was the matter with him?

Hurriedly he dressed and ran down to the pool in the courtyard of the University Hospital, where Sarah worked, and naked he dunked himself in its cold water while on the open balconies the wounded heroes of Jarama and Brihuega and Córdoba cried out in their nightmares, throwing up their bare stumps to ward off the atrocious bombs and murderous bullets, and up there in the darkness somewhere Sarah was sleeping naked to the night.

I'm falling apart.

He returned to his office and room on Calle de Trapería, and in the morning went off on a hot lead a Spanish boy, Rolando, had brought him as to the whereabouts of Daniel Nuñez.

In an old Chevy which had been commandeered for the war, Rolando driving, Jake alongside him, in the rear Heinz Brucker, who had been in Paris when he was there, Struik and Michel, a liverwurst, a pork and a pickle jar, they drove on a narrow pitted macadam road through the *huerta*—mulberry bushes, orange groves, red peppers spread out to dry, long slender fig trees, date trees along the sides of the road, and peasants on bended knee strengthening by hand their pitiful irrigation ditches like kids playing at canal building on the beach. They tended their soil and dribs of water with an adoration only equaled by penitents before the cross.

Behind the old Chevy lumbered a *camión* carrying a squad

of Interbrigaders. They rumbled through the *huerta*, past Monteagudo pointing a challenging black finger at God. The car lurched to a stop, and Jake who had been thinking of Sarah—she was beginning to ask too many questions about the work he was doing, she prattled on about justice like an old Jew—opened his eyes, and smiled. Even the revolution must yield to custom. In the center of the road squatted a peasant who would be neither hurried nor moved. They waited. Rolando would no more think of honking the horn than he would think of drinking water instead of wine with his meat. At last having moved what was to be moved, the peasant rose and slowly adjusted his dusty trousers. At his own time, he ambled to the side of the road, turned about, and with a dignified nod acknowledged the courtesy. To terminate the ritual, he signaled with his hand that they might proceed, a dusty smile broadening his saturnine countenance. Jake laughed—not Rolando—and the car and truck lurched into gear.

An hour later they entered Rolando's village. Rolando was a Murcian peasant boy, sullen, lean, swart, and with hair the color of a blackbird. The village was a hot dusty row of mud huts. Here the green of the *huerta* faded to green yellow. A woman could be seen sweeping her doorstep. A skinny hound slept in the shade of a water barrel. Through the village wound lazily a narrow dirt road which came to a dead halt in the hills of the Espuña range—rocky, arid, scrub. The sun was a pot of melted copper.

The car braked to a stop before one of the huts, the truck having been sent ahead to wait outside the village. Inside the tile floor and the darkness kept the hut cool; a fire smoldered in the hearth over which hung smoking sausages like mottled gnarled intestines. An old woman, barefoot, heavy-gaited, solid flesh in the formless black hubbard, her square face old mahogany and her eyes black walnut, greeted Rolando, her son, with a quick smile. He greeted her curtly, then kissed her proffered cheek. She nodded and said nothing to his introduction of *el capitán* and the others, but to herself she thought, *pistoleros,* without end into eternity, *pistoleros.*

"We are hungry, *madre mía.*"

"*Sí,* son of my heart."

Without further word she set about and soon they were consuming sausages, garbanzos, figs, and passing around a heavy earthen jug of sour *vino rojo.*

Jake thanked her and nodded to his three comrades to leave the hut with him, the mother would want a moment with her son.

"What's the purpose of your comrades' visit to our village, Rolando?"

"We have business in the mountains," he said with attempted nonchalance.

"Between the village and the mountaintop there's but one *granja,*" she stated quietly, holding him with her eyes.

"Yes, I know. This is my village."

"That's why you came to visit with me the past few days?" The way she observed him made him squirm.

"*Sí, madre*—and because I was lonesome for you," and he essayed a sullen smile.

He has no shame, she thought painfully. "You must know as well as I that they are *hermanos,* though of a different political faith from yours."

"They've become *falangistas;* they're no longer brothers," he said curtly, now staring bravely into her eyes.

"So have I heard from those of your political faith in the village, but I've spoken to Lizeta, their mother, who is a friend from childhood, and she swore on the crucifix that it is a lie."

"*Pedo* on her crucifix and on her sons," Rolando snapped, wheeling to go.

Her hand heavy on his shoulder, she yanked him round and spoke harshly. "Then you fart as well on the crucifix of your mother," and she raised her hand like a square spade to strike him.

"I forgot myself, *mamita,* forgive me," he said quickly, lowering his eyes.

"When a boy becomes a man, he's not easily forgiven," she said sternly, dropping her hand to her side. Then, quietly, she continued. "This village has stood as one against the *generales,* yes, even against our Mother, the Church—though I for one will never forgive those who killed the old padre, even those like your father, may the Savior forgive him. It is a small village, forgotten in the *huerta,* yet even in its smallness there have been many divisions into political faiths—as in all España, it is our curse. If you and your *estranjeros* harm our friends in the mountains, the village will never forgive or forget, even after the fascists are defeated, may the devil have them. Remember, Rolando—this is your village."

"Hector and Guillermo have been known to come into the city during the night to distribute papers printed with lies about the *partido.* They say we destroy the revolution and the war. They lie. They now do the work of the *falangistas. El capitán* merely wishes to interrogate them. He is a great man, of much valor—"

"*Sí,* I have read it. The padre taught me how to read, remember? And it was I who taught you."

"If they are innocent, he won't harm them."

"They are innocent; Lizeta herself has told me."

Oh, what's the sense quarreling with an old woman? They know nothing. "No harm will come to them, *mamita.*"

"So say you?"

"So say I."

She searched his sullen eyes—her angel—and saw truth with a mother's love. "I believe you, my son."

He kissed her cheek and departed.

The old Chevy leading, the truck behind, they slowly followed the winding dirt road into the mountains. The pot of melted copper bubbled with white heat, the mountains, the scrub, the yellow sage, and the heath were ashimmer.

"How much more, Rolando?" Jake asked.

"Dos, tres kilómetros."

"Better pull over to the side."

As they sat on the dry heath under a scrub pine which gave no shade, Starr conferred with his men. Concluding, he said, "Since it's siesta, they'll be off guard. They are Spaniards." He merely stated a fact. "No bloodshed unless it's a must." *El capitán:* saint.

He was right, of course. As he and his men circled the mud hut, they saw no guard. They did see Lizeta out in the fields. Fields. A stony mountain ridge, strips of earth, some no wider than a man's back, nurtured by hand, irrigated by a series of ditches leaching a mountain stream trickling as from a squeezed-out stone.

Jake Starr, with Rolando at his side, two others at his back, pistols in hand, quietly entered the door at the front, the grinning Struik and two other men the door at the rear. Three remained outside to guard against old Lizeta. The remaining four covered the corners of the hut.

Four men, sitting feet akimbo on the tile floor, the customary open hearth smoldering under smoking sausages, were listening to an old man straightbacked on a chair plucking a guitar, while an Andalusian girl, standing erect beside him, sang a *canto hondo*. Before they realized they were taken, they had guns at their temples. They sat paralyzed with shame at their foolishness. Not the old man. He hugged the guitar to his chest and spat in Jake Starr's face. Jake didn't blink, his eyes were busy searching.

But Daniel Nuñez wasn't there.

"We'll take what we've got," he said to Struik in French.

"Nuñez is old-fashioned, he will suffer. Leave the old man and the old woman."

As they herded the four men and the Andaluz to the door, Lizeta entered, guarded by a *pistolero.* Her face was like bark, brown and ridged, her broad bare feet solid on the tiled floor. Each hand was an implement for hard labor. She peered nearsightedly from one to another, found Rolando, and raised a hand to touch his face. He blanched and stepped aside. "Rolando," she spoke huskily, "my sons have been your brothers, what will the *estranjeros* do to them and their friends?"

Starr answered for him. "They will not be harmed, old woman," he said calmly, scratching his chest. "We take them to Murcia for questioning. If they prove they are not enemies of the Republic, they will be given their freedom."

"Who are you to decide whether *españoles* are friend or enemy?" she snapped, narrowing her nearsighted eyes and bringing her face close to his.

Before Starr could answer, Hector, her elder son, Rolando's contemporary, intervened. "Remain in the *casa, madre*—look after your father and the farm." Turning to Starr, he said, "Take us, *Capitán.* Nuñez you will never find."

Lizeta first kissed Hector, and then Guillermo, her youngest, sixteen years old he was, then went wearily to the old peasant's side.

As he left the mud hut, Starr glanced back over his shoulder for a moment to Lizeta and her father. She had covered her head with a black shawl and had fallen to her knees before a space on the wall where it was obvious once a cross had hung. As he closed the door behind him, he heard the old peasant spit out, "*Pinga del perro!*"

Prick of the dog.

Hector, Guillermo, the Andaluz, and the two others were taken to the basement of the fifteenth-century Gothic cathedral of Murcia. Neither Carl Vlanoc nor *el capitán* questioned them; it was Red Struik, grinning, who did the interrogating.

He didn't harm them—all he did was have them stand facing a blank wall without food or water; they were not to touch the wall, merely to stand at it, hour after hour. When Guillermo became too tired and fell to his knees, Comrade Struik had him raised to his feet, without violence, not a mark was to be seen on him; humanely. They just stood facing the blank wall. It would be a few days before the interrogation would truly begin. "Where's Nuñez?"

But early the next morning, Capitán Jacobito was roused by a rapping on his door. "There's an *español* to see you, Comrade Jacobito," the guard told him.

Starr smiled drily. "A little thin *español?*"

"*Sí,* Comrade Jacobito."

"I'll see him in Vlanoc's office in a minute."

In precisely one minute Jake looked for the first time upon the consumptive face of Daniel Nuñez. It unnerved him, for it was remarkable how like that of Providencio Morales was the face and build of the Spanish rebel. It was probably a hallucination. Small and slight, tawny, even to the thick black bedraggled mustachios (newly grown), yet where Morales had been blessed with a mean sullen face, totally lacking in naïveté, Nuñez' was almost innocent, and gentle with a gentleness not even his horrible rasp of a cough could deform. The greatest likeness, Starr thought, was in the eyes, intelligent, black, shaped like almonds, and in his mouth, full-blooded and strong, and at which Nuñez continually dabbed his red kerchief to blot up the redspecked sputum of a man dying of tuberculosis.

And indeed, smiling wryly, the first thing he said was, "Don't come too close, my illness has reached the stage of contagion. I wouldn't want the savior of Madrid to become tubercular on my account."

"*Muchas gracias,* Nuñez. You're a fine actor, but you overdo your gentleness. I suppose you think you are the Son of God. Sit down! I was expecting you."

His intelligent eyes wide, Nuñez asked in mock surprise, "You were?"

El capitán did not answer, merely seated himself behind Vlanoc's desk to face the man they had been searching for for months.

Nuñez laughed softly, enough to bring on a hacking cough and spittle of blood to his lips. Wiping his mouth, his chest subsiding, he sat at a chair near the desk. "You consider me a naïve fool, I can see, *Capitán.* You have my comrades and you knew I would be aware that the torture had or would soon begin, one or another of them would break, would reveal my hiding place and then sign a confession that we are in the pay of Franco, perhaps even of Hitler, and, worst of all, Trotsky, Lucifer himself. Therefore you knew I would conclude it to be most humane to present myself to you and at the least save my friends from your Belgian's hands. Besides I will soon die from tuberculosis. *Aie, Capitán?*"

Starr examined the man's face. Playing games, the fool. "If my comrades were as stupid as yours, I would commend them to the wall, for they would deserve it. Not even a guard at the door, Nuñez, and you call yourselves revolutionaries."

"True. We do not possess your discipline and toughness. Therefore we deserve to die. *Sí, compañero,* all the naïve, humane, undisciplined stupid fools of this world deserve to die at the wall, and the world is fortunate at this stage in its historic development that there are such as you, great anti-fascists and revolutionists, who will make certain that we stand at the wall."

"Nuñez, you speak the truth."

They sat quietly for a few moments, both pleased to be warmed by the morning sun striking through the window.

Finally Starr said, "Nuñez, you stand convicted: you have failed. By your political immaturity and misplaced idealism you obstruct our path and thus stand ready to hand the world to the fascists. We have to destroy you. You do not have enough belief in man. I do, Nuñez. And the courage and will to do what must be done. Even if I stand condemned for it."

Nuñez looked into Jake Starr's eyes. A dead man on furlough. "Don't die for my sake," he smiled, "and don't kill me for yours." Now Jake smiled, too. Then Nuñez continued. "When violence is committed in defense of the rights of man and of reason, it is, *mi Capitán,* the ultimate act. To be able to defer it to the ultimate is as good as any a definition of what is civilized. You are about to commit an atrocity on me, and I hope not on my young comrades. An atrocity is not an ultimate act, however, it is a primary act which obliterates all the intervening acts between measured reason and violence as an act of exasperated reason. Your obsessive commitment has led you there; you have leaped without thought to your conscience. Too bad, Jacobo, you have become a man of direct action. A maker of atrocities. You and the fascists are alike in that. There is a taint of rot in the air. Death!" He paused.

Starr merely sat back in his chair, observed the man. Let him talk. The occupational disease of revolutionaries.

Nuñez saw he had made little impression. Well, he would proceed, what had he to lose? "It is no news, *Capitán,* that twenty years after the October revolution its Epigoni commit atrocities in its name. Daily you commit acts of barbarism not only on the Spanish revolution but on the Spanish people through blackmail and terror. Even on your own comrades. You lie to them, you murder them. You are one of the new barbarians—not the wave of the future, but the scum of the past. Everytime you say the word socialism it curls and withers." Again he paused; he felt as if he were talking to himself.

"If we're in error," Starr said icily, and Nuñez shivered in the sundrenched room, "history will destroy us. All of us." Then he said calmly, "There is little sense in arguing, Nuñez. Save your strength, you will need it. The fact is we come to our views each from a diametrically opposed conception of our personal relationship with society. It's obvious you never studied the dialectic seriously. You attribute to some eternal man the contradictions you find in yourself, but they are really those of a class and a social system. I see my problems and contradictions as the problems and contradictions of a social system. I look for the solution of those problems and contradictions in the transformation of that social system." Jake paused, smiled smugly, and, as Nuñez was about to leap to answer him, he said slowly to give what he said proper emphasis, "The *world* is not in me; *I* am in the world."

Now he stood from his chair and stepped around the desk to stand close to Nuñez, who saw that *el capitán* waited for an answer, and that despite himself the answer was important to him.

"The world is in me," the rebel began, "no doubt that is true, and that is precisely why I cannot dissociate myself from the fate of man, of men, even those I most detest. You are in the world, and that is exactly why you do dissociate yourself from individual men, for you can only see them as predetermined statistics on an historioeconomic development graph—as the pockmarks on the iron face of our time."

"But it is precisely I—and my Party—who wish to socialize, collectivize, society—not to pulverize it," Jake interjected, a puzzled look on his face, stepping back from the chair on which Nuñez sat, now wiping his mouth. "The position we take today is merely a tactic, an emergency measure, if you will," Jake said as an aside. Then he returned to the point. "It is you who are so dazzled by yourself and your own uniqueness as a man that you must maintain your individuality or die."

"My dear *compañero,*" Nuñez said with a little smile, "it is not what it seems. It is because I must maintain my individuality or die that I must be reasonable to all men and must yield to them a like right. And for a very selfish reason, which is frequently not merely the most honest reason, but the most sound: if I do not, very shortly—perhaps tonight," and he shrugged his thin shoulders hopelessly—"it will not be yielded to me. That is the essence of freedom and its limits. That is at the core of being a socialist. Socialism is supposed to free man, not shackle him." He saw *el capitán* was listening intently, and he hurried along.

"You are *in* the world, you say. Exactly. You manage to be *in* the Party, *in* the stream of history, *in* the world. You are in everything and take responsibility for nothing. Why should you? It is all predetermined. All you can do is help the predetermined processes along. It is the *partido,* history, the world which dominates your life. Perhaps there is a flaw of character involved there. I do not pretend to know. But why should a man of your intelligence and strength require a readymade haven from the onslaughts of life? Of course, if that is your need, it makes life a little easier. Some people say the masses of humanity—in España we like to call them the multitudes, it is a more vertical term—some say the masses find it easier to have others decide their lives for them, find it easier to be herded together in the center of the world, dominated, overwhelmed, vulgarized, the handservants to history. However, Jacobo, I am not prepared to say that is what the masses want until they have been given ample opportunity to speak for themselves.

"When you are in the world, dominated by history and

manipulated by your *partido*—the leader, the vanguard, the bulwark of the future, the engine, God—you lose your identity as a man, you lose your responsibility as a man to other men—to yourself. How can you possibly be blamed for anything if the world's so big and you are so little? That is why you beat men into seeing the world the way you see it, because you cannot afford to lose your personal investment of emotion and commitment."

Nuñez stopped, hawked up some bloody phlegm into his kerchief. Starr leaned with his back against the desk, waiting for the man to conclude. He was in turmoil, wished to take this little man and shake him to death, for the man was a danger to his very life.

Nuñez said, "I, unlike you, will never give up my freedom in order to crawl around, one of a *sovkhoz* of ants, in some foul, evil cave.

"The world is in me, and I am of the world. I am a selfish man, a vain man, so vain that when I wish to look into the world's heart, I look into my own. I am responsible for myself, and therefore for the world. I am my brother's keeper—and he had better be mine. And that is truth, *compañero mio,* very unrelative truth. I am beholden to no man—yet to all. I gaze into my heart and, knowing myself, know all men. *Un poco.* A little."

Nuñez stood, facing Vlanoc's captain. What was there more to say? It seemed hopeless, they were divided not by intelligence or knowledge, they were divided by themselves. He waited before this man who stood tall before him, his eyes cold, his eyes narrowed murderously, his face frozen. Inside this man Nuñez could discern a rage brewing, a veritable storm. As he tried to reveal himself to himself, this man did all in his obsessive will to conceal his very self—he did not matter to himself. Then how could other men matter to him? His idea overpowered all self—all humanness. And that was their difference—their irreconcilable difference. Despite his anger, his fear for his own life, for that of his comrades, Nuñez felt pity for *el capitán;* and he wanted to raise his hand to touch him—one lonely human being to another. He did imperceptibly raise his hand as he faced Jake, but, no, and he permitted his hand to rest at his side. He merely shrugged, and coughed.

Behind his cold, resolute face, Jake was in turmoil. There was nothing he could find to answer Nuñez. The consumptive rebel had delineated what divided them clearly. The dividing line was as sharp as a honed blade. It appeared to him that not he, Jake Starr, held the knife, but this brave little Spaniard, and he felt in mortal danger. Everything he had ever done and thought could in one flash of assent be rendered null and void. Exactly—he would exist in a void, an eternal nothingness. He had always believed that the very structure of his life, its skeleton, its ligaments, flesh, muscle, nervous system, brain, was held erect by his belief that he himself did not matter, only the cause mattered. Without it he would fall apart in a clatter of bones to the floor. He saw the man's hand flex to touch him, then fall back. Damn him—about to die, *he* pities *me.* Goddam renegade bastard. With a quick movement of his hands he had the little man by the scruff of his skinny neck and raised him off the floor, ready to fling him against the wall, to murder him then and there. But Nuñez, coughing and hawking blood, found somehow the strength to cry out, "At least murder me with dignity, *Capitán,*" and Jake Starr remembered he was human and released him.

Before Nuñez was led away by the guard to join his comrades in the cellar of the cathedral, Daniel, who must have known he was giving himself up to death when he freely yielded himself up to *el capitán* in the hope of gaining the release of his comrades—yes, a naïve, gentle fool—asked Jake Starr to release Hector and the others. "They are young, and besides I take full responsibility. You must have some compassion for them."

"That's not my affair, Nuñez; it's Vlanoc's."

Peering into Jake's cold eyes, the rebel stated bitterly, "They and I will be your affair, my dear comrade, until the day you die. And that day, I can only hope, will be soon."

On the second floor of the University Hospital, in a tiny room off the open balcony, the windows shaded against the afternoon sun, an Italian boy lay naked on his bed. He was dying, his spine having been crushed by a bullet three months before at Brihuega. Somehow he had been kept alive, though no one knew exactly why. He suffered terribly, had not moved finger or toe since his wounding, and morphine was scarce. His immobile, thin, throbbing body was sore and scabrous, his sweat glands issuing its acid to incite the quivering pain even more.

Sarah, sponge in hand, bathed him gently, the sole joy in the boy's never-ending day. He closed his eyes and sighed. She sponged his feet and legs, his groin, his puny chest, his spindly arms, his throat, his lips, his forehead. Again he sighed.

Sarah remembered what Jake had said and done the previous afternoon. She had lain on their bed naked and he had stood at her side. With his finger he had slowly, lovingly traced, starting at her toes, her entire body, following the flow and contour of her womanliness. And she, too, had closed her eyes and sighed.

Then her lover had said tenderly, "Sometime when I'm not around, and you miss me, all you have to do is what I have just done, and there I will be, right at your side. Will you remember?"

She had opened her eyes to find his, and then she had drawn him down to kiss him. "I will remember."

Now she smiled as she sponged again the dying Italian boy. Love gave tenderness not only to her, but to all about her.

When she finished, the Italian opened his eyes. He smiled at her, whispered, "*Gracias,* Comrade Sarah."

Then died.

That night the enemies of the people were huddled in a shadowy corner of the stone basement of the cathedral of Murcia. A kerosene lantern lit the darkness, throwing off a sombre green pink light whose shadows were like long green sinuous fingers reaching out to them. They were scrawny men—three were boys—with skin the color of wet chamois. Even in their huddling, they maintained a certain insolent pride. The Andaluz, if she had been fed, could have been the sister of Sarah Ruskin, with a strong prideful nose, indomitable chin, excepting her eyes were smoke gray and her breasts small and pointed, high on her chest. She had long wild hair and wore a red Andaluz skirt, flared and ruffled, ripped now bodice to hem. Struik.

Vlanoc himself directed the processional. His *capitán* had handed him a victory, now the general must lead the way through the arch. His voice stung out sharply, direct, a leader's.

The procession, without music:

Struik trod solidly to the corner, returned with Hector, whose face was a squashed purple plum. Struik, the victory won, had not been able to restrain his strength's leap of joy. Struik stood the boy with his back against the wall, untied his hands since one must not execute a Spaniard with his hands tied, it is an indignity.

Exit Struik.

Enter Heinz Brucker, bored, Luger in fist.

Hector stood rigid, his lips sullen, contemptuous even, his

eyes like a doe's, big, round, soft, brown. Raising his left fist, Hector declaimed, "Unite, proletarian brothers. U!H!P!"

The gun's sharp roar crashed off the stones of the cellar.

Struik raised Hector's dead body and threw it like a sack of ash into an empty corner. Then he moved again, solid bone and muscle, to the shadows and returned dragging Guillermo, who was trembling from fear. "*Mamita,*" the child cried, "*Mamita.*" But when his hands were untied, shoved with his back against the stones, he became a man, *un español,* one must die with dignity. He stretched his slender body straight, controlled his weeping, quivering lips, ignored the tears slipping down his boyish cheeks, and raised his fist. "U!H!P! *Unios, hermanos proletarios!*" The gun spoke sharply, and his body crumpled to the dungeon floor. Red Struik flung him atop his dead brother.

And so with the two remaining comrades of Daniel Nuñez, each declaiming in death, "U!H!P!"

Now the Andaluz, her bodice and skirt ripped to reveal her high hard quivering breasts, her nipples strangely rigid. She stood straight, her bony knees firm.

Jacob Starr was rigid, his face like stone, and he wondered: Is this courage or madness? He could feel no reality, so he must be totally dead.

Struik untied her hands, placed his thick hand on her belly and pushed her against the wall. Heinz raised his gun to her temple. With rigid stylized grace, she rippled her shoulders and her red dress fell about her feet, and she stood thus, a bony skinny little girl, an exclamation point dotted by a pool of blood. She flicked her tongue, squeezed her small breasts in a definitive gesture of contempt, and harshly cried, "Not brothers. Beasts!"

And died.

Struik threw her among the others, then brought Daniel Nuñez to stand before the massive stone wall of the ancient cathedral. The sombre green pink fingers of light illuminated his haggard face, his lips flecked with blood. Thin-chested, small, not yet thirty years old, intelligent, gentle almond eyes, and he also stood without fear. These goddam Spaniards, Starr thought, take death like a bride on her wedding night.

As Red Struik worked to untie the sweated cord which held Daniel's wrists, the heretic's eyes kept staring at Jake Starr, at him alone.

As he had waited his time at the wall, Nuñez examined one by one Vlanoc and his *pistoleros:*

Carl Vlanoc, a stump of a man, a nose like sharp iron, hero of the October revolution, heir apparent to the leadership of the Hungarian Party, friend of the recently purged Tukhachevsky and of Trotsky before exile, Stalin's agent in China, Germany, Latin America, Spain; educated to be an obstetrician, to bring babies into the world, had for his revolution become a murderer, chief of security, Chekist, gravedigger. Immovable, forever lost as a human being.

Heinz Brucker, sturdy German dockworker, German equivalent of *pistolero* on the Hamburg waterfront for the Party, executioner of enemy, friend, his Party's long finger pressed the button, he responded: a machine. Face blank, eyes blank, stomach full. Immovable.

Struik, powerful Belgian miner, amateur puppeteer, militant fighter in his workers' syndicate, a heroic soldier at Casa de Campo, the San Martín road, fine comrade, but Vlanoc had looked into his eyes and had seen what was to be seen: a grinning redheaded murderer. Forgotten were the days of hunger, injustice. A guillotine. Immovable.

Jacobito, *norteamericano,* capable theoretician of the dialectic, expert on Latin America for his Party, known as an excellent comrade; hero at Jarama, Tajuña, underground fighter *por excelencia,* executioner of fascists; brawny, haggard, scratched his chest, a tic; lover of a beautiful *inglesa,* wife of Professor Rolfe Alan Ruskin, Nobel laureate and scientific consultant to the Spanish Republic; slightly demented by his obsession for the cause, vain, ambitious, a martyr—a dead man on furlough—believes he is a Moses, more, a god. Stone, yet his eyes are still alive. He suffers. He is movable.

I will move him, thought Nuñez; I will marry him as every victim marries his executioner.

Now, as Struik untied his hands, he stared at Jake Starr, who returned his stare, unyielding. I'll move him, Daniel thought relentlessly, suddenly sighed aloud. To his executioners it sounded like a sob. Struik grinned and concluded untying the cord, roughly pushed Nuñez against the wall, then stepped aside. And Heinz, with the impatience of a workman at the end of his day awaiting the factory bell, reloaded his revolver. He was ready; the bell would clang, he would tiredly go home to his meat and beer.

Nuñez suddenly cried out, "A favor in death—a favor in death?"

"No speeches, Nuñez." Vlanoc's voice was bored. But they waited as Nuñez coughed his ugly rasp, the blood from his mouth flowering the cobbles.

The cough contained, the blood spat, Nuñez called out, "Not the German, the American—he is gentler. I prefer him to marry me."

Vlanoc and his two *pistoleros* shouted with laughter.

Jake Starr neither laughed nor uttered a word, only an imperceptible shudder moved him; he withdrew his gun from its holster and stepped briskly to Daniel Nuñez' side.

"You and I, *Capitán*, will be tombs together among the flowers in your universal city of the dead, and the dogs will piss on us."

Jake raised his gun and put a bullet into Daniel's brain.

XVIII

THE FOLLOWING MORNING, an I.B. man appeared at the University Hospital with a note for Sarah. Upon reading it, she asked a colleague to take charge and hurried away. A few minutes later she stood before Jake on the second floor of the Moorish *casa.*

She had never before seen him this way, sitting on the bed huddled in on himself. "What's wrong?" she asked.

"I felt I couldn't live another minute without seeing you, that's all."

She took his head in her arms to crush it against her breast and began to rock him, whispering words of love to him. His hands held on to her tightly, and she felt a moistness at her breast and realized he was crying. For many minutes he wept this way. When at last he stopped, he sat up. He saw her love, no pity, and he took her into his arms, this time with a ferociousness as if he wished to mark her bones as his. It wasn't really necessary, she thought, she was already marked as his. Indelibly.

Abruptly, he released her and stood and began to pace back and forth. For the first time since they had become lovers, in fact since she had first met him, she saw him as an ordinary man—not an ordinary man, as a vulnerable man. Before, even with his sagging shoulder, the scar underneath the dressing like an ugly purplish flower, he had seemed invulnerable to her. Now she saw him vulnerable, subject to the frailties of man, he could be weak and could want her to the point of despair, and he wept—he was a man, as frail as other men, and of course she loved him—oh, she loved him, it wasn't an obsession after all, it was love, tender and gentle.

"There's something I have to tell you—but I can't. It's hard sometimes to talk, to say what's on my tongue, my heart. Lies come easy, truth with difficulty." He hesitated a moment, then continued. "You should go home, Sarah. I'll give you a safe conduct to the border. After that you will have no trouble."

She looked at him with astonishment. "I don't want to go home, I want to stay here in Murcia. Is it because Rolfe is coming?"

"No, not that. He'll come for a few days, and then will go. I wish I could tell you what it is, but I can't." He smiled weakly, turned up his hands. "We've been so close these past weeks, yet there is so little you know about me."

"I'm willing to learn all about you," Sarah said. "Just try me," and smiled.

But he fell silent and she could feel a malignancy in the silence. There were things she hid from herself—saw but pretended not to see. All she knew was that she loved him and that he loved her, and as far as she was concerned that would have to be enough. "I know we love one another," she said, "and that I have been happy with you. Perhaps—"

But he had suddenly decided he had nothing more he wanted to speak with her about, to hell with it, and he stopped her lips with an embrace in the center of the shuttered room, then on the bed, where they caressed one another, he with a violence, a bravado almost, as if he wished to forget the earlier scene, his weakness and frailty, to overcome it with violence and bravado, and she also, wishing to forget the moment of malignant silence, some evil which he concealed. So with the death all around him, the images of death, and the crumpled bodies of death, he somehow, and she too, was able to make love, an odd love—without fire, with a cold violence, a cold passion, necrophilic almost, as though they were going at one another with knives to dissect each other, and he couldn't keep Daniel's words out of his brain, The American—he is gentler. I prefer him to marry me, and the vision of Daniel Nuñez sliding to the floor, dead, the blood from his brain a thin red trickle, and he seemed to be trying with all his strength and passion to pass on his burden to her, to bury it in her, here, you carry him, it's too much for me. And he understood as they fought with each other in this passionate violation that that was why he had wanted to tell her, to have her share his guilt with him because she was so damn blind, loved him with blindness when it was obvious this man she loved was an executioner, how could she love him if he couldn't love himself? She refused to see what was so plain to see, so that he had to carry the guilt by himself, which of course he should—why should he burden her with his guilt, his shame? Because you can't live blind on this earth, you have to see.

And she fought back with passion and equal violence. What was it he wanted from her? She gave him love, wasn't that enough? What is it you want from me? she wanted to cry out in the violence. My life? Or life?

Then, since there is mercy, they slept, nestling, his hands grasping at her splendid femaleness, as if he wished to prevent himself from vanishing, falling into the void, from hearing the wail of her cry.

And he could still hear her wail the next day as he stepped around the dead blond boy Heinz shot in a Murcia whorehouse. The boy's mouth, open in frozen astonishment, dribbled saliva. "The usual," he told Heinz. "The square in the morning. Tag a sign to his chest, 'A fascist killer,' or some such. If there are any more around, they'll get the point."

"And the Pole?"

"The lobby of La Pasionaria hospital, a guard of honor, a Red funeral, that's the least he deserves. Fought for three months at University City with a lousy gun and three bullets and ends up this way, his throat slit by a fucking English fascist. *Salud.*"

"*Salud.*"

Starr stalked out into the *paseo,* a tall bruising man whose sagging right shoulder, one could see through the purple-sweated shirt, was heavily bandaged. He wore canvas *alpargatas* and khaki corduroy ski pants and a thick leather belt from which hung a black Luger, a *memento mori* from some Nazi officer who had fallen at The Road.

Half-naked belly-swollen *niños* scavenging the garbage in the narrow cobbled *paseo* danced frantically before him to beg for pesetas. He scattered a handful of Spanish copper among them and hurried his step, for it was difficult even for him to look at these children with their hunger-deformed filthy bodies and pus-draining eyes. Spain.

As he strolled to his office, he could see the snarled lengths of the narrow *paseos* which connected like bent wire spokes to the hub which was the market square of Murcia. He glanced at his watch. Two o'clock; siesta. She would be waiting at the usual table of the outdoor café of the Reina Victoria hotel drinking orangeade under the torn blue canopy. He realized his back was itching, cursed, but did not scratch. Goddam tic!

He ran up the creaking wooden stairs to his office, washed, changed his shirt, made a note in Verdad's journal concerning the murdered Pole and the English fascist, hurried down again. As he strode into the *paseo* which would lead him most directly to the Reina Victoria, he unconsciously rearranged his expression from the blank sullenness of a *pistolero* to that of a young man on his way to meet his girl. This time his chest began to itch, he started to scratch, caught himself. Damn thing was getting worse. Must be something he was eating, perhaps those idiotic artichokes. Meat and fish had become scarce and artichokes plentiful in Murcia, so for endless days he had been eating artichokes. What I wouldn't do to a steak.

Sarah was drinking orangeade, her eyes impatiently searching for his emergence from one or another of the *paseos* emptying into the square.

She heard a young Spanish voice call, "*Zut, coña, veng' aquí.*" She ignored it as she had long learned to ignore the whispers and the stares. "*La cuñada del capitán.*" "Sssh." Laughter.

Then she saw him emerge from the shadows of the *paseo* into the open sunflooded square and the pain was as it always was, as if his own two angry hands had invaded the privacy of her heart and grasped at it to tear it in two. The terror of his loneliness was too great and she had to close her eyes until his hand touched hers and he sat beside her. "*Naranjada,*" he ordered from the waiter who had leaped to his side, breaking off a conversation with another customer to attend *el capitán.*

They finished their tepid drinks and without speaking rose to stroll *mano y mano* along the Malecón between the palm trees to the *casa moro,* which gleamed white in the siesta sun.

In their room they listened to music, talked. Once, late in the afternoon, she reclined crosswise on the bed, her head cushioned on his lap as he combed her loosened hair with his fingers and she felt an exquisite sadness.

At a quarter to five, the old woman who kept the house knocked quietly on the heavy walnut door. He called out, "*Sí, compañera.*" She entered the cool darkness of the room with

Spanish brandy and little Spanish cakes. He thanked her and she left.

As he sat on the bed watching his love pin her hair with swift driving fingers, she finally spoke. "He's coming tomorrow."

"I know," rising from the bed to come to her. "Carl and the city dignitaries will meet him at the hotel in the morning. You'll be with the hospital delegation waiting for him at the University Hospital. Incidentally, I've gotten you and him a suite at the Reina until he leaves. Rosita will take care of your ward."

He stood at her back so he couldn't see her eyes. "I'll stay with him," she asserted, "but I won't permit him to touch me. Never again. I couldn't."

He took her roughly by the shoulders and embraced her from behind.

She withdrew and sat on the edge of the bed. Bitterly, cruelly, she began to cry.

Coldly, he wheeled and walked to the tall window. He threw the shutters open and stood glaring out over the *huerta,* the fertile plains, to Monteagudo, a shaft of black basalt struck into a crimson late afternoon sky. "Why don't you leave this goddam hole?" he snapped without turning to her. "Go home. I've told you before, I'll give you a safe conduct to the border; before Vlanoc or Roegen learn of it you'll be in France. Quit and forget everything, the movement's not for people like you, too readily driven crazy by an overintensive examination of their asshole." He had spoken more harshly than he had intended.

"Don't give me one of your vulgar lectures. Besides, who was it who was crazy yesterday, clawing at yourself, sick, sending a messenger for me in the middle of the morning with wounded men waiting to be dressed and bathed? Who was crazy yesterday, you or I?"

He kept staring out the window at the mountain peak, his temper reined. "Perhaps we're all slightly nuts. But you hardly less so."

She examined his back. He was right, of course, they were crazy, including herself. "If I go, will you come to me after you leave Spain?"

"You starting that again? I said I love you more than life—not more than the movement. Of course that's my insanity—but being insane doesn't alter the truth. Truth is eternal," he mimicked her. "No obsession ever alters the truth, does it, my love? André Marty's a man of perception—he said I was one of his. I am. I'd even kill for the Party and perhaps—"

She stopped pinning her nurse's cape at the throat, her cheeks suddenly white. "If I thought for one moment you meant that, *Capitán*, my great hero, I would shoot you myself for having touched me with your breath."

He wheeled on her, reached her side in three long strides. How blind could she be? My God, was his love as blind as hers?

She stood to face him, and was startled by the fixity of his stare. Could it be that he was trying to tell her that he had already killed? No, she refused to believe it. That would have been the crossing of the threshold for him. Why did she remain with this man? Why did she love him? There were nights when she awoke and realized how much she hated him, too, and despised herself and thought for certain he was a *pistolero* for the Party. In the luminous clear moment of the night she would whisper the words: *Jake's an executioner.* The point at which love must stop. It took a special breed to kill in cold blood; she had met enough to know: Stepanovich in Paris, Roegen alias General Ernesto at the dinner table in Valencia, Carl Vlanoc—General Truth. Life shriveled in their presence. Was Jake like them? No, she would cry in the dark and force herself to turn to sleep. In the morning, in the bright Murcian sun, she could not believe that Jake Starr, her gentle lover, was a killer. Those poor people like Nuñez lied in their anger because they were treated unjustly. Vlanoc—but not Jake. His love had a purity which was tender and kind, loving kindness. His advising her to leave had been said out of love for her, nothing more.

"I'm sorry," she whispered, lowering her eyes. "No, I won't go home. There is some use for me here—middle-class hands, but quite efficient," and she knew the words had no meaning because it was not for the wounded defenders of Spain's liberty that she stayed, but for her own broken self.

"Then you will have to be his wife for as long as it is considered politically necessary."

"Yes, I know, you've told me a dozen times."

"We have to hurry," he said, taking her elbow and leading her to the door. "Siesta's over, you'll be late, and I love you. Damn me, you make me lose my temper so vilely. I'm sorry."

"De nada, Capitán." She smiled sadly, and he kissed her fevered lips.

The square was drenched in white sun, yet, since it was after five in the afternoon, the mountains had become a deep purple in an insolent red blue sky. The wounded and the nurses hurrying to their hospitals now that siesta was over passed Sarah and Jake without notice. They parted on the Calle de Trapería, he to his office and she to the hospital; they would see little of each other in the next few days, and they were a little sad that they had argued. As she left him she had to admit to herself that he was rarely less than truthful with her. He loved her more than life, he had said, but not more than the Party, and if she stayed she must play out the game with Rolfe who was arriving the following morning on an official visit. The great antifascist professor was coming to Murcia to inspect the hospitals and to speak in the courtyard of the University Hospital among the potted orange trees on

American Independence Day; a simplistic parallel was to be made with the Spanish Civil War. Why, she asked herself, did she refuse to leave Spain as Jake had suggested? Why did she accept the role he and his Party assigned to her to satisfy Rolfe Ruskin's vain self-deception that he had a loving wife. Why? Because love, insatiable, had devoured her self-respect.

At dawn, Heinz and Michel flung the dead body of the English fascist against a post near the open-air café of the Reina Victoria hotel; they attached a cardboard sign to his chest, A FASCIST KILLER, and themselves sat on the cobbles to obtain some rest from too much overtime, for the night before they had been to the *huerta,* near Monteagudo, where they had dumped the bodies of Daniel Nuñez and his comrades into a ditch to be found by the vulture crows and whomsoever.

Jake Starr awoke, ill at ease, unhappy, unable to sleep. Nuñez, Sarah, that stupid English fascist, today's arrival of Rolfe and Sarah's staying with him, how would he be able to rest with the knowledge that Sarah would be sleeping in the same room with another man? Nuñez had been right, he was a dog. How much easier it would be at the front: a gun, the earth, the enemy. No questions asked. In a few days the offensive would begin in the center front, the first major offensive for the newly organized Army of the Republic. The Americans would again be fighting. Their positions at The Road had become stabilized, deep trenches had been dug, dugouts constructed, they played Ping-Pong, had boxing matches, batted a ball around, on occasion went out on patrol, turned back several attempts by the enemy to dislodge them. They were a veteran battalion, with not a few Spaniards in their ranks. And still, according to the letters he received from Joe Garms and the reports from Albacete, there was continual warfare between the rank and file and the battalion leadership, this despite the fact that their new battalion commissar was highly respected and admired.

Mack Berg had written a limerick about one of the comic stars which had caught on and which the men recited whenever the man came among them.

I'm a Comic star named Stu Bland,
Used to sell Daily Workers on Delancey and
Grand.
I'm a party organizer,
An active activizer,
When the workers get wiser—goodnight!

For that they had wanted to hang Berg by his thumbs. Perhaps they should have.

Well, he must find a way to join the battalion, get the hell out of Murcia.

He had a desire to scratch, fought against it with the dialectic—the negation of the negation. It worked and he again had scientific proof of the validity of the genius of Marx-Engels-Lenin-Stalin. Remembered how he had fallen apart the day after Nuñez' execution—yesterday, it had been—no, yesterday he had observed Heinz put a bullet into the English fascist's brain. It was becoming confusing. Lucky for him Sarah had been around to hold his hand. She should leave—he was really hurting her. She'd never learn to live his kind of life. It was his Aunt Eva and Vlanoc all over again. "In our work," Vlanoc had once said to him, "a man can't be bothered"—bothered—"with love, wives, children. We're like monks, married to the Virgin." And Vlanoc had laughed. Rubbed his hands.

Perhaps Sarah would leave with her husband; he ought to arrange it. She would leave with Ruskin, find it impossible to live with him and decide on her own to return to England. A young woman, beautiful, she could make a life for herself. He could never be other than what he was; it was senseless for them to continue. It would be easier for him without her. No matter what he did, he could feel her at his shoulder, stern, indomitable, making judgments. The perfect figure of justice—blind.

He took a swig of cool *vino rojo* from the leather gourd hanging from the post of his bed, punched his pillow into shape. Remembered the English assassin who had refused to give his name. What was the secret?

As he sat up in his bed having this desultory colloquy with himself, he could hear the peasants' carts rumbling over the cobblestones to the square. They would cast their cruel black soft eyes on the dead English fascist and would wonder whether this blond one had truly been a fascist or merely an enemy of the *partido* and would know this was General Verdad's method for informing them that whether they liked it or not the *partido* held Murcia. They would spit; they had been terrorized before—would be again.

Jake stood from his cot, washed carefully, the pain in his shoulder like a thousand toothaches—who cared? Gingerly he dressed, hearing the clatter of dishes in the café kitchen below. He could smell the aroma of brewing chicory, *huevos fritos* for those with the money, fresh bread. In Murcia, the breadbasket of Loyal Spain, there was bread, only in the trenches and among the poor of the cities was there a scarcity. He began to hear shouts and laughter in the *calle* below his window, the shuffling of *alpargatas* on the cobbles like a breathy whistle to the tiptap of high heels; and he heard a boyish voice laugh; then he heard someone piss against the wall under his window, and a shrill childish laugh, "*Aie,* Pablo, y'want some orangeade?"

After a quick bite downstairs, he sat behind his desk, reading reports. The American battalion would be involved in the offensive, he read, and Mulveen, battalion commander, had been promoted to the brigade; Cromwell Webster, presently adjutant commander, was to take over Mulveen's post. Well, Jake hoped Ace Webster would show them all up. Someone rapped on his door. It was an eight-year-old half-starved *niño* with a letter for him. "Where did you get it, *chico?*"

"Un inglés, Capitán." It seemed an Englishman had given the boy a fistful of coppers the previous morning to deliver the letter to *el capitán* this morning. *"Sa-luuud, Capitán,"* and without waiting the boy ran swiftly down the stairs.

Starr tore open the envelope only to find another addressed to Rolfe Alan Ruskin. He rolled the second envelope expertly, loosened its flap, hurriedly read its contents. As he read, he became tense. It had been written, it became apparent, by the English assassin, who, like everyone else in Murcia and half of Spain, had been aware that the professor was arriving that very morning to make a speech.

Most of the letter was the inchoate garblings of a self-pitying madman. Yet in its swamp grew a sickly flower, a limp bouquet, and when Jake reached its very end he squelched a nervous laugh, jumped from the chair, and hurried down to the square.

The dead body reclined against a post like a drunk who had fallen asleep in the middle of a sour belch. Heinz and Michel, half asleep, nodded to Jake as he observed the corpse. The peasants, who had moved their carts and burros from the curb, went about hawking their produce. Who cared if these *estranjeros* killed one another?

Sitting around the tables of the sidewalk café under the torn blue canopy through which poured a blinding ray of white sun were General Verdad and a few dignitaries waiting to welcome the famous scientist. They would escort him to the University Hospital where his wife and a committee of doctors and political commissars would greet him. He would make a brief speech, they hoped, and then have a briefer lunch.

The general and the others sat around drinking coffee or orangeade, ignoring the ugly sight across the street, near the bridge of the Segura River. A necessary evil. The professor would come, they would whisk him away, he would never see it. The sun, its arrogant self, was still rising in the east, skimming the Espuña range. The castle on Monteagudo's uppermost crag still hid behind a morning haze, pink, gold, lavender. As Starr reached the café, he signaled Vlanoc.

At a table away from the others, Starr nodded towards the corpse. "He left a note for the professor."

"WHAT?" Vlanoc almost jumped from his seat.

"His name's Rolfe Keepsake," Jake paused, relishing it. Vlanoc observed him sharply. "He was an English fascist. Also Ruskin's son. Remember? Let's get him out of here."

Vlanoc's burst of laughter bellowed across the square, caromed with a smack off the stone façade of La Pasionaria, and plunked into the Segura. The black turds did lazy somersaults; the square and everyone in it hushed to observe the phenomenon. The river's waters again calm, the market bedlam resumed. Rubbing his hands like a butcher preparing to grab hold of a cleaver, Vlanoc asked, "What does the letter say? Hurry."

Starr spoke quickly. "Keepsake was crazy. He came through the lines with a forged *salvo conducto*, read that his father was coming to Murcia, beat him to it, killed the Pole Witowski, and surrendered to Heinz, pleading to be executed quickly. You know why? For one reason, and only one, or so he writes: so his father could see his body this morning and cry. It seems his father had time for everyone, cried for everyone in the world, but never for him. He wanted his father to cry just once for him. Nuts. Completely nuts."

Vlanoc observed Jake's face through narrowed eyes. Hard,

really hard. He, Carl Vlanoc, shivered for a second. Beware the incorruptible. "You want to see the father cry, don't you?"

"He and Stepanovich owe me a couple of tears." Jake's voice was flat. "But not Sarah, get that body the hell out of here."

For a moment Vlanoc pursed his lips, then said ebulliently, "We will give it a twist even Stalin's eyes will sparkle."

Someone shouted, "General Verdad, he's here," and now it was too late. Carl danced away on his squat radiator legs to greet Ruskin, whose car, the chauffeur mistaking Heinz and Michel for a guard of honor, was being parked near Keepsake's body.

Someone galloped out to the front of the car to signal the chauffeur to back up, but too late. The car door swung open and Ruskin sprung out, a tremendous blue beret flapping about his iron gray head. He turned to the delegation which rose to greet him, his face entrapped by a large white-toothed smile, saw the corpse, frowned, paled, swung away, back, saw it again, and his knees gave way, only Vlanoc's strong arm swiftly hooked round his shoulders keeping him from falling.

A curious silence stifled the square, the sun's shimmer on the cobbles the only movement.

With an abrupt, frantic pull, Rolfe pried himself loose from Vlanoc's hooked arm and ran to his dead son. For a terrible moment he stooped over the corpse, then fell to his knees and began tenderly to caress his dead boy's face. Vlanoc whispered to him, tried to get him to rise, but he flung off Carl's hand and threw himself weeping on his son's body.

For a few fleeting seconds, Jake Starr enjoyed satisfaction. Perhaps Providencio Morales had been right—one morning he would awake to find he had become a hyena.

Carl Vlanoc, an old master, had Keepsake's body dumped into a coffin, draped a red billowing flag about it, had it set in the vaulted foyer of La Pasionaria hospital alongside that of the man he had murdered, Waldemar Witowski, late of the Dombrowski battalion. A guard of honor stood at attention before the red-draped coffins of the murderer and his victim, whose twin funeral would be held on the following day, July Fourth, a good day for a doubleheader.

Vlanoc wrote the report himself, then had it communicated to the Ministry of Information and Propaganda from whence it issued as gospel truth to the foreign correspondents.

Rolfe Keepsake Ruskin, who admittedly had been a fascist, had come to Franco Spain, observed the terror and the lies, realized his error, escaped through flying bullets and barbed wire to Free Spain, journeyed to Murcia to intercept his father on a tour of inspection for the government and ask his forgiveness. In Murcia, he had been assassinated by irate fascist agents, members of Daniel Nuñez' gang, who had also killed Waldemar Witowski, Polish hero, who had leaped to young Ruskin's defense.

Daniel Nuñez, renegade and spy, and his cohorts were slain in a gun battle in the *huerta.*

Disbelievers of the news report were fascist provocateurs who wished to dishonor the antifascist cause, to slander the great Professor Rolfe Alan Ruskin, Nobel laureate, and to besmirch the *frente popular* government of Spain.

Professor Ruskin and his wife, an International Brigades nurse in Murcia, would tomorrow morning attend the funeral of the two heroes. The funeral column of the International Brigades would be led by Capitán Jacobito, the voice of The Road.

Late evening Sarah sat in a shaded room of the Reina Victoria observing Rolfe as he slept. Poor Rolfe. His shocking encounter with his son's dead body had so shaken him that for the first time in God knows how long he forgot about himself.

They had dazzled him with endless flattery and extraordinary attention and honors (and it was rumored beautiful women, too). For months he had been aware of no one but himself. One would have thought that the Spanish Civil War was merely a startling backdrop painted by Picasso before which he could play the great man. Now, suddenly, he stood totally exposed and vulnerable. Sarah was not one to hurt a man when he was stripped bare. She had never envied any man the weight he carried between his thighs; it was said she was old-fashioned, was satisfied with what it was she had been born with—it seemed to her the pleasure was of longer duration and of a more profound quality. Now Rolfe had turned to her and she couldn't refuse him what a wife owes to a husband—a soft breast for his tears.

On the bed Rolfe moaned in his sleep. Sarah rose and with a moistened towel wiped his perspiring brow. She examined him as he slept. Jake had sent Keepsake's letter over to the hotel. She was certain it had not been an act of deliberate cruelty—she knew Jake could be a cruel man, but preferred to believe he wouldn't stoop to such petty meanness. He had sent the letter because Keepsake had addressed it to Rolfe and it belonged to Rolfe, who after all had to face reality no matter how difficult it was. The letter had been the cause of even greater trauma to Rolfe than his sudden encounter with his boy's death.

He read it slowly, cried, "Oh, my God, what he says is true, I had so little time for him. He has repaid me." He wept bitterly, then his body went slack and seemed to shrivel right before Sarah's eyes, as he stared dazedly at nothing. She had been forced to call a doctor for him. The doctor found his pulse was low, his heartbeat sporadic. With the doctor's help she got him to bed; with the help of heavy sedation he slept. Not Sarah.

What would she do? Would she leave with him the following evening, live with him again as his wife? How could she? She loved Jake so completely that she had come to understand at last through her own obsessive love for him his for his cause. It was stronger than tradition, than her moral precepts—there were no depths to which she would not fall for him. She had read the report in *Mundo Obrero* that Daniel Nuñez and his comrades had been slain in a gun battle out in the *huerta* and she related it to the evening before the morning Jake had sent for her and she had found him sick with melancholy. She realized there must have been a connection between his crying of that morning and the events of the previous night. It occurred to her that the report lied (she had not yet read the later, more obscene, report), that Jake and Vlanoc had captured and executed the gentle heretic whose leaflets she had read and admired, never of course daring to speak to Jake about it—another proof of her demoralization—and she had shut off the thought from her consciousness. No, not Jake, not her lover, not the man she had held to her breast and whose hands she had kissed, those loving hands. Still she was unhappy, knowing she was blind and still insisting she perceived all with perfect vision.

She heard Rolfe cry out in his sleep and again she bathed his head with cool water, then softly caressed his forehead. In Valencia she had tried to love him as she had before she met Jake Starr. Marriage after all is not a game. And this man, her husband, was a man who could be admired. No matter what Rolfe had become—a pompous hortatory conspiratorial ass, an extreme egoist who believed that he, *he!*, could transform man—she had always admired his dedication to the search for truth in the laboratory with his accelerators and cloud chambers, for whenever she had seen him at work, whether in London or Valencia, with a discipline he could and would never give up (it was as much a part of him as his fastidiousness), he had to be admired. In his scientific work there was no pomposity, no oratory—only his egoistic dedication—and there his mania for neatness found proper domicile. So he had tried to reawaken her love for him in Valencia, but she knew in Valencia, as she knew now watching at his side as he slept, that she could never again love him. He had changed too much. Besides love cannot be commanded into or out of existence. She wondered a moment, Had she ever loved Rolfe? And she had to answer, Yes, she had. But now she loved Jake Starr, and she realized then and there that she had been living with the belief and hope embedded deep inside her that something would happen which would change Jake—that her love for him would, their love, that raging storm inside her would batter down the walls of his obsessed commitment and, being then freed, he would take up a life with her, a husband with his wife. She supposed, now smiling sadly, that all lovers believe that somehow they are going to live happily ever after. Then she remembered Jake's trying to speak to her that terrible morning a few days before—what had he tried to tell her? Could he possibly have wanted to warn her of his role in the slaying of Daniel Nuñez? To say: *Beware, I am an assassin?* Had he become an assassin? Is that why he lived in that unspoken loneliness of his? How possibly could the man who every day held her in his arms and gave her love, gentle love, yet with such consuming passion that she trembled hours afterwards at the least thought of him, how possibly could that man be an assassin?

Torn though she was by the tragedy of this sleeping man, her husband, she decided she could not leave Jake, not even if she were ordered to do so. Jake would have to tell her to go. And if he did, she would remind him of his offer—the opportunity to escape them both—and she would return to England.

She finally undressed, it was late, and lay down on the sofa to sleep.

In the morning, as they dressed, she asked, "Are you well enough to go? Perhaps we can postpone the funeral until tomorrow."

"I can manage it," he said weakly, pale, wan. Then he asked, "Have you decided, will you leave with me tonight?"

"We will talk about it afterwards." She avoided his eyes, going to the door to open it for the waiter who brought their breakfast.

He followed her with his eyes, then dropped his shoulders in utter defeat. It was obvious, she was no longer with him, was a stranger.

They expected, as they descended to the street, that Vlanoc had arranged a simple quiet funeral for Rolfe Keepsake. Instead, as they entered the square, they were confronted by twin coffins, draped in blinding red flags under a blazing African sun, resting on two horsedrawn caissons, behind which were strung four or five red-bannered horsedrawn carriages waiting to carry them, General Verdad, the mayor of Murcia in a stiff white shirt and red tie, dignitaries of the city, doctors and nurses off-duty, followed by a long column of hundreds of wounded Interbrigaders led no less than by *el capitán*. As Sarah and Rolfe stopped to gape in horror at this simple, quiet funeral entourage, Vlanoc moved toward them. Quickly, he informed Rolfe—Sarah was a mere spectator, to Vlanoc a cipher—of what he had decided to do.

Rolfe looked at him coldly, steeled his spine. "A Red funeral? Though he was my son, he was a———"

But Vlanoc interjected, "None of that bourgeois stupidity, Ruskin. This is politically necessary. We must make the best of a stinking situation. A scandal now is as bad as a political defeat. We must turn it to our advantage. Now get in the droshky and let's proceed."

Rolfe blanched, looked at Sarah, at Vlanoc, took Sarah's arm.

"No," she said. "This is obscene."

Rolfe, hesitant, objected, "Couldn't we have a quiet funeral, just my wife and I? He was my son, but he was also a——" Rolfe could not say the word.

Vlanoc repressed a sneer, became diplomatic. For him. "Your son's a mere sack of bones now, and the man he slaughtered is no different. We can't in the middle of a bloody civil war afford to be sentimental. We can't afford defeats, and neither can you after the plans we have made. Do you understand?" He referred to plans to elevate Rolfe Ruskin to the central committee of the British Party.

How well Vlanoc knew his man. Rolfe hesitated a moment, looked tentatively at Sarah, then nodded assent.

"Come with me, Sarah," he said, observing her with sad, weary eyes.

"No, I am sorry, Rolfe." She wished she could do this for Rolfe, but she had already acceded to too much, and could not go an inch further.

Vlanoc waved her aside with utter contempt. The middle-class is irredeemable. Rolfe glanced at her one more time, then allowed Vlanoc to lead him by the arm through the market to the leading horsedrawn carriage. Sarah went to sit in the café under the torn blue canopy and bitterly observed her husband and her lover meet, shake hands, and the funeral begin.

The caissons began their slow squeaking roll along the stinking Segura, followed by the red-bannered droshkies. Behind them, led by the stiff-backed, shoulder-sagging *el capitán,* the wounded on crutch and cane limped and jerked and slid and marched, singing,

> *Los cuatros generales*
> *Los cuatros generales*
> *Mamita mía,*
> *Se han alzado,* they have betrayed you. . . .

And as they limped and jerked and slid and marched and sang, the brilliant red-shrouded coffins of murderer and victim squeakily rolled along, alternately revealed and hidden by the stinking, winding, murky Segura. . . .

> But your courageous children
> But your courageous children
> *Mamita mía,*
> They did not disgrace you. . . .

When Rolfe Ruskin returned from the funeral he already believed, at least on the surface, that lie was truth. He believed simply because he wanted to believe. It was easier to believe than not. Not an unusual phenomenon. It made the bitter less so. His son had truly deserted the fascist cause to come to plead forgiveness of his father.

Sarah, shocked, saw that he was a man in a trance. She opened her mouth to contradict him, to say, "But Rolfe—"

"Don't speak of it, Sarah," he said in a strangely dead voice, "you have become a bitter, cynical woman."

She closed her mouth dumbstruck, witness to a sleight of hand unique in her experience.

"Rolfe, you must not be blind. You must not." And I? she wondered.

"Sarah, I won't listen," he said fearfully, and walked slowly to the chair near the window, where he sat and stared out into space.

She picked up the letter his late son had sent him and deliberately tore it to shreds. He merely sat on the chair, gazing out the window, absentmindedly unknotting his red tie. Shortly, he napped peacefully on the bed; his son had died a hero's death.

Sarah made a quiet escape from the hotel and went to the *casa moro* where she hoped to find Jake Starr waiting, determined to ask him about Daniel Nuñez. The sight of Rolfe had been enough to convince her that to continue to lie to herself would be just another corruption of self. But no sooner was she close to him than she felt her determination flee. Withdrawn into some private world, he was like a man who by choice or compulsion had decided to refuse all men advent to the wrecked shelter of his being, except for her—the only one permitted to enter—and no sooner had she entered than they were trapped by it together, alone isolated from the world and its reality. Just he and she alone could be witness to the devastation of his being—each depending on the other and no one else.

She flung herself at him and was soon trapped in his loneliness—and was absurdly happy to be there. She loved him as she had never loved him before. She resented every moment of his life at which she had not been present; she resented every woman he had ever touched or even looked on with the hope of possession; she loved him with every part of herself, with every moment of her life. They sat, embracing, and, truly, she found sustenance and strength in that obelisk of loneliness.

After a few minutes, smiling almost bashfully, he asked her if she loved him, almost shyly, perhaps ashamed that he had to ask.

"Of course," she said almost inaudibly, and she saw it made him happy. Then she told him that she had thought about going with Rolfe when he left Murcia that evening, but had decided she wouldn't, and that no one, Stepanovich or Vlanoc, even *el capitán*—and he smiled—could force her to live with a man she didn't love. She would remain in Murcia. "The hospitals can use every available pair of hands."

"There will be many more soon," he said, referring to the coming offensive.

"I'll remain in Murcia as long as you remain."

He smiled gently, pulling her up higher to him so he could kiss her throat. "What will you do if I leave Murcia? I go where I'm told."

"I'll go, too. Nurses are needed wherever one goes in Spain. You won't be able to shake me loose," she smiled.

"And the front?"

"You are leaving for the front?" she cried.

"Sssh, Sarah. I asked you a question."

"There are women at the front, I am no less brave than they—or you."

"Me. I am a coward. I'm afraid of bullets."

"I am afraid, too, but freedom belongs to women as much as to men."

"If you and I were at the front, Sarah, the enemy would have an easy time of it. All you and I would be doing would be making love. I can't be with you ten minutes without wanting to—" and he took her head between his hands and covered it with kisses. "Would you really go to the front to fight? You would carry a gun?"

"Yes."

"To fight for freedom or because you wanted to be close to me?"

"Both equally. Freedom and love are equal."

"You're being romantic. Love is a tyranny."

"Yes," she admitted, "it is." She wanted to ask him about Nuñez but was afraid. Instead she said, "If we cannot risk death together fighting for freedom, then how possibly can we risk living together in love?"

He looked at her in admiration. "You're teaching me the meaning of love, Sarah, and perhaps of freedom. I hope it isn't too late."

"Too late!" she cried. Now she was going to ask him about Nuñez, but his lips had become busy elsewhere. He had gently forced her thighs apart and, leaning over her, had raised her sweet cup to his lips. She parted her knees, and lay back with her eyes closed, one hand to her breast, the other tracing the convolutions of one of his ears. He drank slowly from her, savoring the sweet myrrh, caressing the very nub of her with his tongue. Slowly he drank and slowly he caressed, and soon she was afloat, weightless almost, on a slightly rolling but becalmed southern wind, warm, undulating, the sky behind her closed eyes opening into vast space the color of delphinium, of cerise, of golden yellow, and she loved him with a peace equaled only by the peace they had discovered together the very first time they had embraced that night in Paris, only this time there was no trace of guilt, he was her husband and she his wife, she was more married than she had ever been, and suddenly she was not afloat, and not becalmed, for he had paused to say, "I love you," and then returned to his caressing, his hand beneath her raising her slightly to his lips so that he could drink more quickly, and the vast space behind her closed eyes changed color rapidly, the blue and yellow and cerise merging into lightning streaks of crimson, and her hand clutched violently at her breast and her hand at his ear ripping at it, "Please, darling, come to me," and she heard Jake laugh to himself, refusing to yield up the cup, drinking a long draught without taking breath, the nub of her enflamed by his teeth, until she cried, "My love, come to me, please!" and with a great roaring laugh he threw himself upon her and entered with her into the space behind her closed eyes, pelted by all the colors of both earth and sky.

Then he said in her ear "You're my love, and there will never be another. You're my wife, you're my life, I've tasted your blood and it now courses through my veins."

She kissed him, was about to answer him, to tell him about her love, but they heard the old woman's knock, and it was time to stop speaking of love, it was time to leave. Sarah had to return to the hotel and Rolfe and go with him to the Fourth of July fiesta in the courtyard of the University Hospital at which Rolfe and Jake were to speak. Jake helped braid her hair and they joked and laughed. A change had come over him, he seemed less tense, more at ease, and she felt that somehow they had made an advance in their lives, as if they were concluding a long trek through a wilderness and were approaching a city.

They descended into the street arm-in-arm, and strolled lightheartedly along the Malecón till they came to the bend of the Segura, really a picturesque river, winding among orange and fig trees, then into the empty open square. In the center of the square stood two peasant women dressed completely in black, shawls black and hiding their faces as though they were in mourning and refused even to see the sun. With them stood an old man, also dressed completely in black, and he looked like a thin gnarled blackened cane. About the square in small groups were other men and women similarly in black, all of them in black mourning clothes. Sarah twisted her head about to look for the old horsedrawn hearse, a familiar sight in Murcia. It was not present. As Jake and she entered the square, the two women and the old man spied them and began to move in their direction, the women's black shawls flapping behind them ominously. Like three black angels they advanced across the square towards Jake and Sarah, the faces of the two women still hidden by the black mourning shawls. Confronting Jake, the two women lowered their shawls. They had strong weathered faces, faces of immense dignity and sadness, faces stern with a bitter wrath.

They were Lizeta, the mother of Hector and Guillermo, and Candida, the mother of Rolando. Startled and frightened, Sarah stared at the two women, wondering what they wanted of Jake. Sarah looked at him. His face was stone. His eyes were frozen. Only the pupils were like live black specks in the brash red sunlight. He recognized them, said nothing.

His fingers were crushing her arm.

Suddenly the old man sprung between the two women and spat into Jake's face, and Sarah could see the spittle begin to dribble down his cheeks. That seemed to act as a signal for the others about the square, for they all began to move in their direction, a horde of black angels. Jake began to lead Sarah away from the two women and the old man, but then one of the women spoke, Lizeta, narrowing her nearsighted eyes and bringing her head close to Jake's face as he attempted without touching her to walk past the little group. "Yes, you are the murderer of my sons and of Daniel Nuñez who was a noble man, a *castizo.*" As Jake turned to avoid her, Candida spoke with a harsh whispered anger.

"You have turned my son into carrion. You are a murderer; you are a dog."

Then Jake and Sarah were encircled by the black angels, who now began to shout. "*Perro!* Dog! Prick of the dog! Shit of the dog! *Perro! Perro!* SHIT OF THE DOG! PINGA! PRICK! Prick of the dog! Murdering dog!"

Jake, still holding Sarah's arm, led her through the circle. They passed through, the peasants backing away as if they wished to avoid a leper, still calling him dog and prick of the dog and ran after him to spit on him and spit on Sarah, the bitch of the dog. *Carroña!* Carrion! Followed and spat upon, Jake and Sarah reached the entrance to the hotel.

Sarah looked at him again, and saw him for the first time with clear eyes. It was true, he was a murderer. He stared at her, ignoring the shouting and spitting peasants behind him, and he saw that at last she had seen and understood.

And he also knew it was too late.

With an imperceptible shrug of his shoulders, he wheeled about and left her weeping under the torn blue canopy of the hotel. As he stalked away, she ran into the hotel without looking back, a terrible pain around her heart, and she heard echoing through the square and along the narrow streets as they followed him, *Perro!* Dog! Shit of the dog! *Carroña!* Dog! Carrion! *Oh, I love him,* she cried, and hated herself.

At twilight, when Rolfe returned to the hotel, Sarah told him she would go with him from Murcia. He was very pleased, and with great courtliness kissed her hand. They left within the hour, and she could not remember afterwards how it was she had felt during the jolting ride over the pitted macadam road through the *huerta,* over the Espuña range, into the city of Alicante and then to Villajoyosa, a rest area for the International Brigades. There they were led to a tiny villa on a crest overlooking the beach. Rolfe said nothing; whether he was thinking of his son or his next speech, she did not know and did not care.

She sat for a moment at the window, gazing at the night sea, a silent sea, its waves a mere sibilant sighing on the beach, the moon a white albino eye. From the adjoining room of the villa she could hear the riffling of papers. Rolfe was already at work composing his speech for the wounded of Villajoyosa. All the speeches were alike, why did they bother to make them? Jake was an executioner! She wanted to cry out, to wring her hands. No, that was too easy. He was a murderer. And she? She had lodged him in her breast to give him comfort, she had blinded herself and given ease and warmth to an assassin of the innocent. For that she had no one to blame but herself. He had committed the most evil act a man can commit; and she had committed its twin: she had refused to see what had been obvious to see—and merely because she had wanted to satisfy her love. Now she would give comfort to the sorry man next door. He was becoming a megaphone. No. There was nothing to hold her to Rolfe. Nothing at all. It was hopeless. She must escape—escape the megaphone and the gun. How easily the words had flowed—

they were going to fight and die for love, for freedom. She, too. She had betrayed herself as they had betrayed Spain.

Spain could not escape, but she, Sarah, could. To some dark corner to heal her heart.

As the old men and women of Rolando's village followed Jake through the *paseos* and *calles* of Murcia into the Street of Ragshops and to his office, he willed himself not to hear their taunts. Carrion! Dog! He willed himself to be mute, to be deaf, and to be blind to the stares of his wounded comrades and to their girls who had become hushed with shame at the fall of the voice of The Road. He willed himself not to think of Sarah, his last contact with a life lost forever. He lived now in a different world.

As he approached the little foyer before the stairway to his office, Struik and Heinz, Michel and Tomás, and several of Vlanoc's guards ran out with guns drawn against his taunters, this rabble, but he waved them aside. It wasn't necessary. Lizeta and Candida and the other black-clad peasants had already turned about to leave the city and had begun to sing, several the *Internationale* and several a chant for the dead—a typical Spanish confusion. As he entered his office he could hear the words of the mass: *Agnus dei, qui tollis peccata mundi: miserere nobis* (Lamb of God, who takest away the sins of the world: have mercy on us). And Jake felt somehow that he had not become stone, it was merely a terrifying chill of loneliness, a total isolation.

BOOK THREE

XIX

THAT NIGHT Jake Starr was ordered to report to Madrid, where he was to act as interpreter for the Russian advisers in liaison with the headquarters of General Miaja.

Under the same moon eye, white, red-ringed, the First American battalion lay sprawled among a huge host sharpening its weapons before an onslaught on an unwary enemy. A few days before they had stolen from The Road, left behind their trenches, their mass graves, the olive trees like a ruin of black gnarled monuments, the bones, and the memories. This was it: no time for memories. The offensive at last.

They had been promised furloughs but forgot the promise. They had come to Spain to fight, and believed with half a chance they would win. Freedom must win, fascism must fall. It was very simple. They would relieve the massive fascist press on the northern front, raise the siege of Madrid, transform the style of the war. There would be new rifles, machine guns, an overflowing arsenal of bullets, tanks, artillery, *avión* —excellent stub-nosed Russian pursuits and fighters. And the enemy would be taken by surprise for the first time. This time the Party was running the show. Organization. Discipline. Russians. An integrated, trained Spanish army. No revolutionary bullshit. The real thing. The anarchists would do as they were told. The Socialists were in the bag. Del Vayo was in the War Commissariat. Togliatti was in Madrid. Orlov, Ernö Gerö, Vlanoc ruled the secret police. Roegen ran military security. Miaja had been flattered until he at last realized he was a military genius.

The Americans were no longer fatigued, cynical. They told jokes. Loved everyone. Believed they had enough to win. And win they would.

Now most everyone was asleep after having celebrated the Fourth of July with hot food, cake, chocolate, plenty of cigarettes. Not a few smoked cigars.

Joe Garms, Mack Berg, Greg Ballard, and Archie Cohen sat hunched together having a drinking party of very bad Spanish brandy. Joe was staring sleepily at a lit cigarette cupped in his hand, wondering if at last it was true, really true. The thought of it made him jumpy, anxious, like a fighter in his dressing room before entering the ring. As he sat there he contemplated the chances of victory, defeat, the size of the enemy, his craft, and his own ability to suffer pain. Death? A real fighter doesn't think about death. That's for crumbums. The thought of going into battle made Joe's heart throb swiftly, with fear, but also with an exhilaration akin to that a man feels in anticipation of sleeping with a beautiful broad. Fear, perhaps, of not living up to her own anticipation of the pleasure she will derive from his passage with her, yet exhilaration at the certain knowledge he would succeed, he would win her love and admiration. The *muchacha* in Murcia from whom he had never heard though he had written her often used to cry in his ear that he was a great hombre, an hombre who gave her glory. Glory. Joe Garms lived for battle and glory.

These four men knew each other so well they could sit for hours without talking, each seeming to know what the others were thinking. The heavy roll of artillery fire in the distance meant little to them; it had become part of their lives. There is a rumble, a whine, a crash, screams, death, and what has lain concealed reveals itself with a stabbing anguish.

Archie Cohen abruptly jumped to his feet and trotted away without saying a word. They all watched him disappear in the darkness. String-muscled, tough-fibered Archie Cohen from Chicago's south side and Bughouse Square, with his sandy hair and freckled face and his flute of a voice. Loved women, indiscriminately: Dresden china or brass horse, skewered or parboiled, didn't matter. Women. It was he who had a fight with Joe Garms after a political seminar. "You guys are a covey of whores—sold yourself to an idea, never ask a question, trip round the world or a blow job, it's all the same to you. I ever get out of Spain alive, I'm quitting the Party."

"Once you're in and yuh quit," Joe said right to the point, "we're enemies. There's no in between wit' us. Enemies!"

Archie piped, all the pols and stoolies heard him, "Then we'll be enemies. I stopped being a whore the first time I read a book."

They squared off, and Ballard had to break it up. Joe, a pro, would have killed Archie, and besides the pols' fingers were itching. OGPU Demo was smiling. Greg had learned. For weeks on end after that Archie and Greg and Mack—who hadn't taken any position in the matter, just stared biting his thin lips—kept guard over one another during the night. And Joe Garms? Strangely enough he didn't sleep either. He kept guard over the guard.

"Why?" Archie Cohen asked him. "I thought you said we were enemies?"

Joe Garms didn't answer, just glared at the ground, then shrugged those lumpy shoulders of his. And Archie remembered something Greg had said—There are ninety-nine watertight compartments to a man's brain.

Now Joe Garms watched Archie disappear in the darkness with affectionate eyes. Then he sighed, lowered his eyes. He was troubled. Becomin' a goddam killer. No feelin'. There was that stupid business in Madrid a few days before. Felt absolutely nuthin'. Goddammit, a man oughta feel bad about somethin' like that. But he didn't and was worried. Knew too many punk killers when he was a kid not to know it ain't good not to feel bad when a guy does somethin' like that. If I don't watch out I'll end up like a two bit punk. Joe wanted to be more than a strongarm. He believed he had the brains to study, to learn, to become a leader of the Party. Most of the party leaders he'd met were pretty stupid, why the hell else did they do the things they did with the battalion? To hell with 'em. If Joe Stalin knew what was goin' on in Spain wit' these dumb bastids, he'd shoot the bunch of 'em. It made him feel better for a few moments. He took a puff on his cigarette, carefully hiding the glare in his cupped fists, even though it wasn't necessary here. Looked at Mack Berg, saw his gaunt, furrowed face, his little eyes bright in the moonlight, his sour grimace about which he wasn't even aware. How the pols hated this cunyo. Can't keep his mout' shut, always givin' it to one pol or another. He remembered the latest.

I am a young gunner named Demo,
I don't kill comrades with vino,
Despite their great howls
I suck out their bowels
Then spit 'em all over their beano. . . .

Joe laughed to himself. Stopped. Why the hell am I laughin'? Lookit me. I could of stopped. Had plenty time. Yes, he remembered the whole thing too clearly.

Primero, head of brigade *intendencia,* had sent a runner for him. Once in Primero's office, Joe was informed the battalion was vacating its positions at The Road, and was short a truck. "There's only one way to get it, Joe, and you know it."

They always came to him. "Yeah, I know."

He asked Archie Cohen to come along. They requisitioned

a staff car and drove into Madrid, almost getting hit by an artillery shell near the Jarama River bridge from a field piece on the heights overlooking the river. Joe Garms was an old hand. He stopped in front of a small café on a narrow street off Plaza Mayor, jumped out after instructing Archie to back the car up and wait ready to go. Joe figured some thirsty truckdriver would stop for a drink, a quickie, leave the motor running, then Joe would hop in and off. Archie would follow in the staff car and anyone around at the time would think he was chasing Joe and so lay off. That was exactly what happened, except the driver kept his eye on his truck. As soon as he saw Joe slip behind the wheel, he ran out in front of his vehicle with his hands raised. Joe was already moving and did not stop. Archie just managed to avoid the remains.

After they dropped the truck and car at Brigade, Archie didn't say a word, merely looked at Joe quizzically. Joe knew there had been time to stop or at least time to put on his brakes and perhaps the man would not have been killed.

Now he worried because he felt nuthin'. Not a stinkin' thing. Why don't I feel somethin'? He wanted to speak to Mack Berg about it, or to Greg, but was afraid to, what would they say? Greg, perhaps nuthin'; he would just stare at Joe through narrowed eyes, would purse his thick lips, lengthen his jaw, and guess right. Greg Ballard had a good pair of eyes. Mack Berg, who found it difficult to keep his mouth shut, would probably say, "Try to remember you're a human being. It helps." Suddenly, in the dark, right in the middle of the Castilian mesa, Joe saw the Spanish truckdriver standing in front of his truck, his hands raised, and the look of horror when he realized he was going to be hit. Hard. And Joe moaned to himself and held his stomach. Ah, shit, I'm still human, he muttered aloud to himself, and Mack Berg turned his head from his own thoughts to stare at him. He was about to say something, but Turk Drobny, a huge man with a tiny nose from Jersey City, flopped down in their midst. Archie Cohen was with him.

"I've been counting heads," Drobny said. "There are thousands and thousands. It looks like it's gonna be big."

"Yup," said Greg Ballard, smiling in the darkness. "I hope we have covering fire this time."

"And I hope those green kids of the Second American battalion were taught not to bunch," said Archie Cohen, his voice still like a flute even though he was now a hardened frontline veteran. "Shit, I can still remember February 27th. SPREAD AND RUN! DON'T BUNCH! Remember?"

They all did. And were positive they would never forget it. To the last scream. But Mack said, "I have reason to doubt it. When they came up to reserve positions at The Road in June, Joe and I thought we ought to advise them, impart some of our hard-earned knowledge. So I went to Nevins, the battalion pol—and lucky for us he is, he's the only sensible man we've had in a position of leadership since we came to this hellhole of a country. I'm certain if his hands weren't tied by those mysterious forces which guide our lives that he would have sent Cromwell Webster and Boots Mulveen to Albacete to do paperwork, though I am also certain they would frig that detail up as well as the one of commanding our heroic battalion."

The others settled down to listen, they knew him well enough to know he was launched.

"I suggested to Nevins that it would be a good idea for someone who had been at the front continuously since the middle of February to give at least one or two lectures to the new battalion on what fighting fascists was like. He realized immediately it was a good idea and made out a pass for Joe and me.

"When we showed our pass to their h.q. guard, he, with some embarrassment—and, I should add, with some awe, having I am sure read about our exploits in the *Daily Worker* and come to Spain in an endeavor to emulate our heroism—well, he refused us admittance. He said he would have to inform the battalion commissar. He sent a runner, and shortly the pol strode from the wings. It was Pat Wagstaff, a spunky little man, much like our Joe here, black curly hair, good jaw, but nose not busted. I explained my views to him: after all, the only frontline vets they had were men who had been wounded in early March or late February—with due deference to those bloody blokes, as the English say—and that Joe and I could dispel any notion they had that this little war is a May Day demonstration, besides informing them about the cunning ways of our enemy, the manner in which the African sun distorts distance, and, of course, since it is indelibly etched on our brains, about spreading out and not bunching. Wagstaff listened courteously enough to the end—and refused pointblank, his eyes cold as steel.

"I must confess my usual good nature"—Archie and Joe brayed, Greg giggled nervously—"deserted me, and I mentioned my low regard for 13th Street generals. Well, Comrade Wag the Bag, the little Stag, stretched his full length, all of five and a half feet—with apologies to Joe and Greg—and told us a thing or two. We were from the uncontrollable, undisciplined, unruly, uncomradely, unholy First American battalion (it sure was good there was no *Daily Worker* reporter around), and he was not going to permit *his* highly disciplined troops, with their fine *esprit de corps* and good morale, to be demoralized by us."

"The shitaaass," Greg grunted.

"Joe was about to slug him," Mack continued, "which would have deprived us of a first-class soldier, for I am convinced Joe would have been shot on the spot. This guy Wagstaff is a very tough *puta*. Joe would have been shot and I would have been asked to bury him. I have great expertise in gravedigging."

Turk Drobny scrunched his tiny nose and looked at Mack hard. "What do you mean? You were never on any burial squad."

"Forget it," Mack said sharply, losing his desire to talk.

"Tell him, Mack," Archie said, "he's a good guy." By which Archie of course meant Turk was one of their friends.

Yes, Mack Berg said to himself, go ahead and tell him. Regale your buddies with your war experiences, it makes them feel better about their own and eases the pain in your very own soul. Words, words, the more you use, the less they mean. He reached out his hand and Ballard passed him the bottle of manzanilla from which he himself had just taken a swig. Mack took a long pull, wiped his mouth with his dirty sleeve, passed the bottle on to Joe, who was lying down but sat up to take his gulp.

Turk, in a basso which shook the stars, said, "C'mon, Mack, you're acting as shy as a girl."

Archie piped, "Don't even think the word. Girrrl. Christ, it makes me thirsty. Boy, if I had a broad right now, I'd eat her. Without hands."

They all laughed. Archie, the muffman.

Berg cleared his throat, again wiped his mouth with his sleeve, and they came to attention. Mack Berg, with his mean mouth, his little sharp eyes, his slovenly habits, truly the dirtiest soldier in the western world, was *their* voice. Jake Starr may have been *La Voz y La Mano,* Greg Ballard and Joe Garms among the best fighting men in the International Brigades, no one denied it, but Mack Berg was the voice of the rank and file Americans in Spain. He was their voice against the hideousness of war, its filth, its ghastly corruption of the human spirit no matter how just the cause, he was their voice against the incompetence of their commanders, the arrogant stupidity of their political commissars. And because he spoke out, always asking the question no one wanted to hear, they existed as a fighting battalion. He channeled their hot air, their just complaints, their ordinary soldierly gripes, he was their exhaust system. And the engine, rid of its pollution, a couple of cylinders missing, it is true, somehow ran. The pols hated him, the military commanders despised him, the boy scouts feared his tongue, but they all had an instinctual knowledge that without him the battalion would carbonate, suffocate, and die. So Mack Berg lived where another would long before have been stood against the wall or, at the least, hidden in the Interbrigade dungeons of Castelldefels or the prison camp of Albacete.

So when Mack Berg cleared his throat, they came to attention. They loved to listen to his well-modulated voice, his precise elocution, and the easy flow of his words even when they had heard the story many times before, as all except Turk Drobny had this one. "One morning in April, early, still night, really, I was quietly roused from my innocent slumber by no less a personage than Thomas Demo, OGPU First Class. 'Comrade,' he whispered, filthying the word forever, shaking his rifle, 'come with me.' I was just about to call my friends to arms—you are my friends, I hope—when I saw what I had supposed to be a gun was only a long-handled spade. My mind, with its usual alacrity, concluded there must be an emergency sapping operation underway. But we headed in the wrong direction.

"I followed Comrade Demo to an area some four or five hundred meters behind the lines. Damn, but the marjoram smelled good. There were two other fellows digging away. Demo shoved the shovel into my hands and left for parts unknown. Still half asleep, I joined my comrades in their labors. They dug, I dug. You're my friends, I'll be honest. They dug, I talked." They all laughed. "We were working for something less than an hour in that hard, dry soil, making good headway. I was, you might say, a somnambulant digger; I was sleepily aware that the trench we dug was as long as I am tall, and I am six feet. I say it without pride, knowing how short men like Joe and Greg bridle at the numeral six when it precedes the word feet. Demo rushed up, looked in, said something that sounded like 'Just right,' and galloped away.

"It was still very dark. About fifty or sixty meters to the north there were rifle shots. Thirty seconds later four men came up burdened by a sagging litter. Demo behind them, a nasty pistol in his fat fist. I awoke real fast. I clambered out of the trench—well, it certainly wasn't a latrine, it could never have been used as a machine gun emplacement. It was six feet long, six feet deep, and two feet wide. Obviously it was what it was.

"They plunked the corpse in. It was wrapped in a blanket and it was impossible to see who it was, and I did not ask. Demo ordered us to cover it. We did, smoothing over the earth when we concluded. Before releasing us, Demo said, 'Not one word.' I wanted to ask who it was so ungraciously deprived of life, liberty and the pursuit of his silly shadow, but for once managed to button my lip. That grave was too fucking close.

"For days I tried to determine who it was. Who was gone and didn't return? Finally the puzzle was solved. Why, it was Pete Black. Did you know him?" Mack asked Drobny.

"No, though I heard of him. A union porkchopper on the New York waterfront."

"Yeah. Another little man, stocky, short that is, with good shoulders, muscular legs, strong arms, and a mean puss. Even meaner than mine, it is said."

"Hardly," Greg said.

"He was a man with a bitter anger," Mack continued, "who made himself obnoxious to all and sundry. He had been a high muckamuck in his union, had worked like a dog to organize it, and he expected to be treated like a working class prince, prick that he was. We laughed at him, but apparently the pols, to whom he was exceedingly rude, not a gentleman at all, took him seriously. In Spain *they* are the princes, he was merely a lowly infantryman. I must add he was also a very sharp poker player. His winnings were enormous—one will get you five that Demo emptied his pockets."

"Why did Demo have him killed?" Drobny asked coldly.

Mack laughed. "Why? Because he was rude? Crude? A cardsharp? Why? Did anyone ever tell us what happened to Charlie Flagg? A man asks for a transfer to the French, it is given, he is led away, and when you ask where he was sent, you're told to shut up. I suppose we'll never know. I read in the *Daily Worker* the other day that a plaque was hung in his union's hiring hall in memory of Peter Black who died a hero's death on the battlefield of Spain in the fight against fascism. Long live democracy. Workers of the world, goodnight!"

Turk Drobny, whom they called the Immortal because he had been three times wounded and had come back for more, sagged in on himself, sad. At last he said, "Why do we go on?"

Mack Berg took a swig from the bottle. Greg Ballard began his nervous giggle, caught himself up short. Joe Garms turned away with a groan.

They sat there, dejected.

Archie finally said, "Ah, shit, let's hit the sack. Tomorrow we'll be killing fascists."

They stretched out on the ground wrapped in their blankets and went to sleep.

But Mack Berg suffered from insomnia, the white moon eye seemed to be staring right at him. He was no longer a believer and felt a great emptiness. Except in his bladder, might as well go pee.

He stepped gingerly over sleeping comrades—bony spines curled about rifles—and headed for the latrine trench beyond a knoll to their left. Once there, he reckoned he might as well go the whole hog.

Under such circumstances, he liked saying poetry. He riffled with indecision through the unalphabetized pages of his memory. . . . Mallarmé, Spender, Auden, Yeats. . . . Ah, found a great one. . . .

The unpurged images of day recede;
The emperor's drunken soldiery are abed. . . .

Was disturbed by a scorpion, had to grab for his bayonet, almost fell in, caught himself, stabbed *it* in two. Resumed. Was at the second verse,

Before me floats an image, man or shade,
Shade more than man, more image than a shade;
For Hades' bobbin bound in mummy-cloth
May unwind the winding path—

when he was again disturbed—this time by footsteps, more image than a shade, striding, ramrod, to a knoll overlooking the sleeping encampment.

A man stood on the knoll, ramrod, flicking a swagger stick at his thigh, coolly observing his troops, a mass of blackness, seated before him. With a curt nod, the man began a peroration. Lips moving; hands gesticulating.

Onward! *Venceremos,* my brave men. *Pasaremos!* The day shall be ours.

The peroration concludes, the man bows stiffly, a mere shadow of a nod, an Errol Flynn smile—white teeth in the night—as the black nothings before him rise to their feet, their mute collective voices cheering their heroic commander.

Hip hip hurrah! Their commander stands easily. Napollington. U. S. Granite. Churl Flint of the Bunghole Lances.

Now the commander raises his wrist, all officers do likewise; they synchronize their watches.

The commander strides, ramrod, from the knoll; is now among his troops who give way in awe and respect, laugh heartily as he slaps their asses—hit that line!—cool, bemused. The albino eye is the dawning sun.

The commander positions his troops. Observes them carefully, calculatingly, one eye cold, the other blackpatched, one arm in a sling, the other flicking the swaggerstick. Suddenly he snaps the stick. You there! A man changes his position a notch. The commander smiles, nods curtly. Himself strides, ramrod, to a machine gun emplacement. Himself lifts the gun and emplaces it at another position as his men observe him. A regular guy.

Now he stands, ramrod, before them. His eye of steel observes the sweep hand of his wristwatch, his swaggerstick held high.

Zero hour!

In classic style he leads the charge.

Good show, good show.

A momentary panic. The enemy has made a breakthrough. Without a moment's hesitation he plunges in where heroes are seen to falter. The enemy thrust is thwarted. He raises his left leg. Farts. Twists his lips into a sneer of contempt for the death all about him.

He strides, ramrod, brave, heroic, to the knoll.

Commander of the night.

More image than a shade.

A mouth that has no moisture and no breath
Breathless mouths may summon;
I hail the superman;
I call it death-in-life and life-in-death.

Mack wants to laugh, but he cannot. He wants to weep, but he dares not.

For the solemn night eye turns into sombre light on the image playing at pretend, and he sees that he is Cromwell Webster, the closest he's been to battle in four months.

Mack wants to cry out to him. Webster—Ace.

And then he sees Ace Webster is standing there under that pallid eye. And he is weeping.

So Mack quickly finishes his personal task, taking great care to make no squib of sound. He has no heart to have the man see himself reflected in his pitying eyes. Then Mack sits by an olive tree, waiting for the man to leave.

Soon the moon vanishes behind a black veil, and Webster disappears.

Mack now makes his escape, praying that Ace Webster has made his.

Sadly, Mack ambles on his long legs towards his friends, and near a eucalyptus tree recently gashed by a trench mortar, its blood clotted, still standing erect, a very brave soldier, he bumps into Cromwell Webster.

Mack nods and tries to pass on without a word, but feels his arm held by strong fingers. Ace Webster is a tall man, beautifully built, a model for a classic bronze statue. A soldier, they had all decided long ago, he would never be.

"Mack," he says in his high-pitched choirboy's voice.

Berg doesn't speak a word, just removes one by one Webster's clasping fingers. Twenty minutes before he would have fought a desire to break them one by one. He has a great feeling for the man now—a deep well of pity.

"What y'got against me, Mack?"

"Let's forget it, Ace," Mack says, trying to push ahead, but again his arm is in Webster's grip.

Now Ace Webster whines. "Tell me, Mack—what y'all got

against me?" It is an ugly whine, like hot wire singeing the hair of Mack's neck. It stinks and he wrenches his arm free.

But he makes an effort, for he still sees Webster on that knoll. Napollington. U. S. Granite. Ace wants so hard to be brave. Trying, Mack says softly, "I told you a long time ago. Remember?"

"I didn't ask the pols for a command, y'know that, don't yuh, Mack? Don't yuh?" An ugly whine; an Uncle Tom whine. It stinks.

"Yes, I know," Mack says, still softly, still trying, hoping, therefore believing, it was true.

"So what y'got against me, Mack? What have all the guys got against me?" If only he didn't whine.

"On March 14 when the commander, Mulveen, was off to Albacete to get himself his beautiful handmade Cordovan boots, and the enemy made a sortie and almost broke through our lines you were in command and didn't show your face. Remember? We had to turn them back without a commander. And we lost many men. Remember? When Greg Ballard and Hunt Carrington carried picket signs in the trenches calling for equal rights for whites, you should have known how the men felt, Ace. Those two guys are blacker than you and have fought all their lives for it to be the other way. You should have given it up then, Ace. You're afraid, more afraid than a commanding officer should be. We're going into an offensive, Ace, and we're scared, too. But we want a man who is in the line with us. You'll hide, as you have for four solid months, or you'll panic because you're too scared. That's what we have against you, Webster. Now disappear." Mack finished harshly, breathing hard.

Webster was silent, his face terribly pained, as Mack could see by the moon which had again broken through the clouds. The wounded eucalyptus stood at attention like a guard who hears nothing, sees nothing but his duty. He just stood there, staring at Mack Berg. Deaf-and-dumb Uncle Tom.

Suddenly Berg yelled at him, "Don't you see they're using you for propaganda, a Negro commander of an American battalion consisting mostly of white troops? Give it up, goddam you, just give it up!"

Webster stood dumb, just staring at Mack Berg, his face impassive, seeing nothing. How can he tell Mack Berg that you can't say no to the Party? And that the Party is the world to him? How can he tell him that that very day he'd been promoted to full command of the battalion just in time for the offensive? How? You just can't say no. It is everything to him. How can he tell Mack Berg that even though he had never bucked for a command, that he knows he is terribly afraid, panic afraid, he still is goddam glad he's made it? Yes! he's made it. After all the years of pushing, of wanting, without asking they've given it to him. Commander of the First American battalion of the International Brigades. In the history books. *They* have given it to him. Ace Webster, born an Alabama nigra, moved to Chicago, grew up in shit—shit boy, shine my shoes; shit boy, get your ass movin'; shit boy, you evah fuck your sistuh?—grew up to become a goddam good Party organizer. He's made it! His picture in the papers, Captain Cromwell Webster. Major Cromwell Webster. On top looking down—when he has the guts to open his eyes. Ah, shit, there's no pleasure in life, jest no pleasure. You get what you want, you push, want—wanting all your life to be on top, looking down, to be what you aren't, and there you are without asking, without pushing, and you're on top looking down. And you can't keep your goddam eyes open for being scared. No, life ain't no pleasure; jest ain't no pleasure.

So Ace Webster said nothing, merely stood staring at Mack Berg, seeing nothing.

Mack became impatient, started to leave Webster, decided

to say a few more words. Might as well finish it. "I've heard the phoney rumors started by your stinking pols that I'm envious, that Greg's *politicallyimmature,* the usual line of crap, that Joe's jimcrow, others also. No one ever said a word about you precisely because of your color. 'Leaflets' Webster is all they ever permitted themselves because of that first day you were up in the lines and you yelled leaflets instead of bombs. Well, you were blind then, you are still blind. But none of us ever said a word because of your color. I repeat that so you understand. Except Greg and Hunt. They said we were jimcrow upsidedown. The worst condescension of all. And they're probably right. I'm not saying we didn't want to call you a black bastard, we did, but we didn't. Now you'll probably go back and tell the pols what I've said. Well, tell them for me that all of us, and Spain, too, would fight fascism a hell of a lot better with less help from them."

That was it. He wasn't going to utter another word.

He waited for Webster to speak—to say just one word in his own defense. Nothing. His lips moved, he wet them with his tongue. No, nothing. Dumb. Mack felt a moment's compassion for the man—in truth, a very brief moment—and then it dissipated, went and got lost on the Castilian *mancha.*

So Mack Berg left Ace Webster standing there under the white sad blinking eye, the wounded eucalyptus at abashed attention, sunk in on himself, dumb.

XX

An hour later, the Americans were roused, time to kick off. And there was Boots Mulveen, their commander, and Cromwell Webster, adjutant. A few encouraging words were spoken by Mulveen, then a stutter from the inarticulate Webster. He, they were informed, was their new commander. Mulveen had been promoted to Brigade. The pols and the boy scouts cheered. The rest of them bit their lips, fiddled with their guns. Someone muttered, "Maybe we'll be lucky and he'll be killed right away."

Archie Cohen said, "Amen."

They marched all night towards Valdemorillo, marched through the Castilian *mancha* on roads clogged with troops of the Republic, tanks, *camiones,* staff cars inching forward and back. Once they saw Jake Starr in a staff car with some Russian *consejeros,* advisers, and he grinned and waved to them when they called out to him. "Hey, Jake!" and he yelled, "*Suerte, mucho suerte.*"

And they suddenly felt themselves to be part of a huge army on the move for as far as the eye could see and they forgot everything but the anxiety in their stomachs at what the coming battle would bring; also an exhilaration which came with the hope that victory was at last possible, it was there all about them, a joyful contagion which touched all the men involved in this vast undertaking, many of whom could remember with a distinct and fine recollection the horrors of

February when they had fought almost as individual men with unfamiliar rifles and a poverty of bullets and leaders. They would not now require a voice to give them courage against the enemy, for they had themselves, proven now, tempered, wily, skillful. To hell with Webster, to hell with Mulveen, to hell with the pols, they were now in the hands, they were certain, of men who directed armies and who had the tools of war.

In February they had sparked their will and hatred of fascism into a holy flame which had kept them from defeat and which had helped save Madrid. Now they possessed will, too, and the rumors which flew among them as they marched through the night said there were two or three army corps, perhaps ten divisions, a plenitude of artillery, and with their very own eyes they saw the tanks manned by Russians, German exiles, hundreds of young Spaniards, and at least one American, Bob Gladd, formerly of their own battalion, a brash, blue-eyed blond kid with Tartar cheekbones and a loud laugh. In the sky above them, they could see and hear the rumbling hum of pursuits and fighters like hordes of murderous mosquitoes on a night raid.

It was hot, the scorpions were about, and they marched. In the dawn they bivouacked outside Valdemorillo in a grove of oak, chestnut, pine at the foothills of the mountains. Cool and aromatic, the sun filtering through the leaves like honey. *Café con leche, pan,* sleep scented with pine and the smell of battle, of victory. When they didn't sleep, they talked with excitement, their eyes bright, alternating laughter with fear, exultation with anxiety. Was it possible that they could win?

Night; again they marched. Their mouths were dry, their hearts beat swiftly. The dawn rose and in the distance they could see a dense spiral of smoke from a fire in some town, Quijorna they were told. To its left, closer, they saw a white-walled town, stone blockhouses, stone walls, stone houses, their immediate destination. Beyond, another town, Brunete, and all about them wheat fields, rye, maize, silverleafed olive groves, long slender cypress, and endlessly rolling hills, barrancas, dry rivers, and gullies, the beauty of which was not now visible to their eyes. Their artillery began a continual thumping. Give it to the bastards, give it to them good. They could see tanks spread out in battle formation gently rising and falling as they trundled over the fields, and planes swiftly running to meet the enemy, column after column of Spanish Republican troops deployed for battle. And they themselves began to march faster down the long incline of the Valdemorillo–de la Cañada road, faster, faster, not wasting breath on words, silent in the midst of the cannonading, the rattle and clang of forged metal, honed steel, the explosion of shells, already men were dying, they better hurry, the battle had begun, the enemy, surprised, was engaged.

At the bottom of the long incline, at the foot of a shallow crest, they rested, drank coffee, ate a big chunk of bread. Over and beyond the crest, machine guns were shooting incessantly, there was the snap of rifle fire. A real brawl. Somewhere to the side and below a man screamed. They waited near the road.

Greg Ballard was talking with Garms and Cohen when he noticed everyone staring at a point behind them. He screwed his head about, stared too, pursed his thick lips in disdain. Captain Cromwell Webster, their commander, stood in the shadow of a plane tree, sweating no sweat, lips dry. Webster fumbled with a map, fingering it one way, then another. Lost in a pea-soup fog, Ballard thought. Panic scared. Runners kept coming and going, pointing to the right of the crest, gesticulating wildly, throwing up their hands in despair, turning their backs on him, spitting.

Beyond the crest, the firing thundered, brash, hard, metallic. The Americans observed their commander, waiting, contempt a collective grimace. Three-quarters were replacements, Spanish and American, who had never been over the top. The remainder were from the old days, many wounded at Tajuña returned to the line. The sun rose rapidly, the battle clamored for their guns, and Ace Webster was so blind and paralyzed he couldn't read his map. Well, better to lie there than go into battle led by Uncle Tom. A staff car pulled up, from which alighted Boots Mulveen himself, all shined up, his boots, his pink britches, his gold leaf clashing with the sun. "Stupid," he sneered at Webster. "You so goddam blind you can't read a map? Beat it!" Ace Webster, his sweat glands dried up from fear, stumbled into the staff car, sped away.

Major Mulveen, bucking for general, will lead his troops into battle. With a wave of his hand he led the way around the crest to the right of the town to the edge of a field, near a stone blockhouse. "Battle formation," he cried. "Bayonets!" Erect as a British leftenant, "Follow me, Comrades!" he ordered, leading the American battalion over the shallow crest. For the split second they perched there, they saw the white stone town. Between it and them stretched five hundred meters of an open field, young wheat still green a foot and a half high their only cover. The town, it seemed, was on fire. On either flank, Interbrigaders and Spaniards hugged the earth, shooting and dying.

Mulveen led the Americans, striding erectly, shining like a brand new copper pot. They caught one good look at the battle, fell to their bellies, hoping when they were hit they would die quickly.

The sun was monstrous as they crawled, Mulveen stomping ahead. A general's star is powerful stuff. Zwing! zwing zwing!

Mulveen fell. The men wanted to laugh, but they were just about crying. Mulveen actually was. "Help me, I'm wounded," he wept. Three men went to get him—green men—two were killed, one just stretched there paralyzed. So Turk Drobny, whom they called the Immortal, crawled out and got Mulveen, raised him to his broad back and ignoring those few ounces of steel-jacketed death zwinging about him carried their commander to the rear with a bullet through one ball.

Mack Berg, a nasty bastard, couldn't keep his mouth shut. "Before half a man; now no man." Archie Cohen and Joe Garms laughed.

Greg Ballard snapped, "Shut up!"

Boots Mulveen wept.

They screwed their bellies into the ground, not daring to twitch. That sun was hot. The ground was hot. The fire from those white stone walls down that slope five hundred meters distant had spread over the wheat field and they all thought they were going to burn to death. Just bullets and sun. A command from a voice lost in the fire ordered them to attack. No one moved. Nevins, a pol they respected, commanded them to attack. "We ain't gonna move for nobody." Joe Garms. And he was right.

There was no covering fire from artillery, *avión,* or tanks. They were in an open field. Down below was a town constructed of stone from which poured a solid phalanx of steel bullets. Thus began for them the great offensive. Men had already died. Men were already screaming. It was a romantic war, legendary. Their throats were dry. Canteens were already empty. The sun—that sun. The wheat field already stank from blood, gunpowder. No place to hide. They lay there for an hour.

Now a megaphone ordered them to retire to the shelter of the shallow crest and blockhouse behind them.

They moved then—very orderly.

This wasn't going to be February 27th all over again.

Now they observed the battle from box seats, applauding their team's hits and runs, silent at the errors.

Then, to their amazement, their side sent in a new team.

Americans. The Second American battalion: trained to a fine sharpness, had trained for months they had heard, their morale so high veterans of the First hadn't been permitted to approach them. The new troops slid past the veterans quietly, averting their eyes. Green.

"Bet they bunch up," yelled Garms as the new troops, bayonets unsheathed, took perfect battle positions ahead of them in the open wheat field, flanked by the Franco-Belges with their stogies and guns and the Slav and Spanish troops on the left flank, the English on the right, encircling the town. They did not see the English, they were too far over. The walled town was an endless flame. The tourist sun seemed to be standing stark still overawed by the sight. Fascinating. How quaint are those little two-footed beasts.

"What odds you giving, Joe?" sang out Archie Cohen, pulling out a wad of pesetas—his whore money. Everyone knew and laughed. Archie was the great muffman of the battalion. Once heard that a couple of American nurses had come up to visit the trenches. Went AWOL; stumbled back five hours later, nonchalantly picking hair out of his teeth.

"Ten'll get yuh fifty," Joe Garms called over the battle din.

"Covered," yelled Archie.

They observed the battle.

The Slavs were very good to watch. Very smart. Why not? They had an excellent commander. He was out there with his troops, just slightly behind his battalion at the apex of the triangle they formed, observing his men, the wall, the pattern of fire. Two Slavs would move, then two more, a quick run, a crawl. No big movement, he was taking his time. When he was ready, they would scale the walls with bayonets flashing. They were good. Very good.

The Second American was prettily spread out. They were so fresh, they still shit mustard. Their commander, too. The pol, Wagstaff, Mack Berg had to admit, was very cool. The

First American heard the commander call out an order. A few seconds later, to their utter astonishment, his battalion jumped to their feet, and one, two, three were in very correct battle formation. In that open field, that white stone town aflame.

Every gun in that town took aim in one direction. Their bullets flew like homing pigeons.

"Goddam sonuvabitch!" Mack Berg screamed.

"I tole yuh, I tole yuh!" yelled Joe Garms, collecting his bet from Archie Cohen, as the Second American troops panicked, *bunched,* were slaughtered. Mack Berg howled curses; Greg Ballard merely pounded a stone with his fist, muttering, "Shitaasses, shitaasses."

They could see themselves back in February. It had taken Jake Starr a second to see and to teach them. These boys had never been taught. They bunched. A highpowered rifle bullet can go through seven men ass to belly.

The Second American suffered heavily. Many of those still alive fled in wild retreat, their new gear making up a shiny wake behind them. Wagstaff lay dead.

And in their box seats the veterans laughed hysterically: better them than us, slapped one another's backs, doubled over from the sight. A first-rate entertainment.

Greg Ballard observed them, man to man. He wasn't yet as far gone as they were. Perhaps his chance would come later. "Shut up!" he yelled. "SHUT UP!"

They did. But no one was ashamed.

So it was up to the Slavs, the Spanish, the Franco-Belges, and the unseen English. They had been informed they would have artillery to soften up the town; *avión,* too. Nothing showed. It would have to be rifle fire, machine guns, bayonets, and tin cans against those stone redoubts. It took the entire day, but they took it.

The Americans, too. As the Slav commander inched his men into that safest position of all, close to the wall under the enemy fire, a blind spot, Joe Garms no longer could hold his water. "Let's go get 'em," he yelled, bayonet pointing, and began the long lope down the wheat field, his comrades of the First and Second now impatient behind him. The Spaniards, the Americans, the Slavs went over, bayonets like slender steel spires flashing red and lavender in the blazing twilight. The Franco-Belges followed on their flank, flinging tin cans into the enemy's gullet.

Pasaremos! they screamed. *Pasaremos!*

So they stormed the redoubts, the walls, the gates and took the town. "A town so big, yuh belch, you're out of it." Joe Garms.

The English they did not see at all.

The victorious troops shared the spoils: fat boned sardines, much bread, eggs, canned milk, dates, figs, oranges, casks of *Jerez oloroso*, and slabs of pork and beef from the enemy stores. "The enemy soldiers are starved, will surrender," had lied the pols. A man came to Spain, lived through February and four months in the line without deserting, and they thought they had to lie. Now they kept their mouths shut. The enemy, may he rot, fought well, fought like hell, took his shellacking, retreated. Orderly, too. The only ones starving in the town were its populace. In their patched black, their angular torn faces, their careworn eyes, they greeted the Republican troops with open hungry arms. Liberty, at last. They were fed from the spoils of war.

And then they saw the English. A survivor told the story.

They had approached the town on the extreme right flank. They had approached the gates, prepared to storm them. Before their astonished eyes, the gates opened, by themselves it seemed. They stood a moment in the stillness. From the open gates as from a beggars' cornucopia trickled a bedraggled, bellybloated blight of old knock-kneed men, dried prunes of women, and pus-eyed children. The fruits of war. The English cheered, for now it seemed the battle had been won. But the cheers became a cry of woe, for behind the villagers, guns on the ready, grins on their faces, stood the *falangistas* and their Moorish mercenaries.

Mad, fine Englishmen. They ducked into a gully, didn't fire a shot. Innocent blood is for the carrion crow as the heaven's face stares with its inscrutable eye.

The English died by the score—and fired not a shot.

Greg Ballard plodded ahead. They had left the walled town two nights before, led by Webster and Nevins, the battalion pol. They marched through a vast open country of rolling hills and dried-out tributaries of the Guadarrama River, burros to help carry their tools of war, the rest on their backs. Thank God for the night in this country, a night which never came soon enough. That fireball in the sky dried out a man's blood, scorched and dehydrated the land and the men on it. For two days they had been lost, separated from Nevins and his troops, wandering like the tribes of Israel in the wilderness. Scraggly trees like beheaded men, arms outstretched pleading for life, mesquite, yellowed gorse, scorpion, vicious lizards, desert mice made up their world. Ballard thought of the sea at North Truro and moaned. There the sun yielded to the sea, but here the sun never yielded, only varied its color: yellow, orange, red, white. It made a man wild, hot-tempered, dried him out, yet never enough to kill. That was left for the bullets or the bombs or their clumsy commanders. The enemy had its own variety. The sight of the English outside the walled town made him shudder.

The man in front of Greg stumbled, fell to all fours. As Greg reached him he stopped, helped the man to his feet, kept going. Neither spoke a word. During the day, as they wandered, they encountered enemy tabors, fought, killed, and were killed. At night, unlike this one, they slept. The fatigue was like a plague, yet asleep he dreamt wild dreams derived from the sun and the death and the hatred for the enemy and for the pols and Ace Webster. He hated Webster. In the last day or two he believed he was going mad with the obsession of it. Yet when he slept he dreamt wild dreams, sometimes a bacchanal with all the women he had ever known in reality or in the movies or in books. He laughed to himself at the thought. One night Jean Harlow, another night Ursuline Washington who'd lived next door in Woods Hole and had been as sweet as a caramel. Oh, Christ, those little girl breasts, chocolate kisses—and the harshness of her tongue. Where was she now? The Cape hadn't been big enough for her. She had ideas, to be something big, to be something hurtful, she weren't gonna live with no fisherman. Ah, they all had ideas. Ursuline and Ace Webster and Greg Ballard and Loney, too. To be what they weren't. It was like a nagging leech sucking them dry. A starfish. To be accepted by the world. To be ogled by the world. Look at me. ME! Accepted? No, not him. He didn't want acceptance. He just wanted to be Greg Ballard, five by five, brown skin, smashed black face. He wanted to be himself, at peace with his dreams, no obsessions, no naggings. He supposed that was what most men wanted. But his dreams were wild, and yet awake he found he had lost his sense of touch, his sense of smell. He was a man who needed peace, the universality of the sea, his boat on the galloping sea. How could he be so dried out, so tired and still have those wild dreams? A dog would already have died, its bones dry white in the yellow sage. But he was a man: he dreamt.

Up ahead he could hear Joe Garms singing,

Snatch a little kiss in the mornin',
Kiss a little snatch at night . . .

Greg Ballard plodded ahead, tired, bushed, beat, obsessed. In the distance under a bright night sky he and his comrades could see a group of hills like a herd of fat cows fossilized by time. They had to reach those hills by morning and as they marched the hills didn't seem to come any closer. But at least now they knew where they were going.

A few camouflaged cars rolled past them, trucks, ambulances. A pair of tanks clanked out in the field.

And they marched.

Far ahead, beyond the reach of the night sky, thunder and lightning—enemy cannonading. Few friendly *avión* passed overhead; in three days the enemy had regained its superiority and had cleared the skies.

Tired, dismal, tongues like dirty dry rags, they marched.

No one spoke as they plodded on, the momentum of the man ahead pulling the man behind. "Five minutes," someone called. "Five minutes."

Greg dropped where he stood. His eyelids were weighted with lead. Don't shut your eyes or you'll never open them again.

Mack Berg's long bony body was alongside him. Filthy. "How you feeling, Greg?"

"As usual."

"I'm scared."

"You've been before."

"Very, very scared."

"Ditto."

"Are we going to climb those hills?"

"Yup."

"I'll never make it," Mack said, passing him a cigarette.

"You will."

"Only if we get there before the sun comes up."

They smoked in silence.

They heard someone running towards them. Who had the strength to run?

Joe Garms, of course. He slid to a standstill, rolled from foot to foot like an ashcan emptied of its refuse.

"Take it easy, José José," Archie said, coming up at that point.

"Jake Starr," Joe said.

"Give him a drink," piped Archie. "He's gone nuts from thirst."

A tired laugh from the men around them.

"He's wit' a Russki," Joe said.

"Punchdrunk," Archie snickered. "Get the paddy wagon."

"Yuh dirty bastids, he's talkin' to Webster up there. Warnin' him."

They ran with Joe to say hello to Jake Starr, who had come up with a Russian staff car. There he was, tall, brawny, sagging shoulder, very tan, with a Russian Nagar pistol on his hip, wearing beautifully tooled Córdoban boots, the mark of a leader in Spain. His eyes looked very hard as he spoke in a very calm voice to Ace Webster. Alongside Starr stood a lanky, lean, straight Russian who smelled of perfume and had powder on his face. As Jake spoke to Webster, the Russian kept pulling on his sleeve, hurrying him along. When the boys came up, Jake stopped talking for a moment to give them a quick smile. He was warning Webster to be very careful. "I ran into the Dutchman, the commander of the Franco-Belges. As you know there are tabors of Moors and *requetés* all over the mesa and they know how to fight. He told me he was badly mauled yesterday. A company of Moors showed themselves to him, without thinking, he charged, and they led him into a machine gun trap in a pine wood. Be careful, Ace. Keep your wits about you. Don't go where you don't know." The Russian kept pulling on Jake's elbow, and Jake kept ignoring him.

"Of course, Jake," Webster piped in his high-pitched voice, swishing his swaggerstick. He was acting very much the commander. "Thanks a lot, but I know, yes, thanks."

Starr shook the Russian off a moment. "Those are the heights of Romanillos," Jake nodded in the direction of the hills. "Nevins is already there and engaged. Hurry up, he needs you. *Salud,* and be careful. Okay, okay, Tovarich Lipin, I'm coming," he said to the Russian. But before he slid into the staff car, he hugged Joe and Greg, told the rest of them to be careful. "Watch the *requetés,* they're tough and cruel. Can commit an atrocity and sing a hymn to God simultaneously. *Laudamus te,* they sing as the blood runs."

"Okay, Jake," they said. "Okay, we'll watch out for them."

Before Jake turned to leave, Archie Cohen approached him and with a smile on his face withdrew something from his pocket and showed it to him. It was a lead bullet with teeth marks impressed on it. Jake stopped a moment, looked at Archie, smiled. "I never got to thank you men properly."

Archie became tongue-tied before the great Jake Starr. But Ballard said, "We better move along before the tears begin to flow."

Everyone laughed, and Jake waved and departed, the Russian hurrying trippingly behind him.

The Americans watched the car until it was lost in the night, then resumed their march. With fear. If that could happen to the Franco-Belges led by the Dutchman, he of the red hair and the beard like a burning bush, it could certainly happen to them led by Ace Webster. They were wary now, their fatigue left them. In the distance, near the heights of Romanillos they could hear incessant shooting. They followed behind Webster, also a tall man, dressed in beautiful breeches, highly polished boots, an Ascot tie, a khaki chambray shirt, swaggerstick flicking at fireflies. At three in the morning, they bivouacked, drank hot coffee, ate their usual chunk of bread. The clump of hills was still at a good distance, dominated by a large hump in its center. They would reach it sometime that morning.

"Let's go," ordered Webster.

They followed after him in a ragged line. He was looking more and more like a commander. Well, perhaps he would come around. It had happened to others, why not to him?

It was still night, the moon was very bright, but it was hot. The day would again be a flame, a blast, a furnace, a cauldron. Marched over a shallow hill, into a barranca, up out of it, over another shallow rise.

Spotted a company of *requetés.*

"The trick!" Mack Berg shouted. "The trick!" It was a good thing Jake Starr had warned them. Without waiting for a command they spread out, set up machine guns, beautiful Russian Dikterevs, unsheathed bayonets. They would take these bastards. But the enemy wouldn't fight, merely retreated slowly, sort of beckoning them to come forward.

"C'mon and fight," somebody yelled at the *requetés,* those of the sacred heart.

But perhaps Ace Webster hadn't heard; perhaps he had already forgotten what Starr had told him; perhaps he just panicked; perhaps he wanted to show the world. He ordered battle formation and a charge at the *requetés.* They were soldiers. Many were still green and thought the veterans too damned ornery. They did as they were commanded.

As they charged, bayonets fixed, the *requetés* began slowly to retreat towards some trees. The Americans, led by Webster, scenting a quick victory followed them on the run.

Into a steel trap set in a cypress wood. Into a trap sprung for them; into the wood without knowing what was there. *Hijo de la puta!* Webster had forgotten the first rule of war: Don't go where you don't know.

A slaughter. And they couldn't extricate themselves. The

cypress trees stood in perfect rows, each row controlled by an enemy machine gun. A man stuck out his head, he was dead.

The moon, still out, smiled a silly grin. Communications were lost with Webster. Ace was behind a crest of a hill waiting for his troops to come fetch him.

The wood was now deathly quiet. Should they move the hell out of there or shouldn't they? It would be best to wait. Something would break. Perhaps Nevins would come to look for them with his troops.

The enemy didn't waste a bullet. Just waited.

Fifteen minutes later an order arrived. Cohen, Garms, Ballard, Berg, the most experienced, leave your squads, crawl into the wood, see if the enemy's still there.

"I'm scared," Joe said.

"So am I," snapped Greg. "If you have to sing, make it a chant, the *requetés*'ll think you're one of theirs."

"We'll go in thirty-second intervals," Joe said. "Me, Greg, Mack, then Archie."

Okay.

"Put your helmet on, Mack," Greg said.

"You must be blind, I got it on."

They looked at one another a moment.

"I guess I gotta go," Joe said.

"Before you go," whispered Mack Berg hoarsely, "I want to tell you something."

They stared at him under that silly moon. What the hell did Mack want?

"I never went to college. That was pure bullshit." Their eyes popped, but his back was turned to them as he started crawling into the wood, his helmet plopped over his head to his ears, he never did have one that fit properly, the sloppiest, dirtiest soldier in the International Brigades. Oh, Christ, what a time to make a confession. Must think he's gonna die.

"Who the crap cares, yuh big jerk," Joe whispered after him. If Mack heard, he gave no sign.

The remaining three looked at each other quickly, smiled, shrugged, then followed after him. Joe, Greg, and Archie, in that order.

Ballard reckoned it was about three-thirty when he went in. It was pitch black under the trees except where the moon filtered through. He laughed mirthlessly to himself at his own joke: he'd be the most difficult to see. There were advantages to his color in time of war, and even filtered moonlight couldn't change it.

Inch by inch he crawled, making no more sound than a leaf on leaf. The cicadas' chatter was a blessing. He must have crawled twenty minutes, perhaps more, it was impossible to tell. In that time his only encounter had been with tree trunks. Not even a corpse. They're gone, he thought. Vamoosed. He kept going, always wary, the wood couldn't be more than a couple hundred meters deep.

Saw a form, became abruptly inert. He stared at it for what seemed hours. There wasn't even a breath from the form. Must be a dead soldier. He inched closer, his heartbeat a clatter. Closer. Discerned its contour. Had to hold his mouth to cage an hysterical laugh. A dead burro.

Kept moving. Saw moonlight, a klieg. Was at the other edge of the wood. All he confronted was the moon's silly grin. They were gone. Decamped. Not even a sardine tin remained.

The sky was changing color. Must be four o'clock. Dawn would come early. It was July 9th, he remembered. An early dawn. Must return now. Be careful, they're pros, know their business. War. But he moved faster now, for the darkness in the wood was graying.

Dawn was at the threshold of day when he returned to the beginning of the wood and found his squad. The moon was a pale silver hoop in the gray sky. Long flashes of blue and orange. Archie and Joe were already there. They had found nothing. The enemy had done their work, decamped.

They waited for Mack Berg. Soon he would return, his pisspot, as he called it, down to his ears, and they would laugh. To us you're a Harvard grad. Phi Beta.

"Report to the commander," Joe instructed Archie. "When Mack gets back we'll get the hell outa here."

Dawn now crossed the threshold and daylight was at their backs. Still no Mack Berg.

When Archie returned, daylight had already pushed ahead of them into the wood, and still no Mack Berg.

"The *requetés* are gone," Greg said. "We have to go find him. Stuck by a scorpion. What else?"

In they went, Joe, Archie, Greg. They were breathing hard. Walked now, guns and bayonets on the ready. Went clear through to the very end of the cypress wood. No Mack Berg. They moved over five rows of trees, started back. Each was afraid to look at the other.

Halfway back they found Mack Berg.

His helmet on his head, his head on a stake, his genitalia stuffed in his mouth. His headless mutilated body lay against a tree, emptied of its blood, some of which had been used to scrawl a note now pinned to his chest: *"Buen apetito."*

The *requetés* were very gentle.

Laudamus te, they sang.

Benedicimus te, they sang.

Adoramus te, they sang.

Glorificamus te, they sang.

Greg, Joe and Archie dug a grave, put Mack Berg together again, unweeping buried him.

"Slow," Joe said as they started back.

Neither Greg nor Archie said a word, they were thinking about Mack Berg. The big bastard had known, somehow he had known, and so he had confessed to his great sin. The big fool had never known when to keep his mouth shut. When he was born, he staked out two lines, one for himself, one for life. In between was a battlefield. He raged, he stormed, he was mean, he complained, he was a friend to friends, hateful to enemies, but only the Party could hogtie him. Hot and cold Mack Berg, very, very bold. *Buen apetito,* Mack. They shivved you good.

"Slow, real slow," Joe muttered under his breath as they walked. Still they ignored him. "I'm gonna put a slug in Webster's gut. I'll use the pistol Jake Starr sent me after I left Murcia, it's got a smaller gauge, he'll croak slow. Real slow."

"Shut up!" Greg shouted.

"I won't shut up. Been shut up long enough. Mack Berg did the talkin' for us, now I'm gonna talk. In his gut. Let him die slow."

Greg and Archie stopped, looked at him mournfully.

Joe Garms began to cry.

They sat with him under the slender aspiring cypresses, the sun threading their green with gold, sat with him until his reservoir of tears was dry.

As they stood, Greg said, "No, Joe."

"Okay," he whispered. "Okay, but only for you."

They returned to their squads, what remained of them.

They left their dead for the burial squads and their wounded for the medics.

Sorted their gear, men cursed under their breath, they resumed their march. An inner violence shook them, a violence divorced, isolated from the violence of war itself, the corpses, the fatigue, the firing in the distance, a battle taking place in the clump of hills towards which they plodded. Another ambush and there would be nothing left of them. Many a man raised his gun in the direction of Webster's back, only to lower it, wanting to break it in two at his inability to cross the line into murder, individual murder. They had gone into battle against the walled town three days before under-strength, as it was, and they had lost about sixty men, dead and wounded, in that final bayonet charge led by Joe Garms. They had fought skirmish actions as they marched, lost a few more men. In that cypress wood they left another fifty men, dead and wounded. Here they were at the very beginning of what was to be a major offensive with a battalion at little more than half strength. And where were the fighter planes they had overhead when they left Valdemorillo? Where was the artillery? A couple of light tanks maundered tinnily ahead of them. They plodded behind Webster and wondered what was going on with Nevins at that clump of hills.

They marched. Filthy, their asses bare in their shredded uniforms, led by Ace Webster, a very soldierly man, neat and clean, his boots shined, his Ascot exquisitely ruffled at his strong muscular throat, oh, how they would have loved to strangle him with it. All they wanted was a commander—no Napoleon, no Wellington, just a fucking commander no more scared than they. Brunete had fallen to the armies of the Republic, de la Cañada, too. Quijorna and del Pardillo were about to fall. The enemy had been surprised and almost over-whelmed by the superiority of the Republican forces. Still it was apparent to the men as they marched that the enemy had come charging back in great strength, their *avión* redoubled in numbers, roaring overhead. And they themselves had lost two days wandering about in a daze. Now ambushed. What else awaited them?

But they were told if they helped take that clump of hills the way would be open to destroy the fascist siege of Madrid once and for all. That alone gave them courage as they marched.

Their approach was marked by enemy bullets zwinging overhead. Small flowers of dust sprang up about them. They could see a battle being fought at one sector of the heights. Before them was a series of ravines, rises, gullies, higher rises, all dominated by a hill shaped like a fortress with its tower destroyed by a shell—ragged, steep, and soon easily discerned to be heavily armed and fortified.

They approached in a state of collective rage and madness. Their fury at Webster would be expended on the enemy. In spite of him they would destroy the fascist army for that was their only chance at survival.

"Let's watch that sonuvabitch," Archie Cohen said to Greg Ballard and Turk Drobny. "If he makes a stupid command, countermand it. No more fucking ambush."

Joe Garms called out from the side, "I'm watchin' the fucker, don't worry."

They approached the first short rise, hunched over, guns carried loosely. This time a patrol went over first as they waited among the leaping dust flowers.

Ballard and Drobny observed only Webster. Fantastic how neat the man kept himself, how handsome he was in the sun. That swaggerstick swishing at flies, no sweat purpling his shirt. The man never sweat.

One of the observers slithered over the top of the ravine, waved them on.

The Americans ran swiftly, doubled over. Gorgeous silhouettes for a moment, soldiers poised with guns, wary. They were over the crest, into another barranca.

The sun was a storm of fire. It just poured sun. Hot. Abrasive. Red-hot nails pounded into eyeballs. The firing at their right was heavy, incessant. The enemy on the heights were firing down at them, but the rise of the gully shielded them well.

They could see their comrades led by Nevins on their bellies in the gully at the extreme right firing and moving ahead man by man. There were dead burros around. Dead men. The two tinny Christie tanks took positions at either flank and began pumping their small cannon at the tower on the heights.

Someone among Nevins' troops waved his hand at them, directing them to wheel and turn the enemy line hidden by yet another shallow crest.

"NO!" screamed Drobny, as Webster, without stopping to think, commanded his men to wheel and charge. "A patrol first!"

Too late again, the Americans, seeing their comrades on the right desperately engaged, ran to their aid.

Greg, Archie, Drobny, Joe, all yelling, "NO! NO!" scrambled after their commander.

Over the crest smack into three enemy machine guns.

The screaming was a horror.

They threw themselves into the earth. Ballard fired his gun without end at an enemy machine gun, forgot everything in his rage, just fired, aiming almost unconsciously now. Kill or be killed. For ten minutes the world existed only in Ballard's gun.

It was quiet in the ravine. On their extreme right Nevins' troops were still embattled. To their left, high up, a Spanish battalion engaged another enemy fortification.

The sky was a furnace.

The stillness of death lay on the barranca, an open grave. The grotesquerie of death made a strange, mad picture: the cracked-open head, the upturned palm of outflung hand, the immobile twisted foot of an inert body. Not even the wounded cried out. Perhaps there were none. Perhaps all were dead.

In their barranca, for many seconds: silence.

On their flank the firing was incessant. No one in the ravine seemed to hear.

Suddenly Webster's shrill voice could be heard. "Up and at 'em. Let's go!"

Then Greg Ballard stood on his knees. He turned his head to see the enemy's score. Slowly shook his head. He observed Webster on one knee, resting a neat elbow on the other. Greg's heavy chest was concave, his short body wobbly on his knees, his eyes glazed, fevered. His smashed face, long since not gentle, was screwed up in bitterness and hatred. He rose slowly to his feet, covered by the ravine wall, his short arms dangled at his side, his back humped. With the helmet on his head he looked like the husk of a dead beetle, brown and dried out from many days in the sun. Others about him stood. Thirty men did not stand. They just lay there, immobile, twisted, broken. Bitterness, hatred, madness marked the dirt-caked faces of those who stood. Among them was Archie Cohen. Greg Ballard observed them as they stood, registering them, as it were, counting. If Ballard resembled the brown dried-out husk of a beetle, Archie Cohen in his leanness looked like a gray spider in slow motion, first one leg, then the other, a long arm, the other. Slowly, slowly. Even his blue eyes were gray.

Before him lay Joe Garms, a scooped-out little hole filled with a fat strawberry at his temple.

At Webster's feet lay Turk Drobny, the Immortal, with his fourth wound, his last. He reclined on his elbows, his massive arms his backrest, his belly wide open, his intestines untwining into one of his huge fists. The other held his exposed genitalia which he gently caressed as his blue eyes glared at Greg. "I got it in the gut, Greg," he said unbelieving, his voice a harsh whisper. "I'm gonna die." Slowly he caressed his last treasure, as the blood from his open stomach seeped through his cupped fist down into his blond pubic hair.

Ballard looked at Drobny; then he looked at Joe. Cold to the world. Joe Garms, Hero. Then he looked at Archie. Archie just stood, lean, spidery, gray, staring at the ants eating from Joe Garms. If yuh quit, we'll be enemies, he'd said. And meant it, too. But had stood guard against the pols. After the war, Joe had said. Not here. Now we're comrades. We're buddies. Yeah.

Drobny caressed his penis, dying. "Gut him, Greg," he whispered harshly. "Slow. Let him die slow, before he finishes the rest of you."

Webster stood close to Drobny. He stood easily, a handsome man, sweatless, only his tongue flicking at his lips which were dry. His eyes were innocent. "Let's go, boys," he shrilled in his choirboy voice. "Let's hit the bricks. Let's go, Comrades." He stood erect, soldierly, very neat and clean, flicking his swaggerstick, his boots without blemish.

Those who stood turned their eyes to him. Otherwise they didn't move an inch.

Webster looked from man to man. Where was Mack Berg? Mack would protect him, had promised. He had forgotten Mack Berg was dead. "Let's go," he shrilled, himself standing perfectly still, not moving, covered by the ravine wall.

Archie conferred with two men near him. They looked to Greg, then pointed their heads at a pol who too had stood.

A cavernous voice echoed from down the line, "Fuck 'im, Webster's wore out my luck."

Stepping carefully over dead bodies, Archie approached Greg Ballard. "We've had enough. Too much!"

"Gut him, you bastards," Drobny screamed, pulling hard, bloody. "Hurry up before I die."

Greg Ballard forgot everything in the world, heard nothing in the world, nodded his head, said loudly so all heard him, "Okay, Turk."

Six men, Archie and Greg among them, ringed Cromwell Webster, Drobny at his feet, dying. The silent pol they ignored.

In Cromwell Webster's panicked, frightened brain, it must suddenly have occurred that his life was soon to come to an end. He turned his head from wretched face to wretched face, stood stark still a moment, became again totally unaware. He shrilled his order, "Now, Comrades, let's go. We got fightin' tuh do." He laughed now, unseeing, not wanting to know, no, this couldn't happen to him. Not him. He had worked so hard, had wanted so much to be what he wasn't. No, no, not him. They merely stared at him a few seconds. He stopped laughing, flicked his swaggerstick at an unseen fly. Came out of it with a wild scream. He saw. "It's my coluh, you dirty fuckin' white bastids. It's my coluh. 'Cause I'm black."

Turk Drobny, pulling frantically, looked up into Webster's frightened face. "You dirty bastard Uncle Tom. You sold your color to the pols and they've been peddling your black ass ever since. You're just a fuckin' Uncle Tom."

It was true. They all nodded. The pols were peddling his black ass and they were paying for it with their lives. It's true, Greg Ballard said to himself. He must die so we can live.

The ring tightened around Webster now. He stood there flicking his stick nervously, his eyes bulging, the sun playing about his handsome taut face. On either flank the battle continued. Then he began to scream. "It's my coluh, it's my coluh. You dirty fuckin' white bastids it's 'cause I'm a nigger." On he screamed, and now the sweat poured down his face, into his eyes, and he was raving mad. In one last hopeful scream, he cried, "Black and white, unite and fight."

There was an explosion in the ring and he fell to the ground, his head resting on one of Turk Drobny's massive thighs. Drobny began howling with pain, then grunted, and died.

Not Cromwell Webster. He took his good time.

And those who had killed him, and those who had stood by, became frenzied, mad. They yipped, they danced. Some spit into Webster's dying face. Others kicked him. One man stripped him of his Córdoban boots, Sam Browne belt, and binoculars. Another unpinned the gold bars from his shoulders and placed them on his half-blind dying eyes. Greg Ballard ripped the cap from Webster's head and placed it askew on his own and danced about him. Still another man pissed on Ace Webster's comatose face.

He bloated up from an internal hemorrhage and looked like a six-foot-long worm which had swallowed a hog whole. He turned green, a sickening yellow green.

Then Archie and Greg sat near him, feet akimbo, observing him die. All his blood seemed to flow into his bleeding perforated stomach. They watched him die. Drop by drop. His forehead was no longer black—it was yellow green. Then green white. Then his cheeks, his throat, his hands. Green white. His stomach bloated with blood.

Then, as he approached death, Ballard stood and raised his hand. The singing stopped, the dancing, the spitting, the pissing. Ballard said, "Dig a grave."

"No! No! Let him rot in the sun."

They stuck a pole into the ground near his head, placed his cap and swaggerstick on it, attached a wooden marker. "Cromwell Webster. Black and white, unite and fight."

He died.

Then they looked at one another and no one dropped his eyes. One man who had been in the line since mid-February with a four-day furlough in all that time, a little man, his uniform in tatters, his big toe showing through a canvas *alpargata,* filthy and bone-thin, said, "It was him or us. That's all."

It was midmorning, and the sun was murderous, too. Their comrades on the right flank were still engaged, the Spaniards on their left were digging in.

The battle called.

Leaderless now, they warily infiltrated man by man, cautiously, observant, to their comrades' aid.

Late that night, after having chased the enemy halfway up the big crest of the heights of Romanillos, and then having had to retire to the knoll on the flank of the barranca where Webster had been killed and still lay unburied, they discovered that Joe Garms had not died, and that Jake Starr had returned to the line.

The men cheered, jumping up and down like a bunch of kids.

Cromwell Webster was forgotten, another casualty of war.

XXI

THE VOICE had arrived.

The bitter, angry voice of a haggard man with a sagging shoulder needled with pain, dressed with meticulous carelessness in corduroy ski pants, a faded khaki shirt, a beautifully tooled leather belt for his Russian pistol, a beat-up helmet plunked on his head, clutching a mongrel pooch to his chest. A bruising, sardonic voice, of forced humor or sudden abrupt laughter, prone to rage at inconsequential error or incompetence, contemptuous, arrogant, thus Jake Starr wore the cape and sword of a bullying conscience.

For two weeks Nevins and Starr led the Americans on forced marches over the *mancha* of Castile, over the hills, ravines, gullies, marched with them, crawled side by side with scorpion and salamander, scaled stone walls of ancient cubist Spanish towns and villages, bayonets running red, drove them and themselves with a nervous angry energy, the victories minimal, the defeats major.

One day the battalion, the First and Second combined, hugged the earth for four hours under an oppressive, grinding, murderous Stuka attack with only Starr's brash sharp voice to hammer down the panic; lost one man to sunstroke, one to a scorpion, six to the bombs. And two burros. The Stukas, having dropped their bombs and depleted their machine gun belts, hating to leave, dove to throw the contents of their tool chests; only darkness drove the last of them away. Then, Jake rose to his feet and with a curt quiet command led the Americans on the run up a five-hundred-foot sloping hill to rendezvous with a hardbitten Spanish anarchist regiment to beat off an attack of Moors and Navarrese.

The enemy was competent, did not run, and had the bullets, the guns, the artillery, the aviation, an iron military discipline, and the Navarrese *requetés* at least, a will, a religious fervor not even surpassed by the men of the International Brigades.

At staff headquarters the Loyal Spanish generals and their Russian advisers cursed with a bitter impatience. It was sabotage, it was bad communications, it was lack of matériel.

"It's none of those," Jake Starr said to one of the Russian generals. "We had more than enough matériel at the kickoff. It's the war we're fighting. We had them beaten the first three days—they were surprised, wide open, but we didn't exploit our advantage. Too damn conservative, if you ask me. To hell with the flanks, we should be fighting in depth, using armored trains, guerrillas, small fast-moving combat units. We have the best fighting men in the world for that. And here we are fighting the stupid war of Verdun instead of the revolutionary war you fought in 1917 against the Whites. We can't win this way!"

The Russian, a bull of a man, who had the night before wept drunkenly on Jake Starr's shoulder, grieving the purge of the Red Army, now smiled cynically. "You take it too seriously, *Tovarich.* Before we left for Spain Stalin told us, '*Podalshe ot artillereiskovo ognia.* Stay out of the range of the artillery fire!' This Spain is only a game. What do we care what happens here. What is important are the lessons we learn to take home to the Red Army. . . . Watch your tongue, young man!"

"*Da,* Comrade General," Jake said. "*K Vozhdyu,* to the Leader," as the Russians greeted one another, and departed.

The Republican Spanish army together with the dwindling forces of the International Brigades fought and lost most of the ground which had been gained in the first three days of the offensive. Every evening Starr and Nevins spoke to their troops, edging them on, nagging them, cajoling them, shaming them. Romanillos, del Pardillo, Brunete, del Castillo, the Guadarrama River, wheeling from point to point on the sun-scorched *mancha*. Yet Jake Starr knew they were fighting with a wooden sword. On they fought, thirsty, hungry, uniforms in rags, dizzy with fatigue and defeat.

Bivouacked at night, Jake would swagger off, a lonely romantic hero with the mongrel pooch hugged to his chest. As his comrades drank and sang the biting songs bequeathed to them by Mack Berg, Jake Starr stalked off into the night, the lonely hero, into the arid *mancha,* the crisp tang of gunpowder still scenting the mesquite mingling with the sweet rot of the dead.

Blood must run, he had once said to his mother about the revolution, and she had answered in wry jest, almost as if it had been a curse, it has become a hemorrhage, and it had, with those betrayed in Havana, with the blood of Nuñez, of Hector and Guillermo and the Andaluz and the two others—two others!—nameless Spanish boys crying, Unite, proletarian brothers in the sunless dungeons of an ancient cathedral closed by the revolutionary terror, sandbags at its huge iron doors like the patient dead awaiting grace. Friend to no man now—how dare he have a friend? Friend today, tomorrow, convicted by history, an enemy; the following day, a dead man. *K Vozhdyu.* Long live the Leader. U!H!P!

He thought of Sarah.

Where have you gone, Sarah? Where have you fled, my love? My bones are impressed on your flesh; my mark is on you. My hand has crushed your breast. We are a secret society of two. Our blood has mingled on the white linen of love. Indomitable, passionate Sarah. Hoarder of my love, my sole treasure. My heritage that I have wasted. Onan. Jacob Onan. Wastrel. Here, Sarah, on the desert of Spain I'll sacrifice my dog to love and the law. *Perro!* Jake Starr, revolutionary pro. Their spit was like acid, Sarah. They have maimed me for life. They? Which they? I—I have committed a sin against myself. And now I fast.

Carrion.

Again, the next morning, he led his comrades on a march through the Castilian *mancha,* through mesquite, yellow sage, through the silver green olive groves and grape trees like scrub oak, through scented pine and birches, over soft rolling hills, the sky a bessemer furnace, crawling side by side with scorpion and desert mice. Fighting a battle already lost. *La voz.* Sardonic, bitter, enraged, swaggering, lonely, the bravado of guilt a cloak; the hand a wooden sword. The skinny mangy pooch clutched to his chest, he played the hero of history.

And his comrades? They died. Oh, yes, did they die.

He never spoke to Greg Ballard or Archie Cohen. They existed only as soldiers in one of his squads. He spoke to no one, except to give an order, or to exhort them as a group. Of the combined two battalions there were only a few hundred left now. (The British had eighty. The Slavs, the Poles, the Franco-Belges were almost nonexistent.) Greg Ballard and Archie Cohen laughed at Jake Starr and his stupid dog; or excoriated him to one another for his arrogance. One day the mail pouch had a letter for Greg Ballard from Loney informing him of her marriage and asking him to give her best to Jake. Greg sent him a note with a runner. Jake acknowledged it with a curt thank you and a cold congratulations. Greg hated him. He was one of theirs—the compleat commissar. Thereafter, whenever Jake was close at hand, Greg turned his back and found occasion to snap out an insult about the comic stars or the Party boy scouts to Archie. Greg was swaggering, too, childishly daring Starr to discipline him. If Jake saw or heard, he gave no indication, which of course infuriated Greg even more.

One late afternoon, as the battalion and a regiment of Spaniards found themselves backed against a sharp rising hillock by a fierce fascist attack, Greg and Jake fought side by side, shooting what seemed endless rounds of bullets until the attackers broke and retreated in panic, chased by some Russian tanks, one of which was commanded by Bob Gladd, the American who had been awarded the Soviet Order of the Red Banner for valor in the field. As Greg and Jake reclined, dead tired, with their backs against the side of the hill, Ballard said wryly, "Just yellow dogs, aren't they?"

Jake merely turned his head and looked for a long moment into his erstwhile friend's stubborn brown eyes, then tiredly, as if his body and limbs were weighted with pigs of lead, rose to his feet, scooped out his pooch from under a rock, and straggled off. And suddenly Greg felt remorse at his anger at his friend. For in that short moment when their eyes had caught and held, he had seen that Jake Starr was feeding on a worm and that the worm was spiraling through him like a bore drill, and that his face wore that look of quiet despair which belongs to men suffering from self-hatred. It was obvious the only way the man could function was stiffly and through bravado. Worse, Jake looked like he had come to the conclusion that the best that could happen to him was a fascist bullet in his brain and immediate death, and the worst that could happen was to live in that state of constant torment which his conscience put him to as it faced up to that one rampaging cell in him which all his life had exulted in violence and blood and victory and which thus far had dominated him enough to have led him to this side of the wall, the executioner's. And Greg Ballard knew this and saw with sharp eyes, because he had sensitive antennae, and he too had stood once on this side of the wall.

The campaign wore on. Many thousands of men died. The Slavs, the Poles mutinied against their commanders—a mutiny put down by *Asaltos* with tanks. And one night the Americans told their commanders and commissars they could not and would not return to fight at Brunete retaken by the fascists, they were too damn beat, tired, bushed, weary, enervated, without will. Starr and Nevins argued with them. "If you don't go back to stop them there, they will kill you here tomorrow," Nevins argued. They were camped in the same pine forest outside of Valdemorillos from which they had jumped off for the offensive some three weeks before. Nevins was the only man in the world who could talk them into anything, a man Mack Berg had called the Fulton Sheen of the American Communist Party, he could charm a nun into joining the Bolsheviki. After many hours they agreed, and, as they prepared to make a forced march on the stumps which were their feet, a dispatch arrived with the information that the Spanish marines had taken up the slack outside Brunete, now a pile of stone.

Greg Ballard fell asleep with his legs wrapped around his gun, very drunk. He was dreaming of Ursuline Washington, that same argument with her about going off to make it in the big city, the little bitch, and then suddenly he was snaking around her brown beauty when someone woke him, and he growled out, "Beat it," a part of him not asleep advising him to grab his gun. Whoever it was emptied a canteen of water on his face, shook him loose from his dream, and it was Jake Starr. His eyes half closed, his mouth a rag, he managed to snarl, "Why don't you shoot me when I'm sober?"

"Oh, shut up! I want to talk with you."

"Why don't you do it during daylight, afraid the pols—" He

just couldn't keep his eyes open even though he thought, They've finally come about Webster.

Jake grabbed him by the shoulders, helped him up, led him to the edge of the forest, their sole company the mongrel pooch and a satiny black night.

"I'm leaving in an hour," Jake said quietly; "ordered to Barcelona. The battalion's going to Albares. Those of you in Spain since January are to be repatriated." Greg said nothing, stunned. "You're going home, Greg."

Ballard just keeled over and went back to sleep. It must have been all that manzanilla and the shock.

He did not know how long he was out, but when he came to Jake was sitting alongside him, shaking his, Greg's, head, muttering, "Wake up, Greg. You're going home." And out of the shock and the fatigue and the manzanilla Ballard's eyes suddenly assumed lenslike clarity and precision. Jake Starr's face was a smashed portico and through the debris Ballard could see the inner architecture of the man. He had been hit by a five-hundred-pounder—a disaster, a complete disaster. The dog was whimpering in Jake's arms.

When Jake saw that Greg's eyes were wide open, like a movie running backwards, the portico rearranged itself into its former grandeur, the inner architecture hidden.

Ballard sat up, wiping wet glue out of his eyes.

"In Albacete you'll be told your passport is lost. You'll receive Spanish papers to keep you safe in France until you obtain a duplicate from the American consul—just keep quiet now!" Ballard had begun to rise, his jaw long, his fists like rocks, but he refound his seat, and shut up. "Don't make a big stink about it when they tell you in Albacete, just accept it, even if it kills you, for if you don't it will. They will probably send you to Benicasim on the Mediterranean for some rest. And while you're there just enjoy the sea. Something happened in those hills at Romanillos. So shut up. When you get to

France, don't wait too long, go to the nearest American consular office, tell them you want a duplicate passport, you lost yours."

"You mean I have to lie or inform on myself? You dirty—"

"Tell him whatever you please, who the hell cares. But don't go too far with those phoney papers. You're not one of us—you're my friend—" Jake's voice trailed off. "You'll do as I say?"

Ballard was so enraged he could barely move his lips, so he nodded. He'd lived so long, why give it up now?

Placing the dog on the ground—it promptly became entangled in Jake's feet—Starr shoved his hand into his pocket, withdrew it clutching a wad of francs. "This will hold you in France and buy your transportation home. Don't have anything to do with the Tech-Bureau, handle everything yourself. Understand?" Jake realized he sounded just like Vlanoc.

Greg took the money, angry and yet astonished at Jake's behavior. He was too infuriated and too full of alcohol to really follow.

Then he saw Jake biting his lips, scratching his chest until he caught himself, leaning down and picking up the dog, holding it close. He looked as if he hoped Greg hadn't noticed but Greg had and pretended he hadn't and Jake knew he was pretending. Jake Starr was like a sailing vessel after a hurricane had hit it. Ballard could see Jake was trying to right himself, hugging the pooch closer, until it began to whimper. Greg got the feeling the dog was Jake's heart and he held it so closely for fear he was going to drop it, perhaps lose it somewhere on the Castilian *mancha.* So now he had finally reached into Greg Ballard's war-weary heart and the fisherman felt a joint misery with him. Greg could see Jake wanted to speak and couldn't, and he himself wanted to speak and couldn't, so they just stood there articulating noises with their tongues cut out. Casualties of war.

Finally Greg constructed a sentence out of the misery. "I heard you had a girl friend."

Jake merely stared out into the darkness.

"The gossip's no slower at the front than in the rear—why don't you go get her and make a life for yourself? Don't pols have a right to live?"

Jake turned to him and he had a gentle smile on his wreck of a face. He was silent for a moment, thinking. "No," he finally said, "I can't quit. Not yet." Abruptly he turned away.

Greg started to say something, but Jake interrupted. "It's too late."

"NO!" Greg shouted, as if he were shouting no for himself, too. "A man—"

"Shut up," Jake ordered. "Stop being naïve. Candide in Spain," he snapped with contempt. "The whole lot of you, a bunch of innocent romantics. It's too late," he said dramatically.

"Comic star—" Greg began, but didn't finish.

This time Jake laughed. "Here," he smiled, placing the pooch in Greg's hands. Imitating him, Greg held the dog close to his chest and, dammit, if that warm throbbing little beast didn't give him comfort. Jake was saying, "You and your antennae. Take him out on the *mancha*, make a fire, slit his throat with a clean knife, salt him, then broil him as a sacrifice to God. *Hasta la vista, viejo*, and keep your mouth shut. You'll see Joe in Benicasim, he's all right, just blind in one eye. That's all. When you return to the States, visit my mother, will you, and tell her I love her and that I said she was right, it's already a hemorrhage." Greg peered at him, not understanding, and in fact Jake laughed. "You don't understand—she will. Give Loney a kiss for me, will you. So long, Greg, and keep your damn mouth shut until you get out."

They shook hands and then Ballard watched him till his brawny lopsided back became completely enfolded by the night's blackness.

XXII

"No, THEY HAVEN'T brought her in yet. Don't worry, Vlanoc, I know exactly what to do. *Salud.*" Jake Starr replaced the receiver on the hook. Yawned. Tired. Dead tired. Need some shuteye.

Yawned again, smelled his own bad breath from too many cigarettes, lay his head on the desk and fell immediately asleep.

He was in Barcelona, in his office, a former shop for reliquaries on Calle Fernando, right off the Ramblas. It was now bare except for the old desk, chair, cot in the rear, and a picture of Joseph Stalin, very neat and chipper. Stacked close to Jake's elbow on the desk lay the leaves of a Joe Garms special, hand-delivered from Paris by one of the American veterans who had left Spain four months before only to return again to resume the fight. As Jake slept he could hear Joe's gravel voice ejaculating his very unique, clear, and concise sentences. . . .

Dear Comrade Comic Star,

For three months I been rotting away yuh dirty crud in this fucking frog city waiting for yuh to send Greg Ballard through. So's Archie Cohen waiting. You said he would come right away, what's taking so long? I'm warning yuh, Comic Star, you or they touch a fucking hair on his head and there'll be a new war. He was drinking himself to death in Benicasim and that back a his was killing him from rheumatism and he oughta get out and get home. So hurry it up yuh prick.

Besides that I'm waiting for the party to buy off my U.S. Army desertion papers. A lousy 5 C note and they're collecting all that money for the heroes of Spain. Well I was a hero too witout the voice and the hand.

I'm tired a this frog city even tho I got me a sweet-assed broad who picked me up on Jaures. The same day I got your note I went out and got feelin' pretty high and walked into a café and seen a pretty French dame, sat down besides her and told her what I thought a her and her whole goddam family, race, and all, and after about thirty minutes of hard fast talking she put her hand under my chin lifted it up and kissed me square on the mouth. She didn't know a word what I said but she thought I was wonderful. Anyhow to cut the story I been living with her about 4 weeks and what do you think of that huh? sonuvabitch goddam me if I ain't crazy about the bitch. I give her my 4 francs a day I get from Asshole Liebman, Paris Comic Star. You bastids is all alike—you stink from shit, all that crap that lays between the voice and the hand. ROTC BOYSCOUT COMIC STARS. With that 4 francs and a couple she makes working as a usher in the movies we live in her clean hole near the St. Martin canal muddy as hell. Shit, if it ain't the San Martin road it's the St. Martin canal. It looks like I ain't going no place. She's a real sweet cookie who gives me lots a loving and I give it to her too and I oughta be satisfied. But not me. Y'know what Jakey? I miss the fucking front. That's the trouble. I love war. My blind eye don't hurt no more and me other eye is tiptop so I can still shoot fascists. You're the comic star I love most so send me orders so's I can come back and join the guys on the Ebro. Tell yuh the truth again I gotta yen to die fighting. That's all that's left me after you comic stars took my cherry in old España. My cherry and everybody elses.

How is it guys like Asshole Liebman and all the big comic stars comin' thru from Spain to Paris have all that dough in their kick—big fat dollars and little ole me and the likes of me, the real fighters, we get a lousy four francs a day? Four francs is twenty cents a day. Merde alors! And André Marty and his gang stealing all that cush in Albacete, I.B. money that the working class of the world chipped in for the men of the International Brigades, gypped, stole, copped by those great leaders Marty and Vidal the crap artist who told us at Villanueva that the fascists would turn and run soon as they saw us. Yeah, they run!

I hear the Limey comrades call Prettyman Murderman too after he sent them up that fascist hill near Quinto tellin' them it wasn't fortified when it was like Gibraltar. Another slaughter. The only thing saved them was the fascist avion bombing and strafing their own fortifications. Even the fascist scum have fuck-ups it's good to see. What happened at Gandesa where we lost so goddam many men again? First I hear Generalissimo Prettyman and Brigade Comic Star Mushmouth Moran cowboys & Indians revolutionary with his blue cape shiny boots & silver handled pistol became separated from the troops and end up fascist prisoners. Next I hear one of the communications boys heard Moran call Prettyman it's time we got the hell out a here, and lots of guys say they screwed off. Then I hear Teddy Heller another comic star told that nice American newspaper reporter 30 commanders and comic stars in one group got separated from the men fighting a life and death battle. *The Big Boys in one group?* Funny. Sad. Archie says it's the usual—to hell with the rank and file fighting men. Prettyman and Moran must of got lost and ended up in the enemy lines. I bet the fascists cut them up good.

A confidential tip, my comic star friend, after Spain and Paris here's MY line, I'm a Communist, will be till the day I'm pushing up daisies, right now I don't think very much of the great majority of the party leaders. They are mostly petit bourgeois opportunist bootlicking bastids. They better keep out of my way cause I ain't heard the marxist interpretation on the right and left to the button and I don't give a damn how big or small they are. The Proletariat is the vanguard, what a laugh.

Me and Archie got Skinny Horton thru okay for you and Hunt Carrington the greatest pol on earth before Skinny flipped and got Demoed in Barcelona after we left you in that smelly office. You're gonna smoke yourself to death boy. We went to eat in a good restaurant north of the Plaza de

Cataluña and the head waiter wouldn't let us in. No hay pan he says looking down his nose on us. A dog. We said we didn't care if there was no bread we wanted a piece a meat we was hungry three heroes of the I.B. and he wouldn't let us in. We was gonna pulverize him but he called a guard and I had to pull Archie and Skinny away before we ended up in the can. Before we left tho we got a good look in there. All the big brass and their fancy ladies was eating good. No hay pan for us. Spain's dying, we gave our all, but we ain't dressed good enough—no hay pan for us. And the party's running Barcelona too. Horton, you know how he's getting, he says more bourgeois than the bourgeoisie. Right, I says. So we vamosed to a working class joint and got more fried wood and potatoes. Codfish Greg once told me after we ate it for twenty days solid.

Hey, Greg's bad, get him out pronto. Those days in the hills of Romanillos is killing him. There are things y'don't know and it's good y'don't. It's like a bullet hitting yuh. You don't hardly feel it till after, then it hurts, keereist it hurts. It hurts yuh bastid. You know. You oughta know.

It's dark and we got time to kill and we're walking down Layetana and we pass the American embassy and who's standing outside with his gun looking for deserters but Tom Demo the nogood prick sonuvabitch OGPU. He stops us and asks where yuh goin', comrades. Archie tells him to haul ass. Horton flips and tells him you piece of scum you destroyed the meaning of the word comrade forever and we start to walk away. That Demo is so trigger happy he pulls his gun on us. So there we are. It's come to that. After all those months in the line. Fighting fascists. We get a gun pulled on us. Archie Cohen. The best. Horton—a fascist bullet in his fucking head, a walking corpse. Joe Garms. Me. A comrade pulling a gun on me. We stand in front of him the three of us. We ain't got a gun between us. Archie, he got a bottle a manzanilla in his mits. He's holding it by the neck and he's playing with it. Up and down that fucking bottle goes in his hand. Up and down. Demo's got that gun pointing right at Archie now. He pulls that trigger, Archie's a dead man. Archie's just standing there, that Chicago Jew with his skinny legs and his eyes like diamonds in the dark. You never saw anything happen so fast in your life. Me and Archie is one man. Greg, too. We been buddies in the line off and on for eight months. One can't think without the other knowing it. My foot and Archie's bottle move like lightning. Demo's on the fucking ground one of his balls choking his throat, his head bleeding. I was gonna kick his head in but Horton said cut it out I'm not feeling good. So we grabbed Skinny and run. Well maybe some deserters got thru to the American consulate that night. Who cares.

We still had an hour to make the train for the border. We're walking around. Suddenly Archie says he wants to get laid. You know him. We say aw hell save it for Paris. No he says he wants to get laid one more time in Spain. Something special, he says.

What you gonna say when a buddy wants to get laid? Okay, we say.

So we walk down to the Barrio Chino not too far away from your office. He sees a broad near a doorway, goes up to her, whispers in her little ole ear, she shakes her head. One broad, two, six. Whatever he wants they don't wanna give. It's getting late, we gotta make that train. Go in an alley and jack off Horton tells him, I'm falling off my feet. No, Archie says. He's a burro. When he makes up his longeared brain nothing but nothing's gonna move him. Another broad in a doorway, another no. Just when he himself is ready to give up he glims this fat-assed whore and grins. There's my meat, he says. And sure enough she says yes to whatever he's asking. Up they go, his hand squeezing one of the cheeks of her tail like it's a pot of gold.

Up they go. Ten minutes he's down and we haul ass to the station. We make it just in time.

What exactly, Horton asks him as we sit down in the train, was yuh looking for. Archie laughs that flute a his. We ain't heard him laugh that way for a long time. Something, he says, adequate to meet the historical situation.

Well, what was it, I asks, took so long to get?

These españolas, he says, are real tough. They don't give in so easy. But like the party I'm very very insistent cause I know there's always at least one who gives in. And he laughs again. This time real bitter.

Yeah, I know, Horton says, but c'mon, what was it?

And Archie says, a Spanish broad who'd let me ram it up her ass.

The train's goin' clickityclick now, real fast. And then Archie yells, Arriba españolas, and begins to cry.

Hermanos hermanos, oh, yeah.

That's how we left Spain, three heroes of the I.B.

Now get this in your fucking head, Jake Starr. Get Greg Ballard out a there if yuh wanna live.

Joe Garms, Hero

P.S. I forgot to tell you something. I suppose cause I don't wanna tell yuh. Me and Archie ain't talkin'. We're enemies. He quit the party and I told him he's a fuckin' nogood renegade and he said I'm so fucking stupid I don't know when I'm being screwed or bein' taken for a trip around the world. I love the bastid, he's a good friend, one a the best I ever had, but he quit and the party's all I got, I ain't got no place to go. I ain't blew the whistle to Liebman cause then they won't give Archie his 4 francs a day and he'd starve, they wouldn't even give him his fare home when he goes but he won't go cause he's waiting for Greg just like I am. And the funny fucking thing is when Greg comes out he's gonna be enemies with me too. Y'know what he said before I left him in Benicasim? You guys do the bravest thing a man can do, go out and fight for freedom but you ain't got the living guts to see that your party is a shitass prison. That's not for me.

Maybe he's right, Jakey, huh?

Joe

Jake Starr slept, listened to Joe's clear and concise sentences, moaned and groaned, and was not a little scared.

Sarah Ruskin, walking wearily between two *carabineros* from the train station, was very scared. And why not? Two days before she had finally left Rolfe Ruskin for good in Valencia, left him fuming; without a *salvo conducto* she had taken the train to Barcelona, hoping somehow to reach and cross the border. When she arrived in Barcelona these two men were waiting for her and they asked her to please come along quietly. When she asked them to whom they were taking her, they told her it was *el capitán.* And took her by each elbow. Violently she jerked her arms free. One of the men turned to her, coldly said, *"Por favor, compañera,* come along without any trouble," then roughly pushed her ahead.

And Greg Ballard was no less scared. In Benicasim, in a white villa on the beach, a guard called at his room just as he was turning in. It's come, Ballard thought. "Dress," the guard ordered. Ballard dressed. "Gather your things together."

"I'm wearing them," Ballard said. But he didn't forget the bottles lined up for parade on the console.

Out into the dark, the sea a soughing sigh, he marched before the rifle of the guard, then into a car with a chauffeur just for him, the guard in the back, an old beat-up khaki car driven by a demon of a boy. The boy said his name was Dionisio, and he had a face like that of a shrunken head in a dirty cobwebbed window of a curio shop.

"Where to?" Ballard asked him, as they left Benicasim behind, heading north.

"Barcelona."

"Roegen?"

The shrunken head laughed sourly, the pygmy shoulders dancing violently under the skinny neck. He had pointed ears, pointed eyes, a pointed chin. He drove very swiftly, the car skittering around curves, pounding into potholes. Every once in a while it seemed the car had run wild. But the boy always caught hold of it, then slipped into that sour laugh. Behind them the guard snorted. Ballard was sure he was on his way to hell. He began to drink in earnest from the bottles cradled carefully in his lap, a drunk fondling his habit. His spinal discs seemed to be grinding on each other. The Spanish kid just hit the gas pedal harder and the car literally slammed down the potholed macadam road. Soon Ballard hardly cared, his brain awash with bad brandy—bottled dynamite—his bones and joints aflame, his head a slimy bit of flotsam being annihilated by an endlessly raging sea. Soon he would be dead and he would at last rest his head.

Violence without end. Broken bodies. Pouring blood. The world existed in the hardcased nose of a bomb.

Jake and Sarah ran, he holding her hand to lead her somehow ahead of the cracking explosions which approached closer more quickly than he had calculated. Once Sarah stopped for rest; looked back over her shoulder and saw the flames at their backs and a building caving in, the screams of its inhabitants lost.

He allowed her a moment, then pulled her urgently forward; a half block ahead, off the Rambla de las Flores, there was a massive stone building whose cellar he knew to be a shelter against the bombs.

Earlier, flying across the short span of sea from the Balearics, the planes had cut their engines as they had approached the city to surprise it; now their engines roared dully above the cracking explosions. It seemed there were hundreds of planes but he knew there were probably no more than ten. He had counted six passing overhead, soaring now, empty of their burden, and with luck he could get her to the refuge of stone before one of the still-laden planes would bank over Tibidabo and return to catch them in the naked black-fired boulevard.

But she could go no further, fatigue and fear having stretched her heart beyond its strength; another step and breath would tear it to shreds.

The pounding and cracking explosions crescendoed, closer,

and he could hear the heavy plane motors straining as they banked over the mountains northwest of the city.

Sarah was heavy to his urging, but it was only a few steps more and he held tightly to her hand, pulling her ruthlessly forward; then they were caught by a sudden brilliant flash of white-flowering flame—it appeared now that the entire city was afire—at their backs, huge white spearlike petals, and the planes were overhead and they could hear the screeching of the bombs as they fell away, clear, screeching, and there was no time to go further, so he threw her and himself to the foot of a stone wall at their side, half atop of her to shelter her between himself and the bombs screeching at their backs like cables in a hurricane, cracking suddenly, lifting the city from its roots.

Sarah flung her arms about him, crouching under and against him, and he held her tightly straining with all his strength to hold her to him as the screaming bombs fell closer and closer filling the boulevard above them with their howling whine, bursting beyond them and there was nothing left in the city, the world even, but the screeching and cracking explosions and her heart beat heavily, her lungs choking, and she held him, crouching like an animal, he half lying on her muttering muted curses which fell on her ears like harsh caresses. Her head found his heart, and soon she began to hear his heart's beat; she concentrated wholly on it—a thumping beat, fast and raucous—if they were to die she was bitterly joyous it would be together.

The explosions stopped. A strange muteness filled the city for a brief moment, followed by a steady crackling from the roaring fire over its streets and in the distance the steady whirr of the plane motors as the Capronis fled over the sea to their lair in the Balearics.

Sarah and Jake lay quietly in one another's arms at the bottom of the stone wall, almost lifeless with the fatigue which follows massive fear. Then slowly they began to come alive, the clang and clamor of ambulances and fire wagons a few blocks away destroying their isolation.

As they stood, straightening their clothes, he observed her intently. She was calm now. Indomitable. "You're a remarkable woman, Sarah. A little mad, but remarkable." She smiled through her disheveled hair which fell about her face. "Let's go," he said. "If the tracks are intact, the train will leave. The one for the border's the only train in all Spain which leaves on time—flood, fire or air raid."

His words reminded her of the misery of the past few days, and he saw it on her face, the laughter dying in his throat. A bone. "Yes," she said. "The train."

Holding hands, they walked through the now deafening silence of the city along the Ramblas, stalls shuttered in for the night, towards the Columbus statue, then left down the Paseo Colón towards the train station, the flames at the harbor long frenzied orange fingers beckoning them on. They walked without speaking, sadly. Once he raised her hand to his lips and kissed each fingertip. They were soon at the terminal, dark except for a wan moon and the trainman's blue lantern at the coach's iron steps. As they stepped onto the platform, Sarah tripped over a loosened sandal strap and he knelt to tighten and tie it. For a solitary moment he lost control and clutched at her thighs, burying his head in the folds of her skirt, and her hands gently caressed his head until he regained control and stood.

He meant it, he meant every bit of it.

Steam escaped from the old locomotive's pistons, the last of the passengers—old peasants, young sleepy children, militiamen—were aboard. "Stay away from the *milicianos,*" he demanded in mock sternness, smiling, as they approached the trainman. She said nothing, merely tightened her fingers on his.

"The fascist dung didn't hit the tracks," the Catalan answered Jake's query; "we leave in three minutes."

Sarah showed him the papers Jake had given her; he examined them quickly under his lamp, nodded approval. General Ernesto's very own stamp.

They stood at the iron steps and spoke to one another as lovers do at parting. He reminded her for the tenth time that evening, "Go directly to the Hotel d'Azur at the dock in Port-Vendres, call the nearest British consular office to let them know your whereabouts. Don't speak to anyone else and stay put."

"You will come soon?"

"Yes; it's a matter of a few days. I have to be careful."

She of course believed him.

And why not? After the *carabineros* had left her with Jake, and they were alone, she and he faced one another in the bare shop. She was disheveled, her face white with anger, her eyes blue ice. "You once promised to help me leave Spain," she said coldly. "Now I am your prisoner." He could see she despised him. So he must tell her quickly.

"I love you more than life—more than the Party, history, everything on earth. I love you, Sarah."

Her eyes widened and she had to step back from him, to bite her lips to keep from crying out. Then she spoke harshly. "Against myself, despite myself, I love you. Life's nothing to me without you, which is the way I suppose human beings love. With their life. But you are an assassin; despite all your great beliefs, you are a murderer!"

"Yes," he answered, stepping as close to her as he dared, fearing she would repulse him. "I must tell you what I have done, so you will know it all."

"There are no excuses for murder," she said coldly.

"I know—and I don't intend to make any. It would be obscene. But I have to tell you because there's no one else I can tell. You love me and that's the least you can do—to listen."

"Yes," she said.

Quickly, without fringe or tassel, he told her all of it, from the moment he'd heard for the first time the talk about the universal city of man and it had filled his hungry belly to this very moment, and she stood and listened to all he said, hearing him to the end. "*Abeunt studia in mores,*" he quoted her. "A man lives like a beast, he becomes a beast."

So he told her what she could not doubt was the truth, told her without adornment, yet omitted no thought or even shadow of a thought. His memory was a cave strewn with the relics of his life. She loved him and despite herself she was warm with a lover's pride for him—he had won; her love had worked its miracle.

"I love you with my life," he said, "and that's what I most want to do, love you with my life. That's why I can tell you now I know there will be no paradise on earth because we are only half-men, half-beasts, striving to become men, and I can tell you this because I love you without sentimentality or romance or kisses or fucking though God knows I love to kiss and fuck you and have dreamt that I lay in your arms night and day."

They stood in silence in the bare office which was lit only by a dying twilight, she before him, searching his green eyes in his lean strong face. The arrogance was gone from his face, and though it was a face which wore its turmoil and travail heavily, he appeared suddenly younger to her, his own age—a young man who wanted to live even against the circumstances of his life. She moved towards him and they embraced, whispering words of love to one another, tender, yet bitter.

"You'll go," he said at last. "I'll stay here, serving out my time. It won't be long."

"You can't come with me?"

He answered nothing. Merely kissed her.

She repeated her question.

"We better put the black shades down and the lights on. The twilight's too romantic." He smiled as he pulled himself from her arms.

In the dimly lighted office, the black shades down, she looked tired, haggard. He poured some wine for her from an earthen jug, some for himself. They were quiet as she waited for his answer.

"I can't leave now, Sarah," he finally said. He had to be careful not to frighten her or all would be lost. "The depots, the mountain passes are guarded by Roegen's men, some by Franco's, and others by both together. Comrades in arms. Do you understand me, Sarah?"

She blanched, nodded. Hesitatingly, she asked, "Will your life be in danger from them?"

"If I'm not careless, no. If you go and I remain, do my work, they'll assume I'm still one of them even though I helped you get out. They'll attribute that to my inherited memory of the archaic past. I have to play it their way, or as Vlanoc would say it, horse meat, the glue factory! Ha ha ha."

Sarah shuddered, but he took her in his arms, warmed her spine with his hands. "We'll have a good life together," he promised.

"Yes, my love."

They talked, made plans for the future. It became dark outside. She washed in the lavatory in the back, brushed her clothes. He combed and braided her long brown hair as he used to do in Murcia. Then led her through the narrow alleys of the old Gothic quarter to the Barrio Chino for some food at a sailors' bar, they still had time, the train for the border did not leave until midnight.

After eating the usual fish and rice, he took her upstairs to a dingy room. They never stopped looking at one another, they did everything now slowly, the time to say *hasta la vista* would arrive soon enough.

Later Jake disentangled himself from her arms, sat up in the dark room. She started to rise. "No," he whispered, "not yet. I have something to tell you. When I left Paris and reported to Roegen and he had me thrown into the lines to die, you know what I thought, Sarah? I was getting what I deserved. Hadn't I betrayed the Party by falling in love? Now I feel as if I had humiliated not only myself, but you as well. I feel ashamed. The taste in my mouth is a stench." She pulled him gently down to her lips, kissed his ears. "You know, I found the front boring. Everyone makes so much of it. All it was was death. Death is very boring, Sarah. No challenge—the most simple solution to all the problems of life. Aa, shit, I came to Spain to fight for freedom and I've betrayed myself—how could I help but end up betraying freedom?" She kissed his eyes now, his cheeks, the corner of his mouth, and he could taste her tears. "I want to live now, Sarah. To live with you. Is it banal to say, my love, I want to live with you, a man with his wife, with music and petty quarrels and all the little things? If it's banal, I don't care. That's what I want." She kissed his lips, his throat, his chin, and still he spoke in a hoarse whisper. "I don't speak of you, Sarah, you've made an egoist out of me with your love. All I do is think of me being happy with you. Will you be happy with me? Will you ever forgive me—I can feel deep inside you a hatred for me, for what I've done—will you ever forgive me?"

"I don't know," she said in his ear. "I just don't know."

"Having destroyed life, and now having found it in a few short hours with you, Sarah, I'm greedy, I want to make life, create it. Am I being foolish?"

"No, my darling," she said, her hands becoming light with hunger, a terrible hunger. "Give me your weight then and fill me with your life. Hurry, my love, hurry! and give me life as well. . . ."

It was then they had heard the first bombs falling west of the city and he had forced her to dress so they could leave the firetrap above the sailors' bar in the Barrio Chino.

Now as they stood at the iron steps of a coach headed for the border how could she not believe him when he said he would come to her in Port-Vendres in a few days?

"Take care of yourself," she whispered as he kissed her cheek.

"Sure, honey," he smiled.

"Don't do anything foolhardy," she said. His heart was suffocating and he thought perhaps he ought to make a run for it—but only for a moment. The dogs were about, he could smell them.

The brakeman at the cab of the engine swung his red lantern; the trainman at the iron steps swung his blue; the coach wheels squealed tentatively. "*Pronto, compañera,*" the trainman called.

Once more they kissed, for mysterious time does not hold still, and she eased herself from his clinging arms.

"*Salud,* Sarah," he called after her as she hurried up the iron steps into the blackness of the jolting train.

She turned hurriedly on the platform of the slow-moving train to throw him a lover's kiss; running alongside he shouted, "I love you, Sarah, I love you," and then with a great scream and roar the train hurtled off into the black hole of night, and Jake Starr stood watching as it—and she—disappeared.

As Jake Starr turned to retrace his steps to his office to call Carl Vlanoc, he spoke half aloud, bitterly. "It was all true. I love her."

Twenty minutes later, in his office, he was connected with

Murcia and Vlanoc. "She's gone. She won't talk–she thinks I'm coming after her." As Vlanoc laughed, he waited. At attention.

Then his superior said, "And the black boy?"

"Being taken care of right this minute. They're probably digging the grave."

"Good. Return to Murcia. We have work to do."

"The car's being repaired at the *Intendencia*. I might need an extra day."

"All right. But get your *arschloch* here fast. No monkey business. Understand!"

"Yes, Carl," he said. "*K Vozhdyu,*" and he hung up the receiver.

All night Dionisio drove, his foot really hammering that gas pedal, the guard in the rear slept and snored, and Ballard drank and drank until there was nothing more to drink. Who cared? Once he did say to the Spanish boy at the wheel, "I could hit you with a bottle and escape."

Dionisio laughed harshly. "How far could you run, *moro*? You are marked for life." Then Dionisio hid an eye like a brown button behind a puckered buttonhole, and returned his head to the road, and the car pounded on, whining.

Perhaps Ballard was more frightened than he knew. Throughout Loyal Spain and beyond, General Ernesto was known as a killer, and also that he ruled Barcelona with a ruthless hand, and it was known of course to Ballard that their revenge was always full and complete. But he was a man who when scared sleeps, so with the alcohol and the fear he slept, and Dionisio never once stopped, driving the entire night.

When Ballard awoke, the guard was gone and Dionisio's demonlike face was over his and for a moment Greg thought he had crossed the river Styx. But Dionisio was smiling and he was gently shaking him. "We have arrived," he whispered. "And now you depart."

Ballard shook his head to clear the frogs from his eyes, and stepped shaking from the car. He stood on a precipice. Below were red-tiled roofs hidden among golden mimosa, fresh green cypress standing a guard of honor. Beyond he saw the Mediterranean, yellow crimson from the dawning sun. Dionisio stood at his side, holding a pistol almost as big as himself, and Ballard grabbed for an empty bottle. Dionisio laughed and pointed to their left.

There were the Pyrenees, huge, purple, awesome, and below a railroad station. Port Bou. And there a train waited, headed into the tunnel leading to Port-Vendres in France, and his face must have shown what it had just learned.

"*Sí*," Dionisio said, and he nodded his pointy chin towards the train. "It was a cruel joke, but we did not wish you to look too happy if we were stopped by Roegen's men." He then handed Ballard two envelopes. One contained Greg's papers, the *salvo conducto* and false passport, the other he was to open only when he was in France.

"Now I must leave you," Dionisio said sadly. "I must thank you for having come to help us in our fight for liberty. *El capitán* has told me that you fought well, are a brave man. But that is not of great importance; what is important is that you came to fight. It would perhaps have been better if you had fought in a Spanish battalion, not as one of theirs, because we have come to hate them. Jacobito told me you are not of the *partido* and that is why I have helped you. Free Spain is grateful to all who have come to fight for justice and liberty; she has only hatred for those who betrayed exactly what it is we fight for."

"*El capitán* knows that you hate his Party?"

Dionisio seemed not to hear what Greg had said. He repeated, "I must leave. Jacobito has written what he wishes to say in his letter to you. Just remember, despite all the evil he has done—and he has done much, he has been cruel and mindless—to you he has been a friend. *Salud, el moro.*"

What could Greg Ballard say? They stared into each other's eyes, three feet separating them. Greg didn't know what it was at that moment which moved him, he wasn't a very demonstrative man, had never been—black he was, but New England, too—perhaps it was that shrunken Spanish face or the vivid eyes or the fantastically proud carriage of his head or that impish smile—but he wished to embrace him, to beg his pardon for the evil committed in his name. To weep, head bowed before him. He didn't do any of these. One doesn't, of course, one never does, and one is forever sorry after the moment has passed.

He merely smiled, his face black and itself creased and wrinkled from war, from the terrible agony in his back, from that green-white corpse in the hills of Romanillos. "*Muchas gracias,*" he said. "Tell *el capitán* I thank him but I'll never forgive him."

Dionisio shrugged coldly. "I myself feel the same way."

"*Abajo Franco, arriba España,*" Ballard declaimed and took the Spaniard's small fist in his.

"No, no," Dionisio said. "Down with Franco, up with life. *La vida!*" He smiled, then was gone.

And Greg Ballard was on the train. The train was in the tunnel. He was in France.

The air was fresh and the agony in his back let up. Greg sat down on the creaking wooden station platform of Port-Vendres and read Jake's letter written in his firm, square hand. . . .

Dionisio will have got you to the train in time. He gave you a wild ride, I'm sure. He's an outspoken decent Spanish boy whom I fired from his job because he told me I was a murderer for having executed Daniel Nuñez and his comrades in the dungeon of the Murcia cathedral. He's going to the front to die. That's what he wants. Better to die fighting for liberty than to work in sewers, he said. I agree.

You advised me to go get my girl and make a life together. Not yet. A man doesn't upend a profound commitment as easily as he changes a pair of sweaty socks. A man doesn't look upon his life lived to this point, say "So sorry," and serenely go on to another life. Each second of time ahead of a man is burdened with the years behind him. A child, perhaps, skips lightly ahead, not a man. But let me say to you whom I know and admire, I'm sorry. Sorry most for Webster. He didn't have a chance—we seduced him the way a blind man is seduced by an open elevator shaft.

You suffer, I know. To ask you not to suffer would be stupid and perhaps obscene. Suffer you will—but try to remember that it was we who stuffed him down your throat. You choked near to death on him, so you vomited him up like so much undigested meat. We destroyed him, we destroyed our comrades—live soldiers are the best soldiers, but dead heroes make the best propaganda. I hope we haven't destroyed you. Of course, if white America hasn't, then nothing will, but time and yourself. From personal experience I can say no one and nothing can do as good an ax job on a man as he can himself. I want to tell you, though, if it had been I, I would have shot the pols, not Webster. But of course I'm more radical than you.

I have to get on with this, I have little time. After the fact, there's always little time.

At the dock of Port-Vendres you will find a small inn, Hotel d'Azur. There you will also find Sarah Ruskin. It's my guess she came off the same tunnel train you did and went right there. How she got to France is too complicated to discuss now. It has to do with dealing and doubledealing in the apparatus at which I've become a master. I bow with modesty. I was able to use her as decoy while Dionisio was on his way to get you out. They had something else in mind for you. After you convince Sarah—and you must—that she has to leave with you, you must go to the pier and charter a power boat to take you both to Marseilles. Immediately. Vlanoc and Roegen will know within an hour that you have left Spain and that I have broken discipline. You must act swiftly. Before you leave the inn with Sarah phone the American consul in Marseilles and tell him you are in France without your passport and would he please meet you at the dock. Tell him you are in danger. He will be arrogant, he won't understand, might even be stupid, he will surely be sore, but he will be there.

Sarah knows you're my friend for I've spoken to her about you. Tell her to accept the fact that it is impossible for her and me. Time moves too quickly—there just is no time. Tell her if I beat time, I'll come to her in England. I write you the truth: I'm scared, real shitass scared. I'm like an old barrel on a runaway truck, I can hear the staves rattling. Tell Sarah to go home and to forget me.

You're a seafaring man, go to the sea. I'm a roadman on a oneway road, twenty foot unscaleable walls on either side. I'm going to break the walls down, and you know what that means, don't you? Or are you still Candide in Spain?

Salud! As Dionisio always says, *La vida!* Life!

There followed a few hastily written sheets which looked as if they had been crumpled together to be thrown away then smoothed out with his hand. Ballard read them, though it became immediately apparent they were written to Sarah. . . .

I was supposed to doublecross you. You ran out on Ruskin at exactly the wrong time. In a few days the Party's going to announce to the world his membership in the Party. Spain convinced him. The foremost et cetera has joined the vanguard et cetera. He has insisted no harm be done you—for which you must be thankful. He is still human, but Roegen has been assigned to see that he drops that silly affectation. How bourgeois. It was my job, since the entire world knows you and I were lovers, to trick you into remaining silent long enough so that we could make the announcement to the breathlessly waiting world uncluttered with subsidiary complications. I was able to use your situation to divert attention from Greg for a few days. Now you are both free. Another illustration, Comrade, of the efficacy of the unity of opposites.

Sarah is love is freedom. That's my new slogan. I told you I love you with my life and that's what I want most to do, love you with my life. Once I had an idea and it became greater than all life. I killed for it. But I met you. And you became greater than my idea. Sarah is love is freedom. Is that an idea, too? No. Love and freedom are immutable elements of life. And to me you are life. Sarah. I am crying, my love, forgive me.

Oh, Sarah, if by some good fortune or miracle I seeded you with life our last time together, rear him or her to remember always that it is better to stand at the wall than to concede an inch to the alleged realities of our time—or any time. To live, as one of the Spanish philosophers has said, is precisely to have to do something to prevent our circumstances from annihilating us.

Sweet Sarah, I have never spoken to you of this before, and should have. My father and mother had a very fine love. One that never prevented them from doing what they thought had to be done. My mother by giving generously of herself to her kin, to her neighbors. There were times when she hoarded breadcrumbs for her child, her husband, but never in so selfish a fashion that she could not spare some for a hungry neighbor. And when I speak of crumbs, I speak literally. My father, of course, gave himself unsparingly to the cause of the revolution and of the working man. Yet that which kept them alive as two human beings was their love for each other, a love from which I was never excluded. They didn't trade in love, never used it as a weapon against one another. It was tender, generous, full of laughter, and, I'm sure, of passion. Somehow I came to believe that I could never find a love like theirs, that I could never match my father in his ability to have men listen to him and to be moved to action on their own behalf. I always felt it necessary to reach beyond him in every act I performed. But enough of that now. What remains with me most of all is the remembrance of their ability to give one another a love so generous, so tender that life was made worthwhile despite hunger and the seemingly impossible task of achieving justice in what appears more and more to be an absurd world. I never believed I would find that love—but I did with you. You have sometimes been too smug about your virtue, Sarah, your morality—you've learned that you, too, can become so obsessed that you become blind, but you have given me love without restraint and never with intent to buy mine, and you've never used it as a weapon against me, but only for me. That sort of love can only give life. Forgive me for once having rejected it. But no longer. I cherish your love now, please cherish mine. I have drunk deeply of you, and your blood courses in mine, as I hope mine does in yours. I hope you grow large with me, as I grow large with thought of you.

I love you, my darling, and, yes, I shall try very hard to live. Don't cry, Sarah—no, why do I say that? Cry, my sweet Sarah. Cry.

Greg Ballard sat on the station platform for many minutes, never once looking up to see the faces which belonged to the feet pounding all around him. Finally he urged himself to fold the sheets neatly and to put them in his pocket. He must hurry. He rose from the creaking wood platform and left the station.

It was early dawn and somehow it reminded him of that early day ages ago when he and Archie and Joe had crawled out to get the hand. Gray-streaked dawn like an oyster shell still dripping with sea. Behind him, to the south, he saw the mountains, massive, purple gray, like giant dinosaurs fast asleep. When he reached the waterfront, the gray had begun to recede from the dawn like fading paint. The sea was calm, its grayness merging into a vivid green.

Soon he found the inn, and after some difficulty with the concierge, he got the man to lead him to Sarah's room. He knocked, and she answered immediately without opening the door, asking who it was. "It's Greg Ballard," he called out and in a moment she opened her room, and he could see she had been washing her face.

She looked Spanish to him, not so much beautiful as striking, with a real jaw and a strong nose, softened by long plaited chestnut hair which hung now to below her shoulders, and deeply intelligent blue eyes, reddened by lack of sleep and worry. She was tall, and full, and moved with unselfconscious grace; looking at her, he got a feeling of courage and compassion and a fine, sensitive intelligence. He could understand easily why Jake loved her and why it was she had been able to move him, and knew a momentary pang of envy.

For a brief moment he just stared, but she greeted him with a quick smile, her strong face flickering white from the sun's rays refracted by the sea through the window of her room. "I just arrived myself," she said softly, as they shook hands. "You were on the same train?"

"Just from Port Bou," he said. "Jake got me there by car."

"You saw him in Barcelona?"

"No," Greg said, wondering how to tell her the news he brought.

"What's wrong?" she asked sharply, perceiving his hesitancy.

She wasn't a woman one patronized, he saw that immediately. "We haven't much time, Sarah," he said abruptly, handing her Jake's letters to read.

Sarah gave him a fresh towel, nodded in the direction of the basin and pitcher, then walked swiftly to the window.

He washed, got rid of the stink of manzanilla and bad brandy, straightened out his clothes, and then, first telling her he'd be right back, went down to the tiny lobby of the inn to call the American consulate in Marseilles. Jake was right, the man was sore at being roused so early, was arrogant, didn't quite understand, but said he would have someone meet him and Sarah at the dock. Greg spoke to the concierge about hiring a boat to take them across the Golfe du Lion and the man told him there would be no difficulty, stepping to the door and pointing out a dock a few short steps from the inn.

When he returned to the room, Sarah was still at the window, staring at the letters in her hand, committing them to memory, it seemed.

He was impatient; Jake had written that Roegen would know within an hour that they had crossed the border. Time was insensitive. he had to get her and himself out of Port-Vendres. "We must hurry, Sarah," he said, coming up to her.

She looked up at him, startled, her strong face fragmented by grief. "He told me to cry, but I've run out of tears."

No more tears, Archie had said after they'd found Mack Berg. *Buen apetito.* They were at a time of drought. Greg said nothing, knowing that for her and for him there would yet be many tears.

After a short silence, she asked, "What will happen to him?"

"I don't know," Greg answered truthfully.

"He'll be all alone," she whispered.

So was Daniel Nuñez, he thought, and Cromwell Webster. "Yup," he said quietly, almost coldly, she thought. "All alone."

XXIII

IN MURCIA, in his office, Carl Vlanoc heard Stepanovich's harsh voice grind over the phone. "A mistake, Vlanoc. After all these years."

"Even the *Vozhd* himself makes mistakes," Vlanoc said.

"He has never made a mistake, never once in his life. You miscalculated with that romantic fool. Now he's a renegade. We can't afford mistakes." Stepanovich hung up.

No, Vlanoc said to himself, you're wrong, there will be no mistakes. He had yesterday dispatched a grinning Red Struik and Heinz Brucker to Barcelona in a fast car. There had been something in Starr's voice which hadn't been quite right. *K Vozhdyu.* They would soon be there and would know what to do. And if they didn't, Roegen would set them straight. But it would be his men, not the shiteater's. Roegen and Step had been setting traps for him for a long time; now they thought they had him. Well, they still had much to learn about Carl Vlanoc. They thought they could depose him after all these years because he had allowed himself to be outwitted by a boy for whom he had a sentimental attachment. In his life he had given up much more than mere sentimental attachments—much more! When he had made his decision in '28 after Lev had been exiled, he had made it for better or for worse. It had been his marriage, his life, and his death. There was no turning back, the blood was too sticky. Chop chop went the iron angel and you lost your head. Remember, Eva, the plans we made for our new world? Like children playing at house. There would be dancing in the streets every evening, and potatoes would be pomegranates and all guns would be smelted into playgrounds. What rot. Why was he shaking? What was wrong with him? The man had broken discipline. To break discipline is to be soft, a traitor. He would have to be mashed. The tiniest infraction—mashed. The iron angel ruled their lives. Tiny infractions, like cracks in a wall, become large ones—spread, lengthen, multiply, weaken the structure. Amorality becomes immorality. Immorality acknowledges the existence of morality. Morality gives birth to conscience. With conscience they would be like all others. No others could even contemplate the conquest of man, to remake him in their own image. Beasts kneeling in obeisance before an iron angel. The intellectual cream of Europe curdled before the blank eyes. Bowed to it. Even old revolutionists, men who had dared to attempt the transformation of men into gods, had conquered and found they had constructed—what? Now the old revolutionists didn't want to die. Remaining alive was the only trinket worth the salt. If you're a coward. He, Carl Vlanoc, was a coward. He had known it in '28. He knew it now.

Vlanoc wrung his hands. They were burning, would soon catch fire like two sticks. He threw them heavily against the wall near the desk. Now they dropped loosely to his sides.

He reached for a bottle of whiskey on the table near the open window, the Murcian sun an oven, his own sweat mingling with the stink of the Segura putrid in his nostrils.

Inwardly Roegen beamed. He made his office a few blocks beyond the Plaza de Cataluña in an obscure stone building, sparsely furnished, almost bare. Roegen neither sought nor required the trappings of opulence to advertise his power. His power was real, because wherever he resided there resided power. A gnomish wiry man with sallow complexion, large muddy eyes, a very large narrow head, big yellow teeth in a jaw like the hook of an anchor, he answered to no man in the entire world but the *Vozhd.* In Loyal Spain he had but one peer: Vlanoc.

Right now, early morning, he sat behind a small desk, smoking a long Russian cigarette. All the shades were drawn against the sun, which he detested, and the desk was illumined by a bright lamp, the remainder of the room in darkness. That's the way the *Vozhd* worked, that's the way Roegen worked.

Before him stood Rolfe Ruskin, who had arrived in Barcelona that very day. "I want no harm to come to her. None at all."

Roegen glared, his contempt like ship's garbage caught on the anchor chain. Now he wrinkled his nose, the garbage slipping from the chain and catching hold on the hook of the anchor. "She is an intelligent woman, she will write letters to the newspapers—a scandal, just when we are about to honor you as one of our own."

"It was the American," Rolfe sucked on his lower lip, his gray mustache limp on his chin like a drowned mouse. "He put her up to it."

Roegen measured the man. A fool and yet not a fool. The woman despised him and he refused to face it, yet he was man enough to want vengeance. Starr was the true fool. To give up everything for a woman's ass—for friendship. He peered out of the bright illumination of his desk into the dark periphery where Ruskin stood nervously before him. "What do you suggest?" he asked with a horsey smile.

Rolfe hesitated. He thought he had power in his hands, great power abiding in the tight sallow body of this horrible man with the contemptuous eyes. He knew Roegen did not waste his power, spent it only with purpose. Roegen, Rolfe thought, was a rational man, and Rolfe appreciated rational men. Was he not himself a rational man—a direct descendant from the age of reason? If he expressed his anger and hatred for the American subjectively, Roegen would consider him a romantic bourgeois. And it wasn't hatred—not really. It was anger because a comrade of Starr's stature had shown disdain for the orderly acceptance of discipline. Starr had become an anarchist—a utopian who thought that one's freedom came before the movement. For all he knew, the man was in league with those forces which disputed the party's effort on behalf of Loyal Spain. And Vlanoc? Why else would Vlanoc have given Starr his seal of approval? They had wanted to embarrass him and Roegen just at the moment when his role as a revolutionist was to be publicized. Of course Starr had convinced Vlanoc that she would not speak out; that he, Starr, had tricked her into believing he would come to her free of the Party. They played at hares and hounds, these men, until one became confused as to which were the hounds and which the hares. . . . Still, Rolfe thought, Vlanoc was an old comrade of this man with the cruel jaw. At this point, Starr would be enough. Rolfe hesitated.

Roegen saw. Inwardly he smiled. This was the man about whom the *Vozhd* had spoken with praise, yet here he was befuddled by the hypocritical morality of western society. Afraid, no doubt, of the wrath of God. To himself, Roegen snickered. *He* hadn't hesitated the one time in his life when hesitation would have plunged him into the dunghole. His decisiveness had earned him a name of ridicule among his comrades—those still hampered by vestiges of right and wrong, by vanity, by the romanticism of the nineteenth century. Communards, red flags, barricades. Fools. They would never dare ridicule him to his face. Except Vlanoc. Vlanoc was his equal, and equals can say what they please to one another. Aa, Vlanoc had made a mistake. Absolutely! Well, *el capitán* was a dead man. Yes! Vlanoc was getting old, losing his nerve. Rakosi, the salami butcher, was in a Hungarian jail; besides he had the subtlety of a meat cleaver. Soon he, Roegen, would become the leader of the Hungarian Party. Which meant after the war which was certain to come he would be the Hungarian state. Spain was dead—not the tomb of fascism, but of itself. What the *Vozhd* couldn't totally control, he destroyed. The people of this asshole of Europe were obstinate romantic idiots who thought in politics one could be friends: to give and expect nothing in return. Madmen. Later, after they had eaten fascist dirt for a few years, they would become more malleable and Stalin would return to them. Meanwhile he had written them off. Now he bought time—two-pronged. Keep the war going to hold Hitler's attention and simultaneously prepare for a deal. The unity of opposites on a universal scale. World catastrophe would follow. Then revolution. Hungary would be theirs—and Roegen would be Hungary. Stalin paid his debts—if you didn't die first. Let them laugh.

In '33, after Hitler had seized power, Roegen had been sent with a message from Moscow to the party leaders in Berlin. There was to be no fighting in the streets against the Hitler government, then, at its birth, at its weakest. The *Vozhd* had declared that Hitler was the icebreaker for the German revolution. Roegen brought the message and many leaders of the German Party had questioned the decision. The debate became violent, hysterical. Strong men fell to their knees, wept, begged. *Allow us to go into the streets. We'll beat him—or we'll be annihilated.* It is true, his stomach convulsed in terrible pain, his heart tore itself from its roots and smashed itself against his bones. He believed they were right, but he stood his ground. A decision's a decision. Then one of them snarled, "Is there no end to what you will do for him?"

And he answered, "For him, for the Party, I will even eat shit."

For that the *Vozhd* had given him a rare handshake—an even rarer smile. And his comrades called him the shiteater behind his back.

Now he would permit this new revolutionist, this world-famous scientist, to make the decision. (And he, Roegen, would see to it he made the correct one. Absolutely!) Not that the decision was not already taken, it was—Starr was in Barcelona and how would he get out?—but this fool must be made to take it too, because once he took the correct decision he would be committed for life. Just as Starr was committed for life whether he accepted it or not. No man could run away from the revolution and no man could escape the decision once it was seized. It would follow him to the grave, by which time he would have made a thousand similar decisions, each having given added impetus to the commitment until it was so fast and strong that the beginning was lost from sight. Too bad for *el capitán,* a man with excellent potential. Roegen laughed to himself. He was riding a very sprightly horse.

He smoked his *papaross,* said not a word, waited for Rolfe to commit himself.

Rolfe had by now come to some decision, exactly what he did not know, but a decision. He had made his investment in the cause years before. If he panicked now, sold short, he would take a bad loss. Very untidy! "Starr must be punished," he declared.

Roegen puffed on his cigarette without haste, withdrew it from between his ruby red lips. "And how should we punish him, Comrade Ruskin?"

Again Rolfe hesitated. Wasn't Jake the seducer of his gentle Sarah? And young Rolfe—hadn't he—no, it was confusing—Starr must be punished! Yet Rolfe could not utter the words. Tradition was still strong in him.

Roegen said softly, almost to himself, "Comrade Stalin once said the Central Committee is the dynamo of the revolution." Roegen didn't know if the *Vozhd* ever had said it, but he could have.

Rolfe's heart leaped. One could change the course of the earth. "Couldn't he be demoted and sent into the lines to fight?"

Roegen found it difficult to restrain his snicker. Some day he would tell the Leader and they would have a good laugh together. "If it were I," he said, looking straight into Rolfe's eyes, "who had the decision to make, I would have him put to the wall and have it over with swiftly. It's more honest, don't you agree?"

Rolfe lowered his eyes. He became faint with the horror of it, that he, Rolfe Alan Ruskin, should be responsible for a man's death. He had come to this. It was his decision to make. Sarah despised him, had absconded. Young Rolfe was dead. And here he was at the point of greatness in a completely foreign discipline. No one could declare that he was a narrow scientific specialist who had forgotten humanity. "Yes," he said, his voice low, Roegen could barely hear him.

That won't do, Roegen thought to himself, stilling the laugh which clamored for exit through his large horse teeth. He must say it so the walls can hear him, otherwise he will soon forget he said it. "Did I hear you say yes, Comrade Ruskin?"

Rolfe swept away the image of Jake Starr crumpled at the foot of a wall, dead, and cleared his throat, said in a loud shrill voice, even the walls heard him, "YES!"

Roegen stood ceremoniously from his seat. "You've just been co-opted to the central committee of the British Party, Comrade Ruskin." As he extended a congratulatory hand over the desk to Rolfe standing half-faint before him, he heard a knock on the door. "Well?" he called impatiently.

The door was flung open imperiously, sunlight entering with a blare, followed by Red Struik and Heinz Brucker. "Excuse us, Comrade Roegen. We're looking for *el capitán.* Vlanoc said, 'The glue factory.' "

Roegen, hiding his disappointment, he had wanted the pleasure of taking Jake Starr's life for himself, shrugged. "He's in his office on Fernando. I'll have one of my men take you. I'm glad you have come. Comrade Ruskin and I have just arrived at the identical conclusion."

They heard a rasping noise, looked around puzzled. In a corner of the room, they saw Rolfe Alan Ruskin, Nobel laureate, vomiting all over himself.

Struik and Roegen peered at one another with a knowing smile. "Aaa, Comrade Ruskin," soothed Struik, "the next time you won't vomit."

Jake Starr sat on the wooden chair in his office. Outside he could hear the early-morning crowds on their way to work. He had been sleeping in the chair, and had just awakened. He stood, stretched, brushed his clothes with his hand, ran his fingers through his hair, reached for an earthen jug, and took a long pull of sour red wine. He glanced at the watch. Eight. Dionisio should by now have ditched the car and jumped on the tailgate of a frontbound *camión.* In a few hours he would be shooting at the enemy. Jake lifted his belt and gun from the wall hook, buckled it round his waist. Sat down again, picked up the previous day's *Mundo Obrero,* read it a few minutes, flung it aside. The Nationalist armies were breaking through at Tortosa to the sea, cutting Loyal Spain in two, and they were still talking of victories.

Tired, first Sarah, then Greg, now worrying about Dionisio (sleep had been an elusive abstract theory), he slumped over the desk, his head in his arms, dozed off again.

Struik, Heinz, and Roegen's man had by now crossed the Plaza de Cataluña and were proceeding down the Ramblas towards Fernando.

In the Barcelona telephone exchange, before a special switchboard, sat Constanza Bienquista. She was a young woman of twenty-three, a Valenciana, blond and blue-eyed. After the May provocations in Barcelona the previous year, when the police and assault guards under Roegen had captured the *telefónica* from the Federación Anarquista Ibérica, the shiteater had brought in numerous operators from other cities. Constanza's great love in life was the switchboard over which she ruled from eight in the morning until eight at night. At her fingertips was every major city in Loyal Spain. Even more: the cities of Europe. Click, plug, switch: and there was Madrid or Albacete or Murcia in the south. Click, plug, switch: London or Paris or Port-Vendres. All foreign calls had to pass her board. All that power in her slender agile fingers. True, the magic power reclined behind the board in a mass of wires and metal instruments, but what good all that power without her fingers? She knew it was a special board because, unlike the others, at hers always sat one or another *estranjero* with headphones listening to everything that was said. They were fantastic men who knew many languages. They were also pleasant, kind in their manner, respectful always. They even brought her candy which they received at the hotel where they lived with other *estranjeros.* She often wondered why the *estranjeros* were hated by her new friends and neighbors in Barcelona. *Aie,* these Catalans, they were so vibrant, so talkative. Politics, politics. Who cared? Life changed so little with one or the other *partido* in power. Still, one must oppose the *caudillo* and his *falangista,* for what they had done had been an affront to Spain's dignity, an assault. Spain would never forgive them. *Obedeceremos pero nunca cumpliremos!* We will obey but we shall never comply!

This morning Constanza was extremely busy. Her fingers had to fly. It seemed a matter of great urgency had arisen. Calls to Murcia, to Port-Vendres, several to London and Paris, return calls from Paris. To Murcia. To Port-Vendres. Men with foreign voices. It must be the terrible battle at Tortosa. Yes, there must be some sort of crisis in these days of crises with Loyal Spain soon to be riven in two. She was proud, for her fingers played an active role in this day's happening, whatever it might be. Perhaps later, Louis, *el francés,* the one with the dark smiling eyes and cherry lips, would tell her. He was more talkative than Riccardo, *el italiano,* who was a bitter-faced man, though one could see he had once been gentle. War. He had been wounded twice and an arm was gone. Louis too had been wounded, fighting at Teruel in December. Still, Constanza wondered why they had come to Spain to fight since there were so many Spanish boys to do the fighting—and the Spanish boys were brave too and wanted freedom as much as did Louis and Riccardo.

Click, plug, switch. London, Paris, Port-Vendres, Murcia, Barcelona.

She asked Louis when they were relieved by Riccardo for a few minutes to have *café con leche* what the crisis was and he smiled, wagged his long slim finger under her nose. "A matter of grave importance about which I dare not speak. A marriage contract is being drawn, *bonita mía.*"

"*Aie,* Louis, you are very droll," Constanza laughed.

As she spoke with the cynical Louis, Riccardo played with the board. Happenstance had it that he plugged in Jake's office number. Click, plug, switch.

"*Hola,*" he heard Jake's sleepy voice.

"Jacobito?"

"*Sí,* Riccardo. Quick."

"They know the black man has crossed the border. Dionisio's car has been found. They have turned thumbs down. Struik and Heinz are in Barcelona. *Attenti ai cani!*" he whispered. "*Salud.*"

Click click.

Beware the dogs. *Perro!* He laughed until it hurt, until the tears flowed. Hysterically. Bitterly.

He stood, raised the chair and smashed it to the floor. Enough. Stop bawling and move. No time to think, to contemplate. Words have been spoken; men have become angry; discipline has been broken; more phones will ring; more words will be spoken; orders given—the words like arrowheads tipped in curare.

His life had been decided upon.

He became afraid. He opened the drawers of his desk—wondered why; closed them. He had to jump off. He looked for his gun. He would need a gun. Looked frantically at the hook on the wall. Not there. He could hear himself breathing. Could smell his own stink of fear. Kept turning in circles. Felt the gun at his side. Get out. Heinz and Struik. They would do it grinning. He went to the door, slowly opened it. With a wrench he escaped from the shop, ran jerkily into the narrow, winding streets of the old Gothic quarter; he knew them as well as he knew his face. There was a cruel pressure under his heart, a bitter remembrance of better days. He broke out of the quarter down near the docks, and his eyes came to life with a start as he saw the garbage-foliaged shacks dug into the sand.

In Starr's office, Red Struik, grinning nervously, was on the phone, unhappily calling Roegen. "He's gone!"

"Not far," Roegen said quietly; then coldly, certain of his power, he added, "Where can he go?"

"We'll find him," Struik said, feeling better.

At the beach, among the shacks of the totally poor, the

disinherited, Jake felt the earth reverse its rotation, and he had to spread his feet to maintain his balance; his right shoulder ached as if it were shot with burning ash, his lips were parched. With a tremendous effort he regained control of himself and ran down to the water's edge.

He was scared, tired, felt mangy from loss of sleep and from not having washed, his socks stuck to his feet from sweat, his shoulder ached, he kept worrying about Sarah and Greg, hoped Dionisio had made it to the front. There, surrounded by death, one could hide. Yes. That was it. Of course.

He soaked his head in the sea, felt slightly refreshed. For a second. Wondered suddenly: How does a man pay for his beastliness?

Life's more than hunger, he thought, unless one is hungry, then that's all life is. Life's more than love—unless there's none, then life's nothing. Empty. Life's more than freedom—until freedom's gone, then life's an iron cage.

He stared at the ugly shacks, tin, old wooden crates, garbage, a girl in rags, her eyes pus-filled, her hands like old chicken bones.

What could life possibly mean to her?

Life's a looking glass, because everyone who looks in it sees something different. Enough! Get moving.

Working his way up the beach, then through the docks, he made his way to the rear of the mountain of Montjuich, then up into the park where he hid the entire day, right under the cannon of the fort. At night he headed over the mountain, came down at the other end of town, lost himself in the stream of Catalans as they flowed northward up the boulevards. In the quadrangle of an army barracks which he knew to be controlled by a strange mélange of anarchists and socialists, he found *camiones* loading with fresh Spanish troops of the Republic going to Tortosa to attempt to stop the fascist drive.

He was issued khaki coveralls, a rifle, a cartridge belt, and joined them. He was a free man joining free men and he would repay them for his beastliness by doing what he should first have done—go with them into battle to fight for freedom.

XXIV

When Sarah Ruskin and Greg Ballard left the inn in Port-Vendres that morning, she looked back towards the Pyrenees and murmured, "Time the devourer of things," and began at last to cry.

"We have to hurry," Greg said gently, taking her arm, "the boat's waiting."

She turned to look into his flat, smashed black face, saw the bitterness and the eyes red like two wounds.

"Yes," she said, and continued with him to the dock.

Jake Starr fought as a free man among free Spaniards to the very end, defeat after defeat. Yet he fought as they fought, to win. But they lost, as did he.

For two weeks after the fall of Barcelona, his Spanish comrades and he fought a rearguard action to enable half a million people, vanquished, in despair, but with heads still erect, to straggle across the border.

Then, boneweary and bedraggled, a bearded thin man, unrecognizable except for his sagging shoulder, he himself turned finally to slip into France.

Strung out along the border, in the midst of this disaster and suffering, waiting for such as he—dissenters, mavericks, heretics, both Spanish and International—he knew would be the *pistoleros* of Vlanoc, Roegen, and André Marty.

At the approaches to the frontier north of Junquera, he

stopped cautiously to consider which to choose, then remembered a little-known pass about which Riccardo had once told him. He cut west, then north into the mountains. It was midafternoon, the sun at the beginning of its fall, when he saw the stone frontier markers far below. He forced himself to stop, to rest until the hills would be in shadow. He ate some hard sour crackers, then, fatigued, slept for a few hours. The sun down, he resumed his way.

It was only after he broke free from the last cypress wood, began the descent of the last Spanish hill, that he permitted himself to think of Sarah, to be filled with hope. As he passed under the bough of a mimosa heavy with its spiked yellow flowers, he saw for a moment Sarah with upraised arms, unpinning her hair, the hair falling in heavy braids upon her shoulders, her eyes lovingly upon him. "Hurry, my love, hurry!" she'd said, "and fill me with life as well." He quickened his step, was in the open again, and was confronted by a patrol led by Red Struik, the Belgian miner. Abruptly he knew the terrible fear of a man standing at the wall. He raised his hand, opened his mouth to speak. Struik grinned. It was a bullet from his gun which killed Jacob Starr.

ABOUT THE AUTHOR

William Herrick served in the International Brigades during the Spanish Civil War, and was wounded at the San Martín de la Vega road, some thirty kilometers south of Madrid. He is married to the former Jeannette Wellin. They have three children. He is the author of two previously published novels, The Itinerant *and* Strayhorn, a Corrupt Among Mortals.